The HOUSE of DANIEL

TOR BOOKS BY HARRY TURTLEDOVE

Between the Rivers
Conan of Venarium
The Two Georges (by Richard Dreyfuss and Harry Turtledove)
Household Gods (by Judith Tarr and Harry Turtledove)
The First Heroes (edited by Harry Turtledove and Noreen Doyle)

DARKNESS
Into the Darkness
Darkness Descending
Through the Darkness
Rulers of the Darkness
Jaws of Darkness
Out of the Darkness

CROSSTIME TRAFFIC
Gunpowder Empire
Curious Notions
In High Places
The Disunited States of America
The Gladiator
The Valley-Westside War

WRITING AS H. N. TURTELTAUB
Justinian
Over the Wine-Dark Sea
The Gryphon's Skull
The Sacred Land
Owls to Athens

The
HOUSE
of
DANIEL

HARRY TURTLEDOVE

A TOM DOHERTY ASSOCIATES BOOK
NEW YORK

THE HOUSE OF DANIEL

Copyright © 2016 by Harry Turtledove

A Tor Book
Published by Tom Doherty Associates, LLC
175 Fifth Avenue
New York, NY 10010

www.tor-forge.com

The Library of Congress Cataloging-in-Publication Data is available upon request.

ISBN 978-0-7653-8000-5 (hardcover)
ISBN 978-1-4668-7133-5 (e-book)

Our books may be purchased in bulk for promotional, educational, or business use. Please contact your local bookseller or the Macmillan Corporate and Premium Sales Department at 1-800-221-7945, extension 5442, or by e-mail at MacmillanSpecialMarkets@macmillan.com.

First Edition: April 2016

Printed in the United States of America

0 9 8 7 6 5 4 3 2 1

This one is for Peter S. Beagle.

The HOUSE *of* DANIEL

(I)

It would've been the first part of May. I remember that mighty well. Spring has a special magic to it. Or spring did once upon a time, anyway. I remember that mighty well, too. But when the Big Bubble busted back in '29, seems like it took half the magic in the world with it when it went. More than half, maybe. In the five years after that, we tried to get by on what was left. We didn't do such a great job of it, either.

Other thing the Big Bubble took with it when it busted was half the work in the world. People who had things to sell all of a sudden had more of 'em than they knew what to do with. They tried to unload 'em on the other people, the ones who all of a sudden didn't have the money to buy 'em. They couldn't hardly hire those people to make more things, not when nobody could afford the stuff they already had clogging their warehouses.

It was a great big mess. Hell and breakfast, it's still a great big mess now. And nobody but nobody has the first notion of how long it'll go right on being a great big mess.

Take a look at me, for instance. Not like I'm anything special. You can find guys just like me in any town from San Diego to Boston. More of 'em in those big cities, matter of fact. But take a look at me anyhow. You may as well. I'm right here in front of you, talkin' your ear off.

Jack Spivey, at your service. I know too well I'm not extra handsome, but I'm not what you'd call homely, either. I was twenty-four that May, on account of I was born in February of 1910. Old enough to know better, you'd think. Well, I would've thought so, too. Only goes to show, doesn't it?

So there I was on that bright May morning, walking along Spruce Street in Enid, Oklahoma. I didn't have two quarters to jingle in my pocket. Yeah, plenty like me, Lord knows. Too damn many like me.

I wasn't thinking about much of anything, if you want to know the truth. Maybe wondering how come the leaves on the trees didn't seem so bright as they had before the bustup, and why the grass looked to be a duller green.

Your hotshot wizards, they'll tell you things haven't really changed. They'll tell you it's all in your head. What I'll tell you is, your hotshot wizards weren't walking down Spruce with me that morning.

The flour mill took up a whole block of Spruce. The mill got built a year before things went to the dogs. Timing, huh? It hadn't run flat-out since. It did still run, though. I'll give it that much. Some of the jobs the big bosses were bragging about when it opened up were there to that day. Some were—but not all of 'em.

Sure, I'll tell you what I mean. While I walked by there, a man was rolling a big old barrel of flour to a truck. Only he wasn't a man. He was a zombie. His face was as gray as the slacks I had on, and just about as shabby looking. No, he wasn't rolling the barrel very goddamn fast. To tell you the truth, he was rolling it like he had all the time in the world. If you're a zombie, you do, or you might as well.

But how much do you reckon the rich folks who run the mill were paying him? Right the first time, friend. Zombies work for nothing, and you can't get cheaper than that. Back when times were good, a colored fella or a sober Injun if they could find one would've been rolling that barrel. The rich folks wouldn't've paid him much, but they would've paid him a little something.

Now they had colored fellas and Injuns working inside the mill. They never would have before, let me tell you. They pay 'em a little something, but not much. And some of the white guys who would've earned more, they were out on the street without any silver to jingle in their pockets and scare the werewolves away, just like me.

Difference between them and me was, I knew how to go about it. I'd been scuffling, doing a little of this, a little of that, a little of the other thing, since before I had to shave. Those guys, they thought they had a job for life. They didn't know what the devil to do with themselves after it got taken away.

Some of them drank at the saloons across the street from the mill. Anything stronger than 3.2 beer is against the law in Oklahoma. That doesn't mean you can't get it, only that it costs more. Even before

Repeal, mill hands would drink at those saloons when they came off their shift. Now they were in there at all hours—when they could afford to buy anything, I mean.

Just past the saloons were a couple of pool rooms and a sporting house. The house had to let girls go. *That's* how bad things were. It doesn't get any worse, now does it?

I walked into one of the pool halls. A couple of guys were shooting slow, careful eight-ball at a front table. They looked over when the bell above the door jingled, but they relaxed as soon as they saw it was me. It's not like I was somebody they hadn't seen plenty of times before.

Arnie, the guy who ran the joint, he'd seen me plenty of times, too. He hardly moved his eyes up from the vampire pulp he was reading. He was near as pale as a vampire himself—I don't think he ever went outside. He was wearing a green celluloid eyeshade like a bookkeeper's, the way he always does.

"How you doing?" he asked me. His voice had more expression than a zombie's, but not a lot more.

Most of the time, he didn't talk to me at all. When he did, sometimes it was business. "I'm here," I answered. "What's cooking?" Arnie knew people. He heard things.

Like now. "I hear Big Stu's been asking after you," he said.

"Has he?" I said. "Obliged." I touched the brim of my cap—cloth cap, not ball cap. Then I turned around and walked out.

As soon as I got back on the street, the grass looked greener and the new leaves looked, well, leafier. I'm not saying they were, but they looked that way. To me, they did. Amazing what the thought of some work will do.

It wouldn't be nice work. You didn't get nice work from Big Stu. Some people wouldn't call it work at all. They'd call it burglary or battery or some such name—but Big Stu paid off those people. And he paid the people who did things for him. He paid them good. You can't be too fussy, not since the Bubble busted you can't.

Big Stu ran a diner on Independence, near the artists' gallery. You came in from out of town, you could get the best beef stew between Tulsa and the Texas line. The barbecue was tasty, too. You could get other kinds of things at Big Stu's diner, but you had to know what to ask for and how to ask for it. You also had to know nothing from Big Stu ever came for free. Oh, yeah. You had to know that real good.

Not many cars, not many carpets, parked on Independence when I headed over to the diner. People didn't come into town from the country the way they had in boom times. They hunkered down, tried to do without, as much as they could. So did most of the folks who lived in town. I know I did, and I still do—I have to. I bet you're the same way. These days, who isn't?

So Big Stu's joint was like the pool hall near the mill. It had some people in it, yeah, but it wasn't what you'd call jumping. Big Stu worried about it less than Arnie did, though, 'cause he had the other stuff cooking on the side.

The waitress wasn't too busy to nod at me. "Hey, Jack. What do you know?" she said.

"I'm okay, Lil. How about you?" I answered. Lil's about the age my ma would be if she was alive. She uses powder and paint, though. Ma never did hold with 'em. So Lil looked younger—most of the time. When the sun streamed in through the big front window and caught her wrong, it was worse'n if she didn't bother.

But she had a kind heart, no matter she worked for Big Stu. She set a cup of coffee and a small bowl of stew on the counter. "Eat up," she said, even though she knew I couldn't pay for 'em. "He'll still be in the back when you get done."

"Thank you kindly" was all I had time for before I dug in. Big Stu's *did* make a hell of a beef stew. The bowl was empty—the coffee cup, too—way quicker than he could've got grouchy waiting.

I touched the brim of my cap to Lil and went into the back room. You could hold wedding dinners there, or Odd Fellows wingdings— or poker parties or dice games. Those mostly happened at night. During the day, it was pretty much empty . . . except for Big Stu.

They didn't call him that on account of he was tall. He had to look up at me, and I'm five-ten: about as ordinary as you get. They called him that because he was wide. His double chin had a double chin. His belly hung over his belt so far, you couldn't see the buckle. Somebody who ate that good five years after the Bubble popped, you knew he had a bunch of irons in the fire.

I touched my cap to him, too. One of his sausage-y fingers moved toward the brim of his fedora, but didn't quite get there before his hand dropped again. "Heard you were lookin' for me," I said. Big Stu, he never fancied wasting time on small talk.

"That's right." All his chins wobbled when he nodded. "You're headin' up to Ponca City in a coupla days, aren't you?"

"Sure am. We've got a game against the Greasemen Friday." Back in those days, I played center for the Enid Eagles. Nobody gets rich playing semipro ball—it's a lot more semi than pro. But it was one more way to help fill in the cracks, if you know what I mean. Ponca City's an oil town, which is how come their team got the name it did.

"Okey-doke," Big Stu said. "Something you can take care of for me while you're there. Worth fifty bucks if you do it right."

"Who do I have to kill?" Oh, I was kidding, but I wasn't kidding awful hard. You can live for a month on fifty bucks. A couple of months if you really watch it.

"Not kill. Just send a message—send it loud and clear. You know Charlie Carstairs?"

"I know who he is." Everybody in Enid knew who Charlie Carstairs was. Whatever you needed for your farm around there—a plow, a dowsing rod, you name it—chances are you'd buy it from Charlie.

"That's good. That's better'n good, in fact. Wouldn't want you for this if you were his buddy. I did somethin' for him—never mind what—and now he won't give me what he owes. So what I want is, I want you to rough up his kid brother in Ponca City." Big Stu scowled. "I had to put out a geas to find he had a brother there at all. But I did it." He looked proud of himself then, like a moss-covered snapping turtle soaking up sun on a rock.

"You never sent me out for strongarm stuff before," I said slowly, which was . . . close to true, anyway.

He looked at me. He looked into me. He could see more dark places inside my head than even I knew were there. His mouth twisted. A snapper's mouth doesn't work that way, but seeing him would make you think it did. "Hell, Jack, a hundred bucks."

I was still pretty green some ways. I didn't know I was dickering. He did, or figured he did, which amounted to the same thing. And when he came out with *a hundred bucks*, why, my conscience spread its wings and flew away. "You're on," I heard myself say. "What's his name? Where do I find him?"

Big Stu didn't so much as smile. In his way, he was good. "He lives in a boarding house on Palm Street, not far from the city swimming pool. His name's Mitch." He reached into an inside jacket pocket and pulled out a scrap of paper. He held it out for me to take. "Here's the address."

I had to unfold it. The pencil scrawl read *527 Palm #13*. I gave my best try at a tough-guy chuckle. "Lucky number," I said.

"Lucky for you," he answered. "He opens the door, you clobber him good before he knows what's what. Then go to town from there. And then head on over to Conoco Ball Park and get yourself a coupla the other kind of hits." He laughed.

Well, so did I. I'm not what you'd call proud to admit it, but I did. "I'll do that."

Big Stu reached into a different pocket, the one where his billfold lived. He handed me a sawbuck. "Here. Down payment, like. Buy yourself some groceries so Lil don't ruin my business trying to fatten you up."

How did he know? Part of his business was knowing things. The door to the back room was shut till I walked through it. So what? He knew anyhow.

I got out of there. The sawbuck felt funny in my pocket. Heavy. Not just a printed piece of paper. Heavy as blood, maybe. What else was it but blood money?

Then I went back to the saloons by the flour mill. No, not to drink up my dividend. I like it fine, thank you, but I hold the bottle. It doesn't hold me. I was looking for some of the other Eagles, to let 'em know I'd be going over to Ponca City a day early by my lonesome.

Second place I stuck my nose into, there was Ace McGinty, our number two pitcher. He had two, three empty schooners in front of him, and a full one. You got to work to get plastered on 3.2 beer. Ace, he was working. I told him what I needed to tell him. A slow grin spread across his face. "She must be pretty," he said, and breathed fumes into my face. His hands shaped an hourglass in the air between us.

If he wanted to think that, fine. Then he wouldn't think about Big

Stu. I told a few lies—you know the kind I mean. That grin got wider on his country-boy mug. He smelled like a brewery. I think he'd be our ace for real if he didn't drink so much. I had to hope he'd recall my news.

A blue jay on the chain-link fence around the mill screeched at me when I came out. Behind the fence, that damn zombie—or maybe it was another one; I don't know—was rolling a barrel of flour to a truck. He wasn't going real fast, but he was going. He'd keep going all night long, too. Why not? It wasn't like he'd get tired. Or hungry.

I was getting hungry. Back at the shack I had half a loaf of bread going stale and some beans I could boil up. I'll never make a cook, not if I live to be a hundred. So I headed to Big Stu's again, to spend his money in his joint. I don't know if the barbecue is as good as the stew, but it's plenty good enough.

"Live here, do you?" Lil said.

I kind of grunted and let that one alone. It's one of those jokes that would be funny if only it were funny, you know? Big Stu's was an awful lot nicer than where I did live. If it had a bed, I wouldn't've half minded staying there all the time. Then he could've found even more ways to land me in trouble.

I ate up the barbecue. Since I had that ten-spot and the promise of more, I ate a slice of apple pie with cheese on top, too. I left Lil a dime for a tip—when I've got money, nobody can call me a cheapskate. By that time, it was getting dark outside. I let out a long, long sigh, got up, and went on home.

B e it ever so humble . . . I know you've heard the old chestnut. You want to know what I think, that's a pile of crap, too. If somebody'd burned down the shack I lived in, he would've done me a favor.

It was on the outskirts of Enid, where the town turns into farm country without quite knowing it's doing that. My pa, he lit out for California year before last. A carpet came by heading west, he hopped on, and he was out of there. He took all the money in the place, too. Seven dollars and some-odd cents, I think it was.

Can't say I miss him much. We didn't get along while he was here, which is putting it mildly. No note or anything to tell me where he'd gone—he doesn't have his letters. The old lady across the street let me know the next day. I was doing something or other for Big Stu, so I wasn't around when he hightailed it.

Hell, if I had been I might've gone with him. Then this'd be a different story. I can't say how, but different for sure.

It'd be a different story if my ma were still around, too. I just barely remember her. I was five, I guess, and I was all excited on account of I was gonna have a new baby brother or sister. He would've been a brother if he'd lived. That's what Pa told me. Only he didn't, and neither did Ma.

So it was Pa and me, and then it was only me. I went back to the place to sleep, and to eat when I couldn't afford Big Stu's or one of the other joints, and that was about it. Some guys on their own make pretty fair housekeepers. Not me. Pa used to say I could burn water when I boiled it. I won't tell you he was wrong, exactly, but I will say he was one to talk.

When I got inside, I lit a kerosene lantern. That let me find my beat-up old cardboard suitcase. It's longer and thinner than most, so it'll hold a couple-three bats. I put them in—two Louisville Sluggers, one Adirondack—and my spikes and my glove, and the gray flannel uniform with ENID EAGLES across the shirtfront in red fancy letters. Then I put in some ordinary clothes, too.

And, since I was supposed to send this Mitch Carstairs a message, I dropped a blackjack and some brass knucks into the suitcase. Big Stu's plan looked pretty good to me—get in the first lick and make it count. They'd help. Where'd I get 'em? You do things for Big Stu, you get stuff like that, just in case. I hadn't used 'em much before, but I had 'em.

Across the road, the old gal who'd told me Pa'd headed west had the radio on so loud I could hear Amos 'n' Andy inside my place. She's deaf as a brick. She had power in her house, though. We never did. If we had, they would've shut it off 'cause we couldn't pay the bill.

Power. I laughed, not that that was real funny, either. With any kind of power, I would've been good enough to play pro ball, maybe claw my way up to the bigs, even. I can run. I can catch. I can throw. You play center field, you've got to be able to do those things. But my hitting's on the puny side. Always has been, dammit. I went to a tryout for the Dallas Steers once. Soon as they saw me with a bat in my hands, they said, "Sorry, sonny," patted me on the head, and sent me on my way. They reckoned they could find better.

Worst of it is, they were right.

After I packed, I didn't have a thing to do till I caught the bus for Ponca City the next morning. I carried the lantern into my room, blew it out, and went to bed. I could still hear Amos 'n' Andy from across the street. I didn't care. With a full belly and a little cash, I didn't care about anything, no more than a dog would. You're poor enough, life gets pretty simple.

I ate stale bread for breakfast instead of coughing up another quarter at the diner. Then I lugged my sorry suitcase to the Red Ball Bus Lines station on East Maple. The bus wouldn't set out for another hour and a half after I got there, but I could do nothing at the station as well as I could at home.

Better, even. They set out newspapers in the waiting room—today's *Enid Morning News* and the *Tulsa Tribune* from day before yesterday. Pa didn't know how to read and write, but I do. I'm glad I do. It's handy and it kills time, both. I grabbed the *Tribune*. It had a funny page, and the *Morning News* didn't.

The hour and a half turned into two and a half—the bus came late. I was ticked but not surprised; Red Ball did things like that. The *Tribune* had a story about a king—or maybe he was just a minister—way on the other side of the ocean who promised he'd make everything run on time. Big Stu would've bet against him, I expect.

A guy who looked like a drummer and another one who looked like he'd maybe be a werewolf at full-moon time got off the bus when it finally did chug in. Me and a colored fella, we climbed on. He went to the back. I sat a couple of rows behind the driver. The bus wasn't anywhere close to crowded.

For twenty miles north from Enid, US 81 and US 60 are the same road. Then 81 goes north into Kansas; 60 swings east. The road wasn't close to crowded, either. A few trucks, a few flivvers, us. A few carpets overhead. Costs about the same to ship by magic or by wheels. If it didn't, one would run the other out of business.

Kids played baseball in the fields by the highway. A lot of 'em should've been in school, but they played anyhow. I never did any such thing—and if you buy that, I'll tell you another one. White kids, colored kids, Injun kids, they all just played, together and separate. They'd sort out the rules of how things worked when they got bigger. I must've seen half a dozen games by the time 60 forked off 81. There's Pond Creek and Lamont—little, no-account places—and then, eventually, there's Ponca City. It's about sixty miles from Enid. It only felt like forever 'cause the bus went so slow and stopped at every other farmhouse, seemed like.

Halfway between Pond Creek and Lamont, it stopped in the middle of nowhere. Driver said something that made a lady cluck like a laying hen. I leaned out into the aisle to look through the windshield. A load of rocks was spilled across the highway, and a carpet down beside it on the verge. The only way the wizard on that carpet could've looked glummer was if the rocks had smashed a car and the folks in it. Drunk or just sloppy, he'd fouled up his spell some kind of way.

We wouldn't make it to Ponca City or even Lamont till those rocks got cleared. We all piled out of the bus—even the lady who'd clucked—and started shoving. The unhappy wizard helped some, too. So did a family in a Hupmobile. A couple of farmers brought their mules.

The clucking lady wagged a finger in the wizard's face. "Your company will pay for this!" she said, all angry.

"I am my company," he answered.

"Then you will," she said, which sure didn't turn him any more cheerful.

I wasn't what you'd call happy, either. I muttered some ungodly things while I hauled rocks. Just what I'd need, to mash a foot so I couldn't run or smash a finger so I couldn't throw or hold a bat—or swing a good right at Mitch Carstairs.

But my luck stayed in. I didn't hurt myself; I didn't even rip my pants. We finally cleared a path wide enough for the bus to sneak through. The passengers climbed aboard. The family got back into their car. The farmers took the mules away. And the damnfool wizard just sat there on his carpet with his head in his hands like he'd dropped the last out in the bottom of the ninth and cost his team the game. I know that feeling—I wish I didn't. It's not a good one.

We left Enid late. We had trouble on the road. So we got to the Ponca City bus station later than late. One guy in there waiting for the bus.

Oh, he was hopping mad! He cussed worse'n I did shifting those rocks, and a lot louder. It didn't do him any good, mind, but he was too steamed to care.

I carried my suitcase to the roominghouse where the Eagles stay when they come to Ponca City. It was only a few blocks from the one where Charlie Carstairs's kid brother was staying, so that was handy. I'd made up some song and dance about why I was in town a day ahead of the rest of the team, but I turned out not to need it. Soon as the landlady—widow woman—saw who I was, she nodded and said, "Heard you were comin' early. I'll put you in Seven tonight."

Heard from who? I wondered. But I didn't need to be Hercule Sherlock or whatever his name is to cipher that out. Big Stu knows folks all over Oklahoma—into Kansas and Texas and maybe Arkansas, too. One of 'em must've put a flea in her ear.

Room 7 was a lot less crowded than it would be with four or five of us in there like usual. I picked the bed with the mattress that was less swaybacked. With luck, I'd get to keep it—well, half of it—when the rest of the Eagles came up from Enid.

You stay at a rooming house, you have supper with the rest of the lodgers. That's part of the bill. Not a fancy supper, or they'd charge more. I wasn't fancy. Where else would I go? Ponca City didn't have a diner anywhere near as good as Big Stu's. One of the gals at the table—a secretary or something, I guessed—looked nice. Not *I want to run off to the Sandwich Islands with you, sweetie* nice, but enough to keep my mind off the pinto-bean soup and tinned peas boiled all gray.

She didn't even notice me—she had eyes for one of the other fellows. So I finished eating, I put my dishes in the sink like a good boy, and I went back to my room. Nothing much to do in there, so I did nothing for a while. Not like I didn't have practice doing nothing back at the shack.

Must've been about nine o'clock when I cinched my belt a notch tighter. Then I put the knuckleduster in one front pocket of my trousers and the blackjack in the other. I walked around in there a bit to make sure the pants stayed up all right. They were fine, so I slipped out of my room, out of my roominghouse, and over toward the one where Mitch Carstairs stayed.

Good thing it wasn't far. I didn't know my way around Ponca City real well, and it was dark as the inside of a zombie's brain out there. I wore a cross around my neck to fight off the vampires, but having faith helps, too. I wasn't feeling what you'd call faithful just then, not with the job I had ahead of me.

I might've walked right past the place if a car hadn't picked that second to turn. The headlight beams speared out and lit up the brass numbers—527—on the building. It was yellow brick, two stories high: bigger than the roominghouse where I was.

When I tried the front door, it opened. I figured it would. People still come and go at that hour. More brass numbers over the doorways showed which room was which. I slipped down the hall, quiet as I could, till I got to 13.

Light leaked out under the bottom of the door. That made me let out a sigh of relief—he was home. What would I have done if he'd decided to spend the night playing bridge with his buddies? Wait in the bushes till he came back? I'd had notions I liked better. It was dark out there, and I wasn't sure I'd recognize him at high noon. I mean, I knew what Charlie Carstairs looked like, but I didn't have any promise Mitch looked the same way. Big Stu should've given me a picture. I should've thought to ask for one back in Enid.

But I didn't have to worry about any of that now. I slipped my right hand into the brass knucks. I made a fist in my pocket while I knocked on the door with my left hand.

Somebody moved in the room. I could hear it over my pounding heart—no, I wasn't used to the rough stuff. This was worse than facing a wild fireballer with the bases loaded and the team down two in the late innings.

The door opened, it seemed like in slow motion. Yeah, I was that tensed up. Only I couldn't haul off and coldcock the first thing I saw on the other side. If something had got fouled up some kind of way, if it wasn't Charlie Carstairs's brother, I'd feel bad about whaling the snot out of the wrong guy. Big Stu probably wouldn't pay me the ninety he still owed me, either. Odds were he'd take the first ten out of my hide.

Then the door got all the way open. I started to ask, *You Mitch*

Carstairs? As soon as the guy in the room went *Yeah* or *Uh-huh* or *Who wants to know?*, I'd let him have it.

Only I couldn't. Even the question clogged in my throat. Because it wasn't a guy in the room. It was a girl.

She was somewhere near my age. Dark blond hair in a permanent wave, green eyes, pert nose. Prettier than the secretary-type gal back at my roominghouse. Not actress pretty, I guess, but not far from it. "Yes?" she said to me, her voice deep for a girl's.

God damn Big Stu to hell and gone! He didn't say anything about a girl. She complicated everything—in spades, she did. But I needed that money the way I needed air to breathe. So instead of what I'd meant to ask, I came out with, "Where's Mitch Carstairs?"

Those green eyes got a little wider. "I'm Mich Carstairs. I don't think I know you."

I felt like she'd sucker-punched me, not the other way around. And I realized I hadn't even known what I was doing yet when I swore at Big Stu in my head before. He'd had a magic done, looking for Charlie Carstairs's kid brother, and the wizard said *Michelle* and he heard *Mitchell.* Or maybe the wizard screwed it up. I didn't know, and I still don't.

But I did know that, no matter how bad I needed those ninety clams, I didn't need 'em bad enough to beat up a dame to get 'em. I'm no vampire—I have to be able to look at myself in the mirror. I couldn't do what Big Stu wanted done, not if my life depended on it. That I might be laying my life on the line by *not* doing it . . . I didn't think about that, not then. Fool that I was.

Real fast, I said, "No, Miss, you don't know me. But you're Charlie Carstairs's sister, aren't you? Charlie Carstairs over in Enid?"

"That's right." She gave kind of an automatic nod. "Has something happened to—?" She broke off.

"He's fine—now. So are you—now. If you stick around Ponca City for even another day, though, you won't be." Once Big Stu found out I'd messed up, he'd send some guys who didn't worry about what they hit as long as they got paid. Still fast, I went on, "Get out of town. Get out of state. Go to California." Yes, I had Pa in my head. "Just go, quick as you can. Git!" I might've been shooing a stray dog.

Her eyes got wide again, wider this time. "I can't do that!"

"Sister, you can't do anything else, not if you want to stay in one piece. I know what I'm talking about." I pulled out my right hand with the knuckleduster still on it. If I'd tried to take the damn thing off, it would've looked like I was playing pocket pool. She saw what it was, of course, but she didn't raise any fuss. She must've seen I wasn't about to use it. After I stuck it back in my pocket, I said, "Yeah, I know, all right. Some pieces of work, you just can't do."

"Thank you," she said quietly. Her mouth twisted. You want to know how pretty she was? She was still pretty when it did, that's how pretty. For all I know, she might've got even prettier. When her face cleared, she nodded once more, this time to herself and not to me. "All right. I'll be gone tomorrow. I don't know where. I don't know what I'll do. I haven't got much money, but—"

"Neither do I," I stuck in. "Why d'you reckon I came up here?"

"Thank you," she said again, even softer this time. Then she closed the door on me: not slammed it, but closed it. I didn't mind. We'd already said everything we had to say to each other, hadn't we?

I got the hell out of there. I hoped she got the hell out of there, got the hell out of Oklahoma, come morning. Well, I'd done everything I knew how to do. If it wasn't what Big Stu wanted . . . I was almost to the roominghouse front door when I really and truly realized I'd just crossed the guy who ran a lot more of my home town than the mayor ever did.

The door opened. A man—I guessed he was one of the lodgers—came in. He was skinny and sad-looking, with worn clothes and gray hair getting thin at the front. He could've been anybody. He paid me no special mind—I could've been anybody, too. Some other lodger's friend, or maybe a new lodger he hadn't met yet.

Only I wasn't anybody, not any more, or not just anybody. I was somebody dumb enough to get Big Stu pissed off at him. In Enid, you couldn't get much dumber than that. Big Stu'd wanted to hurt Charlie Carstairs through his kid brother, only she turned out to be Charlie's sister. He couldn't hurt me through anybody else. Everyone I might've cared about was either dead or gone. No, he'd have to pay me back in person.

All of a sudden, what I'd told Mich Carstairs looked like pretty good advice for me to take, too. The farther away from Big Stu I got, the better off I'd be. If I had any smarts, I'd hitch a ride or hop a freight or jump on a carpet the way my old man did. If I had any smarts, I'd do it tonight. I wouldn't wait for sunup. The sooner, the better.

But I didn't have any smarts. What I had was a game tomorrow. I couldn't let the other Eagles down, not even on account of Big Stu. Hal Snodgrass, our backup outfielder, he was slower'n an armadillo after it meets a Model A.

I almost hoped a vampire would try to jump me while I walked back to my boarding house. Maybe I'd fight him off and work out some of what I was feeling. Or maybe he'd get me and turn me into something like him. Then I wouldn't care about anything past my next drink of blood—cow or sheep or coyote blood, or maybe I'd go after people, too, if I was bold.

No vampires, though. Nothing but the stars shining out of a clear, dark sky. The air was cool, close to crisp. Pretty soon it would get hot and sticky and stay that way for months, but that hadn't happened yet. The skeeters hadn't come out, either. Without so much on my mind, I might've enjoyed the walk.

My landlady hadn't locked the front door. I'd timed it all fine—about the only thing I'd done right since I got to Ponca City. I went to my room, laid myself down, and tried to sleep. Took a while, but I did it. I don't remember the dreams I had. I do remember they were the kind you'd want to forget.

(II)

We would play the Greasemen at half past two. We had to make sure we could get the game in before dark. They were already starting to play under the lights even back then. It was risky, though. You really have to tame salamanders or electrics before they get along with wooden stands. So I'd heard of night games, but I'd never seen one and I'd sure never played in one.

Not then, I hadn't. Been some changes made since.

But I'm getting ahead of myself. The widow woman's breakfast was as grim and cheap as her supper. Still and all, you can fill your belly on bread. I'd done it often enough in Enid. The bad, bad times come when you haven't got enough bread or anything else to fill up your empty.

I went down to the room at the end of the hall and took a bath after the folks there who had regular jobs headed off to do 'em. Didn't have to hustle so much that way. Other people weren't pounding on the door and yelling for me to hurry up in the name of the Lord.

I was slicking down my hair and combing a part into it at the mirror on the chest of drawers in my room when I heard a commotion in the front entryway. I knew what that had to be, and it was. The rest of the Enid Eagles had made it to Ponca City.

They all whooped when I came out to say hello. Ace McGinty must've been running his mouth but good. "Hope you're not too tuckered out to play today!" he called to me.

"Ah, stick it," I told him.

Which was the wrong thing to say, of course. "I thought that's what you were doing," Mudfoot Williams said. He was our third baseman. His name was Zebulon, but he'd been Mudfoot since he was a kid. He hated shoes more'n anything, and went barefoot whenever he could.

Him and Lightning Bug Kelly (who always had a smoke going, even when he was catching) and Don Patterson, our top pitcher, threw their bags into the room with me. The other guys got their rooms. Nobody stayed in 'em long, though. We put on our baseball togs, grabbed our gloves and shillelaghs, and headed on over to Conoco Ball Park.

It's on the southwest edge of town, over by US 60. The diamond in Blaine Park is better kept up, but all of the Greasemen except a couple of ringers work in the oilfields, so they play on the company field. We got there a couple of hours before game time, but a few people were already in the stands. Not one whole hell of a lot to do in Ponca City. Well, Enid's the same way.

Rod Graver played short for us, and managed, too. He was about thirty then, not slick, but steady, which you need if you're gonna ride herd on a bunch of ballplayers. He'd got up to B ball in the pros. He might've gone further, but his brother hurt himself and he had to come back and take over the farm work.

Him and me, we threw a ball back and forth to loosen up. After a few minutes, he came over and asked, "You do what you needed to yesterday?" He talked low, but he knew I hadn't come to Ponca City early so I could dip my wick. That meant he talked to Big Stu. It meant Big Stu talked to him, too.

I've always made a lousy liar. I shrugged back at him. "You tend to your business and I'll tend to mine," I answered, not sharp—I didn't want to quarrel before the game—but giving away as little as I could.

He got a double furrow, up and down, above his nose. His eyebrows pulled down and together. "Big Stu won't fancy that," he said, his voice as flat as you wish infield dirt would be.

"Big Stu'll just have to lump it," I said. "I'll pay back the down payment—he doesn't need to fret over that." I hoped I'd get ten bucks from my share of the gate today. If I didn't, well, I'd come up with the rest some way or the other.

Not that that'd do me much good, not with Big Stu. I didn't do what he told me to, so I was dirt to him from then on out. Not dirt—manure. I knew it. So did Rod. He clicked his tongue between his teeth. "Jack—" he started, and stopped right there.

"It's done. I mean, it's not done. The hell with it. The hell with everything," I said. "Let's play ball."

He turned away. *Let's play ball* would do for that day, and maybe for the next one. It sure wouldn't do once I got back to Enid. Like the

Mitch Carstairs who hadn't been there, I'd be an accident waiting to happen, and I wouldn't wait long. I hoped the Mich Carstairs who had been there was somewhere a long ways away by then. I wondered what I would've done if she'd been mud-fence ugly. Lucky—I guess lucky—I hadn't needed to worry about that. Anybody who tells you looks don't count in this old world, he's talking out his rear end.

The Greasemen got to the park right after we did and started warming up alongside us. Their home whites had *Greasemen* across the chest in script, and CONOCO underneath in smaller printed capitals so you could see who they worked for. They razzed us, and we razzed them right back. We were the two best teams in north central Oklahoma, and we both knew it.

People kept filing into the ballpark. Looked like we'd draw 1,500, maybe even 2,000. A quarter a pop, half a buck to sit right back of home, and that's a decent gate. Road team—us—would split forty percent of it. Some money for everybody, but they call it semipro ball 'cause you can't make a living on it.

Two umps, just like in the little pro leagues that pop up in these parts and then die like your crops in a drought. Guy behind the plate was local; guy on the bases drove up from Enid. They'd switch when the Greasemen called on us. I'd seen both of them often enough before. They mostly didn't screw the team from the other side too hard.

"Batter up!" yelled the plate umpire. He was already sweating in his black suit and mask and protector. The crowd whooped and stomped. They were rooting for the Greasemen, except for the few who'd come over from Enid.

Ponca City pitcher was a big redheaded right-hander named Walt Edwards. He'd played pro ball till a sore soupbone sent him back to the oil works. Though he couldn't throw hard any more, he knew what he was doing out there. His fastball might not break a windowpane, but he could drive nails with his curve.

Our leadoff man hit back to the box. Then Mudfoot touched Edwards for a single to left, but he didn't get any farther. Don Patterson took the hill for the bottom of the first. He was the opposite of Walt every which way 'cept they were both tall. He was a lefty, and he could fire the pill through a brick wall. Trouble was, about one game in three he couldn't hit a brick wall with the damn thing.

Conoco Ball Park's got a center field like they say the Cricket Grounds does—it goes on and on. I played deep, too. I knew I might have to cut across. Our guys in left and right weren't what you'd call swift. Even from way out there, the ball went *pop!* every time it slammed Lightning Bug's mitt.

Don walked their second hitter, and the next guy blooped a Texas League single in front of me. But we turned a slick double play on their cleanup man—told you Rod's smooth—so we got out of it.

I was up second in the second. I waited on one knee in the on-deck circle, watching Edwards work. It would've been a pleasure if he hadn't been pitching against us. You need to think on the mound. If you can't blow it by somebody, you need it twice as much. He could do it. Oh, couldn't he just!

Our first man up grounded to short. I stepped into the batter's box. Ponca City fans booed me. They booed everybody in an Enid uniform, so I didn't think anything of it. Edwards threw me a curve just off the outside corner—I thought. The plate ump's hand went up. "Stee-rike!"

"You missed that one," I said. I didn't turn my head toward him. The crowd would've got on me, and he would've thought I was showing him up. Then my strike zone would've been as wide as Big Stu the rest of the day.

"You hit. I'll umpire," he said, which didn't leave me much of a comeback. So I dug in and waited for the next one.

I guessed right. It was another slow curve, only inside this time. I bunted it down the third-base line and beat it out easy. "That's crap," said their first basemen as I took my lead. His name was Mort Milligan. He had arms and shoulders like a blacksmith and he looked mean, so I didn't sass him back. I just grinned.

Lightning Bug swung from the heels and popped up. Our next guy struck out and left me stranded. I trotted to center, picked up my glove—you leave 'em out there when your side hits—and I was ready.

This frame, Don walked their first guy. Then that hulking first baseman came up. Milligan batted left, so I slid a step or two into right-center, just in case. He swung through the first pitch. The next one was a foot off the plate—he let it go by. Don looked in at Lightning Bug, nodded, rared back, and let fly again. This time, the Greaseman connected.

You hear that *crack!* off the bat like a rifle, you start running. You worry about how far later. *As far as you can* is a pretty good bet. You hear that *crack!*, even *as far as you can* may not come close to far enough.

If I hadn't shifted those couple of steps toward right, I never would've had a prayer. I didn't think I had one, anyway. I was running hard as I knew how, but the ball roared out there like a freight on a long downgrade. If it got by me, the man on first would score for sure. Only thing that might hold Milligan to a triple was him being strong and slow. Might. You put a ball over the center fielder's head in that park, you can run for days.

At the last possible second, I threw out my arm. I will be damned if the ball didn't land square in the pocket and stick. They tell you not to catch one-handed, 'cause it's too likely to pop out. You want to say I got lucky, I won't argue with you.

By that time, Mort Milligan was past first. The runner on first was halfway to third—he'd taken off at the crack of the bat. My throw in hit the second baseman. He'd gone out to short right, figuring I'd be flinging from the fence. His relay doubled off the runner easy as you please.

The crowd went nuts. They don't often cheer the visitors, but I got a heck of a hand if I do say so myself. Mort Milligan pointed out at me like I'd picked his pocket. "You *son* of a bitch!" he shouted. I just stood there, waiting to see if we'd get the third out.

We did. I came into the dugout. They clapped for me again. One guy tossed me half a buck, and another a silver cartwheel. I touched the brim of my cap to both of 'em. I always needed money, and right then more than usual.

Well, I won't give you the whole game like a radio fellow. We beat 'em—the final was 5-3. I didn't get any more hits. I did catch the last out. It was a can of corn, as high and lazy a fly ball as you'd ever want to see. Your granny could've put it away without a glove. I caught it with both hands just the same.

When I brought in the ball, Milligan shook his head at me and said, "You wouldn't make that play again in a year of Sundays."

"I made it this time," I answered. Then, because we'd won, I needled him back: "You won't hit it that hard any time soon, either." He gave me a dirty look, but he turned away.

One of the men in the crowd, an old fellow with store-bought teeth, threw me another silver dollar, which I didn't even slightly expect. He said, "I've been playing and watching since before they wore gloves, and that's as good a catch as I ever seen."

"Obliged, friend," I told him, and I meant it more ways than he knew. I felt pretty darn proud—as proud as a guy can feel when he doesn't dare go home with the rest of the team after the game.

Rod Graver was under the grandstand with the Ponca City manager, splitting up the take. More stacks of quarters than you can shake a stick at. Once everything got figured out, my share would be somewhere north of ten bucks—it *had* been a good house. I'd be glad to have it. I would've been gladder yet if it'd been more.

Most of the Eagles didn't know I had things on my mind. Don Patterson pounded me on the back—almost knocked me over—and said, "Thanks, Jack. You saved my bacon out there."

I wondered who would save mine. I wondered if anybody would, or could. All I said was, "Any old time. Part of the service." Don laughed and laughed. His only worry was slathering liniment on his arm once he went back to the roominghouse.

We got paid at the ballpark. Rod gave everybody a roll of quarters and then a dozen more besides. "Thirteen dollars," he said, in case we couldn't work it out for ourselves. That was about what I thought, all right. He kept some extra for himself, on account of he was the manager and did more for the team than just play ball. I don't know exactly how much of a bonus he took. I do know you couldn't've paid me enough to try to keep a bunch of roughnecks like us all heading the same way.

We felt proud of ourselves when we rode back to the roominghouse. You always do when you win, and especially when you win on the road. Win on the road and even 3.2 beer tastes good.

My roomies joined the crowd at the end of the hall to take their turns in the bathtub. Pretty soon, they'd have the choice between dirty bathwater and cold. Since I'd gone in there that morning,

I figured I could let it slip. I got out of my uniform and into my street clothes.

Silver clinked, all nice and sweet, when I moved it from the back pocket of my baseball pants to the front pocket of my regular trousers. The quarters, the half, the heavy dollars . . . I smiled. Money does make things better.

I hefted the roll of quarters Rod gave me. It made almost as good a fist-packer as the brass knucks I hadn't used. Then I frowned and hefted it again. I know what a roll of quarters weighs. I'd better—I've got 'em at enough different ballparks. This one didn't feel quite right. I peeled off some of the orange paper wrapper.

Slugs spilled into the palm of my other hand.

"Well, shit," I muttered, there where nobody could hear me. So it had started already. Ten bucks can take you a ways. Not having it would be bad. Not having it when I thought I did would've been worse.

I went next door to Rod's room. When I knocked, he opened it himself. Made things simpler. "Need to talk to you a minute," I said.

"Sure," he answered, like nothing was wrong. I told you before—Rod's smooth. "What's going on?"

I jerked my head toward the front door. He came with me, easy as you please. When we got outside, I flipped him one of the slugs. "Pay me for the game," I said.

It didn't faze him a bit. He caught the slug—he has good hands—and stuck it in his own pocket. "You told me you'd give back the ten you got out of Big Stu," he said.

"That's between me and him. It's got nothing to do with you," I answered. "Pay me for the goddamn game. Pay me for the catch. Pay me or I'll go back in there and show the guys what you tried to pay me with."

That hit him like one of Don's fastballs in the ribs. If the Eagles found out he'd stiffed me, most of 'em—maybe all of 'em—would be on my side. Semipro teams break up all the time. Something like that could be plenty to break up the one he ran.

He was smart enough to see as much. He never was a fool, Rod Graver. "Okay, Jack. Keep your shirt on," he said, which couldn't mean anything but *Keep your trap shut*. He hauled out his billfold and gave me two fives. "Here you go. You happy?"

"Happy like snow is black," I said. Little old Jew ran the hockshop in Enid I knew too well. I got that one from him.

Rod just looked at me. I bet he was never in a hockshop in all his born days. He said, "If you think ten bucks'll keep you away from Big Stu longer'n ten minutes, you better do some more thinkin'."

"Nuts to that." I didn't want him to see he'd hit a nerve. "I sweat for that money out at the ballyard. I ran for it. It's mine."

"It's yours now," he allowed, "but you better keep runnin'."

"Don't worry about me. Worry about how you're gonna find another center fielder. The guys you got now, they'd have to play it on a bicycle."

He smiled then, just a hair's worth. "Bicycles," he muttered. "Luck to you, you dumb bastard. Anybody who gets in bad with Big Stu is a dumb bastard, but luck to you anyways. You'll need it."

I wanted to ask him how come he was doing Big Stu's bidding. But you don't need to ask a question like that. You only need to think of it, and it answers itself. Rod did things for Big Stu 'cause he knew which side his bread was buttered on, that was how come.

We walked back into the roominghouse together, like nothing was wrong. A little while later, most of the Eagles went out to dinner. Ponca City may not've had a good diner, but it had a chop-suey house, which Enid didn't. Me, I ate another roominghouse supper at the widow woman's sorry table. I didn't want to spend a quarter or half a dollar, not when I was about to pull up stakes. And I wouldn't've been good company for the other fellas, either. They wanted to celebrate beating the Greasemen. I didn't have anything to celebrate about.

All three of the guys I shared the room with went out to eat. When I said I didn't feel like it, Don offered to buy for me. "Least I can do after you went ballhawking for me like that," he said.

"It's not the money," I lied—it was, some. "I don't feel like it, is all."

He could tell I wasn't saying everything I might have. Lightning Bug and Mudfoot dragged him out before he had the chance to get snoopy, though. After I had my supper, such as it was, I went out for a walk. It was heading toward dark, but it hadn't quite got there yet. Maybe the folks at the roominghouse thought I wanted a constitutional to settle myself after the game. That's just my guess—I didn't ask 'em, since I didn't much care. Any which way, I went, and I was glad to be gone.

I wasn't going back to Enid; I knew that much. A mouse doesn't turn around and run straight into the cat's mouth. All I had in Ponca City was in my pockets or in my suitcase or in my head. I could do 'most any kind of odd job, if anybody'd hire me. But things in Ponca City were as rough as they were in Enid or anywhere else. I was a stranger in town, too. Nobody knew me from a hole in the ground.

I chuckled under my breath while I walked along. That wasn't so. The Greasemen knew me, all right, and better than they wanted to. About the only thing I could do better than most fellows my age was play center field. I couldn't do it that much better than the fellow they already had, though. They wouldn't cut him loose so they could take me on.

The one thing I was good at, I wasn't good enough at to do anything with it. Sure looked that way to me then, anyhow. You never know what's comin' round the corner till it smacks you in the chops.

Me, I came round the corner and found myself on Palm Street, a block and a half from the boarding house where Mich Carstairs had been staying. My feet knew where they were going even if my head hadn't a clue. Or maybe my head did know, but decided not to say anything for a while.

When I got to the boarding house, I paused in front of the door, listening. I didn't want to go in if they were still eating in there. Then I wondered why the devil not. What difference did it make tonight? I wasn't going to do anything bad. That had been the night before, and look what it got me.

So I turned the knob and walked inside. A couple of men did sit in the dining room, smoking and shooting the breeze. One of them was the beat-down-looking older fellow I'd passed on my way out before. I nodded to him to show I remembered, and he gave it back. Then I went on down the hall.

No light under the door from room 13 now. Well, that didn't have to mean anything. I knocked, waited, and knocked again. Nothing but quiet on the other side of the door. Oh, maybe she was at a picture show. But maybe she'd listened to me after all. I could hope so—I could, and I did.

Out I went. I got another nod—a suspicious one this time, I thought—from that gray-haired guy. If he never saw me again, it wouldn't break his heart. If I never saw that boarding house again, it wouldn't've broken mine. And I never did. I've had my heart broken a few times since—life is like that. But the boarding house had nothing to do with any of 'em.

It was full dark, dark dark, by the time I left. I was heading back to the place where the Eagles stayed when a voice spoke to me out of the night: "Hey, buddy, wanna take all your troubles away?"

If that voice sounded like it belonged to a pretty girl, I bet I would've gone with her. Chances are I would've spent my cash and got up with more troubles than I'd lain down with. It didn't, though. It was a man's voice, a colored man's, deep and smooth and buttery. He didn't seem to want to knock me over the head or anything. No, he had the kind of voice that could've sold sand in the desert.

"What are you talking about?" I asked him—that's how smooth and slick he was. I knew better. Nobody who calls to you like that is out to do you a favor. He's out to do himself one. I understood that. I answered all the same.

"I work for a conjure man," he said, and I bet he did. Maybe that was how come he sounded so good—his voice could've had a little spell on it. He went on, "Let me take you to him. The way you're stompin' along, I can tell somebody done you wrong. Once my master gets done, though, he'll fix you up so you never care about nothin' like that again."

I didn't know I'd been stomping along. For all I can say, I hadn't been, and he was just spinning out a line like a spider to see if I stuck. But after that I wasn't stomping, and I know that for sure. I was running, running harder than when I chased down the liner that musclebound first baseman tagged. When the colored fella said *fix you up*, he meant *turn you into a zombie*. I sure wouldn't care about anything after that. Being a zombie's worse than dying and going to hell. Looks like that to me, anyway. When you go to hell, at least you know why. Zombies don't—can't—know. That's what makes 'em zombies.

Where would I have wound up? On a farm out West, pulling beets out of the ground forever? More likely at the Conoco works, rolling oil barrels around the way that zombie at the mill in Enid rolled flour barrels. One of the Greasemen might've seen me and laughed.

I tried to cock my head while I ran, so I could hear if the colored fella was gaining. He wasn't—he wasn't even chasing me. The bastard didn't need to bother. Way things are since the Big Bubble busted, getting rid of all your worries looks pretty damn good to more and more folks. Who cares what you do afterwards? You sure won't.

No, the conjure man's helper didn't need me. He'd find somebody else instead, somebody desperate enough to be glad to go with him. Then he'd be happy, and his boss would be happy, and Conoco would be happy, too. Everybody'd be happy—except for the somebody else. He'd be a zombie, sorrier than damned.

I had just slowed down from my wild run to a walk when a vampire jumped out at me from behind a parked Willys. Fry me for a catfish if I can tell you what the police and magic patrol were doing that night. Not keeping an eye on the streets between those two rooming houses—I can tell you that. Twice in a couple of blocks! I might as well've been in New York City, not Ponca City.

"Give me your blood!" the vampire said when he reached out for me. He talked the same way I did—none of that mush-mouthed foreign stuff. So he couldn't've been one of the ones who brought being a vampire to the States from the other side of the ocean. He'd been an ordinary Joe till one of them or one of the ones they got got him.

Which didn't mean I fancied his fangs punching into my neck. I whipped out my cross, quick as I could, and stuck it in his face. The cross flared, bright like a welding torch. I'd had to use it once or twice before, but I'd never seen it do anything like that. I must've had a lot more faith than usual, I guess because I was just thinking about zombies and hell and all.

"Arrh!" The vampire flinched away from the shining cross.

"Go kill a cow if you need blood that bad," I said.

He made a horrible face. "I've been doing that too damn long. It's like eating grits without butter or salt all the time. I want something with some taste to it."

"Well, you can't have me. Go on, git, or I'll make you sorry." I eyed him. He was a miserable, scraggly excuse for a vampire. He'd likely been a miserable, scraggly excuse for a man, too. "Sorrier, I mean."

He said something Pa would've belted me one for if he'd heard it out of my mouth. That didn't do him any good, either. So he slunk off, head down, in the direction I'd come from. Maybe he'd run across the conjure man's helper. I could hope so, anyway. Could the conjure man make a vampire into a zombie? Would the vampire want him to? Could the vampire get the drop on the conjure man's helper and drain him dry, or would the lousy bloodsucker get magicked away before he could bite? All kinds of interesting questions, and I'd never know the answers to any of them.

I came up with another one just before I got back to my rooming house. What would Rod have been telling the other Eagles about me while they were eating dinner? One more thing I didn't know the answer to yet, but there I figured I'd find out pretty darn quick.

Worrying about that might've been what gave me a fit of the shakes after I went into my room. Oh, I expect running across the conjure man's helper and the vampire within a couple of blocks of each other had a little somethin' to do with it, too. I'd got away from them. Could I get away from what I'd done? I mean, what I hadn't done?

I'd give it my best shot, same as I had with the Greaseman's line drive. Maybe I'd get lucky twice. In the meantime . . . In the meantime, I slid under the bedclothes and tried to fall asleep. I surprised myself—I did it.

Lightning Bug and Don and Mudfoot came in a while later. Quite a while, I'd guess. They'd done some celebrating, all right. They tried to keep quiet, but when a drunk does that he only makes more noise.

"See, he's here," Mudfoot said. "Ace was full of it—he don't got no girlfriend in town. He just hung around and hit the sack."

Well, Mudfoot had it partway right. Since that was closer than he usually came, let's leave it right there. I pulled the covers up over my head and did my best to go back to sleep. Damned if I didn't make it, too.

"Nope." Next morning after breakfast, I shook my head at the rest of the Eagles. "I ain't goin' back to Enid with y'all."

Don looked worried. He had a heart as fine as his fastball—and about as wild. "Rod told us you might have troubles in town," he said, and by the way he said it I would've bet that wasn't all Rod said, not by a long chalk. "With us at your back, might be things wouldn't look so bad."

More than half the team nodded. Rod didn't, and he didn't look too happy that so many did. *I* was happy—they really did like me. That made me feel good, but nowhere good enough to go back. "Thanks, boys, but I'll try Ponca City a while," I said. "Nothin' in Enid for me, and not one of you bums can tell me different."

They kind of shuffled their feet and stared down at their shoes, but nobody tried to make me think I was wrong. Don did ask, "How come you reckon you'll come across anything here?"

I shrugged. "Call it a change of luck. One of these days, could be you'll see me shagging flies in a Greasemen's uniform."

They all shook their heads and made hex signs like the ones you use against the evil eye. Then they gathered round me and slapped me on the back and shook my hand and told me what a swell fella I was. One or two of 'em shoved money in my pocket, and it's not like they had a whole hell of a lot more than I did.

Yeah, Rod Graver shook my hand, too. "Shall I tell Big Stu you've set up shop here?" he asked.

"Tell him whatever you please," I said. "You will anyway."

He made a face, as if to say, *Hey, it's not my fault this guy gives me my marching orders. He gives 'em to the whole town.* He wasn't exactly wrong, as I had reason to know. But he wasn't exactly right, either. He stuck out his hand again. I took it. Why not? It wouldn't hurt anything. Of course, it also wouldn't help.

The old cars full of Eagles all started up, which is always a worry when you've got an old car. They pulled away from the curb. The guys waved till they turned the first corner and got out of sight. I stood there on the sidewalk, wondering what the dickens I'd do in a town where I knew nobody and nobody knew me.

I could stay in the roominghouse a while—it was cheap. But it'd be the first place Big Stu looked for me, so I'd best find a different one. I started walking, not going anywhere in particular but sort of heading downtown. Ponca City's a little smaller than Enid; I wouldn't take long to get there.

Downtown Ponca City looked like any other downtown about the same size—well, except that the city hall put me in mind of a Span-

ish mission dropped where one purely didn't belong. The train station. A couple of picture houses. A hotel that looked like it needed
business. A doctor's office, and a lawyer's, and a dentist's, and a
spectacle-maker's. An apothecary's shop.

Some more shops and stores. Most of them looked like they needed
business, too, even though it was Saturday morning and they should've
been jumping if they ever were. Same as you'd see in any other downtown, a good many shopfronts were closed, boarded over. You could
kind of tell how long since each one went under by how many layers of
flyers and posters were pasted on the boards. Some of the old paper was
all raggedy, and fluttered in the breeze. Some of the posters were so
new and fresh, they looked like they'd gone up right before I ambled by.

And dog my cats if they hadn't. BALLGAME TODAY! they yelled,
and underneath it was that day's date written in by hand. The posters
had a picture of two men in baseball uniforms with a big old lion's
head, mouth open and roaring, embroidered on the chest. The ballplayers looked like lions, too. They wore their hair down to their
shoulders or past 'em in a mane, and they had mustaches and shaggy
beards to go along.

THE HOUSE OF DANIEL! the poster said, in letters bigger even
than the ones for BALLGAME TODAY! In smaller type, it went on,
Today, the world-famous touring baseball team comes to your
town! Be there to enjoy the show! More handwriting said they were
playing the Ponca City Greasemen at the Conoco Ball Park, and that
it'd cost fifty cents to get in.

The House of Daniel! I knew who they were. Any semipro ballplayer would have, and does to this day. They were the best of our
bunch, like the New York Hilltoppers are in the big leagues. They're
based in a little churchy town up in Wisconsin or somewhere like
that, but they barnstorm the whole country. They play the year around,
too. For the winter, they head on out to the West Coast, where the
weather stays good. Or they go south of the border, or take ship to
the Sandwich Islands.

They beat the St. Louis Archdeacons once. They've barnstormed
alongside big-leaguers, and had 'em on their team once they got too
old to stick in the majors. They've played against the top colored
teams, too, in places where the laws let you do that.

They aren't part of a league or anything—never have been. So they're semipros, just like the Enid Eagles. But they're semipro royalty, and the Eagles . . . ain't.

Funny how none of the Greasemen said anything to us about this game. Or not so funny, I guess. They didn't want us to know, for fear we'd make our own matchup with the House of Daniel. This way, they got the bragging rights and their share of the big gate, and they left us with hind tit.

No, not *us*. I wasn't an Enid Eagle any more. It hadn't sunk in yet. I didn't realize till that moment how much it hadn't sunk in.

I started west and south, back toward the Conoco Ball Park. I didn't know downtown Ponca City real well, but by gum I knew how to get to the field. I wanted to see how the Greasemen stood up against the House of Daniel, and I wanted to see those traveling hotshots go through their paces.

And . . . I stopped in the middle of the sidewalk, my mouth falling open. I stopped again, at the roominghouse, and stuck my spikes and glove and uniform in a sack I begged from the widow woman. If I could somehow sweet-talk the House of Daniel into taking me along with 'em, I'd go so far and so fast, Big Stu'd never catch up with me. Even if they said no, which they likely would, how was I worse off? You got to try in this old world, or nothing happens a-tall.

(III)

W hat you got in there?" The ticket-seller pointed at my sack when I gave him four bits. "Don't want nobody chuckin' bottles or nothin' at the House of Daniel guys. Could be they wouldn't come back here no more." That would've hurt Ponca City where it lived—right in the old wallet.

"Ain't gonna chuck this stuff at 'em." I showed him my baseball gear.

He recognized the uniform, even from the little bit he saw. "Oh. You're one o' them damn Eagles." His lip kinda curled up. "Well, go on in. They won't be lookin' for no riffraff like you."

In I went, scared he was right and hoping he was wrong. I sat down in the second row back of the first-base dugout, the one the visitors used—the one I'd been in the day before. I sat there, and I watched the House of Daniel loosen up.

The more I watched, the more it looked like the guy who took my two quarters had it pegged. I'd already played with and against some pretty fair ballplayers. The general rule was, the better you were, the smoother you seemed. Oh, not always, but that's how to bet. Takes somebody who knows what he's doing and who's done it a million times to make it look easy.

Those House of Daniel fellas, they made it look so easy, it was like the ball wasn't even there. I needed longer'n I should have to see that part of the time it wasn't. They were doing a phantom infield the likes of which you'd never seen the likes of. They'd catch and throw and pivot and all, as if they were working a rundown or turning a double play or whatever, and you'd follow the ball with your eyes, only there was no ball to follow. It was something to see—or not to see, I guess you could say.

Over by the home dugout, the Greasemen were stretching or playing pepper or having a catch. They were supposed to be, anyways. Half of 'em, though, couldn't keep their eyes off the shaggy men with the lion's heads on their shirts.

When it was Ponca City's turn to take infield, they played it straight as a yardstick. If they'd got even a little bit cute, the crowd—and it was gonna be way bigger than Enid drew—would've seen they weren't as good as the House of Daniel guys. This way, they just looked boring. Not a great choice, maybe, but a better one.

Pitchers were warming up, too. Ponca City's other main hurler besides Walt Edwards was a right-hander everybody called Close Shave Simpkins. Not because his face was so smooth—oh, no. He had almost enough gray stubble to make you reckon he belonged to the other side today. But he'd put one under your chin or spin your cap as soon as he'd look at you.

Closer to me stood Frank Carlisle, who'd go for the House of Daniel. His beard hung down almost to the emblem on his shirtfront. His hair was even longer, and a couple of shades lighter. He was a lefty.

"Let's see what you got, Fidgety Frank!" yelled a loudmouth not too far from me. Carlisle didn't even look his way. He just pegged it back and forth with the guy catching him. He threw somewhere between three-quarters and sidearm, so his curve broke wide but not down too much. Tell you the truth, he didn't look all that tough.

Both sides cleared the field. Some kids dragged it a last time to get it nice and smooth. One of the House of Daniel players bawled into a big old megaphone with a lion's head painted on each side (they didn't miss a trick, the House of Daniel boys).

"Ladies and gents, gents and ladies!" he roared. "Welcome to the latest celebration of America's game by the Lord's team, the House . . . of . . . Daniel!" He stopped there for cheers and boos. He got about a fifty-fifty split—what you'd expect, I suppose. "Today we're mighty pleased to be in Ponca City to play against your Greasemen!"

He waved toward the home dugout. Everybody whooped and raised Cain. I figured it was the first time an outsider ever said he was pleased to be in Ponca City. I also figured they'd whale the tar out of me if I said so, so I shut up.

Out trotted the home team in their white flannels. The Chinamen at the laundry—it's next door to the Ponca City chop-suey house—

must've worked overtime getting 'em all nice and clean again so soon after the game against the Eagles. The crowd cheered some more.

Out trotted the umps, too. The guy behind the plate was the same one who'd worked yesterday's game. I didn't recognize the fella who would work the bases. By the way he talked, he'd come down from Kansas or somewhere like that. Nobody cheered either one of them.

"Play ball!" yelled the plate umpire, and they did.

The first two men for the House of Daniel made easy outs. Their third hitter . . . The fellow with the megaphone called, "Batting third and playing center field, number fourteen, Rabbit O'Leary!"

He was a left-handed hitter. As soon as you saw him, you knew he meant business. About six-one, maybe 175. Yeah, he'd run like the wind. You need speed to play center. And he'd be trouble with the stick, or he wouldn't have hit where he was. I could hope I was as good an outfielder as he was. One look told me I wasn't as good a ballplayer.

Close Shave Simpkins had to be thinking the same kind of thing. On the second pitch, O'Leary hit a mean foul—pulled it past Mort Milligan, the wide-shouldered first sacker I'd robbed the day before, no more than a foot and a half outside the chalk. Pitch after that would have gone in one ear and out the other if Rabbit hadn't flattened out like a snake. That was no brushback. That was a beanball.

O'Leary got up, brushed himself off, and dug in again. He flied out to right, medium deep, two pitches later, and the inning was over. In came the Greasemen, out went the House of Daniel, and we started the bottom of the first.

I found out soon enough why that big-mouthed fan called Carlisle Fidgety Frank. The long-bearded pitcher might've been smooth loosening up, but not once he took the hill for real. He wiggled like an octopus with fleas. All arms and legs and herks and jerks and hesitations, and you never knew where the ball was coming from or how to pick it up till it was on top of you or past.

He struck out the first Greaseman on three pitches. The second guy hit a dribbler to short. The third hitter, Carlisle plunked right in the ribs. Message sent, message answered.

Message answered hurt more. "Ow!" the Greaseman yelled. "Fuck you!"

Polite as a preacher—which he was sometimes—Fidgety Frank tipped his cap. "And your granny," he said. The Greaseman trotted to first. He didn't rub. You never rub, not in semipro and not in the bigs, either.

"Uh-oh," somebody behind me said to his friend. "Gonna be one of those games."

"Looks like," Friend answered. I was thinking the same thing.

Carlisle gave up a squib single then, but he made the next guy pop up, so he fidgeted off the hook. In the top of the second, Simpkins drilled the first hitter up in the behind. "There! I gave you a brain concussion!" he shouted.

He was the one who ended up with the headache, though, on account of the House of Daniel scored four that inning. The guy he'd nailed plated the first run. He looked out at Close Shave when he came home, but only for a second.

Well, you had to know Fidgety Frank was gonna get his own back. He plunked Mort Milligan on the right arm. Mort eyed Carlisle as he took his base, but he didn't say anything. The next batter hit into a force play to end the inning.

There were a couple of more brushbacks after that, but things kinda settled down. It was 5-2, House of Daniel, in the bottom of the sixth. The Greasemen were a good nine—I ought to know—but the traveling team didn't seem to be having much trouble with 'em.

Then Ponca City's cleanup guy doubled to start the inning. The fellow behind him worked a walk Fidgety Frank really didn't want to give away. And up came muscly Mort Milligan, who was the tying run.

Carlisle came up and in, not to knock him down but to push him back from the plate an inch or two. Sure enough, the next one was low and away. Milligan swung and missed to even the count. Fidgety Frank thought he'd go low and away again. That was where the House of Daniel catcher set up, anyhow. Only Frank made a mistake.

Whack! I knew that sound. I'd heard it just the day before. Mort Milligan clobbered this long, low liner to almost the same place he'd hit the one then. Just like me, Rabbit O'Leary was off at the crack of the bat, trying to run the line drive down.

But I'd known I was the only one who had the ghost of a chance of catching the one yesterday. Enid's right fielder could throw fine, but he was slower than some dead people—and I don't mean zombies. I mean dead dead. Unlike the Eagles, the House of Daniel was a high-class outfit. Their right fielder didn't just throw. He could run, too.

It cost 'em plenty.

Rabbit O'Leary streaked after that scalded baseball. So did the right fielder. He was a big, lanky Dutchman called Aaron Aardsma or Double-Double-A or mostly just Double-Double. He was sure he could catch it. So was O'Leary. They both kept their eye on the ball. Neither one thought about anything else.

Till they slammed into each other.

That's the worst collision I ever saw. None of the others comes close. It's the worst collision I ever heard, too. You wouldn't think flesh and blood could make a noise like that smashing into more flesh and blood.

O'Leary went down flat and didn't move. Aardsma rolled over three or four times. When he stopped, he was bent like a bow, both hands clutched to one ankle. The ball shot past them and rolled all the way to that far-off fence in right-center. By the time the left fielder finally picked it up and threw it in, even Mort Milligan had himself the easiest inside-the-park homer anybody could want. House of Daniel 5, Greasemen 5.

A few people in Conoco Ball Park cheered the home-town hero. But those cheers were like ripples on a great big old pool of quiet. Most of the crowd was staring out at the train wreck in the outfield. I can't have been the only one wondering whether Rabbit O'Leary was even alive. He not only didn't move, he didn't twitch.

After getting the ball back to the infield, the House of Daniel's left fielder ran in to see what he could do for his buddies. The bearded second baseman was running out at the same time. They both took one look, cupped their hands in front of their mouths, and yelled the same thing: "Is there a doctor in the house?"

Two men in business suits, one young, the other bald with a gray fringe, came out of the stands. The bald guy had his black bag; the other fellow didn't. The young man went to work on Double-Double. He shouted in to the House of Daniel's dugout. Somebody brought him some boards. After a while, stretcher-bearers came out and lugged

Double-Double off, the way they would have during the Big War. That ankle he'd grabbed had a splint on it.

The Ponca City folks gave him a nice hand. He'd earned it. He'd been going all-out when he got hurt. He never would've got hurt so bad, or maybe at all, if he hadn't been. He managed to wave back before they carried him down into the dugout and away.

Which left O'Leary still down on the grass. The bald doc had him rolled over onto his belly. He was pushing down on his ribs and lifting his arms. "Artificial respiration," somebody behind me said, like we couldn't see that for ourselves.

Only purpose for artificial respiration is when the fella getting it can't breathe on his own. Some of the reasons for that are bad. The rest are worse. It got pin-drop quiet in the ballpark while the old guy worked on Rabbit. The other doctor came over to help him out. I wondered if the next fellow we saw helping out there would be the undertaker.

But that didn't happen, thank heaven. After a long, scary while, Rabbit's motor caught and turned over and he started breathing on his own. Everybody clapped when the bald doc stopped breathing for him and got to work on the other bad stuff that had happened to him.

The guys with the stretcher came back. They carried Rabbit away. His left arm was in a sling. What looked like a whole roll of bandage was wrapped around his head. The crowd cheered him, too—quietly, but they did. Just before he disappeared, his right arm came maybe two inches off his chest in a try at a wave. That took him more hard work than running after Mort Milligan's liner must have. People cheered again, louder this time.

And then? Then the game went on.

Yeah, that smashup gave folks most of their money's worth. Most, but not all. They wanted to see who won and who lost. Plenty of 'em had bets down on who won and who lost. In those parts, ballgames are right up there with cockfights and dogfights for making money change hands.

So the House of Daniel's left fielder moved over to right. A fellow who'd taken grounders at third went into left. And one of the pitchers who'd warmed up back of Fidgety Frank took over for Rabbit in center. Even the fanciest semipro team carries only fourteen, fifteen guys, sixteen tops. The fewer who split the take, the bigger the take is for everybody who does.

They got out of the sixth. The new left fielder made a nice catch—not a great catch, but nice—for the last out. The seventh was scoreless. In the top of the eighth, the House of Daniel scored three runs. They set up the inning with the prettiest hit-and-run you'd ever want to see. Guy on first broke for second. When the second baseman went to cover the bag, the batter slapped the ball through where he'd been. The runner kept on to third, and they were percolating.

Ponca City scored one in the last of the ninth, but only one. The House of Daniel took the game, 8-6. The two teams shook hands. No-body on the House of Daniel tried to deck Close Shave Simpkins. It wasn't like they'd never got thrown at before. In the stands and under them, cash went back and forth.

Then the fellow with the megaphone stood up in front of the visitors' dugout and blared, "Is there an outfielder in the house?" People laughed, 'cause he sounded just like the guys who'd yelled for a doctor after the collision.

Me, I wasn't laughing. As soon as Rabbit and Double-Double train-wrecked like that, I started hoping the House of Daniel would put out a call like that. I could play the field with them—I knew I could. Hit-ting? Well, I wasn't terrible, or the Eagles would've turned me down. Maybe I'd get on a hot streak or something.

You hate to wiggle on to a team because somebody else gets hurt. You wouldn't want anybody else wiggling on 'cause you got hurt. But guys do get hurt all the time. Teams need players all the time. And, by now, Big Stu would know I didn't do what he told me to do. Big Stu, he got mad *and* he got even.

So I was up like a shot. I took my spikes out of the sack and waved 'em around. "Hey, I'm a player!" I shouted. "I'm a center fielder, even!"

The guy with the megaphone looked me over. I wasn't seventy-five years old. I didn't stand four feet ten. Didn't weigh three hundred fifty pounds, either. He couldn't tell me to get lost just by eyeballing me, anyway. "Well, c'mon down and we'll talk," he said.

Down I went. The fellow with the megaphone brought over a couple-three Greasemen, I guess to ask if they knew what I could do. One of them was Mort Milligan. I pointed his way. "*He* knows I can play center some," I said.

Big lug might not have recognized me in my everyday clothes. He did then, though. "Oh. It's you," he growled, like he wanted to clean me off the sole of his shoe. He nodded to the man from the House of Daniel. "Yeah, so-and-so can run 'em down, all right. Robbed me like a bank yesterday playing for Enid." He told him how I'd caught his long drive.

"Huh," said the House of Daniel man. His eyes were sharp in the middle of all that face fuzz. "How come you didn't go on back to Enid, then?" he asked.

Well, it wasn't as if I hadn't figured he'd want to know—him or somebody for the House of Daniel, anyway. Didn't look for it quite so quick, though. I said, "Somebody down there I'm on the wrong side of. Better if I go somewhere else for a while. This here's a way to do it."

"Huh," he said again. "Cops on your tail? They come after you with bloodhounds or wizards or whatever the demon?"

"No cops," I said, which was the Lord's truth . . . unless they were enough in Big Stu's pocket to chase me, too. I added, "I'd be in more hot water with them if I had done what this guy wanted." That was also true, which was good. You want to be straight when you're starting out with somebody. Tell lies at the beginning and they'll always come back to bite you. Later on, when the other folks've shown they don't fly with angels' wings, either, you can do the same. But a bad start makes for a bad finish.

"He can play?" the guy with the megaphone asked Mort Milligan.

"He can play," Mort said, bless his heart. "He's damn good in center—better with the glove than our guy, I'll tell you that. He won't hit third for you like your fella who got racked up, but he's pesky up there."

Pesky is what they call you when you look like you ought to make outs all the time but you don't. I thought I was better than that, but the House of Daniel guy didn't ask me.

He scratched at something under his beard. Then he said, "Tell you what. You've got baseball togs in that bag? Put 'em on. We'll run you around some, see what you look like out there. Oh, and tell me your name, too."

Conoco Ball Park didn't have dressing rooms. Mostly, you put on your uniform somewhere else and then went there. I did kind of a fan dance in the tunnel going out of the dugout. A few people walked by while I was doing it. If anybody looked in, he might've seen something, but he wouldn't've seen much.

A few folks had stayed in the stands. They booed my ENID EAGLES shirt. One of 'em hissed like a rattlesnake. I touched the brim of my cap and waved. They booed louder, of course.

The House of Daniel guy who'd had the megaphone came to the plate with a bat and a few balls. He hit fungoes my way for ten, fifteen minutes. He ran me all over center, and you can do a lot of running there at the Conoco Ball Park. I caught what I could, chased the rest, and threw the balls back to him as hard and straight as I could.

I'd worked up a sweat by the time he waved me in. "You're Jack?" he said, and I nodded. So did he. "Yeah, you're a decent ballhawk, all right. Better than decent." He tossed me the bat, easy and gentle so I could grab it one-handed. "What do you do this way?"

He was bigger and heftier than I was, and the bat was heavier than what I favor. I didn't ask for a different one; I just choked up an extra inch so I could get around faster. Out to the mound came the fellow who'd finished the game in center.

"Wes here will see what you've got," said the guy who'd run me around.

Wes's first one came straight at my nose. I hit the dirt, got up, and planted myself again. "You were watching Close Shave out there," I said.

"Nah." Wes Petersen shook his head. He had a deep, gravelly voice. "I'm a mean son of a gun any which way." To show he meant it, he knocked me down again.

I nodded back to him, as though we were in a saloon drinking beer together. "You can hit me, all right. Let's see if I can hit you."

Next pitch started for my head, too. This one broke so hard, I could hear it spinning through the air. Hell of a curve. It dropped over the plate for what would've been a strike.

I didn't bail out on it, anyway. I did wave out to the mound. "*Nobody* could hit that one," I said. Wes looked pleased.

Then he threw me another one. Maybe it didn't break so sharply. Maybe I was set up and looking for it. Whatever you want to say, I went with it and smacked it into right. It would've been a hit. Wes didn't look so happy about that.

He threw to me for about as long as I'd shagged flies. I did what I could do. I'll never bust fences. When you can't, you're better off knowing you can't. You'll concentrate on the things you can do and get so you do them as well as you're able to.

Wes looked over to the guy who'd hit fungoes. "What d'you think, Harv?" he asked.

"Yeah, he'll work," Harv said. Not a whole bunch of praise, but plenty to make me feel eight feet tall. Harv turned back to me. "So you want to ride with us, huh?"

"You bet I do!" I had all kinds of reasons for saying that. Big Stu was the one furthest up front, maybe, but not the biggest. When the Archdeacons or the Hilltoppers buy some busher's contract after he's knocked around in Rochester or Omaha or Denver or Portland, that's what I was feeling, or some of it. I'd never make the big time. I wasn't good enough. But the House of Daniel reckoned I was good enough for them—good enough to be a blowout patch, anyhow. Long step up from the Enid Eagles. Hell of a long step.

"All right, then. We'll take you along for a while," Harv said. "You can start letting your hair and your whiskers grow."

"I'll do it." I wondered how funny I'd look and how long I'd take to look that way. Because I thought I ought to, I asked, "How bad off are your guys who slammed together?"

"Double-Double busted his ankle," Harv said. His last name was Watrous, I remembered from the game. "Out anywhere from three months to six, the doc said. Have to hope he keeps his speed when he gets back. Rabbit . . . I dunno about Rabbit. His collarbone, that's not as bad a break as an ankle, and it heals cleaner." His face clouded. "But his noggin, his dumb noggin don't seem so good. They're taking him to the hospital for a similarity scan."

"Good they can do that kind of thing these days, anyhow," I said, and Harv and Wes both nodded.

Like everything else, medicine keeps moving forward. A wizard with the right training can cast a spell on a hurt man's skull, say. Then he'll cast the same spell on a regular skull, one with nothing wrong with it. The law of similarity will show him all the places where the two of 'em don't match up exactly. If the hurt guy's got a break in there, the magic'll tell the wizard right where it's at so he and the rest of the docs can decide what to do about it.

Works for other bones, too—not just skulls. And they're starting to use it for the squishier parts, too, though that's not so easy. They can find things and fix things that killed people back in Great-Granddad's time. Quite a world we live in, isn't it?

"First month, we'll pay you ten bucks a game—and we play a lot of games," Harv said. "Hang on after that—we call it sticking around after your beard grows in—and you go on shares like the rest of us."

If they found somebody they liked better, they'd dump me. Well, every baseball team ever hatched is always looking for better players. I'd just have to be good, so they'd want to keep me.

What I said was, "It's a deal, and I thank you kindly."

"You're helping us out of a jam, too," Harv said. "Get back into your everyday clothes. You can hang on to those pants—they're close enough to our road grays. But you won't need that Eagles shirt any more. We'll put a lion on your chest instead. You belong to the House of Daniel now!"

Most semipro teams travel like the Enid Eagles. Guys fill up cars and somebody drives to wherever the next game is. You hope the clown behind the wheel isn't drunk or sleepy or coming off a brawl with his boss or his girlfriend. Players mostly show up where they're supposed to when they're supposed to. When they don't, teams drag somebody out of the stands and hope for the best. Hey, look at me. Even the House of Daniel did that.

But they traveled in style. Waiting outside Conoco Ball Park sat a streamlined bus, modern as week after next. It had enough seats for everybody on the team and enough room so everybody could stretch his legs some and not show up for the next game all tied up in knots.

Each side had that open-mouthed lion's head painted on it in gaudy colors. THE LIONS' DEN was stenciled alongside it. HOUSE OF DANIEL—FAMOUS TRAVELING BASEBALL CLUB.

Most of the seats already had ballplayers in 'em by the time I climbed aboard. I nodded to a fellow with nobody next to him and said, "Mind if I sit here?" It was like your first day at a new job. Well, it *was* my first day at a new job. I'd walk soft till I scouted out how things work.

The guy nodded back, friendly enough. "Go ahead. You gotta park yourself somewhere. I'm Eddie Lelivelt." He stuck out his hand.

I shook it. "Jack Spivey." I stuck my bag on the luggage rack and sat down. The seat was a lot comfier than anything on the Red Ball Line, I'll tell you that.

"Good to meet you," Eddie said. He was three, maybe four years older'n me, his hair past his ears but not to his shoulders, his beard mostly brown but with red streaks on the chin and in his mustache. He went on, "I watched 'em working you out. You can go get 'em—no two ways about that."

"Thanks," I said. "You were playing second, weren't you?" I wanted to make sure so I didn't say anything dumb. Guys don't always look the same once they take their caps off, and all those beards made it tougher.

Eddie Lelivelt nodded, though. "Yeah, that's me."

"You're smooth out there," I said. He wasn't a player who ran all over everywhere snagging things. He tried to put himself in the right place to begin with, so he could make his plays without looking like a showoff.

"Much obliged." He grinned. When he did that, he looked about fifteen.

"I do hate to come on board like this," I told him. "I've never seen two guys run into each other so hard before."

"Me, neither. That was terrible." His grin went away. "I hope Rabbit'll be all right. For a minute or so there, I was scared he'd gone and killed himself."

"People always tell you, 'Keep your eye on the ball,'" I said. "Him and your other fella, they did it too well."

"Boy, you got that right," Eddie said.

While we were talking, Harv and Wes and one or two other House of Daniel men got on the bus. The doors hissed shut. The engine started up. It sounded a lot newer, or maybe just better taken care of, than the one on the Red Ball bus. We rolled away from Conoco Ball Park, heading west.

I had a bad few seconds when I realized we were heading west. Had I joined up with the House of Daniel so I could stick my head in the lion's mouth for real? I turned back to Eddie Lelivelt. "Um, you don't have a game in Enid tomorrow, do you?"

"Nope. We're going way farther than that. Town called . . ." He laughed at himself. "I don't remember what it's called. Somewhere in Texas. Harv will know. Wherever we play next—that's all I can tell you. I don't care where. I'm a baseball bum. What difference does *where* make?"

"Long as it's not Enid, I don't care, either," I said.

"I saw on your shirtfront that's where you played before," he said. "Don't mean to stick my nose in where it doesn't belong or anything, but it sounds like you aren't sorry to give it a miss."

"I was supposed to take care of something for one of the guys who runs things there, but it turned out to be something I couldn't stand to do," I answered. "You can't explain to people like that. They don't want explaining. They just want you to do what they tell you. He'll take it out of my hide if he gets the chance."

"Yeah, I've known a few like that. Everybody has, chances are," Eddie said. "Well, traveling with the House of Daniel's a good way not to give him the chance. We go all over the map, and sometimes we don't know where we're heading till we turn left instead of right. Somebody sets up a game against a strong team in a good ballpark, we'll go. You'd best believe we will."

"How often do y'all win, anyway?" I asked.

That *y'all* made Eddie smile. The House of Daniel fellas, they talked like they came from the North. They did, most of 'em, so I guess they were entitled. He thought for a couple of seconds, working it out. "Two out of three, three out of four, something like that," he said. "It's baseball. You don't win all the time. Their pitcher throws a great game or one of your guys kicks one or the umps are even worse than usual or . . . oh, a million things. But we do all right. Plenty good enough to keep going."

"You sure do," I said. "Only reason Ponca City caught you there was the collision, but you won just the same. And the Greasemen, they're pretty good."

"They weren't bad." Eddie Lelivelt sounded like he was giving them the waddayacallit—the benefit of the doubt. He looked over at me out of the corner of his eye. "How about the Enid team you're off of? How do they stack up against Ponca City?"

"Well, we licked 'em yesterday. That's how come I was in town." That was one of the reasons, anyhow. "But they beat us about as often as we beat them."

He kind of grunted, as if to say, *Yeah, the likes of you could start for a team that good.* He wasn't dogging me or anything, just letting me know what he thought. I couldn't very well tell him he was wrong, either. Rabbit O'Leary looked like a better ballplayer than I am to me, too.

Except Rabbit was back there in Ponca City with maybe a cracked noggin and with a busted collarbone for sure, and I was on the bus. I was on for as long as I could stay there, anyway. That's how baseball works before you ever step out between the white lines.

The bus took us past three or four farms in a row with no crops in the ground, no animals in the fields, empty farmhouses with busted windows, barns and outbuildings fading in the harsh sunlight and starting to fall to pieces. Eddie stared out the window at them, and at the roof-high dust devil dancing in front of one.

He turned back to me. "What went wrong here?"

I kind of shrugged. "Farmers in these parts had trouble making ends meet even before the Big Bubble popped. When it did, the bankers foreclosed on some. A couple of bankers got shot trying."

"Doesn't break my heart," Eddie said.

"Mine, neither. Other folks just upped and left—reckoned they had no hope where they were at. My pa, he was like that. Others yet . . . That dust devil you saw, that's just a baby next to a lot of 'em. You can't grow anything when all your dirt's blowing away and somebody else's dirt is coming down on top of you. So that's prying people off the land, too."

Eddie clicked his tongue between his teeth. "It shouldn't be like this. It isn't right."

I shrugged again. "You know that. I know that. Everybody says the same thing. But it doesn't change. It doesn't get better. You don't need me to tell you so. Playing with this team, you've done more traveling than I have. You can see for yourself."

"I've seen plenty," he answered, his voice quiet. "This is as bad as anything, though."

"How about that?" I said, and whistled a few notes between my teeth. I knew we had it bad—you couldn't very well not know that. But I knew other places had it bad, too. I hadn't known we had it especially bad. Now I did. No wonder Pa headed out West.

Now I was heading out, too. I wondered when I'd come back. I wondered if I would, too.

Before I went out, though, I had to go back through. The sun was sinking when we passed through Enid one last time. Not that many people on the streets. A lot of the ones who were gawped at the House of Daniel bus. Well, that paint job is there to be gawped at. The House of Daniel wants people to know it's coming to town.

The House of Daniel does. I didn't, not for beans, not in Enid. If Big Stu was walking out of his diner and saw me roll by . . . That would've been great, wouldn't it? But he wasn't, and he couldn't have spotted me even if he was. I was sitting by the aisle, since the window seats were taken by the time I got in. No lights working inside the bus. I wouldn't have been more than one dim shape amongst all the others.

I can see that now. I could see it five minutes after we got out of Enid. Did I have palpitations while we were in town? Listen, I had palpitations and a half. And when I saw Ace McGinty staggering down the street like he was already toasted, I had palpitations and three-quarters.

Ace didn't see me, though. I don't think Ace even saw the bus. And he was the last of the Enid Eagles I ever set eyes on. The bus kept on toward the western fringes of town.

Eddie Lelivelt kept looking out the window. I don't know if he would have unless he was sitting next to somebody from Enid. But he was, so he did. Sadly, he pointed and said, "Another one of those lost and damned places."

He was pointing right at my house, the house I'd left a few days before, the house I'd never go back to again. I looked at it, too, but not for long. "Well, you're right," I said as it disappeared behind us.

(IV)

We rolled on through the night. Harv drove and drove and drove. He liked it. We didn't always roll any too fast. Not all the roads in western Oklahoma are paved. Sometimes we kicked up dust. Sometimes gravel rattled off the undercarriage. Sometimes the bus bounced and bucked like a bronco. We rolled on regardless.

Beside me, Eddie closed his eyes and curled up against the iron wall and the window. I thought he was kidding, but pretty soon he started to snore. He wasn't the only one, either. A lot of the time, if guys who played for the House of Daniel didn't sleep on the bus, they went short.

I still didn't know where we were going. Truth to tell, I didn't much care. We were heading away from Enid—now!—which was all that mattered. Almost all that mattered. Other thing was, Big Stu didn't know where I was going, either, and he wouldn't have an easy time finding out.

If I leaned the way Eddie was leaning, I'd end up lying in the aisle. Or I'd snuggle against his shoulder and he'd think I was peculiar. So I tried to stretch out straight in the seat and doze off. I might have got a little shuteye that way, but I didn't get a lot.

We stopped at some little town or other to gas up. When the engine stopped, I heard coyotes howling in the distance. The moon was out, but it wasn't full, so I knew they weren't werewolves. They sure sounded like werewolves, though. Coyotes have some of Old Scratch in them regardless of the moon's phase.

Then we got going again. Hardly any cars came our way. Once we saw a carpet's lanterns up above us. He didn't drop anything on us, so that was fine.

Little by little, light started spreading over the prairie from behind us. We were heading south and west, toward Texas. Hardly any place in Oklahoma west of Enid had a team good enough to give the House of Daniel a game or a ballpark that was worth their while to play a game in. So we were bound for the Lone Star State.

I'd made trips there before. Enid went there every so often. But it's not like I'd been there a lot. The town's closer to Kansas. The people are closer to Texas, though: the way they talk and the way they think. Kansas is the start of Yankee country.

Of course, here I was in the bus with a bunch of guys from Yankee country. Well, they were taking me out of trouble and paying me, too. So I figured I'd worry later about how much I'd let that worry me—if, when later came, I decided it still needed worrying about.

We crossed into Texas just about when the sun came up. The road swung from west to southwest at the same time we did. The bus's long, long, long shadow stretched out ahead of us. We chased after it, but we never caught up to it. When you're chasing shadows, you never do.

Not long after sunrise, Eddie Lelivelt opened his eyes. He yawned and stretched. Something in his back and something in his neck cracked like oversized knuckles. Aside from that, though, he could've been sleeping in a feather bed at the Ritz. He glanced over at me and asked, "You doze any?"

"Maybe a little," I said.

"You'll learn how," he said. "You've got to. We don't get enough time at the roominghouses and motor lodges where we stay for a fellow to catch up there."

"You're used to it. I'm not, not yet." We both talked in low voices, to keep from bothering the other guys who went on sawing wood. I looked out the window. It was all prairie, some farms, some cattle ranches—about like what was in the part of Oklahoma we'd just left. "Know where we're going?"

"Pissant town called Pampa," Eddie answered. I must have stirred or opened my eyes wider or something, on account of he asked me, "You know the place?" He didn't miss much, Eddie Lelivelt.

"I've played there once or twice. You're right—it's a pissant town, kind of like Ponca City boiled down to a pint."

He nodded. "I thought that was how I remembered it, but I wasn't sure. I've been through too many other places since the last time we stopped there, a couple of years ago. We drew pretty good, though, even if it isn't a big place, so here we are again."

You could tell when you were getting close to Pampa. Instead of crops, oil wells and derricks and tank farms started sprouting on the prairie. Once upon a time, Pampa was a no-account cattle town. They struck oil before the Big Bubble busted, so the smashup hurt them less than a lot of other places. Their downtown is tiny, but the shops in it are new and mostly open.

They pay the price other ways. The air smells like everybody's been eating beans for years. There's soot on the walls. There's soot on the ground. I laughed when the bus pulled up in front of a rooming-house and stopped. Eddie, he raised an eyebrow at me. "This is where the Enid team stays when we—I mean, they—come here," I explained.

"Oh." The way he weighed it, he put me in mind of Rod Graver. Well, there was another fella who didn't miss much. When Eddie chuckled, you knew you'd earned it. "Got you. Yeah, that's funny."

The players woke up as soon as the bus stopped. Rattling and banging didn't faze 'em. Quiet? That was a different story. They grabbed their stuff—most of 'em had a sight more'n I did—and got down onto the sidewalk. One of 'em looked up at the sun trying to poke through all the stinking crap in the air and said, "Just as pretty as I remembered it." He held his nose. Yeah, that about summed up Pampa.

As we started filing into the roominghouse, Harv said, "Eddie, you and Jack'll get a room by yourselves. You'll need to climb out of the sack earlier'n the rest of us so you can pretty him up."

"No worries," Eddie said.

"Pretty me up?" I asked him.

"Get some sleep first," he answered. "Plenty of time to take care of it then."

I shrugged. "Okey-doke." In we went, all those shaggy guys with their manes and their face fur and me feeling like a kid—a kid who could use a shave, but a kid just the same—beside 'em. The landlady didn't even blink at the way they looked. Their money spent as good as anybody else's.

She did blink when Harv asked for one more room than she'd expected. Cash money kept her from getting too fussy, though. It has a way of doing that.

Our room was about like the one I'd had with the Eagles in Ponca City. With only two guys in it, it felt, well, roomy. Eddie took an alarm

clock out of his bag, wound it up, and set it on the nightstand. Then
he went next door and came back with another one.

"You'll buy yourself one of these, first chance you get," he told me.
"We all have 'em. We all set 'em, too. Can't afford to miss wakeup, so
we don't take any chances."

I was too busy yawning to worry about alarm clocks. I lay down on
one of the beds and sacked out without even shedding my shoes. Tired?
Me? Oh, just a little.

Next thing I knew, it was like a bomb went off next to my head. A
few seconds later, another one started bang-clanging away, too. No,
not bombs. Those blamed alarm clocks. Eddie killed 'em before I
could fling 'em against a wall.

"Rise and shine, sweetheart," he said. "Time to pretty you up." Way
he talking, we could've been canoodling in there, not flopped out like
a couple of stiffs.

I told him where he could stick his rise and shine. I told him how
many corners he could fold it into before he stuck it there, too. He just
laughed. Then he pulled a bottle and a little painter's brush and what
looked like the hair that goes into furniture cushions out of his bag.
"What's all that?" I asked.

"Spirit gum and fake whiskers," he said. "You play for the House
of Daniel, you got to look like you belong."

"How about my hair?" I ran my hand over it. It wasn't what you'd
call long. Not too many fellas wore theirs shorter, matter of fact.

"We'll slap a wig on you, too, but that can wait." He didn't get excited, any more than a grocer would if you asked him how much his
soap flakes cost. "C'mere and sit on my bed. The light's better over
here."

So I went. He started painting spirit gum on my cheeks and my chin
and my top lip. Smelling it made me half drunk, or maybe just woozy.
The stink was something like moonshine and something like ether.
I went under ether one time, when the dentist yanked my wisdom
teeth. I was there, and then I was gone, till I woke up sore, with holes
in my head. I wondered if the spirit gum would knock me out, too.

Soon as Eddie painted the gum on, he started bearding me up.
"Tickles," I told him.

"Don't talk," he said. "I'll do a better job if your face doesn't fidget."

When the gum dried, it started to itch. Or maybe it was that uphol-stery all over my face. I started to scratch. He slapped my hand down. "This'll drive me crazy," I said.

He kinda looked at me. "Look where you're at. Look what you're doing. You've got to be crazy already." He made me sit there till every-thing was ready. Then he let me get up and take a peek into the mirror over the beat-up chest of drawers.

Don't know who that was on the other side of the glass. A stranger. A mighty strange stranger, too, let me tell you. "Looks like some-body slapped shredded wheat all over my face," I said. The fake beard was darker'n what I grow on top of my head, but I didn't grumble about that. Plenty of real ones are the same way.

They handed me Double-Double's uniform. It fit tolerably well. Then Harv did stick a wig on me. That was about the same color as the whiskers. It was even hotter than they were. I started sweating like a fool. I hoped the spirit gum was waterproof. If it wasn't, my beard would start falling out in clumps. That'd give the folks in Pampa something to talk about!

"We playing at Gulf Field south of town or Road Runner Park?" I asked Harv. He seemed to know such things.

"Road Runner, against the All Stars. It holds more people, so the gate will be better," he said. I nodded. The Eagles had gone down to Gulf Field against the Oilers, who got their name the same way the Ponca City Greasemen did. There was another team in town, too, the Plainsmen. All those guys who pulled oil out of the ground needed something to do when they weren't working. They drank or they played ball, same as in most places.

The landlady had a big chicken stew going—well, more potatoes and cabbage and carrots than bird, but you could find some. We ate up, piled into the bus, and went on over to Road Runner Park for the ballgame.

Hitting eighth," Harv shouted through the megaphone, "in center, number fourteen, Jack 'the Snake' Spivey!"

Nobody'd ever called me *Snake* before, never once. Harv didn't care. He wanted folks to notice you and to remember you. The Pampa fans noticed, all right. They booed and they whistled. For me, some of them hissed, too. Fans do that stuff. I paid 'em no special mind, not unless they started throwing things. Razzing the road team's part of the fun.

We got a run in the top of the first. We might've got more, but their third baseman took a double away from us and left the bases full. I was in the on-deck circle when that happened. I got my glove and trotted out to center field.

They went down in order. Nothing came my way. They could've put a doorknob out there and it wouldn't've made any difference. I trotted back in, took a few cuts while their pitcher loosened up, and climbed into the box.

I took a ball. I took a strike. Next one was a belt-high fastball. I swung, but I got under it a little. Lazy fly to medium left-center. I hustled down to first, hoping their left fielder would drop it. Happens every once in a while, even in the bigs. Didn't happen then. I went back to the dugout. Would've been nice to do something good my first try. No such luck, though.

"Tell you something?" Eddie Lelivelt said when I sat down beside him.

"Sure."

"Your bottom arm looks kind of floppy when you're up there. You might pull the bat back a little, straighten the arm out some. Maybe you'd drive the ball better."

I'd hit the way I hit for as long as I'd played. Nobody'd ever said anything about it. It was good enough for the Enid Eagles. For the House of Daniel? I was batting eighth. They saw I wasn't likely to scare many people the way I was. So what did I have to lose? "Thanks," I said. "I'll give it a try."

Next inning, I cut off a single before it could sneak through, and got the ball back in quick enough to make sure it stayed a single. The All Star who hit it took a big turn, but he had to jam on the brakes and back up. Eddie flashed me a thumbs-up. That felt good. I caught the last out, too, not that it was any kind of tough play.

When I went to the on-deck circle again, I tried the new stance. I pulled the bat back till my left elbow almost locked. It felt different, all right, but not too bad. I came up with a man on second and two outs. Did I want to drive in that run? Oh, maybe a little bit.

Ump said the first pitch caught the inside corner. "Wish you'd give that to our guy, too," I said without turning my heard.

"Nobody cares what you wish, furry boy," he told me. What I wished then was that I'd kept quiet. I could tell I wouldn't have a skinny strike zone from then on. Well, I hadn't had one before, either.

He did call the next one a ball. It was higher than the button on my cap. The one after that wasn't, so it turned into a strike no matter how wide it was. The All Stars' pitcher kinda grinned. He saw what was going on. He came in on my hands, figuring anything halfway close would be a strike.

But you've got to make your pitch. Guys who play for big money can't do it all the time. This was just an oil-field worker picking up spare change on the diamond. It was over the inside corner, not six inches inside the way he wanted. I hit a hard grounder into the hole between third and short. The third baseman dove. The shortstop tried to backhand. The ball squirted into the outfield. The runner on second scored. I scooted into second myself when the throw from left went over the catcher's head and the pitcher, backing up the play, kicked the ball around.

Guys from the House of Daniel whooped and hollered in our dugout. The crowd at Road Runner Park sat on their hands. Crowds come out to see their team lick you. They don't like it so much when you lick them.

The Pampa All Stars got a run back, then tied the game on a homer that may be going yet. Hang a slow curve and that's what happens. Wes kicked at the dirt on the mound. But we got three in the seventh—I chipped in with a bloop to right. Looks like a line drive in the box score, they say. We took the game, 5-3.

"We'll get you next time you come to town," a grumpy All Star said.

"Maybe you will," I answered. You don't want to tick 'em off any more than beating 'em already did. And who could say? Maybe they would. They weren't as good as my old Eagles, but maybe they would anyhow. Their pitcher hot, ours off, a few balls falling in, an error where it hurt most . . . That could do it. It could, but odds were it wouldn't. Even with me in center and Fidgety Frank playing right, the House of Daniel was a better ballclub.

"You bums!" somebody yelled from the grandstand.

"Yankee bums!" somebody else added.

They could yell—they'd paid their four bits. House of Daniel didn't go for quarter seats, the way a lot of semipro teams did. They figured they were good, and people would pay more to watch 'em on account of they were. They were right, too. We had a nice house. Only three or four thousand folks in Pampa, but there are some farms outside and littler towns not too far off. We made decent money.

Harv paid me my ten bucks before I even asked him. Can't hardly ask for better than that. I tucked the bill into a little suede pouch I wore under my shirt on a thong around my neck—a grouch bag, they call it. Lots of semipros have 'em. Best way to keep your money safe.

"Good job," Harv said. "You've got an idea out there, don't you?"

"Well, I try," I said, feeling better than good. I don't have all the tools to play top-level ball, so I have to make the most of what I do have. Nice to see somebody noticed.

Eddie Lelivelt ambled over. He got more than ten dollars—I know that. "What do you think of straightening your arm that way?" he asked.

"Didn't hurt. I'm sure of that," I answered. "Might've helped. I'll keep doing it for a while, see what I think—see if I get used to it, too."

"All right. Glad it didn't mess you up, anyway," he said. "Sometimes when you do something new, it's like you're screwing yourself into the ground." He turned to Harv. "We going over to Miss Louise's after the game?"

"Once we clean up? Sure," Harv said. I felt like cheering. No, Miss Louise's isn't a sporting house, even if it sounds like one. The meat they serve there's already cooked—falling-off-the-bone barbecue, some of the best anywhere. I was going to tell the House of Daniel fellas about it if they didn't already know, but they did.

Bathroom in the roominghouse was down at the end of the hall. Yeah, one of those places. By the time my turn came—I was low man on the totem pole, naturally—the salamander that hotted up the water was plumb tuckered out. On a May afternoon in the Texas Panhandle, you mind that less than you would some other places.

Some of my fake whiskers came off in the tub, but nowhere near all. I went back to my room looking like a sorry case of mange. "Have anything to make your blasted spirit gum say uncle?" I asked Eddie.

"Try some of this. Rub it on a cloth and then over your face." He handed me a bottle of greenish gunk. When I pulled the cork, it smelled something like witch hazel and something like what a colored herb woman'd cook up if she didn't like you so much.

But it worked, whatever it was. "Thanks," I said, and started to give it back to Eddie.

"Hang on to it," he told me. "You're the one who'll be using it till your own whiskers get long enough so you don't need the false ones."

So we ate. And we ate. And we ate some more. By the time we got through, you could've built a cow and a pig and a flock of chickens from the bones on the table. Miss Louise had smiled when we came in. She'd said, "Good to see y'all. Not a lot of folks with money to spend."

"Even in an oil town like this?" Harv asked.

"Things are better here than some places," Miss Louise said, "but they ain't what you'd call good. People hunker down, fix their own eats—it's cheaper'n goin' out. So customers are hard to come by."

Pampa was better off than Ponca City, no doubt about that. The oil wells here were newer, and paying better. But if a place as good as Miss Louise's had trouble staying full, it was hurting, all right.

I rubbed my stomach. If I ate like that all the time, I wouldn't fit into Double-Double's uniform for long. "Where do we go next?" I asked. I figured maybe Borger northwest of Pampa—the two little towns get along like Ponca City and Enid. Anything one does, the other reckons it does better. When the Eagles played Pampa, they usually played Borger the same weekend. Not even forty miles from one to the other.

But Harv said, "Amarillo. We've got a game tomorrow against the Metros."

"All right." I sounded as easy about it as I could. Amarillo's not a great big city. It's bigger than Enid, but not by a lot. The Eagles never dared square off against the Metros, though. They were out of our league too many ways.

Back before the Big Bubble popped, the Metros played in the Western League for a couple of years. That's real pro ball—Class A, same as the Texas League, the league where the Steers wouldn't sign me 'cause I wasn't good enough. Even after they didn't stick, they barn-stormed against teams in both those circuits.

I must not've been as calm as I tried for. Harv kind of grinned at me. "If God wants us to beat 'em, we'll beat 'em," he sad. "And if He's got other plans, His will be done."

"Amen," Eddie Lelivelt said, and some of the other guys nodded.

I knew the House of Daniel was a churchy team, but they hadn't done any preaching to the heathen that I'd seen. They hadn't done any preaching at me. I knew that for sure. I'm not a heathen, but I'm on that road. Hey, anybody who's seen a salamander or a dust devil knows there are Powers. Just what those Powers are and Who calls the shots amongst 'em—that's where the arguing starts.

"We'll sleep here tonight, go on over in the morning," Harv said. I liked that idea. I'd sleep better at the roominghouse than on the bus. It wouldn't have been a trip like the one from Ponca City, though. Amarillo's farther from Pampa than Borger is, but just a little.

When we were walking back from Miss Louise's, somebody stuck his head out the window of a flivver and yelled, "Crazy longhairs!" But he kept going. He went faster after he yelled, matter of fact. We might've been crazy longhairs—well, except for me, and I was gonna head that way—but there were more than a dozen of us. Bad odds for a would-be tough guy, even in his home town.

Amarillo! The Metros! I should have got into trouble with Big Stu sooner. I came up in the world because I did. Who would've thunk it?

Metro Park is a real ballyard. They built it when they went into the Western League. It has a big old wooden grandstand—they figured they'd pack 'em in for Saturday games and Sunday double-headers. What you look for isn't always what you get, though. I knew about that—too right I did. Not putting enough fannies in the seats was part of why they dropped out of pro ball.

Because it's a real ballyard, it even had dressing rooms. The visitors' clubhouse was about as big as an outhouse, but it was there. We could dress in it if we didn't mind elbowing each other while we did. Bigger places have lockers to stash your street clothes. Metro Park had nails in the planking. It was still better than no place to dress at all.

We got booed when we went out to limber up. You always do on the road, and the House of Daniel was always on the road. I took my swings at the plate, then went out to shag flies. I caught one and threw it in. Then I said, "That's funny," to Wes, who was standing pretty close to me out there.

"What is?" he asked.

"They've got a colored section down the line." I pointed to the black folks sitting there. Amarillo has quite a few coloreds. They've got their own ballclub—the Sandies, they call it. They play in a little park on the edge of town against other Negro teams. They're nothing fancy, any more than the Metros are in the white scheme of things, but they play.

"I know. All the parks down here are like that." By the way Wes said it, he didn't much fancy it. Well, he was a Yankee. To me, that kind of thing was water to a fish. I honest to Pete thought the coloreds felt the same. I hadn't seen so much then as I have now.

But I wasn't thinking about that then. I pointed again, this time toward a seat right behind the Metros' dugout. "You're right. All the parks down here are like that. So what's *he* doin' there?"

He was high yaller. I might not have noticed him but for his kinky hair—he wore it longer and fuller than most colored men. Or I might have. His suit was the color of a lime that just got hit by lightning. He had on a pumpkin shirt and a blood-red tie with something on it—from that far out, I couldn't tell what. No white man would ever have put on an outfit like that.

All Wes saw was the clothes. "He's a piece of work, all right. Some places I know, the cops'd toss you in a cell for what he's got on. An offense against morals, they'd call it, and they'd be right."

"They might put him in a cell, but could they keep him there?" I said. "If he's not a conjure man, what is he?"

Wes sat up and took notice then, so much so that a fly ball almost skulled him. "Wake up, sweetie!" yelled a fat fan in the bleachers. I would've told him to go stick an apple in his mouth if he called me sweetie. Wes just trotted in. The next fungo came my way. So did the one after that.

When I could pay attention again, Wes was chinning with Harv. Things are tough enough on the road when the game is pretty much honest. Honest or not, the umps won't give you a break. The home team knows the field and the fence angles better than you do.

If they put a hex on you, too . . . Amarillo's a tough town some ways. You heard stories about the Greys, the team that was on top there before the Metros got good. They brawled all the time, sometimes so bad they couldn't finish games. When they did finish 'em, they had their own kind of fun afterwards. They'd bury live chickens in the dirt up to their necks, all in a row. Then they'd gallop by on horseback, one player at a time, and lean down and yank off the chickens' heads. Whoever tore off the most won.

So a little magic to help the home team along wouldn't have surprised me one bit. If you had some serious side money down on the game, wouldn't you do whatever it took to make sure you didn't blow it? Sure you would.

Anybody would think I used to do business for Big Stu or something. Yeah, anybody would.

I watched the Metros getting loose after we came in. They might not have needed a conjure man. They were slick as boiled okra. Their pitcher was a big southpaw who'd been around the block a time or three. He wouldn't beat himself. That's half the battle right there.

Oh, and I got a look at what was painted on the high yaller guy's necktie. It was a skull—a skull in a yellow fedora. Wes had it right. That fellow was a piece of work. Dirty work. Dirty work he'd pull on us.

Nobody sat anywhere near him. It wasn't because the crowd there was white and he was colored, either. Oh, no. Whatever color he was, that was the least of people's worries.

We went down in order in the top of the first. The stuff the Metros' pitcher was throwing, either it fell off the table or it came in hot enough to broil steaks on. Back behind their dugout, that conjure man was wiggling and twisting like he had a swarm of fire ants inside that stupid silk suit. He might have been sweating harder than the guy on the hill. Of course, if you can't sweat in Amarillo, you aren't half trying.

They touched us for a run in their half of the frame. Two singles and a long fly to left—nothing much to do about it. We got a scratch hit in the top of the second, but that was all.

We watched the Metros' pitcher. We watched the conjure man. "I bet he's a fake," Wes said. "They're playing games with our heads, like—gave that clown five bucks and told him to play at being a wizard."

"I dunno," Eddie said. "I don't remember their guy being anywhere near this sharp last time we were here."

"Me, neither," Harv allowed. "But have no fear, friends. The Lord provided for Daniel. If He's so inclined, He'll provide for Daniel's House, too."

"If," Eddie said.

"Have no fear," Harv repeated. "Just go out there and play good ball. You take care of your end and the Lord'll take care of His."

But Eddie booted one to start off the bottom of the second. He looked down at his glove as if it were playing tricks on him. Me, I thought the ball took a crazy hop right when it got to him. The infield was baby-butt smooth—it shouldn't have bounced like that. It shouldn't have, but it did.

Metros didn't score, though. I ran down a drive in left-center to make sure they didn't. It was a good catch, yeah, but not a crazy one like the one I made in Ponca City. A guy doesn't make this play, he's got no business out there. Way the conjure man clapped his hands to his chest and screeched, I might've swiped his life's savings, if he had any.

I led off the top of the third. First pitch was high heat, straight at my coconut. I sprawled every which way. Wes hadn't buzzed me anywhere near that hard. I got up, picked up my bat, put my cap back on, dusted off my behind, and stood in again. If my head was thumping, their pitcher didn't have to know.

"Didn't mean to throw a beanball," he said. He sounded as though he meant it. But I bet the conjure man meant him to.

I wanted to hit the next one nine miles. That'd learn both of 'em! I swung hard, and missed. Then I grounded to third. Yeah, what you want and what you get are different. If nothing else shows you that, baseball sure will.

When I got back to the dugout, I was muttering to myself. "Hang in there, Jack," Eddie said. Eddie's all right.

Harv was muttering to himself in there, too. Not the way I was.

He was muttering things like, " 'And in all matters of wisdom *and* understanding, that the king inquired of them, he found them ten times better than all the magicians *and* astrologers that *were* in all his kingdom.' "

Good Book talk. You heard it all the time in Enid. I used little bits and pieces myself sometimes. Harv talked as if he grew up going on like that. Well, he did. And it wasn't just Good Book talk, I found out later. It was Book of Daniel talk. He was pickled in it like a cuke in vinegar.

I looked across the field at the conjure man back of the Metros' dugout. He was wiggling and twitching some more. Different now, though. When I wiggled like that, it was because I swallowed a big old dose of castor oil. And wouldn't you know it? Right about then, he lit out for the gents', and he wasn't what you'd call slow about it, either.

"Harv?" I said.

"What you want, Snake?"

"Did you have anything to do with that?"

"Who, me? I'm just a dumb ballplayer." *Dumb like snow is black*, I thought. That old pawnshop man's crack came in handy all kinds of ways. Harv went on, "Anyways, whatever happens, I'd sooner chalk it up to the Lord. He gets the credit. I get the blame for not being good enough."

All at once, without the conjure man there, the Metros' pitcher wasn't good enough. Oh, he still had smarts. But now his curve was just a wrinkle, not an old-time drop. He lost some giddy-up off his heater, too. You could hit him. We scored two runs, and then two more. I bunted those last two along. I thought I was safe at first, but they called me out. I jawed a little. You won't win—you never win— but you feel a little better afterwards. And maybe they'll get the next one right.

Then the conjure man came back. He looked drug through a knot-hole, but he was still game. And I'll be blamed if he wasn't carrying a live chicken. I thought about the Amarillo Greys and their notion of after-the-game fun.

Whatever the conjure man did with the chicken, he held it down so we couldn't see. I don't *know* that he killed it, but the Metros' moundsman started throwing bullets again, and the ball took some more funny bounces off their bats. They closed to 4-3 on us.

" 'That we would desire mercies of the God of heaven concerning this secret,' " Harv muttered in the dugout. Book of Daniel says *they*, but he was talking about us. " 'He revealeth the deep and secret things; He knoweth what *is* in the darkness, and the light dwelleth with Him.' "

I watched the conjure man. I hoped he'd get the trots again, but he didn't. I don't believe he did any more conjuring after that, though. His head kind of lolled back and to the side, the way your head will when you take one on the button and you're trying to recollect who you are. He was a *good* conjure man, mind, same as the Metros were a good ballclub.

But the House of Daniel was better that day. And Harv might not've done anything to a chicken, but he was better that day, too. He didn't do anything to the Metros, or I don't think he did. Without their fellow in the lime and the pumpkin and the skull with the fedora, we ended up whupping 'em good. Final was 9-4. I got one hit—not the homer I wanted, but a single. It would do. It would have to.

"Good game," the Metros' manager said when he came over to shake hands after the last out. It didn't quite sound like *Now go swallow rat poison*, but it was on the way there.

"Why, thanks," Harv said. "Nice to see you let one of your colored brethren out of their section so he could sit with the white people."

The Amarillo man's face congealed like fat in an icebox. "Cornelius, he sits where he wants to," he said.

"Shits where he wants to? Well, ain't that nice?" Harv went right on smiling. I would've punched the Amarillo guy, swear I would. Now I look back on it, though, Harv's way was better. It hurt worse, and it would sting for longer. He hardly ever cussed, but he couldn't resist that one. We gave old Cornelius something fresh to think on, too. Well, ain't that nice?

(V)

Tulia's fifty miles south of Amarillo. Only a couple of thousand people there, but Eddie Lelivelt told me they had themselves a pretty fair town team. It was one of the outfits the Amarillo Greys used to tangle with, and you can take that however you want—I guess they did.

But the House of Daniel felt right at home when the bus chugged in there. Quite a few of the Tulia men were raising whiskers along with their wheat and cows. "Good thing you fellers won't be here for Old Settlers' Day month after next," one of them said. "They give a prize for the best whiskers, and y'all've got yourselves a running start."

"How big a prize?" Wes asked. "If it's big enough, maybe we'll come back." He smiled so the local could think he was joshing if he wanted to.

The bristly man from Tulia said, "It's only twenty-five smackers. Wish it was more, but times is tough all over."

We'd seen that on the way down from Amarillo. Plenty of what had been farms weren't any more, on account of nobody lived on 'em. Tulia wasn't like Pampa; it didn't have the oil fields to keep it going. It was hurting so bad, it could've been in Oklahoma.

Maybe there were folks with nothing to fear but fear itself. I'll tell you, though, plenty more with getting thrown out of work to fear, or getting foreclosed on and tossed out on the street, or not finding a new job if you'd already lost the one you used to have, or not being able to feed your kids and put clothes on their backs, or not being able to feed yourself and put clothes on your own back.

Shack I'd lived in, getting foreclosed on would've just been a laugh. I'd been all those other places, though, and more besides. Would I have taken up with Big Stu if I hadn't? Well, I like to think I wouldn't have, any road.

Tulia team called themselves the Ravens. No, I don't know why.

Because they did, that's why. Socks and caps and uniform letters and piping, those were all green. Ever seen a green raven? Me, neither.

But they beat us. They had a spotty-faced kid throwing for 'em, and he just rared back and flung, and we never could catch up to him. We managed one run, but they got three.

I almost made the last out. I purely hate doing that. It's like everything's my fault then. I was proud of myself when I worked the kid for a walk. A round-tripper would tie it. A groundout to second wouldn't, and that was what we got.

After the last out, the Ravens started yelling and pounding on each other like they'd just licked the Wolves and they were all gonna get fat Series checks. Folks in the grandstand weren't what you'd call sedate, either. Looked like the whole little town was there, or pretty close.

Well, what else did they have to do? Whole flock of 'em had no work to go to. They'd sit wherever they'd sit, and they'd stew. Or they'd cough up a quarter and go to the pictures. They could do that all day, every day. House of Daniel came through once every couple of years. The hope of beating us ought to be worth half a buck, hey?

And then the Ravens went and did it. Happy days for Tulia. One happy day, at least. If that kid kept pitching and his arm didn't blow up, he'd go places for sure.

This was the third game I'd played for the House of Daniel, the fourth I'd seen. I felt mad about losing, and I felt bad about losing. We were the House of Daniel! We were supposed to charge on into these no-account hick towns and *win*.

It's funny. I didn't feel the same way when I played for the Enid Eagles. I wanted to win then. I tried to win. But I knew sometimes we wouldn't. We were good. We weren't *that* good, though.

When I looked at the other fellas with the lions on their shirts, I needed a few seconds to cipher out how they felt. Then it hit me: they were *embarrassed* to lose a game to the Tulia for heaven's sake Ravens. You play baseball, you'll get embarrassed every once in a while. The game does that to you. Doesn't make it any more fun when it happens.

Harv walked over to the Tulia dugout. He was a better sport than that so-and-so in Amarillo. When he said, "Well, you got us this time," he didn't sound like he wanted a tornado to blow the Ravens and the ballpark and the whole town straight to nevermore. He may have felt that way, but he didn't sound like it.

"I'm much obliged," the Tulia manager said. "Sidd pitched his arm off out there today, didn't he?"

"Hope not, for his sake. I don't know how long you'll be able to keep him," Harv said. "A year from now, he could be in the Texas League. Three years? Maybe the bigs, if he stays sound. He's trouble, all right."

"That'd be something, wouldn't it?" The guy from Tulia turned his head and hollered, "Hey, Sidd! The House of Daniels reckon you got the stuff to pitch in the big leagues!"

"I'd sure like to." Sidd's uniform was all soaked and soggy with sweat. Well, so was everybody's, but the pitchers and catchers had it worse. He went on, "You pitch up there, your name goes into the record book all official, like, and you're in there forever so they can remember you."

"The Lord always remembers you forever," Harv said, but even he sounded kinda halfhearted about it. What we did would go in the local paper—a guy from the *Tulia Herald* was talking with some of the Ravens and scribbling down what they said—but who except the ballplayers and their kin would recollect the game and what all went on longer than Tuesday after next?

Baseball. It's the same game, semipros or the bigs. Oh, they play it better—they play it real well a lot more often—up there. But it's the same game. Only in the bigs everything everybody does between the white lines gets written down for all time, almost as if they carve it in stone. Sidd said it: play the game there and you're part of history.

Play in Enid or Amarillo or Tulia and everything you do is written on the wind. The dust devils will grab hold of it and rub it out or blow it away, so it might as well've never happened. Same thing for the House of Daniel, or near enough. Being the best semipro team around— what's that? It's like being the best cook in Enid. Even if you are, who's gonna remember you fifteen minutes after you're gone unless he knew you beforehand?

I wondered why the demon I bothered. Come to that, I wondered why anybody bothered working hard to be the best cook in Enid, or anything else where they forgot about you as soon as you weren't there doing it any more. What's the point?

Harv went under the stands with the manager from Tulia to split the take. When he came back, he handed me two five-dollar bills.

If you could get 'em to pay you for whatever you did, that made a pretty fair start on things. Remembered? You could fret about remembered later on. You'd have some grub in your belly while you were fretting, too.

If you played in Pampa one day, in Amarillo the next, and in Tulia day after that, how could you *not* go on to Lubbock for a game on the heels of the one in Tulia? The House of Daniel couldn't. That's how we wound up squaring off against the Hubbers. It was an afternoon that made me think, *Well, hey, I guess maybe Texas is hotter'n Oklahoma after all.*

"You got to watch out for these fellas," Harv told us before we went from our boarding house up to Hubber Park in the north end of town. "This is a town like Amarillo, and it's a team like Amarillo. They been in real pro ball before. Chances are they will be again one of these days. Some of the guys who played for 'em in the West Texas League before the Bubble popped, they're still here. Maybe not as quick as they were then, but they'll be sneakier for sure. So play smart, you hear?"

I stuck up my hand. When he nodded at me, I asked, "Reckon we have to worry about a conjure man here, if they're just like Amarillo?"

"Hope not," he answered. "Even for a ball team like the Metros, that was a lowdown thing to pull. But if they try it, well, I do hope we'll come out of the Hubbers' den without getting eaten up, same as we did farther north." He grinned.

Some of the ballplayers grinned back at him. Some groaned at the bad joke—and it wouldn't be the first time he'd told it, or the dozenth. It might've been a joke, but it made sense to me just the same. What could you do but go on and try to take care of whatever came your way?

Hot? Oh, I mean to tell you it was hot. Outfield fences had signs for a butcher and a baker and a tailor no candlestick maker, can't say why. When I took my cuts at the plate, those signs shimmered as though I was looking at 'em in a ripply little creek.

I didn't see anybody in the stands who put me in mind of Cornelius. There were a fair number of colored folks in their section down the line. Four men sitting together there had on ball caps like the ones the Hubbers were wearing. They looked as if they could play for 'em, too, if they weren't too dark to get away with it.

After I finished swinging, I asked one of the Lubbock fellas, "Who are those smokes in your hats?"

He looked down the line. "Them's Oree and Jake and Wilson and Big Mike."

I hadn't guessed he'd know 'em by name. "They ballplayers, too?"

"Every one of 'em," he said. "They're on the Black Hubbers—they play colored teams from around these parts. We give 'em our hand-me-downs. We ain't got a lot of money, but they got even less."

"That's how it works, all right," I said, and trotted out to broil in the outfield before the game started.

Then we came in and the Hubbers hit and took infield and outfield. Their pitcher warmed up in front of their dugout. I had all I could do not to start laughing when I saw him. "He looks like he ate up half the gate receipts," I said.

"More than half," Eddie Lelivelt agreed. You can be pretty porky and still play ball. Plenty do, especially the pitchers and catchers, who don't have to run so much. But this guy was fatter than Big Stu, and that's not easy.

He didn't look like he had much, either. Oh, he put the ball where the guy catching him put his glove, but he didn't throw hard enough for it to matter. "This may be easier than you thought," I said to Harv.

"Or he's got somethin' up his sleeve," he answered. You run a team, you never think anything'll be easy. Most of the time, you're right.

The fat guy waddled out to the mound. He threw some more warm-ups. Still nothing. "Play ball!" yelled the ump behind the plate. Our leadoff hitter dug in.

Fatso wound up. He let fly—slower than ever. His wrist kind of snapped when he turned the ball loose. Ball staggered to the plate like the drunkest drunk in town (only Lubbock's dry, dry, dry, and always has been). Azariah Summers, who was playing left that day, took a swing that missed by a foot.

"Stee-rike!" the umpire said.

Second pitch was just as staggery. Azariah let it go by. Last second, it hopped back over the outside corner. The catcher dropped it, but the ump called it a strike anyway. The third one was a ball—it stayed outside. Then Azariah swung and missed, even wider than the first time. He might have got it with a butterfly net . . . or he might not. He came back to the dugout with his head down.

"Oh, that's a nasty knuckler," Harv said. "He went and sandbagged us, too—didn't show it till it counted."

You don't throw a knuckleball with your knuckles. Well, you can. A few people do. But most of 'em dig in with their fingernails instead, and push the ball out of their hand with no spin at all. It does whatever it wants after that. Flutters, wiggles, or herky-jerks—that kind of thing. Catchers hate it. Batters hate it worse. Even the pitcher doesn't know where it's going or how it'll get there. But if he's got a good one that day, he'll drive the other side wild.

If he doesn't, if he throws 'em so they tumble instead of knuckling, they're long balls waiting to happen. But Fatso set us down in order—two whiffs and a little dribbler straight back to him. I wondered if he'd throw the first baseman a knuckleball to keep him on his toes. He didn't, though.

If we didn't let them score, they couldn't beat us. That's what I was thinking when I walked out to center. It was too hot for me to run if I didn't have to. I hoped the spirit gum holding my whiskers on wouldn't catch fire. Almost muggy enough to swim in, too.

Out on the hill, Wes had to be feeling the same way. They didn't score in the bottom of the first, anyway. We got another shot at their guy. He walked a couple of people. No, he couldn't tell where it was going, either. A double play bailed him out of the jam. When he took off his cap to wipe his forehead on his sleeve while he went back to the dugout, I saw he was almost bald. Well, so what? If you can throw a knuckler at all, odds are you can keep throwing it till you're fifty.

Wes held 'em in the second, too. Fatso walked our leadoff man in the third. That put me up there with a man on first. Maybe the pitcher'd make a mistake. And he did. It came in as juicy as a roast on a platter. I creamed a bullet of a liner—straight into their shortstop's glove. Only good news was, he couldn't double off our runner.

I went back to the dugout cussing. Not all the House of Daniel men went in for that. Harv mostly didn't, like I've said, but he didn't get mad to hear other people do it. He found ways to let folks know how he felt any which way. He got more mileage out of *Shucks!* than I did with a whole raft of blanks and blankety-blanks.

"Do it again same way next time, Snake," was all he said when I slammed my bat into the trash can that held 'em. "You hit it good. It just didn't drop in."

I fanned the next time, fooled as bad as Azariah had been to start off the game. But in the bottom of that inning I threw a Hubber out at the plate to make the third out. Throw beat him by five feet. He saw it coming in and tried to knock our catcher back to Tulia. Amos held on to the ball even so. When he took it out of his mitt to show it to the ump, even the Lubbock crowd clapped for him. You've got to be brave to want to catch. You've got to have a screw loose, too. They don't call the mask and chest protector and shin guards the tools of ignorance for nothing.

Scoreless through seven. We really didn't fancy losing two games in a row. Losing wasn't what the House of Daniel was all about. Fatso looked ready to keep serving 'em up till it got dark. Why not? He wasn't working hard. Smart, yeah, but not hard.

Nobody on, one out in the eighth when I came up again. You're gonna beat smart, you better play smart yourself. I figured I'd bunt, the way I had against Ponca City. The Hubbers' third baseman was back and tight to the line, guarding against doubles into the corner. Bunting also gave me more time to wait for that damn flutterball. If I could get it down, I'd beat it out.

I could. I did. And I took off on the first pitch to the next hitter. A knuckler's easy to steal on. It goes in slow, and the catcher has trouble corraling it a lot of the time. That's what I was thinking, anyhow. But the throw came in to second like something shot out of a gun. The second baseman slapped the tag on me right as my spikes hit the bag.

We both waited. "Safe!" the base umpire said, and held his palms flat to the ground. The crowd booed. The second baseman cussed hard.

He thought he'd got me. A pop bottle flew out of the stands. It missed the ump by three feet, no more.

He just stood there, a skinny little guy sweating like the rest of us. His black suit didn't show it as much as our flannels, but black held the heat worse. Pop bottles and bad language were all part of the day's work for him. Hard way to make five or ten bucks, let me tell you.

I had planned on lighting out for third as soon as Fatso went to the plate again. Now I wondered if that was a good scheme. Their back-stop threw *hard*, even if Fatso didn't. Harv would stretch *Shucks!* some more if I got hung out to dry. Would he ever!

But we had to grab a run some kind of way. We couldn't win if we didn't score. So I lit out.

Another strong throw. Strong and about three feet over the third baseman's glove. It sailed into left. I scrambled up and dashed home.

Everybody punched my arm and pounded my back and patted my behind when I went into the dugout. "A home-run bunt!" Eddie said.

"Good work," Harv said. "You pushed 'em, and you rattled 'em, and they broke." He would've said a few other things if they'd thrown me out. But I had plenty of bigger might-have-beens than that to fret about if I was so inclined.

We beat 'em 1-0. Their second baseman gave the base umpire an-other piece of his mind after the last out. That did him as much good as you'd expect. I might have told the ump a thing or three if he'd called me out. Or I might not have. We still could've won some other way if I were out. My being safe was pretty much why the Hubbers lost.

In their dugout, the catcher and the fat pitcher were talking. I couldn't hear what they were saying, but I didn't need to be Sam Spade to work it out. The catcher was telling the pitcher he was sorry he'd heaved one into left there. When Fatso put a hand on his shoulder, you knew they'd be playing together again any day now.

After Harv handed me my money after the game, he said, "Looks like you're earning your keep, kiddo."

"Don't jinx it!" I said. He laughed, but I was only a quarter joking, tops.

★   ★   ★

Where do you go from Lubbock? If you weren't born there, *anywhere—and quick!* seems like the right answer. Oh, that's not quite fair. Lubbock brags about being the cleanest town in Texas, and it didn't look too dirty to me. They farm outside of town. They raise cows and chickens. Cotton, too. Reason enough to stay if you already live there, I guess. Not reason enough to settle there if you don't.

Only we couldn't get away as fast as we wanted to. I told you how hot it was during the game, and how sticky. It got stickier and stickier, too, and clouds started filling the sky so it looked black as night an hour before sundown. I knew what was coming. So did everybody else. "Gonna pour," Eddie Lelivelt said.

It didn't just pour. It came down in buckets, hogsheads, barrels. We listened to it drumming against the boarding house's dining-room windows. We might've gone out to celebrate the win—Wes was talking about a steakhouse he'd been to before. But when you might have to swim back, the widow woman's supper looked like a better idea, even if it was longer on dumplings and sauerkraut than it was on beef.

Rain didn't let up, either. Thunder boomed like big guns. Devils' pitchforks of lightning played flashbulb tricks outside the windows. The wind screamed. There'd be tornadoes spawning somewhere—I hoped nowhere close.

When we were going upstairs to our rooms, Wes said, "Forty days and forty nights." That wasn't Book of Daniel, but it didn't seem so far wrong, either.

Harv kind of sighed. "I don't think we're gonna play in Sweetwater tomorrow." He sighed again. "Dunno about Big Spring the day after, either. Parks'll dry out pretty fast once the rain blows away, but it don't look like it's blowing away. Looks like it's blowing in, doggone it."

I heard what he wasn't saying. If we didn't play, no money came in. But money still went out. We had to pay for the rooms, and for whatever food didn't come with 'em, and for everything that went with the bus, and probably for a bunch of other stuff I didn't even know about. I'd lived on a frayed shoestring myself, same as half the country, and got used to knotting it back together when it broke.

When something I'd counted on fell through . . . well, that was when the shoestring got some new knots in it. That was when I started taking care of this and that for Big Stu, too.

If I hadn't started working for him, and then stopped the way I stopped, I wouldn't've been there in Lubbock right then, part of a better ballclub than the one I'd jumped. You try to track all those things and how they fit, life starts looking like a plate of spaghetti with the strands squiggled together.

After we got to our room, Eddie poured a glass full of water from the pitcher on the dresser. He didn't drink it or anything. He just set it on the window sill. "What's that all about?" I asked him.

"Supposed to keep twisters away," he said.

"Oh, yeah?" I didn't see how it could. But I didn't see how leaving it there would hurt things, either. So I kept my mouth shut.

No tornado picked up Lubbock and carried it away, not during that storm. If Eddie wanted to credit his glass of water, he could. But the town's been hit before. I expect it'll get hit again. Same as Enid, it's in the right part of the country for twisters. Maybe nobody there knows Eddie's trick. Or maybe the trick doesn't work. But don't tell that to Eddie.

It was still raining next morning, maybe not so bad as in the night but too hard to give us any chance to play a game that day. Harv said to our landlady, "Ma'am, may I use your telephone to call Sweetwater and see how we can rearrange our schedule? Of course I'll pay you back for the call."

"You talk so purty, I'd be right glad to let you use it if only I had one," the widow woman answered, "but I ain't."

"That's . . . too bad." The way Harv skipped a beat there said he was thinking harder things than what he came out with. He did tack on, "I'd guess it might come in handy for a business like this."

"No, sir." The gray-haired gal shook her head. "People calling me up all the time to pester me when I don't care to talk to them? Slick-talking fly-by-nights trying to sell me things I don't want and I don't need and I can't afford? I've got enough of them scoundrels knocking on my front door. I send 'em off with a flea in their ear, let me tell you. You can go to the drugstore or the post office to palaver on the telephone if you feel like it, but I don't want one. So there you are."

"Here I am, all right." It was raining plenty hard enough to soak Harv, even if he went out with an umbrella and a slicker.

But he was less put out than he might've been. Not everybody's got a telephone—nowhere near. Only people I knew in Enid who did were Big Stu and Rod Graver. Well, I guess Charlie Carstairs, too, but I knew him just well enough to nod to him when I walked by his store or we passed each other on the street. And not to beat up his kid sister when neither one of 'em had done anything to me.

Come to think of it, I read in some newspaper or other that there's one telephone for every seven or eight people in the country. Newspaper wasn't sad about that—it was crowing. We've got more per head than anywhere else in the whole wide world. If you believe that paper we do, anyhow.

None of which did Harv a red cent's worth of good. It might explain why the widow had no telephone—though she'd done a pretty fair job of that all by herself—but it didn't make one pop onto the table in her parlor. Harv splashed out to do what needed doing. We were only a couple of blocks from a Rexall, so he didn't have to go too far. And the lightning and thunder had eased off with the rain. You could still hear thunder growling to itself, but it was off to the south now. It put me in mind of a mean dog chained up to guard a still out in the woods, and you hear him when you're walking down the road at the edge of the trees.

After they finished their oatmeal and toast, some of the House of Daniel players went back to their rooms for more sleep. Why not? We weren't going anywhere any time soon. Some of them played cards. The widow woman eyed them as if they were sacrificing babies to Moloch, but she didn't say anything.

I stayed out of the poker game. If you know beforehand you'll lose money, why give yourself the chance? Eddie Lelivelt had a little traveling checker set. He beat me two out of three, but it didn't cost me anything. Our landlady didn't look at the two of us like she expected devil's horns to pop out of our foreheads. I kind of wished she would have.

Harv finally came back. Maybe to get even with the widow woman, he dripped all over the rug and the wood floor in her front hall. "What's the news?" Eddie called.

"If the rain stops, we'll play in Sweetwater tomorrow morning and Big Spring tomorrow afternoon," he said. "We won't draw much for a morning game, but what can you do? If the rain doesn't stop . . ." He shook his head. More water flew from his hair and his beard. "Even if the rain doesn't stop, Daniel and his brothers had it worse. I always got to remember that."

"It's a fact," Eddie said.

"I got to remember it anyway," Harv said. "Just 'cause something's true, that doesn't mean so much. You got to know it's true. You got to know what its being true means." That was too deep for me. But then, I never ran a ball team, or wanted to. Harv could do it. He could play, too, which was even better.

The rain did stop, so we took off for Sweetwater at sunup the next day. It was still hot. Still muggy, too. When the sun hit the ponds and puddles and ditches, you thought you were in a steam bath. When you were in our bus, you for sure thought you were in a steam bath. We opened up the windows. Then we might as well have been in a windy steam bath.

We went southeast down US 84 till we came to US 80, and then east a few miles into Sweetwater. There were a couple of refineries along the way—nothing like what they've got around Pampa, but a couple. Sheep grazed by the highway. We saw buzzards feeding here and there on the shoulder, so some of those sheep must've tried to cross when they shouldn't have. Sheep don't have the brains to look both ways before they start. Well, neither do some people I know.

Game was due to start at half past nine. We got to Swatter Field with, oh, forty-five minutes to spare. That's the town team: the Sweetwater Swatters. They're another one that had played pro ball when times were good. Now that times aren't so good, most of the Swatters work in the gypsum mines outside of town or in the factories that process the gypsum once it comes out of the ground.

They wouldn't have to work today, of course—at least not the morning shift. They were loosening up, throwing the ball around, when we came in. Infield still looked muddy, but they'd put down enough sand so there weren't any puddles on the dirt. There sure were in the outfield, in the left- and right-field corners and one maybe twenty feet back of where the center fielder would stand.

"Gonna be one of those exciting days." Wes spat a stream of tobacco juice into a little puddle by our dugout. We were all trying to get limber after the bus ride. Easy to hurt yourself when you didn't have enough time to stretch. Pull a hamstring on that muddy infield and Harv would start yelling *Is there a shortstop in the house?*

Wes was going to pitch this game. I knew he had good stuff. He'd worked me out with it. How long he could keep it on a day and a half's rest . . . Well, we'd all find out.

"The Swatters'll eat you lion guys up!" yelled a fan a few rows back of our dugout. "Eat you up, you hear?" We heard. They could probably hear him inside the gypsum works across town. Every little place has one of those fans. Sometimes he's a drunk, sometimes just a loud-mouth. He shouts for the town team and cusses out whoever they're playing. He never shuts up, no matter how much everybody else wants him to.

You pretend not to hear. If you answer back, you're playing his game and letting him get your goat. If you go into the stands and knock his front teeth down his throat after he talks about your mother, three to two you'll find out the sheriff is his brother-in-law. In that case, you'll be a while getting out of town.

Grandstand wasn't packed, the way it was a lot of the time when the House of Daniel came calling. Half past nine was too early to start a game. The Swatters didn't have much of a chance to spread the word about the new time, either. We drew some people, though: I'd bet at least as many as they got for a game with some other North Texas team.

We didn't score in the top of the first. I felt better than I expected going out to center. I wasn't used to playing day after day, or to riding the bus the same way. Two nights on the same saggy mattress in Lubbock had put some gas back in my tank.

When the first ball the Swatters hit was a grounder, I took a closer look at the little lake behind me. Not deep enough for gators, but a snapper or water moccasin wouldn't've surprised me. Even that early, mosquitoes buzzed around. Swallows swooped down to catch some, but plenty were left. I knew I'd have welts before the game ended. Mosquitoes are nothing but little vampires with six legs.

Of course the Swatters' second guy up hit a long fly to center. Would have been an easy catch but for the puddle. I splashed on into it—what are you gonna do? Water soaked my shoes and socks, but I made the play. Wes waved out at me when I threw the ball in to Eddie. Getting drenched like that on a cold day would've been worse. Well, a cold day in Sweetwater was something we wouldn't see this year.

My first at-bat, I paid the Swatters back. I hit my own fly ball out toward the center-field fence. Their outfielder ran it down. Splashed it down, if you really want to know, same as I had. I hoped he enjoyed squelching around out there just as much as I had.

Next inning, I was on my wet feet yelling. With two men on, Wes hit one that skipped into the pond before their center fielder could run it down. We plated both of 'em, and Wes wound up on third because the Swatter threw what was worse than a spitter back to the infield, and the relay man couldn't handle it.

We scored two more that inning, and ended up coasting to an 8-3 win. That was good. The thing Harv dreaded most of all was extra innings in Sweetwater. Play fourteen or fifteen there and we might not have made the game in Big Spring. We climbed back on the bus in our dirty, sweaty, smelly uniforms and tooled west on US 80. Fifty miles? Seventy-five? Something like that. More than an hour. Less than two.

You want to play baseball every day? You want to try to make a living at it? People who do—well, people who say they do—think about the big leagues and nice hotels and fancy steaks and showgirls and bottom berths in Pullman cars. You aren't in the bigs (maybe even if you aren't a star up there), chances are you've got to do something else besides to make ends meet. And playing baseball every day means bus rides through hot country in stinking wool flannels and a boardinghouse that waters the oatmeal when you get to the next little town.

I took off my shoes. Then I peeled off my socks, too, and wrung 'em out on the floor of the bus. I'm not sure I was ever wet enough before to need to wring out my socks. I left my dogs bare after that. I'd put the socks and spikes back on when we parked next to the Big Spring ballpark.

Countryside changed about halfway there. It went from ranching country with sheep and a few cows to cotton fields as far as the eye could reach. Workers changed, too. Lot more colored fellas—gals out there with 'em—than we'd seen farther east. Most of 'em kept the sun off their noggins with straw hats. The brims on those were as wide as something a Mexican'd wear, but not shaped the same way.

Then we drove past a couple of work gangs in rags with no hats at all. They didn't move real fast, either. They were zombies, and already dead, so of course they didn't care about the sun. Their bosses weren't paying 'em anything, so they didn't care—too much—if things went a little slow. Even coons and greasers cost a little something to hire. Not zombies.

Eddie Lelivelt saw 'em, too. "I don't like those shuffling stiffs," he said. "They ain't natural."

"That's kind of the idea," I said.

"No, not like that," he said. "I mean, nobody likes 'em when they put real people, live people, out of work. Nobody but the people who use 'em, anyhow. But I mean, *really* not natural. They're dead, right? But they're still movin'. So some kind of something's gotta be going on inside their heads. Only stands to reason. But what else is going on along with it? Somebody did that to me, I wouldn't be mighty happy about it. Would you?"

"I could've been one of those—things," I answered, shuddering when I remembered. "I ran away from a conjure man's tout not long before the House of Daniel took me in."

"Hey, you make a better center fielder than you would a zombie."

"Thanks a lot," I told him. Better he should've said it like that than the other way, but even so. . . .

Harv kept looking at his watch. He pushed the bus as hard as he could. Not a lot of traffic on the road, so that was pretty hard. Only thing that slowed him down even a little bit was worrying a Texas Ranger on a motorcycle would pull him over and give him a speeding ticket. He wouldn't have cared about the ticket, mind, but the time he wasted jawing with the lawman would have eaten up every minute he saved by stomping on the gas and more besides.

Big Spring is a new enough town, most of the trees are still little. It's a big enough town to own a few traffic lights. Harv had to stop for those, even if he didn't like it. But hey, we got to Hutch Field half an hour before game time. What more do you want?

(VI)

Two bus rides, a ballgame in the morning . . . Was I tired? Oh, just a little. Only people who wonder how you get tired playing a game haven't tried it. Stand and run around in the hot sun for a couple of hours so your uniform sticks to you like glue and see how you like it. Then turn around and do it again that afternoon. Think that won't wear you out some? Good luck, buddy!

"Oh, my," I said when we got inside Hutch Field. Grandstand was nice enough, and we would have a bigger house than we did at Sweetwater. I didn't see any standing water anywhere—the colored groundskeeper knew his business. But I did see right away it was gonna be one of those games.

Conoco Ball Park in Ponca City, they fenced off a fair stretch of prairie and called it a field. In Big Spring, it looked more like the idea was to put a fence around an outhouse. I guess that was the lot they had to build their ballyard on, and they did what they could with it, but oh, my!

Left was 306, short but not crazy short. Only 380 to dead center, though, and 265 down the right-field line. Right-field fence was twenty-five, thirty feet high, and made out of pressed tin, to try to keep some of those balls from sailing out. Every ball that hit it left a dent. That wall was dented plenty.

The home nine was the Cowboys. Big Spring was another one of the nine million places that got into pro ball when times were flush and got flushed out after the Big Bubble went ker-pop. Some of their old guys stuck around because they still liked to play and they still liked picking up extra cash. The younger ones had those reasons and the hope somebody who knew somebody would notice 'em, like what he saw, and give 'em a chance at the brass ring.

Their pitcher was one of those kids. He was a southpaw, and he threw BBs. He didn't aim real well, though. He put me in mind of Don

Patterson back in Enid. I hadn't hardly been homesick since I joined up with the House of Daniel—I hadn't had time to be, tell you the truth—but I was then.

He got a couple of outs in the first and walked a couple of guys. Harv came up, swung late on one of those fastballs, and lofted a high, lazy fly to right.

Cowboys' right fielder went back, back, and then the wall stopped him. *Clank!* It picked up a new dent. Harv got a double, but we only scored one. They would've thrown out our other runner by twenty feet if he'd tried to come all the way around. Didn't matter, though. Eddie drove in both ducks on the pond with a single up the middle.

And Fidgety Frank gave back two of 'em in the bottom of the first. One was a homer to dead center. I jumped—the fence in center was low enough to give me a chance—but it was long gone. The Cowboys rattled the tin once themselves, too.

We were all shaking our heads when we came back to the dugout. "Last man standing," Wes said, and that was about the size of it.

We beat 'em, 15-11. Not pretty—nowhere close—but we made it work. It would've been 15-12, only I purely stole a home run from one of their fellas. Another one where I jumped with my back against the 380 sign. My glove must've been a foot over the top of the fence when I hauled the ball back in. I think the catch I made in Ponca City was better, but even the Cowboys' fans clapped some for this one.

All I wanted to do when we got off the field was go on over to our roominghouse and clean up. And all I wanted to do was grab something to eat, on account of my belly was grumbling like some of that faraway thunder. And all I wanted was to go to sleep. Two bus rides and two games—that's a long, long day.

And I couldn't do any of the things I wanted to, at least not right away. A reporter for the *Big Spring Daily Herald* wanted to talk about the home run I took away. "What can I tell you?" I said. "I jumped as high as I could, and the ball stayed in my glove till I could get my other hand on it."

"That wasn't a semipro play," he said. "That was a play they'd be glad to see in a big-league park."

"Thanks. Obliged." I left it there. You see plenty of great plays in semipro ball. Trouble with guys who play my kind of baseball is, they've got a hole in their game somewhere. They don't hit enough—like me. Or they're terrible slow. Or they'll make some great plays but foul up too many everyday ones. Or if they're pitchers they're wild, like the Cowboys' twirler or Don back in Enid.

Higher up the ladder you go, the more everyday plays get made and the simpler the game looks. Just in my handful of games, I'd seen that the House of Daniel stood on a higher rung than my old Eagles. Not a way higher rung—the Eagles stood a chance against 'em, same as the Greasemen had. But you'd have to be a fool, and a fool from Enid at that, to bet against the House of Daniel in the matchup.

"You made the play of the game, no question about it." The reporter showed me his scoresheet. He'd put two stars by my catch, so he liked it, all right. He'd even spelled my last name right, which doesn't happen all the time.

I never saw the story. We were on the road the next morning, and nobody bought a paper. If I'd known how much trouble it would make me, I would've told him my handle was really Eddie Lelivelt.

We set out for Midland and Odessa from Big Spring. We played in Odessa, even though Midland's the one that used to have a pro team. They both reminded me of Pampa. Neither one of 'em was real big, but they had oil wells. Only from Odessa you could see mountains against the western skyline, blurry and purple in the distance.

There's gold in them there hills. They say there is, and I guess they're right, since a miner got rich in them. But he never told anybody where or how, and the secret died with him years ago. People still go out and look for his strike every now and again. Nobody's ever found it, though.

Anyway, we didn't have to worry about being late for this game, not unless the bus broke down, and it didn't. We played on a field in the city park. That made Harv unhappy: the stands didn't hold enough to suit him. "Next time we come through here, we'll go to Midland instead," he said, and he wrote it down in his notebook to make sure he didn't forget.

Watching him tend to that reminded me of something that was on my mind anyhow. "Are we just playing our way through Texas, or what?" I asked Eddie.

"Huh? You don't know?"

"If I did, would I be asking?"

He kind of laughed. "I guess there's no reason you ought to. I forgot how you joined the team. We're playing through West Texas, yeah, and then into New Mexico, and then on up into Colorado. The *Denver Post* semipro tournament starts the twelfth of June, and we're gonna be there."

"The *Post* tournament!" I knew about it. The Eagles had talked about it back in Enid. Talk was as far as we ever got. Not a chance in church we could've scraped together the money to get there. If we won the tournament, that would've paid for the trip and then some, but what were the odds? Bad, worse, and downright ridiculous, that's what.

Post tournament's open to any team not in the bigs or regular minors. You can't use ringers who played in pro ball this year or last. But there are plenty of good ballplayers outside that tent. I was in a bus full of 'em. And . . . "They let colored teams play in that one, don't they?"

"I'm not sure they have before, but they're going to this year—I know that." Eddie cocked his head to one side and eyed me like some funny new kind of bug. "We've played those teams before. Why? Does the idea bother you?"

"Not so you'd notice. I think it'd be interesting to see what they can do." I tried to give him back his own stare. "How come you reckon it would? On account of Ah tahk lahk thiyyus?"

I stretched out the last few words, and turned the very last one into two syllables. That was more Texas, and hick Texas at that, than Oklahoma. We drawl some—plenty for a Yankee to notice, but less than our Lone Star neighbors. They get more up in arms about colored folks—and greasers—than we do, too. Well, they have more of both to get up in arms about.

He had the grace to look embarrassed. "I'll shut up. Some of the stuff I think about where you come from is probably just as dumb as some of the stuff you think about my neck of the woods."

Everybody creaked and groaned when we went out there against the Odessa Coyotes. Harv called 'em Kye oh-tees. In Odessa, they were Kye-oats. Whatever you called 'em, we should've licked 'em easy. Just watching 'em take infield and shag flies, you could see they weren't as good as either the Swatters or the Cowboys.

We weren't so hot in Odessa ourselves that afternoon, even if the weather was. We'd played solid ball in Sweetwater and Big Spring the day before. I'd though it would catch up with us in Big Spring, but it didn't. We'd played two solid games . . . and it came back to haunt us in that sun-blasted ballpark in Odessa.

Wes did the twirling for us. He wasn't what you'd call rested, but he was fresher than Fidgety Frank. He could get by on junk and smarts. He could, yeah, only not that day. And we made four errors behind him, which'll kill anybody deader'n belt leather. We kicked it around so much, you would've thought we were playing football out there.

"Shucks!" Harv said. He said it again a couple of innings later, too, only louder. It was one of the few times I saw him where he looked as though he wanted to tear loose and cuss for real. And when the last out came and we were on the short end of a 7-2 thrashing, he said, "Doggone it!" Strong words, from Harv.

The Coyotes didn't go over the moon at beating us the way the Ravens had, but you could tell they were happy about it. "We must've been lucky," their manager said to Harv. "I've seen you guys before. You're sharper than that most of the time."

"You like to be sharp all the time," Harv answered. Then he said "Doggone it!" one more time. Then he yawned.

"Been on the road some?" the Odessa manager asked. Yeah, he was a gent. He was doing his best to let us down easy.

"Some," Harv allowed. He quickly added, "But we're on the road all the time, too." Harv was never one to make excuses. As far as he was concerned, there was no excuse for losing anyhow. He went on, "You got some good ballplayers here. That's how come you beat us."

"Obliged to you for saying so." The Odessa man touched the brim of his cap. He was an older fella, with gray hair sticking out from under the cap. He hadn't been in the game. Looking at his soaking uniform, though, you would've guessed he'd gone about sixteen innings behind the plate. He gestured back toward his dugout. "Let's play like a couple of thieves and divide the loot."

"Okey-doke." Harv went over there with him. He looked unhappy a different way when he came back. First thing he did then was take me aside. "Snake, I know I said you'd get ten a game till you went on shares, but nobody's share today comes that high. I'm gonna give you five for the game. I'm sorry, but there you are."

He waited to see what I'd say. Did he reckon I'd pitch a fit? Not likely! I had more money in my grouch bag than in I don't remember when, I was playing more ball than I ever had before, and I'd got clean away from Big Stu (well, I thought so, any road). Yeah, I could've gone *You so-and-so, you promised!* and either got the money or jumped the team. But I'm not that kind of natural-born damn fool. Other kinds, sure, but not that one.

All I did say was, "Seems fair. If I stick with the House of Daniel, I know I'll make it up."

He punched me on the arm, not too hard. "You're all right, Snake."

We got back on the bus and drove to the boarding house where we'd clean up and spend the night. It was getting on toward suppertime. We went past a couple of soup kitchens, one in some sort of county office, the other—with a longer line outside—at a church.

I only got five dollars that day? The scrawny men and the worried women and the hungry kids in those soup-kitchen lines, they didn't have anything. They hadn't had anything for quite a while. Chances they'd get anything any time soon didn't look real great, either. They had to know it, too. No wonder the women in those faded dresses, washed too many times and patched and darned, looked worried.

If I had thrown a fit about the money, seeing those lined faces and sorry clothes would have shamed me. I hope like anything it would, anyway. I felt a little ashamed even as things were. Here I was, making money playing a boys' game, and those folks couldn't find work to save their souls. The world's a cruel place sometimes.

Tomorrow we'd be gone. Harv knew where, and I'd find out. They'd still be right here. So would their troubles. Tomorrow, we'd see somebody else's troubles. Not everybody could stand life on the road. The more of it I saw, the less sure I was that I could.

Odessa bragged about having night clubs. It didn't brag about all the folks who couldn't afford to set foot inside one even if they wanted to, but never mind. The House of Daniel guys didn't go out to cut a rug. After we cleaned up and put on regular clothes, we walked across the street to a joint where we could get a big bowl of chili—spicy enough to barbecue your tonsils—and a Shiner Bock or a Coca-Cola for thirty-five cents. Then we came back, went up to our rooms, and did our best to sleep in the heat. Each room had a little fan that pushed the air around some, but they sure didn't cool it much.

So much for night life in Odessa, Texas.

No, I take that back. We did have some night life . . . one more time, no. That's not right, either. Let me tell it instead of trying to explain it ahead of time. That way I won't get it all twisted up. And if the Odessa Rotary Club doesn't like what I have to say, too bad. It's as true as everything else in here.

Some time in the middle of the night, something started tapping on the window glass. You hear noises like that if you've got a lighted window and moths fly into the glass. But it was black as black in there, and what tapped on the glass, that was no moth.

I was asleep. Then I was a little bit awake. Then I was awake awake, if you know what I mean. Awake clean through. How else are you gonna be if you look toward the window—a second-story window, mind—and you see somebody pressed against it beckoning to you to open up and let him in?

"Eddie?" I whispered, none too steady.

"I see it, too, Jack," he whispered back. Nothing fazed Eddie. He'd made one of the errors that afternoon, and a bad one, but I knew he'd be fine tomorrow. A vampire at the window wouldn't rattle him.

"Let me come in," the vampire said. Like the one I'd bumped into in Ponca City, it talked like anybody else. Had a West Texas drawl thick enough to slice, in fact. "Let me come in, and I'll make you free like me."

"Tell me another one," I couldn't help answering the undead thing. The conjure man's tout tried to sell me freedom, too. It's as American as apple pie—if you're dumb enough to buy it. Or if times are hard enough for you.

The vampire should have sold Pierce-Arrows or something. Maybe it had, back before it got bit. "I mean it," it said. "Freedom from want, freedom from sorrow . . . All you need is a neck, and you're as rich as a Rockefeller. In the brotherhood of blood, you're as good as everyone else. You won't have to scramble for steaks any more."

"No—you have to scramble away from stakes," I said, and mimed pounding one into the vampire's heart. It flinched back from the window glass. The room might've been pitch-dark, but it could see in there fine.

A neck, and you're as rich as a Rockefeller. The brotherhood of blood. Ever since the Russians went and slaughtered their Czar, people who aren't in Russia have wondered if vampires are running things over there. The Russians sure talk like that a lot of the time. And is it an accident their new flag is red?

"Let me in," this one said. "You won't need to worry about the fancy new convertible, either. You'll fly like me." I wasn't so sure about flying. It could hang outside the window without visible means of support, though. I had to give it that.

Eddie Lelivelt laughed at it. "Fat lot of good a convertible'd do you now, huh? First touch of sun and what are you? Dust in the wind."

That made the vampire flinch again. But it didn't quit. It must've been hungry itself. "Don't you want to live for yourselves, by yourselves, with no one to tell you what to do any more?"

What I wanted to do was go back to sleep. I pulled the cross out from below the undershirt I was wearing. It flared, the same color as the lightning a couple of nights earlier. In the dark room, it seemed about as bright as a lightning bolt, too.

"Go away!" I said. "You aren't invited in!"

When my eyes got used to the dark again, the vampire was gone. I stuck the cross back where it belonged and rolled over in bed. Five minutes later, I was sleeping some more. Eddie beat me to it, though. I heard him snoring before I dropped off myself.

West again on US 80 the next morning. The farther we went, the paler and the more sun-scorched the country got. Cactus. Sagebrush. Gray dirt. White sand. I've seen some sad and sorry prairie. This here wasn't prairie. This here was desert. I hoped we had a couple of extra jugs of water in case the radiator overheated—or in case we did.

The little town of Barstow was like an oasis in that desert. They raised all kinds of crops around there, on account of they got the water they needed from the Red Bluff dam not far away.

Four or five miles farther on, we crossed over the river on an iron bridge that hadn't been painted in too long. Big streaks of rust ran down it. It was still strong enough to take our weight, yeah. How long would it stay that way, though, if nobody cared for it?

As soon as we got to the far side, Wes let out a whoop: "West of the Pecos! No law here!"

Some of us laughed. Some groaned. From behind the wheel, Harv said, "Let's go out there and steal us a herd of buses, then." He got himself some laughs and some groans, too.

Town of Pecos is right on the west side of the river. Like Midland and Odessa, it's a cow town and an oil town. It's about the same size as each of them, too. I don't think Pecos ever had a team in a pro league. Didn't mean they didn't have three or four clubs that played on weekends and split the gate. We were playing the Pecos Peccaries—a peccary is a little wild hog.

"Not the Pecos Bills?" I said.

"There is a team with that handle," Harv said. "The Peccaries are better—and they promised us a bigger share of the money."

So much for my try at a joke. We went out there to swing the bat and chase flies. The infielders would practice on grounders, and then they'd go through their phantom infield drill to give the crowd something to ooh and ahh about. You need to liven them up any way you can.

Watching us, some of the Peccaries seemed ready to ooh and ahh, too. I heard one of their men going off say, "I've got trouble believing I'm on the same field with the House of Daniel."

I hoped more of them felt that way. I hoped they'd go right on doing it. If they figured we were bound to beat 'em, it would mean as much as if they started every at-bat with a strike already on 'em.

We batted around in the top of the first and scored four times. I doubled in the last one myself. If they hadn't thought we were world-beaters before then, we did our best to convince 'em.

Fidgety Frank took the hill. He'd pitched afternoon before last, but he didn't care. He was like Walt Edwards back in Ponca City. Not being able to throw real hard didn't bother him one bit. He couldn't throw all that hard even with plenty of rest. Hey, raw speed counts, but only so much. Put a little on, take a little off, vary when you do it, and you'll have the other side swinging at shadows and talking to themselves when they go back to the dugout after a popup or a roller back to the box.

Fidgety Frank was puffing and blowing out there. He was working hard even if he wasn't throwing hard. He got a hit of his own in the third, a booming, run-scoring double into the gap in right-center. He might have been happier to sit on the bench with the rest of us while the inning played out.

But another double cashed him in. That made it 6-0. You could watch the air go out of the Peccaries as though they were so many leaky inner tubes. If any of them had thought they were going to whip us, they started to see that it wouldn't go their way today.

Sure enough, we breezed home, 11-3. Fidgety Frank got tired in the late innings and served up a few fat ones. Or maybe he did it on purpose, the way a card sharp'll let a sucker win a hand once in a while to keep him in the game. I don't know. Didn't matter one way or the other.

After the game was over, the Peccary who couldn't believe he was playing against us brought around one of our advertising posters and had us all sign it.

"I'm gonna get it framed. I'll hang it on my wall when I do," he said.

"Most of the time, our flyers get hung right on top of a POST NO BILLS sign," Harv said. We laughed about that, for all the world as if it weren't true. When you win a game by eight runs, laughing comes easy.

A kid came up to me with a sheet of paper and a pencil. "Will you sign this?" he said. He couldn't have been more than nine.

"Here you go." I did it. I'd never signed an autograph in my life, and now I'd done two in five minutes. I thought that was pretty funny, too, in a different kind of way.

"I want to play for the House of Daniel myself, when I can grow me a beard," the kid piped.

"Maybe you will," I told him. He had a while to wait.

The Peccaries' manager came over to make nice with Harv. Since they hadn't thrown at us or tried to rack up our infielders after we got the big lead, Harv made nice with him, too. "Maybe you'll get us next time," he said.

"Mebbe." The other guy sounded as though he wished he could believe it. "You Pecosed us but good today, though."

Harv stuck a finger in his ear, the way you will when you aren't sure you heard right. "We did what?"

"You Pecosed us," their manager repeated. "In the old days, when there really wasn't any law in these parts, you'd shoot somebody, then you'd fill his carcass with rocks before you chucked it in the river so it wouldn't come up again. That was Pecosin'."

"How about that?" Harv said. "Nice little town you had here, huh? They don't do that any more, do they?"

"Not over a ballgame, anyways," the local answered. "Not with you fellas—y'all are famous. If we were playin' a team from Fort Stockton, though, say, and it was one of those games where the benches cleared two or three times, well, some folks might get a tad upset over somethin' like that."

"Do tell?" Harv said tonelessly. "Do they, um, Pecos people in Fort Stockton, too? We've got a game there tomorrow."

"Nah." The Peccaries' manager shook his head. "Oh, they might shoot you. Fort Stockton's about half greaser, and they got themselves some excitable boys. But they wouldn't chuck you in the river afterwards. They ain't got no river. They draw their water from Comanche Springs instead."

"Thanks. That takes a load off my mind." Harv sounded as mild as milk. The Peccaries' boss man kind of scratched his head, wondering whether Harv had just needled him and this whole part of Texas on the sly.

Fort Stockton is about fifty miles southeast of Pecos down US 285. If that's not the lonesomest stretch of highway the good Lord ever made, I don't know what would be. Empty in Texas seems emptier than anywhere else, on account of there's so much of it and it stretches so far. Desert and sun and every once in a while a dust devil swirling and grinning.

We could tell when we got to the ground Comanche Springs watered—ten square miles of it, maybe more. Wherever the ditches reached, the gray and the yellow and the faded tan turned green. It's good enough land if only you can irrigate it. Most places, they couldn't.

Without the friendly water elementals and the free-flowing spring, Fort Stockton'd be one more dance floor for the dust devils.

Wherever the ditches reached, shacks popped up beside 'em like toadstools. Packing crates, scrap lumber, tar paper, rocks, corrugated sheet iron for a roof if they were lucky, all kinds of junk slapped together any old way . . . You wouldn't believe how many Mexicans lived in each one. I sure didn't.

Power? Running water? They didn't imagine that stuff, much less have it. They didn't even have outhouses. I watched a kid squatting over the edge of one of those ditches, doing his business happy as you please. His mama would draw water out of that ditch to wash with, and to cook with, and to drink.

When I lived in Enid, I was poor. I knew it. Everybody else did, too. In case I hadn't, plenty of other folks would've been glad to point it out to me. But you know what? Till I saw those shacks, and that kid crapping in the irrigation channel, I didn't have any idea what poor meant.

Don't get me wrong. It's not just greasers living that way these days. If anything, the Mexicans may cope with it easier, on account of they didn't have it any better south of the border. But you can find shanty-towns outside of a lot of cities, and hungry, miserable people living in 'em, too.

No wonder folks want conjure men to take away whatever it is that makes 'em people. Zombies don't care about being poor—or anything else. No wonder vampires recruit more vampires, and no wonder so many are willing to kiss sunshine good-bye. Every vampire's as good— or as bad—as every other one. The thing outside the window in Odessa had that much straight.

No wonder even the people who stay human, which is most of 'em, can't figure out what to do next. Nothing seems to help much. No wonder politics are so fouled up. The questions look bigger than the answers. Since the Big Bubble popped, it's like we've fallen and we can't get up.

But you know what else? Some of those skinny, dirty, raggedy Mexican kids were playing ball. Oh, not with a real baseball, not unless they stole one. Not a real bat, either, or I don't think so— whatever they or their fathers could fix up from more scrap lumber. Gloves? Gloves were for people who could buy them.

They made do without 'em. They played. They had fun. You watch something like that, you remember baseball's a game. Play it for money and it's a different game. They played it 'cause they liked playing it. That was reason enough for them. More than reason enough.

Harv was eyeballing those shacks, too, while he drove past them. What he said about it was, "I wonder if anybody in this whole place will be able to shell out four bits for a ticket."

If the crowd didn't come, he wouldn't pay us after the game. Well, he would, but not much. The team would lose money on the stop. If you went on losing money, you couldn't keep going. Yeah, baseball for the House of Daniel wasn't the same game as it was for those shantytown boys.

Things looked better when we got into the real town of Fort Stockton. They still looked kind of Mexican, because some of the buildings on the town square were made out of mud brick. Adobe, they called it. Put an overhanging roof on it so the rain can't melt it down and it'll last about as long as the other kind of brick.

There was the Hotel Fort Stockton, too. No mud brick there—all columns and fancywork. It would have been something to see twenty years earlier, I guess, when the gilding hadn't peeled away from the plaster yet and the sun hadn't bleached the paint. Now it just looked as though they ought to run up something new to take its place.

The train station looked the same way. So did the ballpark, which sat right behind it. I don't think it was as old as the Hotel Fort Stockton, but it wasn't much newer. Crows sat on the edge of the roof that kept the sun off some of the grandstand. They weren't buzzards waiting for something to die, but they might as well have been.

You always wonder what the team you're gonna play against calls itself. The Fort Stockton nine were the Panthers. A panther is a painter is a cougar is a catamount is a puma is a mountain lion. It would've been fun if they had a cat's head on their shirts like us. But they just spelled out PANTHERS across their chests in blue block letters. Hard to get less exciting than that.

Three or four of their players had dark skins and black, black hair and funny angles in their faces. Mexican Panthers, that's what they were. The white men on the team didn't seem to mind. Texans will let Mexicans get by with things they wouldn't take for a second from colored folks. Sometimes they will. When they feel like it. They didn't make the Mexicans in the crowd sit down the line by themselves in the hot sun—I will say that for them.

We had to work to beat the Panthers. They didn't roll over and play dead, the way the Peccaries had in Pecos. One of their greasers couldn't have been more than five-six, but he was built like a brick: he was almost as wide as he was tall, and it was all muscle. He hit one so far over the left-field wall, it just disappeared. Maybe it broke a window in Pecos when it finally came down.

But we were knocking the horsehide around, too. It wasn't a little tiny ballpark, but it played like one that day. We came out on top, 8-6, but they had men on second and third in the bottom of the ninth with that short, strong Mexican at the plate. Wes threw him a pretty changeup, and everybody on our side let out a sigh of relief when he got out in front and Eddie Lelivelt caught the popup. The guy slammed down the bat and cussed in English and Spanish.

"Thought José would nail you there. He's mighty tough in the pinch," the Panthers' manager said. "That would've been a feather in our caps."

"You guys played a good game," Harv told him, and he wasn't saying it for politeness' sake. "You would've made us sweat in an icebox."

"No icebox here," the Texan said, which was plenty true. "Besides, making you sweat isn't the window they pay off at. We came out here to win."

"Well, so did we. Take any one day and only one team can," Harv said. "But you fellows can play with anybody around here."

"Kind of you to say so," the man from Fort Stockton answered. "Pecos, Midland, Odessa . . . yeah, we can hang with any of the teams from those towns. But have you been down to Alpine yet?"

"Not this year," Harv said. "We're heading there next. I remember right, they were tough the last time we came this way. What's their name?"

"They're the Cats," the Panthers' manager said. "If you beat 'em this year, I'll tip my cap to you. Rancher down there, fella by the name of Kokernot, he's put some money into their teams, paid for good ball-players. They're a handful and a half."

"Fellow by the name of Coconut, you say?" Harv kinda chuckled.

So did the Fort Stockton manager. "Yeah, we call him that some-times. Call him worse things, too. You've been around the block, I know—seen more'n I have, for sure."

"Around the block? Me? Oh, maybe a time or twelve."

"Well, then, you've got to know how it goes. A team in one town starts spending on players. Pretty soon, the other teams for miles around, they get sick of losing all the time. They get sick of hearing about how they lose all the time, too. So then they start throwing their own money around. It's like one country builds battleships, and then their next-door neighbor does, and then everybody's doing it."

"Uh-huh." Harv nodded. "And then they all sail out and blow each other to smithereens."

"That's about the size of it," the Panthers' manager agreed. "They spend and spend till they go broke. Then the leagues they built up fall apart, and then they pick themselves up and start over without the expensive fellas from out of town. Right now, Alpine's the one laying out the cash. Way it looks, though, everybody else will be playing catch-up pretty darn quick."

Enid and Ponca City and some of the other Oklahoma towns had played that boom-and-bust game not long before I joined the Eagles. Got so people said they were better than some real pro ballclubs. Then, just like the Big Bubble, that little bubble busted. They went back to being pretty much town teams.

Town pride's a scary thing. If one team starts whaling the stuffing out of its neighbors, everybody in those places wants to do something about it. People get sick and tired of losing, and sick and tired of get-ting the horselaugh from the town with the hot team. No matter what it takes, they've got to get even.

Good thing they play baseball instead of war. Otherwise, they'd be shooting at each other somewhere all the time. Oh, wait. They do that, too, you say? Well, there you are. And there they are.

(VII)

South and west to Alpine out of Fort Stockton. The land climbs as you go down US 67. I wasn't sorry to get away from Fort Stockton, not even a little bit. I saw more ditchside shanties while we were on the irrigated land around the town. Had any of the peons who lived in them scraped together fifty cents to watch the Panthers play us? Had they yelled their heads off when fireplug José hit that one out of sight? I sure would have, in their shoes . . . if they had shoes.

We got back into ranching country pretty quick. Signs along the side of the road said WATCH OUT FOR CATTLE. Every few miles, though, you'd see a dead cow on the shoulders. Sometimes buzzards flapped up from one when the bus roared by. Sometimes they'd be too busy chowing down, and didn't bother.

I saw a truck and a car that had taken a beating, too. Cows always lose when they get hit on the highway. But they can let your old DeSoto know it's been in a brawl.

Green mountains rose, off in the distance. We got closer and closer to them. Then we got in amongst 'em. Alpine's almost a mile up, but it sits in a valley between a couple of those peaks. Because Alpine is higher than Fort Stockton or Pecos or Odessa, the weather there wasn't quite so hot and sticky.

We passed a road sign pointing the way to Kokernot State Park. I had no idea if it was named for the fella pumping money into the Alpine Cats, but it had to be named after somebody in his family. I mean, how many Kokernots are there on the tree?

Roominghouse where we stayed was nicer than most. Ballpark was . . . well, a ballpark. It wasn't much different from most of the other parks in Texas where we played. The grandstand had a roof on pillars that shaded the section behind the plate and partway down the lines. The rest baked in the sun. Alpine might have been cooler than some of the other towns where I'd played lately, but if you stayed under that sun too long the buzzards would be flapping up from whatever was left of you.

We warmed up. Then we watched the Cats go through their paces. They looked good, all right. They looked good in a way that worried me. Baseball is like a lot of other things. When you do it very well, it looks as though you aren't working hard at all. If it seems to take a lot of effort, you ain't that good, even if you think you are.

The Cats scooped and caught and threw as if it were all as simple as you please. The House of Daniel plays like that. Good pro teams play like that. Teams that aren't so hot make it look harder.

Their pitcher was around the plate except when he felt like knocking us down. We put a man on in the top of the first, but they turned an around-the-horn double play that was slick as motor oil.

Fidgety Frank threw the first pitch in the bottom of the first behind their leadoff man's noggin. You throw behind somebody when you want to hit him, because the natural thing for a batter to do when he sees a ball coming his way is to lean back. Frank didn't quite bean the Cat. He picked himself up and dug in again. Next pitch was right at his head. It ticked off his bat when he bailed out, so he got a strike to go with his scare.

That sent a message loud and clear. If they wanted a beanball war, they could have a beanball war. The next two pitches sent a different message. They were both on the outside corner at the knees. The Cat took the first one for a called strike two. He swung at the next pitch, but he couldn't've hit it with an oar.

He walked back to the dugout shaking his head. If I were him, I would've been glad it was still attached to the rest of me. The Cats batting second and third were, well, call it loose up there. They didn't get buzzed, but they were leaning away from the plate anyhow. Neither one of them hit the ball hard.

We went down in order in the top of the second. Their guy had a nasty curve and a fastball that hopped when it got to the plate. He was tough. He didn't try low-bridging anybody, so I figured we could settle down and play ball.

And we did. They got a run in the bottom of the second on a double and a couple of ground balls. We tied it in the fourth when Wes hit a homer down the left-field line. It barely got over the fence, but nothing in the rules says you've got to hit 'em as far as that Mexican in Fort Stockton did.

It was 3-3 after nine. We got a run in the top of the eleventh. They tied it again in the bottom of the frame. We got another one in the twelfth. So did they.

It went nineteen innings. We were ready to take the field for the twentieth, but the plate umpire held up both hands. "Game called on account of darkness!" he shouted.

Sure enough, the sun was going down behind what they call Twin Mountains. I thought we could've played one more inning, but I wasn't ready to argue about it. In the gloaming, their pitcher might hit me when he didn't mean to.

Both sides kind of milled around. So did the crowd. Nobody knew what to do. You don't have a lot of draws in baseball. Rain or darkness will make 'em once in a while, but not very often. We couldn't be happy, the way we would have if we'd won. But we couldn't be too unhappy, either, because we hadn't lost. What do the Catholics call it? We were in Limbo, that's where we were.

I nodded at one of the Cats. "Good game," I said. And it had been. A game that's played well brings its own kind of enjoyment even if you don't win.

"Yeah." He nodded back. "Y'all can play, even if you're funny-looking." He looked like a cowboy himself, face lined and tanned brick-red, big hands, long chin, a chaw in his cheek.

By then, I was starting to get used to my own itchy cheeks. Part of that itch was from sweat and spirit gum, part from my own whiskers coming in. I hadn't shaved since I joined the House of Daniel. Even after I got the false beard off, I was starting to look like I lived in a shantytown. Pretty soon, I'd have a real beard, but I didn't yet. I looked like somebody who couldn't afford a new blade for his razor, is what I looked like.

"It's a free country," I said, and glanced over toward their pitcher. He had his uniform sleeve pulled all the way up so he could rub liniment on his tired soupbone. "We showed you headhunting wasn't such a good notion, anyways."

He coughed a couple of times. "That wasn't my idea."

"Didn't say it was."

He coughed again, spat out a ribbon of tobacco juice, and chuckled deep in his throat. "After that second fastball from your guy came in high and tight, I bet Zeke wanted to stick his head down in his neck like a turtle."

"He figured we only got one to a customer?" I asked.

That pulled a real laugh out of the cowboy Cat. "Somethin' like that, I expect."

I turned away then. I wanted to get back to the roominghouse and clean up. Play nineteen innings anywhere in Texas, even in Alpine, and you'll need cleaning up afterwards. I wondered if I'd have to wring out my socks again, even with no puddles in the outfield. That's still the longest game I ever played in, and not by a little bit. I wanted supper, too. Play nineteen innings anywhere and you'll be hungry.

There was a diner down the street from the roominghouse. Kind of a pretty place—different-colored bricks in patterns. Beef stew wasn't bad, either. Not as good as Big Stu's stew, but not bad. Along with bread that tasted fresh-baked, it filled up the empty fine.

We were just getting back to the roominghouse when a Consolidated Crystal delivery man—well, a kid in a uniform on a bike—came up and stopped. "Any one of you-all named Harvey, uh, Watrous?"

"That's me," Harv said.

"Got a message for you."

Harv signed for it and tipped him a dime. The kid in the gray-blue jacket with the brass buttons pedaled off. We all went into the roominghouse. The rest of us drew back a little to let Harv read the telegram by himself. You get a crystal message when you're in some strange little town, it's liable not to be good news. In case it wasn't, we gave Harv room to pull himself together some before he passed it on to the rest of us.

But he was smiling when he folded up the sheet of flimsy green paper and stuck it in his inside jacket pocket. "Message from Ponca City," he said. "Rabbit and Double-Double both got on the train this afternoon, bound for Cornucopia."

"Good!" Azariah said. "That's good news!"

Cornucopia's the little town in Wisconsin where the House of Daniel has its main church and its lands and its I-don't-know-what-all. It's on the shore of whichever Great Lake it's on the shore of. They told me which one I can't tell you how many times, but I don't remember. *Cornucopia* means *horn of plenty*. I remember that. The town was built and named before the House of Daniel settled there. They took it for a lucky sign. Reckon I would have, too.

And Azariah was right. It *was* good news. I'd seen those two out-fielders smash together. When Rabbit went down, I figured he'd be lucky to get out of the hospital at all, much less in only a bit more than a week.

I said so. Wes answered, "Rabbit always did have a hard head."

"Not too hard to crack," I said, at the same time as Harv went, "Like you don't."

"You bet I've got a hard head," Wes said proudly. "Would I still be playing a kids' game at my age if I didn't?"

"You could go out and get a regular job instead. That's easy as pie, right?" Harv said. Everybody laughed then. We all knew how easy it was . . . n't.

Wes scratched his chin. His beard had a couple of gray streaks there. He'd been at it for a while, all right. "I'm eating doing this," he said. "I'm sleeping in a bed, and under a roof—even if they're different ones almost every night. What more do I want?"

A wife? A family? A house? A car, even? I wondered. I sure wanted all of those things. I would've thought Wes wanted them more, since he was older. But he didn't seem to care.

All I'd wanted in Ponca City was the chance to go somewhere, any-where, that wasn't back to Enid. I'd got that. I'd already traveled farther than the Enid Eagles ever got. Big Stu wouldn't have any notion of where I was, where I'd been, or where I was going. I'd jumped into a hole and I was growing a beard over it.

I thought so, then. What did I know? Not much about how sharp Big Stu could be, or how far his arm could reach. Well, I'd find out.

From Alpine west to Marfa, US 90 and US 67 are the same road, the way US 81 and US 60 are heading north out of Enid. It's a short haul, hardly more than twenty-five miles, and it goes through moun-tain country all the way. Even the pass through the mountains is a mile high, or close enough so it doesn't matter. The mountains tower over the valleys. But the valleys are pretty high up themselves, or the mountains would seem to loom even higher.

Marfa's another cow town, about the same size as Alpine. It's the last place of any size along the highway till you get to El Paso. That's a couple of hundred miles of not very much. El Paso is a real city, bigger than Enid and Ponca City put together. We were hoping for a big crowd there. They'd had a team in the Arizona–Texas League till a couple of years earlier, when the league went belly-up. The hope was that they'd be hungry to see some good ball. The hope was that we could give it to 'em, too.

But Marfa first. It's a cow town, like I said. There are ranches in the valleys the mountains shelter. Cowboys came out of those ranches to watch a ballgame. Some of 'em were suntanned and wore Stetsons. Some were darker to begin with and wore sombreros. Mexico does a lot of slopping over the Rio Grande in that part of the country.

The team was called the Marfa Indians. As a matter of fact, most of 'em looked more like cowboys, the Stetson-wearing kind. They were lean and tan, some with their hair bleached almost white by the sun. But the pitcher loosening up in front of their dugout was shorter and stockier and browner. He wore a big, bushy mustache, black as shoe polish.

We all watched him to see what he had. He didn't cut loose with anything real hard, but his curves broke quick and sharp. He was hitting the catcher's glove with every pitch, too, so the guy hardly had to move it.

Eddie Lelivelt clucked like a worried chicken. "We better watch out for that guy," he said. "The rest of the Indians wouldn't let him play with them unless he was way better than anybody else they could find."

That made more sense than I wished it did. When you're the wrong color or you talk the wrong way, you've got to work twice as hard to get half as far. It isn't fair, but who told you life was fair?

Finally, the Marfa pitcher broke off a curve so nasty, the catcher couldn't handle it. He kinda laughed and trotted after the baseball. The other Indians laughed. They clapped their hands. "Way to go, Pablo!" one of them called.

"Long as I don't do it with a man on third," Pablo answered, and they laughed some more. He sounded like a Mexican with a drawl. Maybe he hadn't grown up speaking English, but the kind he'd learned came from around there.

The crowd cheered when the Indians took the field. It was another city park, but Harv couldn't beef about the gate today. The grandstand was packed, and they'd roped off space behind the chain-link outfield fences for standing room. The crowd was about fifty-fifty, whites and greasers. The cheers for Pablo when he warmed up on the mound sounded different from the ones for the rest of the team.

Everybody whooped it up when he got us out in order to start the game. He could throw harder than he'd shown warming up. Well, no surprise there. And his control on the hill was as good as it had been on the sidelines.

"Another day where we've gotta bust our tails," Harv said sadly when the House of Daniel took the field. Marfa was another town that never had a pro team. They didn't have a rich man spending money on 'em, the way the Alpine Cats did. They had players who liked to play, that was all. And they had Pablo.

A good pitcher will give you fits no matter who you are. Good pitchers are harder on a traveling team than in a league. In a league, you see them over and over and get to know what they do. Not when you come through once a year at most. Of course, they don't know your guy, either, so that evens out . . . unless their guy is good that day and yours isn't.

It was scoreless in the third, one out, when I came up. Neither side had got anybody on yet, as a matter of fact. Pablo dropped a hook on me that could have caught Jonah's whale. "Strike one!" the umpire said. I stepped out of the box to think it over. When I got back in, he threw me a fastball near the outside corner. "Ball one!" the ump said. The crowd hooted. He could have called it a strike. I gave him credit for going against the home team.

Another curve, another strike. Another fastball. This one ran inside. Pablo didn't like to throw it for strikes. Okey-doke, even count. I stepped out again. He'd feed me another curve. Where, though? Start it over the heart of the plate and bust me inside? Or make it look wide and come back over the outside corner?

He hung it. First mistake he'd made all day. Instead of diving down around my ankles, it came in belt high. And I belted it. When you hit it square on the sweet spot, it doesn't feel like anything coming off the bat. But it scooted between the left and center fielders and out to the fence before they could cut it off.

I took a big turn around second, then hustled back. Their center fielder could throw. An infield out got me to third. And a fly ball to right meant I stayed there.

Next time I saw Pablo, in the fifth, the first one came in under my chin. Not trying to hit me, but to let me know he remembered me. Fine, Pablo. I remembered you, too. He got me to swing too soon at a changeup, and I rolled out to third.

Scoreless through six and a half. Some games are like blowing up a balloon. Pressure inside builds and builds. Then, like the Big Bubble, it pops, and leaves one side or the other unhappy. The Indians got two guys on in their half of the seventh. Up came their cleanup hitter.

The count went to two and one. Wes let fly again. As soon as the pitch left his hand, even before it got to the plate, he yelled, "Shit!" Thigh-high would-be fastball with nothing on it, right down the middle.

Crack! You know that sound when you hear it. All you can do is turn your head and see how far it goes. It went quite a ways. Somebody at the back of the standing-room folks in left field made a sign-him-up catch. Three-nothing, Indians. A couple of dozen people must've scaled hats onto the field. A sombrero flew almost all the way to the mound. Wes stomped it. Was he ticked off? He might've been.

We got one back in the eighth on a walk and a two-out double, but that was all we could do. Pablo stayed strong the whole game, and we lost, 3-1.

"I should've shut 'em out," Wes snapped. Yes, he was steamed. "One lousy pitch! One, goddammit, the whole game!"

Pablo made one, too. He made it to me. I hit it good, but I didn't hit it out. I do think straightening my left arm helped my swing, but it sure didn't help enough to make me a number-four hitter. I haven't got the power, and that's all there is to it. Their guy did. He got his chance, and he took it.

The Indians were proud of themselves. Some people in the crowd here had watched the game in Alpine the day before. The Indians knew the Cats hadn't beaten us. Now *they* had. They got bragging rights next time they faced Alpine.

I tipped my cap to Pablo. I took care, so my wig didn't come up with the hat. "How come you aren't pitching in the Texas League?" I asked him.

"What you talking about? You clobbered me," he said.

"Once," I said. "Anybody'll mess 'em up once in a while. You sure didn't mess up many. I bet you could pitch pro if you wanted to."

He shrugged. "I don't want to. I got a ranch job I ain't gonna lose. Got a wife and two little kids, too. Pro ball's a crapshoot. With the Indians, I pick up some extra money and I don't go far from home."

I've heard plenty of other good semipros say the same things. I mean, guys who could play in the top minors if they had the itch bad enough. Maybe even in the bigs—I dunno. But they're happy where they're at, doing jobs they like, so they don't care if they go up higher. I'd do it in a red-hot second, only I'm not good enough myself. In Enid, I thought I might be. That tryout in Dallas taught me I was wrong.

I wouldn't've been good enough for the House of Daniel if they hadn't needed somebody bad in Ponca City. They got somebody bad, but I was doing my doggonedest not to let 'em figure it out. I didn't hurt 'em in the outfield, and nobody expects much from an eighth hitter, anyhow.

They might cut me loose when my cheap month was up. They might find somebody with more pop in his bat. They might drop me when Rabbit healed enough to play again. I'd be somewhere new if they did. I'd have myself a stake. I could start over. No—I could start. Except for the baseball, I hadn't done anything in Enid I wanted to bring along with me.

We set out early the next morning. The sun wasn't up yet. It's two hundred and some miles from Marfa to El Paso, like I said before. US 90 curls north and west up from Marfa to Van Horn, where it runs into US 80 again and goes on to El Paso. We could gas up in Van Horn and put some water in the radiator. From what Harv said, that was about what it was good for. But it was the only place worth calling a town till we got where we were going.

On the way to Van Horn, we drove through some of the most

terrible country I'd ever seen. What looked like snow was the sun shining off salt in a dry lakebed. By the way the landscape seemed, that lake'd been dry for a million years. I bet the buzzards circling in the sky had to go in to Van Horn to buy gas and water.

Dust and I don't know what all else had scoured the mountainsides into weird, peculiar shapes. The desert lower down had greasewood and prickly pear popping up every so often. The rest of it . . . well, it tried to pretend nobody ever ran a road through there.

When we made it to Van Horn, we got out to stretch our legs and put nickels in the Coca-Cola machine and line up to use the toilet back of the filling station. "Hurry up, you lugs!" Harv yelled when the attendant finished pumping gas. "We're late to El Paso, I'll know why!"

The rest of the players had known him longer than I had. When they didn't hustle up, I decided he was just venting steam, so I didn't, either. The stop wasn't what anybody would've called long.

It was mountains and desert again, except in a few places where they could get water. Everything by the roadside greened up then. And, along with the crops, more of those shacks made of junk and scraps sprouted from the ground. Animals in a zoo live better than the people in those places—and animals don't know others have it better. It shouldn't be allowed.

Getting close to El Paso, we went past what was left of some old Spanish missions. You had to be mighty sure of your God to want to bring Him to a place like that. I guess they were back then. Maybe they were even right. The longer I go on, the less I know I know about anything like that.

Every now and then, I could see across the Rio Grande into Mexico. Another country! You don't think about other countries in Enid, Oklahoma. You're too close to the middle of your own.

Irrigation channels brought water from a dam upstream on the Rio Grande and from deep wells in town out to what would've been desert without 'em. The peons' shacks in the fields blended in with the shanties on the edge of El Paso. And the shanties and shacks blended in with the poorer neighborhoods till you couldn't tell where one left off and the other started.

Part of the trouble is, everybody's hurting since the Big Bubble busted. And part of it is, El Paso was somewhere between half and two-thirds Mexican. The folks who ran the big farms kept the people who worked on 'em as poor as they could so they'd make more money themselves. Texans don't keep Mexicans separate, the way they do with colored folks, but they keep 'em down.

Right across the Rio Grande from El Paso is Juarez, in Mexico. Juarez was hurting, too. Since Repeal, not so many Americans came over the border to drink. Most of the guys on the House of Daniel team had gone down into Mexico to play against greaser teams in the wintertime. From what they said, the poor parts of Juarez made El Paso look like heaven—and the poor backwater farming towns down there made Juarez look like heaven.

I waved out the window at the crummy shacks we were passing. "How could anything be that much worse than this?"

"Snake, till you've seen it, you just can't imagine it," Fidgety Frank said. "Thank your lucky stars that you can't, that's all I got to tell you."

Everybody knew I didn't fancy the nickname Harv hung on me. Maybe I shouldn't have let people know quite so much. They all called me Snake every chance they got. Ballplayers are like that. And if you show they've hit a nerve, they'll only do it more. So I just nodded and made like I was easy with it. If I kept doing that long enough, they might give it up.

We got into El Paso in good time. I'm sure Harv credited his hustling and his fussing for that. You ask me, we would've done it without all that mother-hen business. Even I'd traveled enough playing ball to hit my marks without thinking about it much. The rest of those fellas could go around the world twice with what they could cram in a duffel bag, and not miss a bus or a boat or a train even once.

We each got two keys for our roominghouse doors. Well, each door had two locks on it. That right there told me everything I needed to know about what part of town we were in. I didn't have much worth stealing, but I got the feeling some of our neighbors wouldn't be choosy.

At least we could change at the ballpark. The Texans played in Dudley Field till the Arizona–Texas League folded. Before they joined that league, El Paso had good semipro ball and played in an outlaw league or two—pro, but not hooked in with the bigs and the regular minors.

Now they were back to semipro, but they still had that nice park to play in. It was in the south part of town, not far from the Rio Grande. A lot of buildings there were Mexican style, and Dudley Field fit right in, as much as a ballyard could. The entranceway was built from the mud brick they use in those parts. You got your tickets there—well, unless you were playing you did—and then you went past the people selling hot dogs and beer and what they called tacos and other Mexican stuff on the way to your seat.

The grandstand was shaded partway to first and third, like it is most places. Bleachers out past the grandstand on both sides. More bleachers back of right field. Nothing behind the fence in left but a street.

It was long down the lines—340 each way—but only 390 to dead center. The alleys were short, too. It wasn't quite the bandbox we'd seen in Big Spring, but there are plenty of bigger parks. The left-field wall was pretty high, the one in front of the bleachers not so much.

The Texans' home whites had the team name across the chest in blue letters, with red numbers on the back. Their caps were blue, with a red EP on them. They wore red socks with blue and white rings on the calves. Texas colors are the same as the country's, so naturally a team named for the state wore them.

Most of their team was white—a bigger share than the town had. But there were some Mexicans on it, too, not just one star (or pet, depending on how you looked at it) the way there was in Marfa. Guy playing third couldn't have been anything but a Jew. El Paso was about the last place I would've expected to find one playing ball, but I guess they're all over.

We got a run in the top of the first. Fidgety Frank took the hill for us. If he was tired after going nineteen in Alpine, he didn't show it—and Wes had pitched the day before. You do what you've gotta do, that's all.

Their leadoff man singled. The next fellow hit a perfect double-play ball to short. We turned it, but the lead runner bowled over Eddie at second even after he'd got off his throw. A calling card, you might say. Fidgety Frank called back. He stuck a fastball right in their third

THE HOUSE OF DANIEL

hitter's ribs. The Texan let out a yell, but he went on down to first. Their cleanup guy made an out, so we came up again.

We all watched to see how things would shake out. Sometimes one apiece is enough, and the game goes on. Sometimes you need more. Every once in a while, things get out of hand. When their pitcher threw at our first two guys that inning, I had the bad feeling this'd be one of those afternoons.

And it was. What made it even worse for the Texans was, we jumped all over them. By the end of three and a half, we were up 8-0. They could see they weren't gonna win. The crowd was on them in English and in Spanish. I was in the middle of things when they blew. I slid into second kind of hard to break up a double play—not a patch on what their guy did earlier, honest. I did break it up, too. Their second baseman couldn't get off his throw.

We both wound up sprawled in the dirt by the bag. "You hairy Yankee asshole!" he said, and hauled off and punched me in the ear. Hurt like anything.

I believe I said something about his mother. I know I punched him back. Then we were rolling and wrestling and thrashing. Their short-stop jumped on top of both of us. The dugouts emptied, and we had ourselves a rhubarb.

"Break it up!" the umpires bleated. But there were two of them and maybe thirty of us, so we didn't have to break it up if we didn't feel like it. And we didn't, not for a bit. The crowd screamed while both sides banged away. A few bottles came flying out of the stands. Only a few, though. This wasn't baseball, but they liked watching it just the same.

When it wound down, the umps threw me out of the game. They tossed the Texans' second baseman, too, so that was fair. Harv thumped me on the shoulder. "Attaboy," he said. My ear still hurt. But you've got to stand up for yourself on the road. Nobody'll do it for you if you don't.

We ended up beating them 12-2. Might've been different some other day, but that was how it wound up then. Their manager didn't look happy when he and Harv talked after the game. He was also their left fielder. He'd been in the brawl; he had a mouse under one eye.

About the most he could say was, "What the hell—you got us."

"We don't usually play it that way," Harv said, which was true. He added, "If you want to, though, we can." And that was also true.

Their manager looked up at the stands, which had been packed and still had a lot of people in them. "Ah, screw it. You guys put fannies in the seats. If you come back next year, we'll be glad to take you on again." He knew he liked money, whether he liked us or not.

"Glad enough so you don't have to show you got Louisville Sluggers in your jocks?" Harv didn't cuss much, but he got his point across.

He got it across so well, the Texans' manager turned red under his tan. But he grudged a nod. "Yeah, yeah. You can take care of yourselves." He rubbed his cheek. Somebody'd tagged him a good one.

And that was the story there. We showered under Dudley Field, changed into our street clothes, and rode back to the roominghouse. Harv hung on to the proceeds. By the look of things, they were safer with him than they would have been anywhere he stashed them.

We ate at a Mexican place. Wasn't any other kind near where we were staying. We had those tacos and enchiladas and tamales and beans and spicy rice and all kinds of funny stuff like that. I washed it down with a Mexican beer. That was *good*—it had more taste than the American stuff. Can't get it anywhere but right by the border, though.

Then we trooped down the street to a movie house. It was one of those Fred-and-Ginger singing-and-dancing shows. They could cut a rug, all right. Some of the things they did had to be harder than turning two with an El Paso Texan trying to knock you into next week.

Laying a quarter down for a ticket without worrying about it felt funny. I couldn't remember the last time I was able to do that. I liked it.

I liked it till just before the end, anyway. Then there was a horrible scream right outside the theater—a man. A couple of seconds later, a girl screamed, too. The house lights came up. The movie stopped. A little man—the manager, I guess—came out and said, "Please exit the building in an orderly manner." Then he said what had to be the same thing in Spanish. Peculiar to think Mexican farm workers and factory girls'd want to watch Fred and Ginger, but plenty of 'em did.

We hustled out. A man lay in the middle of the street. You could see right away he was dead. The streetlight showed blood in three spots on his white shirt. *"Aii!"* Kind of a cute Mexican girl beside me crossed herself. *"Chupacabras!"*

I didn't know what that was. Before I could even think about asking, three paddy wagons and an ambulance pulled up, all of 'em with lights flashing and sirens wailing like banshees. The cops bailed out of their cars with pistols in their hands. One of 'em carried what they call a riot gun instead: a sawed-off double-barreled shotgun. You didn't want to get on his bad side, no, sir.

"That way!" A young gal—maybe the one who'd screamed out there—pointed down a dark alley. "It went that way!" She had to choke out the words.

"You can smell the stink of the thing," a cop said. I'd thought that was only the Rio Grande wafting over the city. Maybe I was wrong.

Two cops had flashlights on their belts. They shone them down the alleyway. Something in there let out a hissing screech. All the cops started shooting at once. The riot gun boomed twice, the shots close together. One of the cops yelled. More pistol shots then, and another one from the riot gun after the guy with it reloaded.

A cop came back to the street. He didn't seem to notice he had blood on his face and more on his hand. "We got the damn goat-sucker!" he said.

Several Mexicans crossed themselves then, and a gray-haired white woman. The fellas from the House of Daniel wanted to see what this thing was. One cop started to wave us back. Another one had been at the game that afternoon and knew who we were. He let us go on.

I wasn't sure I felt like thanking him. The thing was as big as a cougar, maybe bigger. It had a hide like a lizard or a gator. Spines ran down its backbone, all the way to the end of the tail. It had big, pointy teeth and big claws. Close up, the reek made my stomach want to turn over.

"There's a dead wetback," a cop said, and he laughed.

Listening to them talk, I worked out that these things killed livestock—and sometimes herders—down in Mexico. They sucked out the blood in nothing flat. *Chupacabras* and *goat-sucker* meant the same thing.

Mexicans sneaked over the border when they got hungry, whether they had papers or not. This *chupacabras* thing had, too. But it didn't work for its supper. It killed. It was big and tough and hard to dispose of. It took I don't know how many revolver rounds and three barrels' worth of double-aught buck before it died. It did die, though.

So did that fellow on the street. The ambulance men had covered him over so we didn't have to see his blind, dull stare at the sky. They'd have to find out who he was and who loved him. Some lives were about to have a tornado tear through them. I remembered when my mother died. The dead man was of an age to have little kids. The goat-sucker didn't care. It was just hungry. But they'd be as ruined as if it had hunted down their daddy on purpose.

(VIII)

We weren't even a little bit sorry to say good-bye to El Paso, let me tell you. That *chupacabras* thing left me thoughtful. Well, what it left me was scared, if you want to know the truth. We've had werewolves as long as we've had full moons. It's in the blood, they say, and for once I expect they're right.

We've had zombies a long time, too. Ever since we brought over colored folks to slave for us, it would be. We make more of 'em now and we use 'em for more and different things, but they've been around.

Even vampires . . . They crossed the ocean some time not too long before I was born. They've spread through the whole country by now. They're a nuisance. Some places, the ones where there are a lot of 'em, they're worse than a nuisance. But you can keep from getting bit if you're careful. Eddie Lelivelt and I sure did. Wasn't the first time for me, or for him, either.

But that goat-sucker thing, that threw me for a loop when I saw it. Threw me for a worse loop when I smelled it. I guess those critters have been running around loose in Mexico for as long as there've been people there, however long that is. Maybe longer—I dunno. To run into one on our side of the Rio Grande, though, that rocked me back a little. More than a little.

So we were glad to head up US 80 out of El Paso, out of Texas, and into New Mexico. Our next stop was La Mesa. Then we'd go on to Las Cruces. Eddie told me Las Cruces means The Crosses in Spanish. I liked that. Oh, you bet I did. I liked it fine. If ever a name would keep those vampires away, that was the one.

La Mesa first, though. It was a tiny little town, but what they called the La Mesa Town Team did its own barnstorming. It didn't go all over the place like the House of Daniel, but it traveled in Arizona and New Mexico and Texas and down across the border into Mexico. The Town Team and the Las Cruces Blue Sox and the Tortugas Red Caps and some other clubs down there had what they called the Old Pro League. They'd play ball and they'd play brawl with one another and with anybody else who came along. Us, for instance.

Some of the guys on the Town Team were Mexican. Some weren't. Some could've gone either way. One thing I saw straight off was that whites and Mexicans were a lot easier with each other in New Mexico than they were in Texas. Farm workers who followed the crops played alongside grease monkeys from the garage and college kids out for extra dough.

We had a good game in La Mesa. It was another place where we played in the city park, but it was also another place where Harv didn't care. The stands were full, and there was standing room around the outfield.

The Town Team played hard, but not dirty. It didn't turn into a beanball war or anything. Maybe some folks from La Mesa went down to watch the game in El Paso the day before and told their ballplayers we knew how to do whatever needed doing. That kind of word does get around.

We won it, 9-7. I got a couple of hits and threw out one of their guys trying to stretch a double into a triple. The next batter doubled, but Wes wiggled out of the inning. He swatted me on the rear when we came into the dugout—actually, it was just a bench behind a chain-link fence, with some more chain-link in back of it to keep the fans from throwing too much at us.

"Way to go," he said. "That would've been a bigger inning if you didn't shoot him down. Dunno whether Rabbit could've made the throw."

"I'm glad I did." I left it there. I knew I couldn't hit with Rabbit— they weren't about to bat me third. I also knew I could get the job done in the outfield. The House of Daniel would've latched on to someone else in a hurry if I couldn't. This was the first time, though, that anybody'd said I might be better out there than their man who'd got hurt.

After the game, the La Mesa manager told Harv, "Now you gotta go up and whip the Blue Sox right outta their shoes."

"Well, we'll sure give it a try," Harv said.

"You gotta *do* it," the La Mesa manager said. "Otherwise, the Blue

Sox, they ain't gonna let us forget it. We always play 'em home-and-home Fourth of July weekend. Those games, man, they're wars." He grinned. He liked it.

To show us they had no hard feelings about the game, the Town Team went out to supper with us. Not a lot of places to eat in La Mesa, but if all you were after was chili and beer you could do fine. And we did. We filled up the place, all of us still in our sweaty uniforms, and told stories about ballgames and road trips.

Some of the House of Daniel players were temperance. From what they said, their church didn't hold with drinking. But not all of them followed all the church rules, any more than folks who listened to any other preacher did. And not all the ballplayers belonged to the church. Everybody on the team had to look as though he did, to draw notice to the House of Daniel. But I wasn't the only one there because he could run and throw, not because he believed in the sermons coming out of Cornucopia.

The boarding house had crickets. Crickets aren't as disgusting as cockroaches or bedbugs, but they're about as annoying. For one thing, the little bastards kept chirping all night long. I've heard they do it 'cause they want to meet lady crickets. I wish they went to dances or promenaded in the town square instead.

And for another thing, crickets hop. They end up in bed with you instead of with a lady cricket. You yank a cricket off your eyebrow in the middle of the night, you won't go back to sleep right away. Believe me, you won't. And if you fling it against the wall hard enough to splatter it, the spot it leaves there will make the landlady screech at you while you're leaving.

She was screeching at a bunch of us when we left the next morning. We were mostly yawning. I wasn't the only one who'd had a crummy night. We went back to the chili joint for breakfast. They scrambled eggs and peppers and spicy sausage all together and wrapped 'em in those flat corn things they call tortillas. And they made coffee strong enough to pry our eyes open before we went on to Las Cruces.

Las Cruces is a real town, almost a city. Six thousand, maybe eight thousand people—bigger than a place like Pampa or Big Spring, though not a patch on somewhere like Ponca City. It sits alongside the Rio Grande. Wherever they can make the water from the river stretch, everything's all green and growing. Cotton, corn, beets, asparagus, sweet potatoes, pecans . . . I don't know what all else. Go six inches past where the Rio Grande reaches and you're out in the desert again.

They said the La Mesa Town Team was older, but the Blue Sox had their own ballyard. They didn't have to play in the city park. They may have had it, but I didn't much like it. Lions Park was, well, a sight to behold. It was only about 290 feet down the right-field line, and the fence was low.

Center was something else. That was why I didn't like it. There was no fence at all out there. If somebody hit one over your head, it would roll as far as it rolled, and all you could do was chase it.

"Snake, you better play deep," Harv told me.

"Thanks, boss. I never would have worked that out on my own," I said. He kinda laughed. I went on, "How come you didn't warn me it was like this?"

"I've seen too doggone many ballparks, that's how come," he answered. "I remember every one of 'em real good, but I don't always recollect which one's where, if you know what I mean."

I hadn't thought about it, but it made sense once I did. He'd taken that team over most of the country and down south of the border. He'd been doing it for years and years. How could you blame him if he misremembered whether a park was in this town or that other one fifty miles farther down the highway?

Then I stopped caring about small stuff like that. When the Blue Sox went out to catch flies, the fellow who patrolled that fenceless center field for 'em was black as moonless midnight. He looked like a center fielder, tall and skinny. He ran like a center fielder, too, and threw like one. But he was *black*.

That jerk of a second baseman in El Paso called me a Yankee just before he hauled off and punched me. All of a sudden, it struck me funny, almost laughing funny. I never felt less like a Yankee than I did that afternoon in Lions Park, not in all my born days.

Don't get me wrong. I knew colored folks played ball. I never had any trouble with that. I knew some colored teams were mighty good, too, likely about as good as some of the clubs in the real bigs. But where I came from, after folks got grown whites played with whites and coloreds with coloreds. That was how things worked. I didn't wonder about it, any more than I wondered that water was wet. I just took it for granted.

Oh, I knew they did it different in other parts of the country. But knowing that was one thing. Seeing it was something else. And playing against a colored fella on a mostly white team, that was something else again.

I sidled over to Eddie. Then I sorta nodded toward that colored outfielder. I didn't want folks to see me pointing at him. I didn't want him to see it, either. "We really gonna go up against him, Eddie?" I asked. I must've sounded like I had trouble believing it. Well, I did.

"Sure we are," Eddie said. It didn't feel like *sure* to me. He went on, "You aren't in Oklahoma any more. You aren't in Texas, either."

"Yeah, I know." I spat on the ground. It was so dry, the glob soaked in in nothing flat. "But it feels wrong to me. Know what I'm saying?"

He looked at me out of the corner of his eye. "You want to tell Harv you won't play against him?"

Part of me wanted to. Playing against coloreds wasn't how I was raised. But I could guess what would happen if I did. I wouldn't play. I wouldn't get paid. And when the bus went up the road to wherever the House of Daniel had their next game, I wouldn't be on it. Because this smoke wouldn't be the only one playing side by side with white men here. He was just the first.

So I spat again. I let out a long, long sigh. And I said, "No, I don't want to tell Harv anything."

He nodded. "Probably a good idea to keep your trap shut. Less you say, less you've got to be sorry for afterwards."

"Uh-huh." Ballplayers go, *He's a good guy. Wouldn't say shit if he had a mouthful.* I understood it better now than I ever had before.

"Okey-doke. It's just a ballgame, Snake. Jack, I mean." Eddie called me by my right name to show he was serious. "In between the white lines, only thing that counts is whether he can play or not. The field doesn't care what color he is. I'm not telling you to marry his sister. I'm not telling him to marry yours, either. But if he whacks one out to you, you catch the son of a bitch, all right? 'Cause he'll sure be trying to catch yours."

"It's just a ballgame. Right." I tried to sound as though I believed that. I didn't have an easy time of it.

The man who called out the lineups to the crowd said the colored guy's name was Willard Something-or-other. Weren't more than a handful of black faces in the stands. But the hand he got sounded about the same as the ones the fans gave the rest of the Blue Sox. They booed us. They wouldn't have booed any louder if we were all black—or green, come to that. They couldn't have. We were Goliaths, come to take on their Davids. They wanted to throw us all to the lions.

Out went the Blue Sox. The crowd cheered some more. Their pitcher warmed up from the mound. He threw hard, but he could put it where he wanted. You go up against somebody like that, you're liable to have a long day. I hoped Fidgety Frank would have his good stuff.

We went down in order to start the game. Willard came in toward the infield to catch a fly ball. I saw where he was playing out there: deep, deep, deep. I'd already made up my mind to do the same thing. Now I decided to take even a couple more steps back.

Nobody hit the ball my way in the bottom of the first, so it didn't seem to matter. I had a long jog in. The Blue Sox's colored center fielder trotted out to take my place. You get an edge any way you can. As we passed each other, I said, "How's it goin', Tarbaby?"

He stopped. He was bigger than I thought. Bigger than me, and he looked tougher, too. I wondered what I'd bigmouthed my way into, and if I'd get out of it in one piece. But he just said, "Up yours, Snowball," and went on to take his position.

All right. We split that one, near enough. The House of Daniel got a single in the second, but that was it. I was in the on-deck circle when we made the last out. The colored guy didn't say anything to me when I came out, and I didn't say anything to him.

He did say something to the Blue Sox's pitcher when they were in the dugout. I didn't know what, but I could guess. Sure enough, when I came up to start the third, the guy got me right in the ribs. "Oof!" I said.

"Take your base!" The plate ump pointed down to first. I breathed tiny little sips of air till the ache eased back some.

Azariah was coaching first. "He meant that," he said. "Don't worry—we'll get even."

"Don't bother," I told him. "Reckon I had that one coming."

Azariah sent me a funny look. So did the guy playing first for the Blue Sox, only his was a different kind of funny look. "Now you know better than to give Willard crap," he said.

"Just riding him some," I answered. "Hey, he's a ballplayer, too, right? You can't wrap him up in excelsior."

"Being colored's hard enough. Getting crap for it's worse," he said.

I didn't say anything to that. Instead, I lit out for second as soon as their pitcher went into his stretch. Stole it easy—he wasn't paying much attention to me. My ribs hurt some more when I slid, but I didn't show it.

Two pitches later, I swiped third. Thought it was one to a customer, did they? Okey-doke, they had their reasons for plunking me. But I'd do my doggonedest to make 'em pay. Man on first, no outs, that's nothing much. Man on third, no outs, and they've got worries.

Sure enough, I scored on a fly ball to center. Willard put everything he had into his peg, but the ball went deep enough so Big Bertha couldn't've shot me down from there.

When I got back to the dugout, they patted me on the back and swatted me on the rear. "Keep an eye on the smoke," I said. "If he gets on, you bet your backside he's gonna run."

Willard singled with one out in the fifth. Did he take a big lead? What do you think? Fidgety Frank threw over there. The colored guy dove back to the bag. "Safe!" the base umpire yelled. Willard took another hefty lead. Frank threw over there again. "Safe!"

This time, Fidgety Frank seemed to forget about the runner. Willard took off . . . but Frank was pitching out. The batter swung anyway, to try to protect the thief. It didn't help. Amos turned loose a perfect throw.

"Out!" the umpire shouted. Willard couldn't even beef. The ball was waiting for him when he got there. He got up shaking his head, brushed himself off, and left the field.

The guy who'd been in the box launched an enormous drive to center. It would have sailed out of a lot of parks, and I don't mean small ones. Here, I was already so deep, I took half a dozen steps back—I didn't even have to turn around and run—and caught the ball. He kicked at the dirt. He'd killed that one, and he had nothing to show for it but a big, fat out.

We got another run in the seventh, when Wes swung late and lobbed one just over the short fence in right. The ball the guy from the Blue Sox teed off on went a lot farther, but Wes' counted for more. Baseball's like that sometimes. Not only how far you hit 'em, but where.

Fidgety Frank kept getting into trouble and wriggling off the hook. He gave up seven or eight hits and walked three or four more, but nobody scored. The Blue Sox loaded the bases in the bottom of the ninth with one out. Their batter hit a line drive back at Frank. He caught it—probably to keep from getting smacked in the kisser—and doubled their runner off first. That was the ballgame. Not pretty, but we'd take it.

First thing out of their manager's mouth was, "Well, at least you beat La Mesa, too. We won't hear about it on the Fourth of July."

"They told us to take care of you so they wouldn't have to," Harv answered.

"Why'd you have to go and listen to them?" Their manager was one of those guys who couldn't stand losing and didn't know how to hide it. A lot of people like that are good at whatever they end up doing. A lot of them end up dead sooner than they might otherwise, though.

"You've got a good ballclub here," Harv said, and he wasn't joshing to make the other fellow feel better. "Will we see you in Denver?"

"We'll be there," the Blue Sox's manager said. "I hope we don't run across you long-haired so-and-sos till one of the late rounds."

"Long-haired so-and-sos. That's us." Harv patted the lion's mane embroidered on his shirt. He sounded proud of being one of those.

They went on gabbing for a while after that, but I lost track of what they were saying. The colored guy, Willard, came up to me and jabbed a finger in my chest. "You want to make something out of what you said before, buddy, we can go back behind the right-field fence and settle it now."

A black man who said something like that to a white in Oklahoma would've been asking for a hemp necktie. Or if he got shot on the spot, no jury in the state would convict the white man. But I wasn't in Oklahoma any more. Things here were different.

You can't back down. That never changes anywhere. I didn't care to fight, but you can't back down. So I said, "We can if you want to. Your call. I've got no quarrel with you outside the white lines. If you've got one with me, we'll go take care of it, that's all."

He'd had some time to simmer down after I razzed him. He wasn't so steamed any more. After a couple of seconds, he said, "Hell with it. Johnny got you pretty good there. That'll do for payback."

"Cost you a run," I said. I wondered if I'd have the stitches from that baseball printed on my bruise when I stripped down. That's also the kind of thing where you don't let on, though.

The corners of Willard's mouth turned down. "Yeah, you ran on us. I wanted to get even."

"Reckoned you would," I answered.

He thumped his forehead with the heel of his hand. "Godalmightydamn!" he went. "No wonder you pitched out! I shoulda figured on that." He walked off scuffing through the dirt and kicking up dust.

"You havin' trouble with that fella?" Azariah asked me.

"Nah. We fixed it," I said. And since nobody chucked a rock through my window or set fire to the bus or anything like that, I guess I was right.

Seventy miles, more or less, from Las Cruces north and east to Alamogordo. It's another one of those lonesome roads. Not a lot of traffic on it, and the countryside is mostly desert. A few ranches, but none close by the road. They stick to the water holes that spawned 'em. Without those, they'd be nothing but sand and rock and rattlesnakes and roadrunners.

A dust devil tall as a three-story building paced the bus for a while, sneering down at us. He wasn't big enough to pick up the bus and throw it away, and the Federal Wizards' Administration wards the highways anyhow. But wards wear out, or they aren't quite right, or sometimes a devil's too mean and strong to be warded. Then you end up in the newspapers, maybe even on the radio. Not here, though. He finally blew off to bother something else.

Right outside of Alamogordo, the road goes through what they call White Sands. It's that gypsum stuff that they mine in Texas. Only here it's not down in a mine with the earth elementals and all. It's spread out over acres—no, over whole square miles—of ground. It shines in the sun, which is how the place got its name. Hardly anything will grow in it, and what does is strange. Not like the plants in ordinary dirt and sand just a few miles away, I mean. Even the lizards and bugs and things are peculiar.

Alamogordo is bigger than La Mesa, smaller than Las Cruces. It's a lumbering and railroad town. There's a marble works, too; they get the stone from a canyon a few miles away. And they've got the New Mexico School for the Blind there. I never would have found out about that if we hadn't driven past it on the way to our roominghouse, which was only a few blocks farther east.

When we did drive by it, Harv started laughing fit to bust a gut. "What's so funny?" Eddie asked him.

"Now I know where they get 'em," Harv said.

"Where who gets what?" Eddie sounded a touch peevish. Can't say as I blame him, either. When somebody answers your question by not answering it, you've got the right to be annoyed. But Harv wouldn't explain. He seemed to think he already had. And he kept cackling like a chicken after we got to the roominghouse.

Even though it's not a big place, Alamogordo's got a couple of semi-pro teams. We were playing the Rebels. I didn't know till I got there that they fought in New Mexico during the States War. The South tried to take it away from the North. They couldn't manage, which I guess is how come Willard played with the white guys and Mexicans on the Blue Sox.

No colored fellas on the Rebels. They did have a Chinaman, though, playing third base. Harv remembered him from the last time he came through. "Listen, Mike, you better get our uniforms clean!" he yelled. The Chinaman—Mike—grinned and waved back at him. Turned out Harv wasn't just trying to get under his skin. Mike and three of his brothers ran the best laundry in town. To me, Harv added, "A team called the Rebels has to have Mike on it—his last name's Lee!"

I chuckled. "Good thing you didn't say it was Beauregard." Harv shied a pebble my way.

Place we played at wasn't even a city park. It was the high school's baseball diamond. It wasn't quite so bumpy and rocky as a cow pasture, but it came close. The grandstand was none too big, either. I was starting to get a feel for such things. Breaking even here would be the best we could hope for, and this was liable to be another place where Harv cut my pay so I didn't make more than the regulars.

Most of what I remember about the game is, we won. The other thing is, Mike the Chinaman smoked one over my head and all the way out to the chain-link fence. I tried to throw him out at third, but I couldn't do it: he tripled standing up. He wasn't a big guy or broad-shouldered or anything. Big or not, he could hit. Maybe working the laundry gave him strong wrists. I dunno.

Oh, and we found out why Harv laughed so much. The base umpire called Azariah out at first when he beat the throw by half a step, easy. "I know where you came from, dad-gum it!" Harv shouted from the dugout.

That ump walked right into it. He asked, "What do you mean, where I came from?"

"You came from the New Mexico School for the Blind, that's what!" Harv bellowed.

He got to watch the rest of the game from the stands, because the umpire screeched "You're gone!" and gave him the thumb. But it was worth it. Everybody heard him, and everybody busted up.

I nailed the kind of crowd it was—I sure did. After the game, Harv gave me four singles and a silver cartwheel and said, "Sorry, Snake, but this is what I've got for you today."

"Hey, it's better than nothing," I answered. People have said that a lot since the Big Bubble busted, and they mean it every single time they do.

"You're all right, Snake," Harv said. He was all right in my book, too—better than all right.

"What is there to do in Alamogordo?" I asked him.

"They've got a movie thee-ay-ter, if you feel like that," Harv said.

I shrugged. I'd seen the film in El Paso. I didn't know if I wanted to do that again so soon. I didn't know if I wanted to shell out another quarter, either. I was making better than decent money playing for the House of Daniel, but I'd been broke so long that it didn't seem real to me. I socked away every penny I could, against the time when the well ran dry.

"Or you can sit around and watch the railroad ties grow," Harv said.

"That sounds exciting," I told him. We kinda rolled our eyes at each other. I suppose, if I'd felt like looking a bit, I could've found a sporting house. Alamogordo was big enough to have one. But that would've cost more than a movie. And I don't care for bought fun unless I've got the urge so bad I purely can't stand it any more. You'd rather lie down with somebody who cares about you, not about the money you just set on the dresser.

For supper, we could pick either Fred Harvey food at the train station or Mexican stuff closer to the roominghouse. The Mexican was cheaper, but I had a craving for fried chicken, so I went to the station with Eddie and Azariah and a couple of other guys. It was good, I will say. Cost me forty cents with a slice of cherry pie.

We got back to the roominghouse at the same time as the fellas who'd eaten those enchiladas and beans and tortillas. A card game started, but most of us went to bed. Another bus ride tomorrow morning. Another game tomorrow afternoon. I was sure ready for sleep. I'd just started finding out what a grind playing every day was.

I woke up with a start in the middle of the night. Eddie snored away in the other bed. Not a vampire at the window this time. I knew it was a dream. But what a dream! The whole northern skyline exploded with light, the brightest light anywhere, brighter than the sun, brighter than anything. The roar that went with it sounded like the end of the world.

For all I could tell, that flash and that roar *were* the end of the world, or at least the end of Alamogordo . . . in the silly dream. Can't imagine why that kind of crazy stuff boiled up in my head then. That and one word, just one, to go with it. Trinity.

Isn't it all the silliest thing you ever heard? If I was dreaming of the Trinity, shouldn't I have done it in Las Cruces? And like I've said, I'm not even Catholic.

We had a long haul the next morning, all the way east to Artesia. We went more than a hundred miles, through the Sacramento Mountains and the national forest in them and then down to the high plains country that looked as though it belonged to West Texas. I do believe it's even barer and drier, though.

They named Artesia for the first well they dug there. They made a bargain with the water elementals deep underground. That well's been going for years and years, and it's never run dry. They cooked up a sweet deal with the earth elementals, too, because Artesia's as big an oil town as Midland or Odessa. Sheep graze on alfalfa near town, and Angora goats gnaw anything that grows on the hillsides farther away.

Brainard Park in Artesia is a peculiar place to play a ballgame. It's a real baseball park, with a partly roofed grandstand and all. But they plopped it down on a funny-shaped piece of ground and did the best they could. It's 360 down the right-field line, but only 350 to dead center. I don't know how far it is out to left. The distance sign's fallen off the tin wall; a rectangle of darker green paint shows where it used to hang. Farther to left than it is to center—I'm sure of that.

The tin wall is higher in center than it is down either line. They tried to keep balls from flying out of there, yeah. But that wall would need to be as tall as the Pierce-Arrow Building in New York City to stop all those Chinese home runs.

When I said so, Harv came back with, "Yeah, I bet that Mike Lee on the Rebels has hit one or two out of here."

Did I wince? Did I groan? I know darn well I did. Sometimes you get topped, that's all. Harv topped me there.

And then the Artesia Drillers topped us. Fidgety Frank was on the mound for the House of Daniel, and he didn't have anything. His fastballs ran straight—no dip, no dive. His curves hung up there in the strike zone, just asking to get creamed. When he tried to change speeds, the Drillers waited on him and hit the slow stuff as though they knew it was coming.

For all I knew, they did. They got plenty of runners on second base to peer in and steal signs. Those tin fences already had lots of dents. The way the ball kept clanking off them, they got some more. And two or three sailed over that joke of a wall behind me. You say *I hit the ball out to dead center*, it's usually quite a poke. Not at Brainard Park.

We were hitting some, too, enough to keep the Drillers interested but not enough to catch up. The guy running the scoreboard had plenty of zeroes and ones painted on flat sheets of tin. He wasn't using those much, though. I wondered if he'd run low on fours and fives. It wasn't a tidy game. It wasn't anything like a tidy game. I will say the fans got their four bits' worth. By the time the dust settled, the Drillers beat us, 17-13.

Looking out at the final, Harv shook his head. "By the score, anybody'd think we were playing football out here."

"Did we make a couple of field goals or miss an extra point?" Eddie asked.

"Way we were kicking the ball today, I'd bet on the field goals," Harv said. Our glovework had been about as bad as the rest of it. A pitcher doesn't give up seventeen runs all by himself, not even in a joke of a ballpark like that. The whole team has to help out, and we did. Booted grounders, throws to the wrong base, bad throws to the right base . . . I made one of those. That day, it wasn't as if I stood out from the crowd.

The Drillers' manager was so tickled, he slapped Harv on the back almost hard enough to knock him down. "I don't expect we'd get you every time, but we got you today," he said.

"Yeah, you did." Harv kept it short. I could see why. The Drillers weren't a bad team, but they didn't come close to the Las Cruces Blue Sox. That was a solid outfit. They played the game the way it ought to be played, even if they did have a colored guy in center.

Even if Fidgety Frank were sharp, this would've been a high-scoring game. In a place like Brainard Park, you won't get pitchers' duels. Well, you will, but you'll never know it by the scoreboard. Since Frank was about as flat as a mouse under a steamroller, we didn't get it done.

"We had a good gate, too," the Drillers' manager went on.

"Yeah, we did." Harv still wasn't talking much. No, he didn't like to lose, not for beans. But he sounded a little less end-of-the-world gloomy. Brainard Park had the ridiculous little playing field, but the stands held 4,500 people. They hadn't been full, but they hadn't been far from it.

Artesia's never yet had a minor-league team. Semipro ball was as good as those folks knew. And when it comes to semipro ball, the House of Daniel tops the heap. And here they'd gone and trounced us.

Over in the dugout, Fidgety Frank had his sleeve rolled all the way up to his shoulder. Wes was slathering liniment on his arm. It smelled something like mint and something like moonshine and something like hot peppers. If you put it on spare ribs, it would probably cook 'em without any fire.

Fidgety Frank looked up into the burning blue sky. "Don't see any buzzards circling," he said. "Danged if I know why. That thing is dead. Somebody oughta cut it off and bury it." He sounded embarrassed. Get clobbered the way he did and you would, too.

"I got me some plumbing work that needs doing," the Drillers' boss said. "With what we brought in, I can just about afford it."

"Good for you, then," Harv said. "We're on the road so much, the only plumbing I worry about is what's hooked up to the radiator on the bus."

"Must be nice, playing so often." The man from Artesia sounded as if he wished he were riding with us.

"Well, it's a living," Harv told him. "Not an easy one all the time. Sometimes we have days like today. Sometimes the bus breaks down or the road washes out. Sometimes we get a rotten crowd, and we lose money for the stop. Can't take too many of those. Sometimes we get the other kind of rotten crowd, the kind that throws stuff at us. And all the greasy spoons we eat at, I guzzle more bicarb and Bromo-Seltzer than you ever seen."

"Hey, I can do that when my wife makes pot roast and onions." The Drillers' manager chuckled, but then he frowned. "Been a while since she's done that. These days, it's oxtail stew and boiled tripe when it isn't noodles and cottage cheese."

"Times are tough all over," Harv said. "I've seen more of it than you—oh, you bet I have. Oil wells, they kinda keep you from knowing just how rugged it can get."

"I wouldn't be surprised," the Artesia man answered. "My brother-in-law, he headed out to California. Now he's scuffling there instead of here. Where do you fellows go next?"

"Hobbs," Harv said. "Do I remember straight? Isn't the ballpark there even smaller'n this one?" He waited for the Drillers' manager to nod, then cut loose with a sigh. "We'll have to see what we can do about that, I guess."

We cleaned up and found one more greasy spoon for dinner. I've had worse, but I've sure had better. When we came out, the full moon blazed low in the eastern sky like a twenty-dollar goldpiece. It was gorgeous, but you don't always want to be out on full-moon nights.

The howl came from right around the corner. A second later, so did the werewolf. It charged right at us. No matter we were a whole team—nothing much can hurt a werewolf. But it can sure hurt you, and it wants to when the fit is on it.

Nothing much can hurt it. Not nothing, it turns out. Fidgety Frank reached into his pocket and flung something at the critter. Caught it right in the nose. And the beast let out another howl, a horrible one, and turned around and ran like the dickens.

Fidgety Frank walked over to where it had been and picked up whatever he'd thrown. "What did you do?" I asked him. I wasn't the only one, either.

He opened his hand. A half-dollar sat on his palm. "Werewolves hate silver," he said, "so I gave him some."

"Sweet Jesus!" Wes said. "Where'd you get an idea like that?"

Frank looked faintly embarrassed, as though he'd got caught looking at dirty pictures or something. "Read a story in a rag called *Amazing* by a hack named Iverson, I think it was. Some guy drove off a werewolf that way in it. I thought it was a good idea, and I guess I was right."

"I guess you were!" Wes said. "I gotta remember that."

"Yeah." Fidgety Frank stuck the coin back in his pocket. He sighed. "Best fastball I threw all day, too, dammit."

(IX)

Go to Hobbs and you're almost back in Texas. I didn't even think about that when the bus chugged out of Artesia early in the morning. It's, oh, seventy miles from one place to the other. A couple of hours on the highway. Only you don't stay on the highway. If you do, you end up in Lovington instead.

Nope. A few miles after you go through the tiny little town of Loco Hills, you swing onto the right fork of the road instead of the left. The left is the one that keeps on being US 82. The right . . . You go on for a ways, and then the paving stops. It's not dirt all the way from there to Hobbs, but it is for something close to twenty miles.

We had to stop once, to jack up the bus and fix a blowout. It was hot. The sun sledgehammered down. It was dryer than dry. I was helping to work the jack. I've done things I enjoyed more.

We were about through when the car under an oncoming cloud of dust turned out to have cops in it. I was glad to see 'em, which'll tell you something about how frazzled I was. "Sorry we didn't get here sooner," one of them said.

Harv wiped his sweaty forehead with his sleeve. "Oh, yeah," he said. "I bet you are."

"We would've lent a hand." The cop turned to his partner. "Wouldn't we, Winslow?"

"Sure. You bet." By the way Winslow said it, he was lying and didn't care if we believed him or not. The other cop gave him a look. Winslow sounded a little friendlier when he went on, "Wouldn't want the buzzards and the coyotes squabbling over your bones." He mostly didn't talk like a Texan, but he said *kye-oats* the way they did.

Buzzards *were* circling up above us now. They weren't after Frank's arm. They were hoping for the whole team. They'd flown over this road often enough to know that, when cars and things had to stop along it, they got a decent chance for the blue-plate special.

The cop who wasn't Winslow said, "I've seen the House of Daniel play before. You're good. You heading for Hobbs?"

"Sure are," Harv said. Where else would we be going on that horrible road?

"I'm from Artesia myself," the cop said. "I hope you knock the stuffing out of the Boosters. Now, as long as you're all okey-dokey, Winslow and me are gonna mosey along."

"You do that," Harv said, along with something less charitable under his breath.

Off drove the cops. They left their own trail of dust behind. It wasn't a dust devil, but it made you think of one.

We piled back into the bus. One thing playing ball every afternoon will do is give you a suntan. I knew a fellow back in Enid who was so blond and so pink, he couldn't do it. He wouldn't tan at all. He'd burn and peel and burn and peel till finally he had to hang up his glove— he couldn't stand it any more. These days, a lot of towns have lights for their ballparks and play under 'em as often as not. Wasn't like that even those few years ago, though.

Our adventure with the tire cost us half an hour. Harv couldn't step on the gas, the way I know he wanted to. On that rutted dirt track, he would've had another flat in jig time, or else pieces would've started falling off the undercarriage. So he just drove along, taking things easy even if he didn't like it. When somebody going the other way came by, he slowed down even more till he got past the dust the truck or the Model T kicked up.

I know those twenty miles on dirt only seemed like forever. If they really were, I'd still be on 'em, I guess, like the Flying Dutchman only in a bus instead of a boat. I also know we all cheered when we got on US 62—which is the same as US 180 on that stretch—to finish the run to Hobbs. Could be asphalt's never got itself a bigger hand.

Hobbs isn't even five miles from the Texas line. We were closer to Midland and Odessa again than we were to Las Cruces and La Mesa. When I wondered out loud about that, Eddie said, "Don't try to keep a map of where all we're going in your head, Snake. It'll drive you screwy—well, screwier. It looks like the belly marks a real snake leaves in the dirt. It does if he's drunk before he starts going, I mean."

"When I want to know what you think, Eddie, I'll kick it out of you," Harv called from the driver's seat, so he'd overheard us. "Long as we're in Denver for the start of the *Post* tournament, everything's fine."

We stayed at a motor lodge in Hobbs. US 62 (or 180, if you'd rather) runs west and a little south toward Carlsbad, so there is a paved road there. It just wasn't the one we'd been on. The old man running the motor lodge was glad to see us. Most of his cabins stood empty, so I expect he would've been glad to see anybody.

"People been askin' about y'all, askin' when the House of Daniel was comin' to town," he told Harv. "They want to know what y'all are up to." Yeah, we were by the Texas line, all right. By the way he talked, he'd grown up on the other side of it.

Harv puffed out his chest. Any farther and he would've busted off some buttons. "Everybody wants to know when the House of Daniel is coming to town," he said grandly. "It's true in plenty of places bigger than this."

I was proud of myself, to be part—even a little part—of such a famous team. I was when I heard the old man go on like that, anyhow. Later, I had me a different notion about why those people were asking about the House of Daniel. But that was later. I didn't have it then, when it might've done me some good. You never have those notions quick enough to help you. It's always later, when you can see why you should've had 'em sooner.

We got into our uniforms and went aboard the bus one more time. You spend more time riding here and there and back and forth than you do playing ball, let me tell you.

Well, it wasn't a long trip from the motor lodge to League Park. Hobbs is growing like a weed—that was what the guys who'd been there before said—but it's not big enough for anything in town to be too far from anything else. Don't ask me why they call their ballyard League Park. They've never been in a pro league. New Mexico semi-pro ball is hot stuff, though. We'd already seen that.

When we got inside, everybody groaned. Yeah, it was another one of *those* ballparks. Honest to Pete, I don't know why they built so many of 'em that way out in West Texas and New Mexico. They're high up out there. The air's already thin and dry. The ball flies like nobody's business. So how come they play in so many stupid little bandboxes? I guess they just like to watch balls sailing over the fence.

"Hope you got your hitting shoes on, boys," Wes said when he saw the numbers painted on the outfield wall. It was 340 down the left-field line in League Park. Okey-doke, that's an honest poke. Not long, but honest. But it was only 345 to center and 290 to the right-field line. They plopped another field on a lot too small to hold it.

"Just play your regular game, guys," Harv told us. "Don't air it out swinging for the fences. You don't got to. Plenty of balls'll leave this yard any which way, and you won't mess up your swing trying to do too much."

Harv was full of good advice. He usually was. Here, though, how could you talk somebody into *not* whaling away with all his might? It was like putting a turkey dinner in front of a starving man and telling him to take little bites and chew his food real good.

I watched the Boosters taking their hacks before the game. They all swung with an uppercut. They were sure going for the downs with every cut. Well, this was their home grounds. They played half their games here. The House of Daniel couldn't afford to try and smash everything. That style just doesn't work when you use it in a bigger place.

"Maybe even we'll pick up some homers here," I said to Eddie. Along with Azariah, we were the smallest, slimmest guys on the team.

"Maybe we will. I don't know if I want to or not, though," he said. "I start trying to hit 'em out, most of 'em won't make it." Anybody'd think he'd been listening to Harv or something.

Harv wasn't watching the Boosters, not right then. He was looking into the stands. He didn't fancy what he saw, either. "We've got a full house, and that's good," he muttered. "But I don't think this place'll hold more than thirteen hundred, fourteen tops, even if they stuff 'em in sideways. Miserable park's too small all the way around." I would've guessed the crowd for bigger—it was plenty loud—but you couldn't beat Harv at counting the house.

A few of the faces in the crowd were swarthy and Mexican. There weren't any faces like that on the town team. No black faces, either. Well, even the one on a mostly white team had surprised me plenty. But I remembered again that Texas started just the other side of Hobbs.

We got three in the top of the first. One ball went over the fence and one banged off it. In the bottom of that frame, Wes served up his own gopher ball. But it was a solo shot, and the Boosters didn't get anything more then. Still, you could tell what kind of game we'd have.

I led off our half of the second. I hit a fly to center. I hit it pretty hard—didn't crush it or anything. Most ballparks, it would've been a medium-deep out. There, it ticked off the top of the fence and went over. The Boosters' pitcher flipped his glove in the air—that's how disgusted he was. I hustled around the bases. Not like I had much practice at a home-run trot.

Nobody talked to me when I got back to the dugout. Nobody even looked at me. Then all the guys pounded on me and made a racket. It was my first long ball on the team, and they made sure I'd remember it.

A couple of innings later, I went hard into that center-field fence, trying to catch a liner that should've been an easy out. It banged into the wood a couple of feet over my glove. Fidgety Frank was playing right. He got the ball and held their runner to a single. Center and right were so short, if any outfielder had the ball you couldn't go for second 'cause you'd get nailed.

"You all right?" he asked me after he threw it in.

"I'll live." I'd have a new bruise to go with the one from where the Las Cruces pitcher hit me, but what can you do? Was I thinking *Wouldn't say shit if he had a mouthful*, too? Oh, you bet I was.

Frank swatted me on the can with his glove. "Way to hustle, Snake." He walked back to his spot in right.

We staggered through that inning without giving up any more runs. I felt like a guy in a saloon brawl when a haymaker just misses his chin. Another one'll be coming his way any second, likely from an angle he doesn't expect.

In the bigs and the top minors, they play 1-0, 2-1, 3-2 games all the time. Well, we'd had a 2-0 game ourselves back in Las Cruces. Most semipro matchups aren't like that, though. It's next to impossible to play a 2-0 game in a place like League Park. And, even if I hate to say it, semipro players aren't as good. They won't get balls that big-leaguers can reach. If they do get to 'em, they're more likely to kick 'em or throw 'em away. More runs go up on the scoreboard when they do.

Baseball is hard to play well. You watch most big-league games, they go so smooth they almost make you forget that. You watch semipros and it shows more. Hate to say that, too, but it's true.

So we didn't have one of those neat, tidy games in Hobbs. It wound up 12-8, with us on top. The Boosters started throwing at us the last couple of innings, when they saw they wouldn't catch up. Wes took care of that. He hit their cleanup man right in the knee. The guy had to hop down to first base on his good leg. He never once rubbed it—I will say that. But they had to take him out and put in a pinch-runner. I hoped Wes didn't break his kneecap . . . but I wouldn't have cried if he did. They started it.

Things got a little testy after the game, too. We didn't brawl the way we had in Texas, but there was none of the *Good game* and *Attaboy* and things like that that you hear a lot of the time. They didn't like us, we didn't like them, and neither side tried very hard to hide it.

We didn't go out to supper with 'em, either, the way we do some of the time. They went their way and we went ours. We'd leave town the next morning, and they wouldn't miss us one bit. I wondered whether Harv would come back to Hobbs next year. For them, this was a big crowd. For us? Nope. Harv didn't dock me, so we must've made expenses, but we couldn't have done better than break even.

Somebody knocked on my door in the middle of the night. Took a while to wake me. You're tuckered out after a long bus ride and a ballgame, especially when you know you've got to get up early for another bus ride and another ballgame the next day. When you helped fix a flat on the bus and baked your brains out in the sun for that, you're double tuckered.

"Who the devil is that?" Eddie sounded as far underwater as I felt.

"Beats me." I know I sounded blurry, 'cause I was yawning while I was trying to talk.

"Well, tell him to go take a flying leap at himself," Eddie said.

I might have told him to do it, but I didn't. I staggered out of bed instead. He was a veteran. I was a replacement, and a new replacement at that. A baseball team has the same kind of pecking order chickens do. Eddie could peck. I was way down at the bottom. I got pecked.

The knocking went on while I lurched to the door. I wondered how long it had taken to wake us up. Then I yawned again. I opened the door.

Two guys I'd never set eyes on before stood outside the cabin. One of them said, "You What's-his-name—Spivey?"

"Uh-huh. Who the—?"

That was as far as I got. The fellow who'd asked my name hauled off and gave me a right to the jaw. His buddy dished out a left to my belly. I folded up like a concertina. I was on the floor when one of them kicked me. The other one said, "Big Stu says, that'll teach you to get your name in the papers. And he says, you gotta take it if you won't dish it out." Then he kicked me, too.

They walked away. They weren't laughing or anything. They didn't beat on me for the fun of it. They did it because they needed the money. It was a job, the way me going out and playing center for the House of Daniel was a job.

If I'd given Mich Carstairs a right to the jaw and a left to the belly and kicked her a couple times, I wouldn't've been playing center for the House of Daniel, of course. I would've still been back in Enid, doing more jobs like that for Big Stu. And if Mich had been Mitch, that's just where I would have been and what I would have been doing.

Instead, I was on the floor in a motor lodge cabin in Hobbs, New Mexico. The inside of my mouth was bloody. I ran my tongue around in there, but I didn't seem to have busted any teeth. If Big Stu ever found out, he'd be disappointed. The muscle men hadn't kicked me in the face, either. Once in the ribs, right where the bruise from that plunking was, and once not quite close enough to my family jewels to crack 'em.

"What the demon was *that*?" Eddie said. When I didn't answer right away—on account of I couldn't answer right away—he got out of bed and came over to me. He almost tripped on me, since I was trying to get up then. I wasn't having much luck yet, but I was trying. His voice got shriller: "What did they do to you?"

"Pounded on me." Talking hurt. That was when I realized my tongue was cut. "I told you I was getting away from some trouble. I guess it went and caught up with me."

"I guess it did." Eddie found the light switch. I managed to make it to my feet. He winced. "Wash your face," he said. "You've got blood dribbling down your chin."

I went to the pitcher and basin on the dresser and did. I spat into the bowl once or twice, too, and rinsed out my mouth. Then I tossed the basin water outside. It was pretty gory. But I didn't look too bad. My beard was coming in pretty thick by then. It hid most of the bruising and swelling.

"I hope not," I answered. "Sounded like it's done. Well, almost." There was something I still needed to take care of. Big Stu's bully boys hadn't thumped me to make me think of it, but getting thumped made me remember.

"Should we call the cops? Should we wake up the rest of the team? If we catch those skunks, we can give them more of what they gave you." Eddie mimed connecting on somebody's ribs with a baseball bat.

But I shook my head. "Forget about it. They're gone. And like I told you, I'm pretty sure it's over. I just want to go back to bed."

"You won't go to sleep," Eddie said.

I figured he was right. I hurt too much, and in too many places, to make shuteye a good bet. I could just lie there in the dark, though, and try not to think about anything. So I said, "I'll give it a shot." Took a while to talk Eddie around, but I did it.

Out went the light. I lay on my back. They hadn't done anything to me there. My mouth hurt. My jaw hurt. So did my ribs, and my belly, and my thigh. I hoped like anything I didn't have a Charley horse. I had to be able to run the next afternoon, doggone it. We still didn't have anybody else who could do even a halfway decent job in center field.

So much for not thinking about anything. All that stuff went round and round in my head. After a while, my hurts weren't quite so sharp. After a while more, I did fall asleep again. Doesn't mean the goons didn't beat on me. Just means I was mighty tired.

I was still tired when Eddie's alarm clock and mine (yeah, I had one by then) went off together. I was sore, too, and stiff. But I thought I could work out the kinks in my leg. I'd drooled more blood and spit down my beard. The pillowcase wouldn't make the geezer who ran the motor lodge very happy. Well, that was his hard luck. I poured more water into the basin and washed my face again. This time, the water wasn't quite so bad, but I chucked it anyhow.

If I looked funny, nobody on the team said anything. When we came back from breakfast, I gave the fellow at the motor lodge a nickel for an envelope, a piece of paper, and a three-cent stamp. I went back to the cabin and wrote Big Stu's name on the envelope, and the address for his diner. Then I folded the paper around a ten-dollar bill so nobody could see what it was and I sealed everything up.

A mailbox sat on the street outside the motor lodge. Tourists and salesmen and people passing through could drop reports and letters and whatnot in there. I'd told Rod Graver I'd pay back the ten bucks I got from Big Stu to do what I hadn't wound up doing. I'd forgotten about that till now, but I got reminded. Oh, yes, just a little.

I wanted to write something on the paper to tell Big Stu where to head in or where to stick the money. I wanted to, but I didn't. That might've kept him sore at me. If he figured I'd got my licking and he'd got his cash, maybe he'd decide it was all over and forget about me.

Or maybe he wouldn't. Big Stu didn't get to be what he was by forgetting things. I hoped Charlie Carstairs was all right. I hoped Mich Carstairs was in California. I hadn't heard any Oklahoma news since the House of Daniel made the long jump from Ponca City to Texas. I'd almost forgotten about Oklahoma, tell you the truth. Well, I had bruises and bumps and a cut on my tongue to show how Oklahoma hadn't forgotten about me.

"You good to go, Snake?" Eddie asked me when we got on the bus. We weren't heading back into Texas. I thanked my lucky stars for that. No, we were going the other way, west and a little south on US 62/180 to Carlsbad. If we'd headed straight down to Carlsbad from Artesia, it would only have been about twenty-five miles. But then we would've had to go to Hobbs from there and come back west over that unpaved stretch. We would have done the whole triangle any which way, in other words.

And we would have done another stretch without paving. They may call US 62/180 a highway, but close to thirty miles of it are nothing but gravel and dirt. Harv said "Shucks!" and "Doggone!" more than I'd ever heard from him before. Some of the guys said stronger things than that. I know I did. We got through it without a flat. I don't know how, but we did.

Some of the land around Carlsbad is irrigated. The rest sits on top of potash mines. They just found the potash a few years earlier. It wasn't quite a gold rush or an oil field full of gushers, but it must've been the next best thing. Carlsbad's got it almost as good as though the Big Bubble'd kept getting bigger.

The semipro team was called—guess what?—the Potashers. They were a company team, like the Greasemen in Ponca City. Some of 'em really worked in the mines. Some played ball well enough so they didn't have to do much else.

They've got a nice ballpark in town. Nothing was built up around Montgomery Field, so they could make it a decent size. It's 345 in left, a good 415 to center, and 320 to right. Because of the thin air and heat, it sounds bigger than it plays, if you know what I mean. We saw that as soon as we started taking batting practice there.

When I wasn't swinging, I was trotting from home down the foul line and back, loosening up my sore leg. Once the blood got flowing, it wasn't too bad. I didn't think I'd be as quick as usual, but I'd still be better in center than anybody else Harv could put there.

He noticed me trotting that way, of course. It wasn't part of my usual routine before a game. "You good to go, Snake?" he asked.

"Yeah, I think so," I said.

"Honest injun? Talk straight with me, son. I hear you ran into some trouble last night—or it ran into you."

He'd heard from Eddie. I hadn't seen Eddie talking with him, but I don't have eyes in the back of my head. Eddie cared more about the team than he did about me. One more reminder I was still a spare part bolted on to keep the machine running. Nothing I could do about that except keep it running as well as I could.

"I'll be all right, Harv," I told him. "Even sore, I move better'n anybody else you've got healthy, and you know it."

He didn't try to convince me I was loopy. He couldn't. I went out to center to catch some flies and see how it felt when I had to turn fast. It was sore. So were my ribs. So was my belly. I could play, though. As long as I could, I would. Big Stu's plug-uglies would've had to stomp me a lot longer than they did to knock me out of the lineup.

By the time the game started, there were a couple of thousand people in the stands. Not quite a full house, but close. Harv said Montgomery Field held 2,250. He knew things like that, so I didn't try to argue with him.

The Potashers were good. I'd seen that watching their hitting and fielding drills. They knew what to do out there, and they could do it. The mining outfit that backed them had the money to go out and find good ballplayers. Maybe their reserves weren't so hot; I don't know about that. But the men they put on the field could've been pros. Some likely had been. One or two of the kids might be in a year or so.

Their pitcher reminded me of Fidgety Frank, only he was a righty. He was tall and lean, all arms and legs, with everything going every which way. The one trouble with a motion like that is, it's not easy to fix when something goes haywire. He walked our first two guys, and Harv smacked a double into the left-field corner on a get-it-over fastball. Both runners scored.

Their first batter hit a fly into left-center. I caught it. If I couldn't have caught it, I didn't belong out there. You always feel better after you do catch one. You're in the game, not waiting for something to happen.

We got another run in the third. They got two back in the fifth when their left fielder knocked one over the fence just to the right of the 415 sign. I got back on it fine. I would've made the play if it stayed in the park. But it was long gone. I'd seen that that guy was slow and had a glass arm, even for a left fielder. He could swing the bat, though.

They tied it in the eighth. We went to extra innings. I got up there with men on first and third and two outs. I hadn't done much—I'd walked once, but that was it. I guessed their hurler wouldn't worry about me. He'd come in with fastballs and try to get out of it. I took one for a strike. He wasted a curve, and I laid off. Then he threw me another fastball. I dropped down a bunt.

I'm not a power hitter. I never will be, not even in Hobbs. I haven't got the muscles or the fast bat. So I have to do the little things better than I would if I could swing for the fences all the time like Mort Milligan or the Potashers' left fielder in this game. And their third baseman was playing back of the bag to try to cut off extra-base hits.

I got it down. If it stayed fair, it'd be a hit, 'cause I knew I laid it out there too far for their catcher to reach, and their pitcher fell off toward first every time he threw. I ran as hard as I could. It hurt, but I didn't care.

I didn't look back till after I crossed the bag and turned around. The ball had gone about fifty feet up the third-base line and stopped. I couldn't have rolled it out there any better. We had ourselves a 4-3 lead.

The Potashers' first baseman looked disgusted. "What a crappy thing to go and do," he said.

I shrugged. "We needed the run. You would've liked it fine if one of your fellas went and did it."

"Take your hacks, man," he grumbled. "You don't fight fair." He could say things like that. He was even bigger and wider through the shoulders than their left fielder. He was bound to be even slower, too, or they would have put him in left. When he took his hacks, the ball would jump.

"I wish I could hit hard," I told him. "I've got to get it done some other way. It's all part of the game."

"Phooey," he said. Any first baseman would have. First basemen are hitters first. When it comes to defense, first is the easiest position to play. You don't have to run fast or throw much. If you can hit but can't field, that's where they put you.

He said *Phooey* again, or maybe something ruder, when he flied out to me with a man on second to end the game. I had to run some to get it, but not too bad. One of the Potashers yelled out from their dugout: "You shaggy bums went and stole that one!"

Harv smiled. We'd won, so he could. "They don't count how you get the runs. They count how many you get. Back in the deadball days, they would've said hitting a homer was stealing one."

Eddie swatted me on the behind when I came in with the ball still in my glove. "They don't know how tough that was," he said, not too loud.

"Nothing hurts when you come out on top," I answered. That wasn't quit true, but close enough. I knew I might be more sore and swollen the next day and the day after that, but I figured I could play through it if I did a good job getting loose beforehand, the way I had here.

Harv patted me on the behind, too. "You get the most out of what the good Lord gave you, don't you, Snake?"

"I'd better, on account of He didn't give me big muscles or anything," I answered. Did I wear a silly grin right then? Oh, I just might have.

"Snake, huh?" The Potashers' manager had been the man on base when their first sacker made the last out. "You went and bit us, all right."

"He's a troublemaker, the Snake is." Harv sounded proud of me, the way a father will when his kid does something good. It soaked into me the way irrigation water soaks into the thirsty ground around Carlsbad. I sure never heard much in that vein from my real old man.

Next day, we went up to Roswell on US 285. It's paved all the way between Carlsbad and Roswell. We liked that fine. Beat-up dirt roads that beat up the bus's chassis and the passengers' chassis, too—I could do without those.

Artesia sits halfway between Carlsbad and Roswell. So we played there and went through from west to east on the way to Hobbs, then went through again from south to north on the way to Roswell. We'd finally gone and tied a knot in our own tail, you might say.

The Roswell Giants played in what they call League Park. They'd been in the Panhandle–Pecos Valley League for a season about ten years earlier. The league fell apart, and they went back to semipro. The name of the ballpark and maybe a player or two, those were about all that was left from those days.

Roswell's a bigger town than Hobbs or Carlsbad or Artesia. It's been there a while, and looks that way. Not just cottonwood trees on the streets, but willows, too.

Grandstand wasn't big enough to suit Harv. "If we get fifteen hundred in here, it'll be a miracle," he said. "This place is big enough— we oughta do better'n that."

"This outfield is big enough," Fidgety Frank said. "I'm supposed to play right today, ain't I? Can I have the day off, or a motorcycle to go get the ball?"

"You grouse about the little ones the same way," Harv said, which was true enough. But for the grandstand, a little one League Park wasn't. It was 330 to left, but then it went out and out and out. Dead center was 500 feet, and it was 425 to right. I wouldn't have minded a motorcycle myself.

Fidgety Frank wouldn't let go of it. "These blasted New Mexico parks are like Goldilocks and the Three Bears. They're either too big or too small. None of 'em's just right."

"They've got to play in it, too," Eddie put in.

Fidgety Frank gave him a look. "Oh, keep quiet, you, you—infielder, you." Frank wasn't that young any more, and he wasn't that quick. Playing right out on that wide stretch of lawn wouldn't be much fun for him. And any ball that got over him or between him and me was a sure triple, maybe a homer.

In the top of the first, I saw how the Roswell center fielder shaded over into right-center to try to cut off those gappers. The left fielder gave up the line and swung a few steps into left-center, which was also long. When we went out there in the bottom of the first, we played it the same way.

Hits dropped in anyhow, for both sides. With that much acreage, what else would you expect? We did what we needed to do. The Giants were a respectable team, about as good, say, as the Enid Eagles or the Ponca City Greasemen. The Potashers were better. That mining company had more cash to spend on the team than anybody in Roswell did. The House of Daniel ought to beat a ballclub like the Roswell Giants most of the time. We won this one, 8-5.

It wasn't neat. Fidgety Frank did have to chase a couple of long drives all the way to that far-off fence in right. One went for a triple. The other was an inside-the-park job.

After he got that ball back to the infield—too late to do any good—he turned to me and said, "I'm getting too old for this. Wes serves up another one of those, he can come out here and I'll take the mound. Let's see how he likes that."

"Let's see how the Roswell guys like it after you stick one in somebody's ear," I said with a kind of a wink in my voice.

"Who, me?" By the way Frank talked, butter wouldn't've melted in his mouth. But I'll tell you, if he had started pitching I wouldn't have wanted to dig in at the plate if I played for Roswell. You'd be digging your own grave, is what you'd be doing.

He stayed in the outfield, though. Nobody threw at anybody on purpose, not that I could see. It was only a ballgame. That suited me fine, day after I'd been on the wrong end of a punching out.

We went to supper with the Roswell team, in fact. They raised a lot of cattle around there, and they had good beef. The Roswell Giants knew a place that served big steaks and fried potatoes and draft beer and didn't try to gouge you. Can't hardly ask for better'n that, not as far as I'm concerned. Not everybody on the House of Daniel drank, but the ones who didn't didn't ride the ones who did, not unless somebody put down so much it hurt the way he played.

"C'mon, boys," Harv said at last. "Long drive tomorrow."

We got up. So did the Roswell fellas. Most of them had to go back to their regular jobs, poor bastards. We'd been in the steakhouse a while. It had got dark outside. The night was clearer than clear. You could see a million stars in the sky.

You could see other things, too. Azariah pointed up at them. "What the devil are those?" he asked.

"Oh, good!" I said. "I'm not the only one who sees 'em." I'd wondered if that sock on the jaw did scramble my brains. There were, I dunno, eight or ten little shining circles flying through the air in a V as though they were Canada geese. They were dead quiet; they didn't buzz like aeroplanes. They flew too fast and turned too sharp to be carpets, and flying carpets aren't round. So I was like Azariah—I had no idea what they could be.

The Roswell guys just laughed. "We call 'em flying hubcaps," one of them said. It was a good name—they did look like polished hubcaps with the sun shining off 'em. He went on, "They come around every so often. They fly by—that's all they ever do."

"But what are they?" I asked.

"Beats me," he said. "Nobody knows. Nobody outside of Roswell gives a hoot. World's got more important things to steam about than stupid lights in the sky." I couldn't very well quarrel with that. Along with my teammates, I went back to our boarding house.

(X)

We got up before sunrise. We had to. It's two hundred miles from Roswell to Albuquerque. Harv would've liked it better if we'd left Roswell after supper and driven through the night, the way we did from Ponca City to Pampa. Everybody else bellyached so much, though, that he threw up his hands and let us sleep where we were at.

More flying hubcaps in the sky when we got going. They didn't pay any attention to us. They just zoomed around minding their own business, whatever that was. I wondered if the Army Air Corps knew about them. If it did, it sure didn't do much to shoot 'em down.

Up US 285 we went. It was cold when we started out. It wouldn't stay that way, but it was. We stopped in a little no-account place called East Vaughn for breakfast. Instead of potatoes or grits, they gave us pinto beans and chilies with our ham and eggs. Wasn't bad, but it wasn't what I was looking for, either.

Then we piled back into the bus and got going again. US 285 swung from north to northwest after our stop. In a while, it ran into US 66. That would take us west to Albuquerque. Route 66 had taken a whole pile of folks west, especially since the Big Bubble popped.

I expect my pa took Route 66 west to California or wherever he wound up. Not like I'd heard from him since he took off, so I didn't waste much sleep time fretting over that. Still and all, he was my flesh and blood, as much of it as I had anywhere. So I did wonder every now and again.

Sleep time . . . I got half an hour or so on the bus. First time I'd ever managed to do that. Only goes to show you can get used to anything. Some of the guys just turned out like light bulbs as soon as they climbed aboard. I never got so I could do that, but a little shuteye comes in handy however you grab it.

Albuquerque's just under a mile high. "It'll help us get used to

Denver," Harv said about three different times. It's the biggest city in
New Mexico, and New Mexico's a big state, at least on a map. Well,
turns out *biggest city in New Mexico* makes it a little bigger than Enid.
Next to Oklahoma City or Tulsa, Albuquerque's hardly there at all.

But like the fella said about the skinny gal, not much meat on her
bones but what there is is choice. You could see the mountains from
anywhere you looked. We'd crossed over 'em; we were on the down-
hill of the other side. They used a lot of adobe to build with, and some
of the places that weren't made from the stuff looked as though they
were. Everything blended together, I guess you'd say.

The cabins in our motor lodge were made of adobe. Till I opened
the door, I had nary a notion about how thick an adobe wall was. All
that mud does a decent job of keeping out the daytime heat. I will give
it that.

We put on our uniforms and went over to Tingley Field. It was in
Rio Grande Park, not far from the river. And doggone me if it wasn't
made from adobe, too, adobe and timber. I'd seen that ballpark in El
Paso with the adobe entranceway and walls, but this one was all adobe,
just about. What they called box seats were folding chairs close to
the field. The grandstand was just for the seats back of home—most
were bleachers.

The field looked as though it was half adobe, too. The grass grew
kind of by fits and starts. It was a big park—not a monster like League
Park in Roswell, but big. It went 348 down the lines and 480 to
straightaway center. Just to make things exciting, a telephone pole
sprouted inside the center-field fence.

"Is that in play?" I asked an umpire, pointing out to it.

"You bet it is," he answered. "Ball goes behind it or bounces off it,
you've got to chase after the thing. I've seen it happen a few times."

"Okey-doke," I said. "Pole was there first? Is that it?"

"Uh-huh." He nodded. "They only built the ballpark year before
last." You could've fooled me. Adobe looks old even when it's new. The
ump frowned. "They put it up for the Dons, in the Arizona–Texas
League. But the league folded halfway through the season. What are
you gonna do?"

"Hang on tight. What else can you do?" I answered, and the umpire nodded again.

The team we were playing had DONS across their chests in big square brown letters—almost adobe-colored, but darker. The uniforms didn't look new. They'd likely belonged to the pro team, and the guys kept 'em after it went bust. When they got new players, they'd alter old uniforms to fit. One way to hang on tight is not to waste anything.

They knew what they were doing out there. You could tell most of 'em would have been good enough to play pro ball. Their third baseman might have been good enough, but I knew darn well he hadn't played in the Arizona–Texas League. He was lighter than that Willard fella in Las Cruces, but darker than the team name and number on his shirt.

I didn't feel as funny about playing against him as I had in Las Cruces. First times are always strange. After the first, you think, *Well, all right. I've done that before. I guess I can handle it again.* I wasn't in Oklahoma or Texas any more. There weren't any laws against it here.

Weren't any in Denver, either. I had to remember that. There wouldn't just be colored ballplayers in the tournament. There'd be whole colored teams, and fine ones. They'd want to show the white man's world they could play the game a little bit, too.

Harv beamed like a brown-bearded Santa Claus at the crowd filling up the bleachers and the grandstand. "Swap me pink and call me Bluey if we don't have better'n three thousand here today," he said. I don't know what he meant, exactly, but that's what came out of his mouth. Kinda like *dog my cats*, I suppose.

He hit a hard smash at that colored third baseman in the first. The guy vacuumed it up and threw him out. It wasn't a great play, but it was a good one. A pro third baseman wouldn't have made it every time. Well, I don't know that this fella would've made it every time. He made it that time, though.

I played deep. This was another park where you didn't want one going over your head. Too much room for the darn thing to roll in, and never mind the stupid pole out by the fence. If a single or two dropped in front of me, swell. You'd rather have a runner on first than on third any day.

Fidgety Frank gave up a run in the bottom of the first. Eddie, of all people, hit one out to tie it in the second. When I came up in the third, I thought I'd drop another bunt. I'd had good luck with 'em, and maybe I'd catch the colored guy napping.

Only I didn't. He charged in, scooped it up barehanded, and threw me out by half a step, all in one motion. He had a good arm, too. I kinda looked at him when I walked to our crowded little dugout. He grinned back at me. He knew he'd stolen a hit from us.

The Dons kept making the plays. You couldn't get anything past that guy playing third. He went into foul ground back of the bag to snag a hopper from Wes, then somehow planted himself and nailed him at first. Wes isn't what anybody'd call fast, but even so. . . . He shook his head when he came back. "Gotta keep 'em away from that son of a gun," he said, or something like that.

The colored fella could hit, too. I cut off a drive into the gap before it could go through, but he got a double out of it anyway—he slid, but the play wasn't close. One out later, he scored on a single.

They beat us, 5-3. They were better than we were that day. I don't know what else to tell you. I think we would've been better than they were more often than not, but they don't pay off at that window.

After it was over, I went up to their third baseman and said, "You got a mask and a gun? You robbed us blind out there."

He grinned again. His teeth looked real white, the way colored folks' do against their dark skins—except for one in the top center. That one was gold. "Hey, I got lucky," he said. He'd come from some-where in the South. You could hear it when he talked. It made me homesick.

"Lucky, nothing," I told him. "You can play down there."

He touched the brim of his cap. "I thanks you kindly." One of his eyebrows went up. It changed the shape of the grin. He could hear where I came from, too. "Mighty nice of you to say so. You ain't too bad yourself. I thought I got that one by you in the sixth, and you almost threw me out."

"Nah. You had the bag." I stuck out my hand. Hey, in for a penny, in for a pound. After a beat, he shook with me. If you didn't think about it, it was just like shaking hands with anybody else.

They had showers under the grandstand. Those were tiled—adobe showers wouldn't be smart. We got into our street clothes. Harv didn't know how to feel. He was gloomy 'cause we'd lost but happy about the gate receipts. A split of the doubleheader, you could call it.

When we came out to walk to the bus, a couple of Indians were sitting with their backs to the adobe outer wall, enjoying the shade. One of them had a pint in his pocket. He took a drink, then passed it to his friend. They didn't look likely to go anywhere except to sleep for quite a while. I'd seen the same thing in Enid. It's sad, but there you are. Too many of 'em don't hold their liquor well. It ends up holding them instead.

A kid—thirteen, fourteen, tops—popped out of nowhere and said, "Spare a dime?"

I never had to beg in the streets. I came close a few times, which helped get me started doing this and that for Big Stu. I don't know if I could've done it. I've got a funny kind of pride, but it's pride just the same. If I got hungry enough, though . . . Well, you never know for sure.

This kid was so scrawny, he had to be plenty hungry. I reached into my pocket and gave him a quarter. I hoped somebody would've given me a little something if I had to beg. "Here," I said. "Get yourself some food."

"Thanks, Mister!" By the surprised way he said it, he'd had a lot of people tell him to dry up and blow away. Times were hard for him, but times were hard for darn near everybody. He scooted off with the silver clenched in his fist.

"That was a Christian thing to do, Snake," Harv said.

Well, I went and did it anyway was the first thing that came into my head. I didn't let it out, which was bound to be just as well. Harv tried to live what he believed. He said that was how he preached, by example. "Kid looked like he could use a hamburger or something" was what I did tell him.

"That he did," Harv agreed. "But not everybody would have given him the chance to get one."

I kinda shrugged. "I know what empty feels like. I ought to. Playing ball for the House of Daniel, this here is the most money I ever made in my life."

"You've had it rugged, all right." That was Fidgety Frank. He was half joking, half not. He was like the rest of the team—he didn't care to lose. Made him sore as a bear that swatted a hornets' nest instead of a beehive.

You will lose some of the time. You know that going in. The House of Daniel plays the best semipros. Some of 'em could be pros. Some of 'em were pros only a couple of years ago, like the Dons. Sometimes the House of Daniel plays real pro teams. Hard to get matches like that, though, because the pros know they can lose to us, same as we can lose to good semipros. Losing to us embarrasses pros the same way losing even to good semipros embarrasses us.

The door to the bus creaked closed. It was supposed to hiss closed, but the bus sounded as tired as we were. We'd come a long way from Roswell, and we'd lost. Somehow, you're twice as tired when you lose as when you win.

But Harv didn't take us straight back to the motor lodge. He stopped at a Consolidated Crystal office first. "Be right back, boys," he said. "Gotta send me a message." And in he went, as sneaky as though he were playing a spy in a thriller.

He came out with a big old grin on his face, the kind of grin you get when you know something and other people don't. "What's going on, Harv?" Fidgety Frank asked him.

"Not a thing, Frank, not a thing," Harv answered, which was such obvious bushwa that we all hooted at him. Even Azariah hooted, and he's as churchy as Harv.

But Harv didn't say anything more. He kept that I-know-a-secret smile on his mug all the way back to the motor lodge. He kept it all the way through supper at a chop-suey house down the street. And he kept it when we walked back to the lodge from the chop-suey house.

It was getting dark by then. I looked up into the sky. All I saw were a bunch of stars coming out. No flying hubcaps. They must've been back in Roswell, doing whatever flying hubcaps do. Flying.

Most of the guys went into their cabins. I stayed out for a while. So did Eddie. So did Wes. So did Fidgety Frank. We talked baseball. We talked life on the road. We talked about everything under the sun except how come Harv needed to send a Consolidated Crystal message, and how come he looked as though he had canary feathers in his beard.

No, we didn't say anything about any of that. No, not a word, not one single, solitary word. We just stood around killing time. We mostly kept our hands in our pockets like kids pretending to be tough guys. Wes and Fidgety Frank smoked a few cigarettes. Eddie and I didn't use 'em. I never got the habit. When I was back in Enid, it cost too much money. Anything that cost any money at all cost too much in those days.

A shooting star sparked across the sky, there and gone before you could be sure you saw it. There are more of them after midnight, but you get some in the early nighttime, too. "*Not* a flying hubcap," Eddie said. Was that also in my mind? Oh, just a little.

So we talked about flying hubcaps for a while. Since even the fellas who lived in Roswell didn't know what they were, we didn't find any answers. Sure came up with some interesting questions, though.

Fidgety Frank had just lit another coffin nail when a carpet came up the road toward the motor lodge. We all watched it, all of us trying to make as though we were doing no such thing. The carpet stopped in front of the cabin where Harv was staying. By the light over the cabin door, we could see that the fellow riding it wore a gray-blue jacket of a cut everybody knows. We couldn't see that the brass buttons on the jacket were stamped CC for Consolidated Crystal, but we didn't really need to.

The deliveryman gave Harv the message. Harv closed the door. The CC man got back on the carpet. Casual as could be, Wes asked him, "Where'd that message come from? Do you know who sent it?"

"I can't tell you anything like that," the deliveryman answered. Wes handed him a folded-up bill. When he unfolded it, he coughed. No, I don't know how big it was. Big enough to make him cough, that's how big. Real fast, he said, "It's from Pittsburgh, from some guy on the Crawdads, whatever the Crawdads are. But you never heard that from me." He sailed out of there faster than he had any business going.

"Huh," Fidgety Frank said when the Consolidated Crystal deliveryman was gone. The CC fella might not have known about the Pittsburgh Crawdads, but we sure did. They were only one of the two or three best colored teams in the country. They traveled in a couple of big old limousines. People had been telling stories about Carpetbag

Booker, who pitched for them, as long as I could remember. Job Gregson, their catcher, hit balls farther than anybody, and I mean anybody.

"Are they coming out for the *Post* tournament?" I asked.

"Don't know," Fidgety Frank said. Wes and Eddie both shrugged. If they did come out, they'd have a good chance of winning. We all knew that.

"What's Harv cooking up?" Wes answered his own question: "Whatever it is, it's gotta be something juicy. But what?"

"Can't ask him," Eddie said. "If he knows we know, boy, will we catch it." So would the CC deliveryman, but we didn't waste any time caring about him.

"I almost wish we didn't find out," I said. "Now we've got more questions about this than we do about the flying hubcaps."

"We won't ever get answers about those, though," Wes said. "This stuff with the Crawdads, we'll find out pretty quick, whatever's going on."

"But I want to know now," Eddie said. I was thinking the same thing.

Wes let out a smart-aleck chuckle. "Gives you something to look forward to, don't it? Me, I'm going to bed. We've got another game tomorrow. We've always got another game tomorrow."

He had that right. I thought curiosity would keep me up. It did, too, for a good three minutes, maybe even five. Another game tomorrow. Always another game tomorrow. Well, I knew what I'd be doing, anyway.

What I'd be doing was getting on the bus and going up to Santa Fe for a game there the next afternoon. Nobody said a word about the Pittsburgh Crawdads. Harv didn't think anyone else knew. Oh, wouldn't he have reamed us out if one of us asked him something like *Hey, Harv, gonna get Job Gregson to catch for us?*

When you go up from Albuquerque to Santa Fe, you go up every which way you can. You go north—you go east, too, but you do go north. And you go up, as in up. Albuquerque's just under a mile high— I think I said that before. Santa Fe's at 7,000 feet.

And you notice the difference. At a mile up, you feel pretty much the way you always do, especially if you've been in high country for a bit, the way we had. Climb another couple of thousand feet on a two-hour bus ride and all of a sudden every staircase feels as though it's got three or four extra steps in it. You stop to catch your breath when you shouldn't need to. If you do something where you really need to, you mostly can't.

It's so high up, it's not even hot. But you can sunburn lickety-split, on account of there's less air between you and the sun. Hit a baseball and it goes and goes. Pitch one . . . Well, you can try. Curveballs don't want to curve. Fastballs won't hop the way they do down closer to sea level.

It was a pretty place. It was old, too—settled from Mexico more than three hundred years ago. On this side of the ocean, that made it ancient. I don't reckon anything in Oklahoma is even one hundred years old, let alone three. And it looked old. It was like Albuquerque, only more so. Everything either was made of adobe or else wasn't but looked as though it were. That kinda grows on you after a while. It makes a town look like it belongs where it is, not like it just got plopped down there by happenstance. Santa Fe's the state capital, too.

Some of the mountains around the town still had snow on them. If Santa Fe was high, they were higher. Every so often, you'd see an eagle circling maybe even higher yet.

Santa Fe'd had semipro teams for as long as anybody. It's never been in a pro league. The Santa Fe Saints played at Fort Marcy Park. No adobe there. Chain-link fences and wooden bleachers. If the bleachers were smaller, it would look like a high-school field.

It was too small to be as high up as it was. Only went 302 in left and 318 in right. Center was 395. That wouldn't be a big ballyard at sea level. Up 7,000 feet, and even I started looking like Job Gregson. Well, hitting like him, anyhow. From what I heard, he was twice as wide as me and more than twice as black. But I had no trouble clouting 'em over the fence in batting practice.

Wes said, "Why don't you let Frank pitch today, Harv? I don't want to get blamed for a mess of a game." I don't know whether he was grousing about my batting-practice homers or his own curves that wouldn't.

"I'm still pooped from yesterday," Fidgety Frank said. "Give the ball to Eddie. He can throw a few innings."

"I'll do it. If you aren't scared of what'll happen, I'm not, either," Eddie said. Some position players are convinced they can pitch. Once in a while, they're right. More often, what happens is something to be scared of.

"Wes, you'll run your fat behind up on the mound, and that's all there is to it," Harv said. "If you get knocked around, I expect we can jump on whatever they've got chucking, too." He rolled his eyes. No, I'd never want to manage a baseball team.

More than half of the folks in the crowd looked Mexican. When they chattered or yelled, you heard Spanish with the English. But New Mexico isn't like Texas. You saw that even more in Santa Fe than you did anywhere else. In Santa Fe, the Mexicans looked down their noses at the Yankees for being Johnny-come-latelies. They were the old families, and some of 'em were rich old families, too. Gringos? They didn't need any miserable gringos, or they didn't reckon they did.

The Saints were split the same way as the crowd. I heard some of the Yankees on the team calling each other gringo when they practiced: "Don't boot that one, gringo, or you'll warm the bench!" Stuff like that. They laughed. They thought it was funny, the same way colored folks will call each other names where they'd pull out a knife if they heard 'em from a white guy.

Harv turned out to know what he was talking about. He usually did, which was one reason he did a good job of riding herd on the House of Daniel. We landed on the Santa Fe pitcher with both feet. We batted around in the first inning, and scored five runs. Nothing makes a pitcher happier than taking the hill with a big lead. Wes gave one back in his half of the first, but you think you ought to get a medal if you only give up one in Fort Marcy Park at 7,000 feet.

We got three more in the second. Their manager—he was a fat little Mexican guy who I found out later was the assistant attorney general for the state of New Mexico—made a slow, sad walk out to the mound from the dugout. Their pitcher made a slow, sad walk into the dugout from the mound. A new guy came in. He got the last out.

The Saints answered back with a run again. Then we beat up their new pitcher. When you're leading 12-2 after two and a half, the rest of the game doesn't seem so important. You know what's going to happen, and so do the players on the other side. All you want to do is collect your share of the gate and leave town without anybody getting hurt.

When it got to be 15-4, the Saints' third pitcher threw one at Harv's ear. That kind of thing can happen in that kind of game. Harv got out of the way. Next inning, that pitcher came up. Wes hit him right on the ankle bone, the one that sticks out. I could hear the clunk all the way out in center. The Saint went down in a heap. After a bit, he stood up and hobbled to first.

Nobody threw at anybody else the rest of the game. One more time: message sent, message answered, answer received. The end.

"You were too much for us today," the Saints' manager told Harv after it was officially over. "You had your hitting shoes on."

"Play in this place all the time and you probably gotta talk your pitchers down offa tall buildings like they was stockbrokers or something," Harv said—as much sympathy as he'd show after he got decked like that.

The fat little Mexican heard what he didn't say. "Just so you know, I didn't tell Ike to spin your cap."

"Okey-doke. We took care of it any which way."

"I guess you did!" the Saints' manager said. "He'll limp for two weeks. That one caught him solid. He's got luck with him if he didn't break something in there."

Good luck or bad? I could see the question on Harv's face. He might have been as good a Christian as he could be, but he believed in an eye for an eye and a tooth for a tooth. Not many ballplayers are ready to turn the other cheek. If they do, somebody may fire a fastball at that one, too.

Harv knew what kind of a big shot their manager was. He told us over supper, which is how I found out. "You better believe I went over everything three times and made sure I saw a cash box from every concession stand in the place," he said. "With a lawyer for a manager, you bet the Saints'll never be short for money."

"Are you sure you got it all?" Wes asked.

"I'm sure I gave it my best shot," Harv answered. "If he was out to diddle me, he had to work hard."

"Sounds all right by me," Wes said after a bit of thought. "Going against lawyers is like playing the Hilltoppers. Chances are you won't beat 'em, but you hope you can give 'em a good game."

When we came out, we all stared up at the stars. We couldn't help it. We saw a lot of 'em in Roswell, and even more in Albuquerque. But you never dreamt you could see as many stars as you could in Santa Fe. The Milky Way looked like milk, honest. It wasn't just a smudge in the sky, the way it is most places. I never saw it like that before, and I never did again, either, not even in Denver later that year.

"'But there is a God in heaven that revealeth secrets,'" Harv murmured, gaping up like the rest of us. Book of Daniel language? Sure it was. I've read the passage since—I hadn't then. Daniel was talking about dreams, not stars, but so what? Seeing the stars that night was like revealing one page from a big book of wonders you don't usually get to open.

Then something flitted across those stars. You could follow it by how it blocked them. I pulled the cross out from under my shirt. It was glowing a little, so that was a vampire, the way I thought. A couple of other guys were doing the same thing at the same time.

"I think maybe we'd better head on back to the boarding house," Fidgety Frank said.

"Pronto," Wes added. They say that in New Mexico—some in Texas, too. Means something like *and step on it*.

That seemed like a good idea, so we all *pronto*ed. And none of us got bit that night, or crumbled to dust or caught fire when the sun hit him the next morning. Back on the bus we went. Another ballgame, coming up.

From Santa Fe, we went down to Madrid. When I saw the place, I wondered whether Harv had lost his marbles stopping there. It couldn't have held much more than a thousand people. And it wasn't a town, or not exactly a town. It was a company town. If not for the coal mines, there wouldn't have been any Madrid.

They put us up in company housing. We had time to kill before the game. For one thing, Madrid isn't far from Santa Fe. For another . . .

Well, I'll get to that in a little bit. The company housing was about like you'd think. It had everything a person needed, and none of what he might want.

We got some extra sleep. That was all right. They fed us lunch. Company lunch was like company housing. I didn't have to pay for it. Just as well, 'cause I wouldn't't've wanted to. They showed us around. I know more about coal mining than I did before, I will say.

Then we changed into our uniforms and went to the ballpark. And as soon as we got there, I understood why Harv brought us to Madrid. The Oscar Huber Ballpark was fancier than the one they had in Albuquerque. Bigger, too—they said it would hold 6,000. The grandstand had a tin roof.

And the ballpark had lights.

It had had them for almost fifteen years when I was there. They'd replaced some of the first salamanders atop their towers with bigger, brighter ones that didn't eat so much. The kind of people who run coal mines will save money any way they can. If that happens to make the baseball better, too, well, they don't mind.

So the Madrid Miners were the same kind of ballclub as the Ponca City Greasemen or the Carlsbad Potashers. The coal company paid for their travel on the road. Watching them work out, I would have bet that the coal company paid for some ringers, too. They were an outfit that knew its business.

I wanted to get out there and catch some flies by salamanderlight myself. I could tell right away it was different. The ball looked like a white pill against the sky that got darker and darker. No, not like a flying hubcap, if that's what you were thinking. Those flattened out when you saw 'em edge-on. The ball stayed round.

Under that hot white glare, the grass and the infield dirt seemed greener and redder than they would have in the daytime. The stands almost disappeared into the deepening night. You could still hear the people in 'em, but you couldn't see them any more. It felt peculiar.

When I came in for our first at-bats, Eddie said, "If they start playing lots of games at night, teams will hire vampire outfielders to fly up and grab home runs before they go over the fence."

"What'll they pay 'em in—necks?" I asked. "I don't want to go on the road with a bunch of coffins stacked up in the back of the bus. Do you?"

"Well, no," he allowed.

"What's the world coming to?" I went on. "Zombies stealing jobs that just take a strong back, and now you're talking about vampires in the outfield? Isn't there anything left for a poor, ordinary human being?"

"Doesn't look that way," Eddie answered. "If a zombie or a vampire can't do your work, chances are some kind of a machine can. People are obsolete."

"About the only thing machines can't do is make more people," I said, "and they'll probably figure that one out Wednesday after next."

"Even if they do, I bet it doesn't catch on." Eddie tipped me a wink. "The old-fashioned way's too much fun."

The Madrid Miners took the field. People in those invisible stands cheered them. They had their team name on their chests: MADRID in an arc that went up and then down, MINERS under it in an arc that went down and then up, so it almost looked as though they made a baseball. The letters and their caps and socks were black. It was all about as plain as plain could be, but it made sense for a bunch of guys who grubbed coal out of the ground.

By the way they played, some of 'em didn't work too hard when they went underground. They were good. They were the kind of semipros who were ballplayers first and had their job jobs, if you know what I mean, to make it look as if they weren't for-true pros.

Fidgety Frank was on his game, though. The way he'd lost in Albuquerque, I'd worried about it. You couldn't curve people to death here. Madrid was up almost as high as Santa Fe. But Frank never threw two pitches in a row the same speed. Take a little off, put a little on, keep the hitters looking for what you aren't throwing . . . He made it work.

Their pitcher was a skinny Mexican kid who threw hard. Their team and their crowd were split like the ones in Santa Fe. More of the rich people in Madrid, the mine owners and such, were gringos, though.

It was a tight game all the way. We hit into three double plays. Their infield was as good as you ever saw. The shortstop and second baseman played as though they'd been married for years. They knew each other's moves in their sleep. After eight innings, it was knotted up, 3-3.

Their guy started to wear down as the game went on, but their defense kept saving him. In the top of the ninth, we had men on second and third with two out and Eddie up. I knew what I would've done then—I'd done it before. But if I yelled it out to him, the Miners would know it, too.

Turned out I didn't need to. He saw their third sacker playing back and laid down a sweet little bunt. The third baseman rushed in, grabbed it, and tried to make an impossible play at the plate. The run would've scored any which way, but he hurried the throw, and it went wild. That let our guy on second come in, too.

Sometimes you've just gotta know when to stick the ball in your pocket. If you try to do what nobody can, you only make things worse.

And was I glad we had the two-run cushion, because one of their guys homered with two outs in the bottom of the ninth. Nobody on, so we kept the lead. Their last batter hit the ball pretty good, but not good enough—and right at me. I caught it with both hands, trotted in, and set the ball on top of the mound.

"Final score—House of Daniel 5, the Miners 4," their announcer said sadly, and stepped away from his microphone. Yes, they had a microphone. Along with the lights, that made the Oscar Huber Ballpark as modern as they came.

We did trade handshakes and *Attaboy!*s and *Good game!*s with the Miners. Nothing wrong with their team at all. We won the game, but it could have gone their way just as easy. They knew it. So did we. Play baseball and somebody's got to come out on top. That's how the game's set up.

Eddie was so happy with himself, his spikes hardly dug into the dirt. He walloped me on the back. "I saw you do it, Snake, so I figured I'd give it a try," he said. "If I got it down, it was a hit for sure, and I got it down. The second run seemed like icing on the cake, but we ended up needing it."

"You did great, man!" I walloped him back. I'd rubbed off on somebody! On a team as good as the House of Daniel, who would've figured that?

XI

W e'd gone through Artesia twice, once on the way to Hobbs and once on the way to Roswell. Now we went through Santa Fe twice, too. Las Vegas was on the far side of the capital from Madrid, east through the Santa Fe National Forest and some no-account little towns.

Yeah, I know there's another Las Vegas in Nevada. That's the one where you can gamble and carry on if you're so inclined. Reno's better set up for such things, but you can do them in the Nevada Las Vegas, too. The one in New Mexico is a farming town and a railroad town. People may think of the one in Nevada first, but the one in New Mexico's bigger.

It used to be a rip-snorting place. Billy the Kid spent a little while in jail there. They had outlaws with nicknames like Caribou and Dirty-face and Hoodoo and Flapjack Bill and Jimmie the Duck. The only people who get to wear handles like that nowadays are ballplayers. Fair enough. We're on the road even more than Billy and the rest of the gunslingers were.

The Las Vegas Maroons have been around for about as long as I've been alive. They and the Miners and the Saints and the Dons play each other a lot every year. They call it the Central New Mexico League, but it isn't hooked in with real leagues and real pro ball any way I know of.

When we got to Maroons Field, the Las Vegas players shook our hands and gave us cigarettes and chocolates because we'd whipped the Miners. "Those guys got more money than they know what to do with," one of the Maroons grumbled. "Well, no—they pay players with it. About time somebody took 'em down a peg."

"You won't like us so much if we beat you the same way," Harv said.

"Nope, sure won't," the Las Vegas fella said. "But we'll like the payday all right."

Sure enough, the stands were filling up. Only a thousand people in Madrid, but their ballpark held three times as many as the one in Las Vegas even if Las Vegas had a dozen times more people. I guess the answer to that is, there's nothing else to do in Madrid. Las Vegas is a real little city. You can see a film or go shopping or go to a restaurant the mining company doesn't run or do anything else you feel like.

Still, this wouldn't be a bad crowd. Harv wasn't looking as though he wanted to cuss in spite of belonging to the House of Daniel.

Like the Miners and the Saints and the Dons, the Maroons looked as if they knew what they were doing out there. They were kitted out in the color that gave 'em their name. It made 'em seem less somber than the Miners did.

We won the game, 6-2. No thanks to me, doggone it. I didn't get a hit. I struck out once. And I dropped a fly ball. I didn't do anything stupid. I tried to catch it two-handed. But it popped out of my glove before I could get my meat hand on it. Next thing I knew, it was on the ground. The guy who hit it wound up on second, and the crowd laughed and laughed.

He didn't score. I still felt like a jerk. When I got back to the dugout, Harv said, "Hang in there. Nobody's perfect."

"I should've had it," I muttered.

"Yeah, you should have," Harv agreed. "Just catch the next one, and the one after that, and. . . ."

"Gotcha," I said, or he would have gone on for a while.

We were still in our baseball togs when we left the ballpark. It didn't have showers; we'd have to clean up when we got back to the roominghouse where we were staying. The take was enough to keep Harv happy, even if it wasn't enough to make him jump up and down.

But we had to run a gauntlet of beggars to get to the bus. I handed out a couple of quarters. So did most of the guys. You knew they wouldn't help with anybody's real troubles. If you don't have a job, if you don't live in anything better than a packing crate, a quarter will get you a supper, but then you'll be hungry again tomorrow and you still won't have work or anywhere decent to stay.

Decent . . . I ask you, friend, what are you supposed to say when kind of a pretty girl sidles up to you and goes, "For five dollars, Mister, I'll do anything you want all night long"?

Women can always do that, because some man or other will want what they're peddling. But can they do it without wanting to bust every mirror where they're staying? It's a rotten old world sometimes, it truly is.

I didn't much want to, but I coughed up another quarter. "Go on—get out of here," I told her. "You don't know what you're talking about." Maybe this was her first time trying it. Maybe she'd decide it wasn't such a hot idea and wouldn't try it any more.

Yeah, and maybe the stork finds babies under cabbage leaves and takes 'em to the hospital. Her mouth twisted. "Devil I don't," she said. "I ought to, by now. But I got to feed my little girl some way or other."

She hadn't found her kid under a cabbage leaf. I wondered what it would think of her when it found out how she'd fed it. Or maybe it never would. Maybe, when she saw a better chance, she'd move away from that town and hope she never ran into anybody from Las Vegas, New Mexico, again.

"Here. Now scram." I coughed up one more quarter. She was plenty pretty for that, even if she wasn't enough of a beauty to make me such a fool that I'd give her all she wanted.

She didn't scram, of course. But she did leave me alone—she went off and rubbed up against some of the other House of Daniel guys. Nobody walked away from her. I bet she collected five bucks easy from the ballplayers, and she didn't even have to give back what she'd said she would.

When we finally made it onto the bus, I sat down by Wes. He chuckled, not in a nice way. "How much did you give her?" he asked.

"Half a buck," I said. "How about you?"

"Six bits," he answered. "Go ahead, call me stupid."

I didn't. I said, "She was like a vampire, sucking money out of us."

"I'd sooner have her suck me than a vampire any day," Wes said. My ears got hot. Back in Oklahoma, you could go to jail for something like that. A crime against nature, they called it. People did it just the same—I'm not saying they didn't—but they hardly ever talked about it. When Wes saw it made me nervous, he laughed and laughed. He had maybe eight years on me. That's not so much, honest. But he was way older.

Times were hard for everybody. That was the thought in my mind as we pulled away from Maroons Field and the beggars and the girl who wanted money and didn't care how she got it. That was the thought in my mind, yeah, but I didn't come out with it. Wes would have had some more ear-burning things to say if I did.

A nother early start the next morning: we were heading east again, bound for Clovis. The road had been paved, but not any time lately. We couldn't have gone as fast as we did if there'd been more traffic. I didn't care to think about breaking down, especially right after we passed a bleached-out cow skull near some rocks. A roadrunner was sitting on it.

When we got about halfway to Tucumcari (Tucumcari is about halfway to Clovis from Las Vegas), the road improved. Pretty soon, I saw why: they were damming the Mora River. A big billboard said the Conchas Dam would make the desert bloom and stop the Mora from flooding whenever it got the urge. It also said the dam was putting I don't know how many people back to work. Pick your own big number.

They were driving trucks and tractors and backhoes and bulldozers and steamrollers. Way more of 'em, though, were using picks and shovels and sledgehammers to dig and to break rock. A private company building a dam these days'd likely use zombies for the pick-and-shovel work. It'd go slower, but it'd come out cheaper in the end. Companies care about stuff like that. The government cared about votes, so all the workers out there in the desert were real, live human beings.

They had their own little town of shacks and tents by where the dam was going up. Chances were they had their own town team, too. No sooner had the thought crossed my mind than Fidgety Frank yelled out, "We gonna play them on the way back, Harv?"

Harv laughed along with everybody else. "Nah," he said. "They ain't got enough of a ballpark to make it worth our while." Nothing fazed him—nothing the guys on the team could do, anyhow.

Past the regular workers' town was a smaller one for the engineers and wizards. I watched one wizard in a wide-brimmed straw hat smoking a pipe while he palavered with a water elemental. He'd built a canvas shade to protect it from maybe boiling away while it came forth in the burning sun. You change how the water's going to go around and what it's going to do, you've got to make it right with the Ones tied to the water. I'm sure some of the other wizards were dealing with the earth elementals. Put all the weight of a dam on top of them, plus all the water backed up behind it, and you'd better keep them happy. If you don't, pretty soon you've got a big earthquake and no dam.

Tucumcari turned out to be a bigger town than I'd guessed. "How come we don't stop here?" I asked Harv when we went through. I tried to pitch my voice so he could tell I wasn't razzing him the way Fidgety Frank had—I really wanted to know.

"We ain't stoppin' in Tucumcari on account of Tucumcari don't care enough about baseball to have a team worth playin'." Harv bit the words out between his teeth. He might have sounded more disgusted if he'd talked about blasphemy and abominations against the Lord in Tucumcari. Then again, he might not. To Harv, not caring about baseball *was* blasphemy and an abomination against the Lord.

We went south out of Tucumcari. Soon as we left it behind, Harv sat up straighter in the driver's seat. It was as though he was glad to shake the dust of the place off his tires—well, off the bus's tires. So, south for a while, and then east, and then south again. And I will be fried for eggs and bacon if we didn't find ourselves in Clovis, and in plenty of time for the game.

When we pulled up in front of the motor lodge to change into our uniforms, Harv hopped out from behind the wheel. He wasn't just ready to go—he was raring to go. He'd herded that bus, and us yahoos, across 170, 180 miles of rugged road. I would have been all crippled up after that. I creaked like an old man even though I hadn't been driving. I'd be fine once I got loose, but I wasn't loose yet.

In our motor-lodge cabin, Eddie looked me over. "Y'know, I think we can skip the false whiskers," he said. "Your real beard's long enough so people can see it from the stands."

"Sounds good to me!" I said. "That spirit gum still makes me woozy. I won't miss it, not even a little bit."

"Okey-doke. You still better put on the wig, though."

"I'll do that. The wig's just hot. I'd be hot without it, too."

Eddie nodded. "Can't be much else down here this time of year."

Harv looked at me twice when I went back to the bus without the shredded wheat glued to my cheeks and chin. Then he nodded, too, I don't know whether to me or to himself. "Yeah, you'll do," he said. "Sorry to put you through that. We don't always. When Benjamin Harrison Caesar pitched for us a couple of years ago, we let him stay clean-shaven." He kinda frowned. "Didn't help. He drank his way off the team."

I wished he hadn't told me that. Benjamin Harrison Caesar was as good a pitcher as ever lived (except maybe Carpetbag Booker, I supposed). He played for the Philadelphia Quakers and the St. Louis Archdeacons for years and years. So he ended up pitching for the House of Daniel after he couldn't get 'em out in the bigs any more, did he? I wondered if he'd left the bigs on account of the bottle. If he had, he took his time about it. He stayed up there for twenty years.

"Don't worry about it," I said. "I know I'm not Benjamin Harrison Caesar. Nobody's gonna come to the park because he hears Jack Spivey will be playing."

"How about Snake Spivey, the world's slickest center fielder?" Harv didn't just play for the House of Daniel and manage 'em and drive the darn bus. He promoted the team, too.

"If that's what I am, you aren't paying me enough." I said it with an egg-sucking grin, so he'd know I was joshing.

"Get on the bus, you no-good, worthless bum," he growled. I hoped like anything he was joshing. And he was, because he went on, "Pretty soon you'll go on shares like the rest of the guys, you know. That's better money."

"I'm not losing sleep about it, Harv," I said. And I wasn't.

Bell Park was a nice place to play a ballgame. It was newer than most, and held about 2,500. That's what Harv said, anyway, and what Harv doesn't know about seats at a baseball park isn't worth knowing. And it was different from a lot of those parks in Texas and New Mexico. It wasn't too big or too small. Nope—it was just right. Goldilocks would've glommed on to it for sure. It ran 330 down each line and 410 to straightaway center.

The Clovis Pioneers were just right, too. We knocked them around the same way we did with the Santa Fe Saints. The scoreboard didn't show it, because their yard was bigger and they were only—only!—at 4,200 feet. It wasn't a pinball score, but we won going away, 8-2.

Guys who'd been there before expected a tougher game. Clovis had fielded a pro team for a couple of years in the Twenties. They'd played in a ramshackle field on the north side of town then; Bell Park wasn't there yet. But the Pioneers didn't have it when they took us on that afternoon.

Their fans let 'em hear about it, too. Anybody called me some of those names when I wasn't between the white lines, smiling when he said it wouldn't help. But when you buy a ticket, you buy the chance to tell the ballplayers what you think of 'em. And that crowd did. Some of the ladies in the stands didn't talk as though they were.

Still, I have to give Clovis points. They had better manners than the Saints or their own fans. Even after the game got out of hand, they didn't start aiming beanballs at the team from out of town.

"They're good sports," Harv said when I remarked on that sitting in the dugout in the bottom of the eighth.

"Huh," Wes said. "They want us to come back next year so they draw another big crowd. This'd be an easy enough town to skip, and they know it. We'd get thrown at a lot worse'n we do if the town teams didn't like the money we bring in so much."

"Sometimes we get thrown at, anyway," Azariah said.

"Sometimes we do," Wes agreed. "But it would be worse if we were a lousy draw. It would be worse if we didn't give as good as we got, too." Wes was almost as much of a hardnose as he thought he was.

After the game was over, the Pioneers took us to a barbecue. They were no-kidding semipros; their shortstop ran the joint where they fed us. He wouldn't take our money, either. "That's not fair," Harv said. "We beat you. Least we can do is pay for our supper."

"Unless you're stickin' a rib bone in there, you shut your yap, you hear?" the Pioneer said. Clovis is like Hobbs. It's another one of those towns by the state line. In that part of New Mexico, you might as well be in Texas. A lot of the settlers came from Texas to begin with. They still talked like it, and they still acted like it. Weren't any Mexicans on the baseball team. I didn't see many in town.

Nothing wrong with the barbecue, not even a little bit. I was glad I only had my own whiskers to get all gooey. That fake stuff would have been a horrible mess. When everybody who drank had had a beer or three, the Pioneers' catcher got a guitar out of a back room and started singing.

He was good. He was plenty good enough to make some money on the side with his singing and playing. A semipro ballplayer and a semi-pro music fella. I never did find out what his regular job was, or if he had one.

You'll never see me playing center field for the Titans in the Cricket Grounds. I'm a pretty decent outfielder, but I'm not good enough to do that. You won't hear the fellow from Clovis—they called him Rocky—on the radio any time soon, either. He was fine at a barbecue place after a few beers. But he wasn't good enough for the big time, either.

One of the things I remember my pa saying was that folks used to make music by themselves and for themselves more often before the radio came along. They knew how they sounded and how their friends and neighbors sounded, but they only heard top people when they went to the theater for a show, and they didn't do that very often.

When most houses got radio sets, all that changed. You just had to twist a knob and there they were: the best singers, the finest bands, right in your parlor playing for you. And you listened to them for a while, and then you thought about how you sounded singing with your sister at the piano and the fat guy from across the street sawing away on the fiddle. If you weren't embarrassed to open your mouth after that, you were either mighty good or you had a lot of brass.

The Pioneers' shortstop may have been too proud to feed us for money, but their catcher pocketed what we gave him between songs. Maybe he figured he'd earned it. Or maybe he was looking for what-ever he could get his hands on because semipro ball and semipro music left him stretched to make ends meet.

I thought about that gal in Las Vegas. She was a pro, a pro at something she couldn't want to do. Thinking about her made me feel rotten, so I got to the bottom of my beer bottle in a hurry.

Then I thought about Mich Carstairs. I hoped she made it to California. I hoped she found a job there, too, a for-true job. If she didn't, I hoped Charlie Carstairs could help her out. She looked good enough, she could have made a go of it as a pro if she had to. But you don't care to imagine that for somebody you like, so I hoped for the for-true job instead.

"You feeling good, Snake?" Eddie asked. "You look kinda unhappy, like."

"Must've eaten too much." I put my hand on my belly. I *had* eaten too much—we all had—but that wasn't what griped me. Well, when somebody asks *How ya doin'?*, you don't tell him everything that's gone wrong with you for the past month. Or if you do, you got to reckon he won't ask you again.

Harv patted his belly, too. "You can roll us back to the motor lodge tonight, we're so stuffed," he told the Pioneer who ran the barbecue place.

"That's the idea." The shortstop sounded proud of himself. "Have some more if you want. There's plenty." If you can brag on how much food you've got now that the Big Bubble's busted, you're doing all right for yourself. You want folks to know you are, too. I mean, unless you just want them to think you are.

When we staggered out of the restaurant, a garbage truck was coming up the street. The fellow driving it was a man. The two picking up trash cans and dumping them in the scoop were zombies, though. You could tell by how slow they moved—and, when they got in the glare of the truck's headlamps, by how gray they were.

"I hate those things," the Pioneers' shortstop said. "I don't believe they're as dead as everybody thinks. Doesn't stand to reason anything'll slave all the time and not want anything for itself. Doesn't stand to reason it won't want to get even with the folks who make it slave all the time, either."

Eddie'd said the same kind of thing. But I wasn't thinking about Eddie right then. I'd already noticed that shortstop was one of the fellas who sounded all Texan. He'd've had grandfathers or great-granddads who'd worn gray during the States War. How many of them had owned colored folks? I'd had kin in the States War my own self, but no slave-holders. Us Spiveys, we were never rich enough for that.

"Hasn't happened yet," Azariah said.

"I know," the Clovis man answered. "I hope it doesn't, too. We won't have ourselves a good time if it does."

He had that straight. We all found out how straight he had it. But I don't care to miss a bag in the story. They call you out for that.

When we got back to the motor lodge, the old coot who ran it came out of his office and asked, "One of you beards called Harvey Watrous?"

"That's me." Harv ran his fingers through his whiskers. He was proud of 'em. He should've been, too—he had some humdingers.

The coot gave him an envelope. "Consolidated Crystal guy brung a message for you."

"Thanks." Harv opened it. He read the green paper inside, smiled, and stuck it in his hip pocket. "Well, ain't that nice?"

"Ain't what nice?" Fidgety Frank and I asked at the same time.

Harv smiled again. This time, he looked like a dad smiling at a three-year-old who keeps asking *Why?* all the time. "When everything's ripe, you'll know. I promise," he said, and ambled off to his cabin. This side of clouting him with a bat or a tire iron or a jack handle, we had to go off to ours, too.

And we had to get up too blasted early the next morning. We were going all the way up to Raton, near the Colorado line. It would be a long trip—250 miles, something like that. "Tell me again why I'm doing this," Wes said around a great big yawn when he got on the bus.

"Because if you don't, we'll leave your sorry behind right here in Clovis." Harv sounded as cheerful about it as if he'd already had three cups of coffee.

"That's a good reason," Wes allowed, and he sat down.

I thought it was a terrific reason after we had breakfast at an all-night greasy spoon. They vulcanized the eggs. The coffee tasted as though they brewed it from adobe. I've had plenty of better food. I'd need to think for a while to decide whether I've had worse.

Out of Clovis, we headed north and north and north some more over roads almost as bad as that greasy-spoon breakfast. You go and you go and you go. Every fifteen or twenty or twenty-five miles there's a tiny little town in the middle of the desert for no reason anybody can see.

Harv stopped for gas in a little place called Nara Visa. If he'd turned right from there, he would've been in Texas in ten minutes.

But he didn't. He went straight ahead. We chugged past red sandstone bluffs—mesas, they call 'em out there—that either the wind or some crazy god with too much time on his hands spent eons carving into shapes nobody who hadn't seen 'em would believe.

I didn't see all of 'em myself. I was on-and-off dozing in the bus, coffee or no coffee, jounces or no jounces. By then, I was getting the knack. It wasn't as good as a bed, but it was a lot better than nothing.

I was awake again when we went through Clayton and swung from north to northwest. That was a sign we were only an hour and a half away.

If the bus didn't break down, I mean. That was always the dread. Not just a blowout. We could deal with those. Harv built in time to fix one in every long haul. But if we threw a rod or something . . .

It was one of those places where every so often you'd see buzzards circling overhead. A lot of the time, they'd be the only moving things you'd see. Cars and carpets were few and far between.

Yeah, we had some guys who knew their way around an engine. Yeah, we had an iron box full of tools and another one with spare parts for some of the things likeliest to fail. But that didn't kill all our worries. Some breakdowns you just can't fix without a shop.

Past Clayton was Rabbit Ear Mountain. Don't ask me why they call it that. It looks like a mountain, but not much like a rabbit ear. Ten miles farther on, Mt. Dora was a village at the foot of the mountain called Mt. Dora. Half of it was boarded up. Looked like the Big Bubble got it but good.

After another ten miles, we went through Grenville. It was about the same size as Mt. Dora, and looked just as broke. From what Fidgety Frank said, though, Grenville busted even before the Big Bubble popped. They struck oil near there right after the War to End War. Then, a few years later, the well dried up. So did Grenville, and it didn't seem anyone had watered it since.

Here and there in the desert, you'd see one or two of those made-of-anything shacks like the ones that farm workers and foreclosed folks lived in. I don't know what the people who ran 'em up lived off of.

They hunted some, I suppose. If they had a little water close by, they might scratch out a vegetable plot.

All I can tell you is, I wouldn't want to try it. Pretty soon, you'd be down to roasting lizards and grasshoppers and crickets. Even a soup kitchen and a flophouse are better than that, aren't they? It was plain enough that the folks in those shacks didn't think so.

"Why would you want to live out here?" I asked after we went by another shanty like that.

"Because the whole goddamn world leaves you alone, that's why," Wes answered right away. "When the world's knocked you down and kicked you, just getting it to leave you alone is more precious than rubies."

Behind the wheel, Harv clucked. "Wes, do you have to take the Lord's name in vain and quote from the Good Book in back-to-back sentences?"

"Sorry, Harv," Wes said. Harv sat up a little straighter, so you could tell he was pleased. As soon as he did, Wes went on, "If I'd known you were minding me so close, I would've done 'em both in the same one."

Not many of us needled Harv. Wes would do it, and Fidgety Frank. Well, they were the pitchers. Harv had to give them more leeway than the rest of us, on account of he needed them more. But Wes would have needled Harv if he'd played the outfield all the time, not just when he wasn't out there flinging. He was a natural-born troublemaker, Wes was.

Next place after Grenville was Des Moines. "Harv, you took a wrong turn somewhere!" Fidgety Frank said. "How in blazes did you land us in the middle of Iowa?" We all laughed.

"That'd be funnier if you hadn't said the same blamed thing on this road last year," Harv shot back. We all laughed louder—well, all of us but Frank. Harv didn't cuss, but he had a good needle just the same.

In more time than it takes to tell you, we made it to Raton. We got there fine for the game, because we'd left so early. Raton, the guys told me, is a Spanish name that means exactly what you'd think. Great name for a town. Unless you're a cat, why would you want to move there?

To raise cattle, maybe. Or to work on the railroad. Or to mine coal. Those are the things folks around there do to make a living. We heard as much Spanish as English. There were some colored folks in Raton, too. You don't see that many in New Mexico. Eddie told me they sprang from the Buffalo Soldiers who fought Indians around there in the old days.

The boarding house where we put on our uniforms was . . . a boarding house. You could have put it in Enid or Amarillo and nobody would have looked at it twice. We played the Raton Mice in a ballyard called Elks Park. It was old and made of wood and looked as though a fire was the best it had to hope for.

Nobody'd painted the little grandstand behind the plate or the seats or the outfield fences for a long time. The fences had advertisements on them, so badly faded you could hardly make out what they said. The one right behind me, I figured out at last, was for a funeral parlor. That did everything you'd think it would to cheer me up.

Distance markers? If there'd ever been any, they were long gone. The field was short in left and long in right. The left-field fence must've been twenty feet high. That would keep some balls in play, but not all.

As for the Mice, they looked like the town. Quite a few of 'em were on the swarthy side. A couple wore bushy black mustaches. Another guy had a thin one, so he looked as much like a lounge lizard as somebody with MICE across his chest in big letters could. The shortstop and first baseman weren't swarthy—they were colored. The first baseman stood six-four, easy, and he was almost as wide as he was tall. Not fat. Muscle. He batted left. Right field was a fifty-cent cab ride from home plate, but he launched half a dozen balls over the fence limbering up.

"Oh, yeah!" he'd yell every time he got hold of one good. Kids on the far side of the wall chased down the baseballs and brought 'em back for a dime. Well, one kid chased down a baseball and ran off with it. He decided he'd sooner have the ball than the money. I hope he had fun with it.

The Mice didn't look like anything special before the game. Not bad, you understand, but nothing to scare you, either. The crowd was big enough to keep Harv from putting on his my-hound-dog-just-died face, but no bigger'n that.

This sure wasn't the Texan part of New Mexico any more. The

colored fans who'd come out to watch their guys and the rest of the Mice sat scattered amongst the others. Nobody fussed about it. It was how they did things, that's all. They took it so much for granted, you wondered why people all over didn't do it the same way.

I knew we were in trouble as soon as we got two batters into the game. They had a tall, lanky sidearmer, a white guy, on the hill. He leaned to the right, too, so he looked as though he was coming straight from third base. He'd bust you inside twice and then put the next one just off the outside corner. You'd swing and you'd miss by so much, you'd look like you were trying to hit a golf ball with a broomstick. He set us down in order, and our guys came back shaking their heads.

"Keep us in it, Wes!" Harv chirped. Sounded like good advice to me. We might get something, but I didn't think we'd score much. If the Mice jumped out ahead, coming back wouldn't be easy.

But a walk and a Texas League single put Raton men on first and second with one out and that great big black first baseman coming up. His name was Luke. Wes tried to jam him, the way their pitcher had with our first three hitters. He got it inside, all right, but not far enough inside.

"Oh, *yeah*!" Luke yelled. The ball headed my way. I ran back a few steps, in case I was wrong. Then I stopped, because I wasn't. It went over my head and way over the fence right where the old funeral-parlor sign was. That seemed fair—Luke killed it.

He took his time rounding the bases. He wasn't trying to show Wes up. It was just that somebody that big couldn't move too fast.

"Oh, Luke! Yeah, Luke!" a colored gal behind the Mice's dugout hollered, over and over. She blew him kisses. If she wasn't Mrs. Luke, she sure wanted to be.

We got one back in the third. Their sidearmer walked me and then left one over the middle of the plate for Azariah, who was hitting last. Azariah split the gap between Raton's guys in center and right, and the ball rolled to the fence. It's a long way out there; I scored standing up.

But in the bottom of the third Luke came up with two on again. This time, nobody was out. Wes didn't try to come in on him again. That hadn't worked so well the last time. Instead, he pitched on, or off, the outside corner. Luke worked the count to two balls and a strike. Wes went outside again, but he left it up a little higher than he wanted.

Luke didn't try to pull it. No—he went with the pitch, and hit a high fly to left. And the big fellow was so strong, he sailed it over the high fence out there. "Oh, *yeah!*" he shouted, and went into his home-run trot. Go down 6-1 to a team with a sharp pitcher and you're in deep water. And we were.

It was 6-2 when Luke came up again, this time with the bases empty. They didn't stay empty long. Wes drilled him right in his big behind. Luke flipped away the bat and looked out to the hill. I think that, if he'd decided Wes hit him because he was colored, he would've tried to tear his head off. But to get hit because he'd slugged two three-run homers? That was part of the game. Luke went on down to first.

Next inning, their pitcher plunked Wes. That was part of the game, too. Even Luke chuckled, and swatted Wes on the butt when he took his base.

They ended up beating us 7-4. The crowd cheered their heads off. That colored gal jumped out of the stands and gave Luke a big kiss. She was pretty and then some. *I am black, but comely*, the Good Book said. It knew what it was talking about, all right.

When Luke detached himself from her, Harv went over to him and said, "You big galoot, you ruined us."

"Sometimes you have good days, sometimes not so good." Yeah, Luke was a ballplayer. He pointed over to Wes. "Did you have to hit me so damn hard, man?" Now, for a joke, he could rub at his posterior.

"Not as hard as you hit me," Wes said. "I don't think that first one's come down yet." I looked out toward center. I wasn't sure it had come down, either.

XII

Colorado!" Harv said when the bus crossed the state line. You know what, though? Except for the sign that told us we were out of New Mexico, not one thing changed. The landscape didn't—still mountains and rocks and pines. The people didn't, either. The next town up, not far over the border, was Trinidad. It was bigger than Raton, but just about as Mexican. You don't think about Colorado belonging to Mexico back in the day, but some of it did.

Only about twenty miles from Raton to Trinidad, so we could sleep in that morning. After the long haul from Clovis to Raton, we needed it. Nobody blamed the long drive for our loss, even if it could've had something to do with it. We were supposed to travel and play and win. That was what the House of Daniel was all about.

They mined coal in Trinidad. The streets crossed at funny angles; the place was built on a chain of foothills. The center of town had some regular brick buildings. More of the ones on the outskirts were made from adobe. Yes, they did things here the same way as they did farther south.

They called their ballyard Round-up Park. The city ran it, but semipro teams could use it. The folks in Trinidad knew the Raton Mice had beaten us. They were wild for their club to do the same. Trinidad and Raton didn't like each other any better than most towns twenty miles apart. That they were in separate states only made things worse.

Remember what I'd been talking about with Eddie a few days earlier? That was before I found out the Trinidad team really did call itself the Vampires. "Good thing it ain't a night game!" Wes said when he saw that across their shirts.

Me, I made sure none of their players was wearing great big sunglasses and that none of 'em had slathered every inch of skin that showed with ointments and lotions. They looked like a bunch of ballplayers, was what they looked like. As long as they didn't start lick-ing my ankle if I got spiked, I was ready to go.

We all were. Trouble was, so were they. The game could have gone either way, but it wound up going theirs, 3-2. Now both those towns that couldn't stand each other had bragging rights over the House of Daniel.

That was the first time since I joined the team that we'd lost two in a row. Harv was not happy, which is putting it mildly. He read us the riot act when we got back on the bus after the game. " 'They shall drive thee from men,' " he said, madder'n I'd ever heard him, " 'and thy dwelling shall be with the beasts of the field, and they shall make thee to eat grass as oxen, and they shall wet thee with the dew of heaven, and seven times shall pass over thee, till thou know that the most High ruleth in the kingdom of men, and giveth it to whomsoever He will.' "

No, Harv didn't read the riot act like anybody else. I've heard some lulus in my time, but up till then I never had a manager ream me out Book of Daniel style. I'm not saying it didn't work. The guys on the team who belonged to the House of Daniel hung their heads. The rest of us, I guess, wanted to laugh, only we didn't dare. Harv might not have been cussing the way a lot of managers would have, but he was hot enough to melt lead.

He glared at us from the driver's seat. "We'll be in Denver pretty soon," he said. "We'll be playing in the *Post* tournament. We want to be playing our best ball then, don't we? Are we playing our best ball right now?"

Nobody said anything. If anybody had said anything, Harv would've kicked him off the bus and around Round-up Park, I mean kicked him so he had spike scars on his behind the rest of his life.

"We lost two straight games!" Harv roared, as though he were one of those lions in the den. "We lost to the Mice, and we lost to the Vampires! Those teams ain't fit to shine our shoes. Am I right or am I wrong?"

"You're right, Harv," I said, along with two or three other fellas. That seemed safe enough, on account of he *was* right. You didn't need field glasses to see it. They weren't as good as we were. They beat us anyhow.

Harv breathed out through his nose, hard. Now he sounded like a bull about to charge. "All right, then. You listen to me, you lunkheads. You listen good, you hear? *You hear?*"

We nodded—all of us, I think. We couldn't help it. I don't know if Harv ever was a drill sergeant. If he wasn't, the Army let a good one get away.

"When we go up to Pueblo tomorrow, I expect to see some players who care about what they're doing, then," Harv said in a voice that warned he was ready to bite nails in half. "If I don't, I expect I can pull in some off the street who do. We got Snake that way. We can get more. You wear the lion on your chest, you better not have a pussy cat's heart."

"Teacher's pet," Fidgety Frank whispered to me.

"Oh, shut up," I whispered back. I wished Harv hadn't singled me out like that. I wanted to be like the rest of the guys. That's how you fit in on a team.

"Did I hear something?" Harv shouted.

"No, Harv," Fidgety Frank and I said together. Along with everything else, Harv had rabbit ears. He would.

"Mm, okey-doke," he said, as if he knew we were lying but didn't want to call us on it. He went on, "I want you to whip the tail feathers off the Pueblo Chieftains tomorrow. Not just beat 'em—whip 'em. Whip 'em good! And if you don't, I'll know the reason why."

He turned around and started up to the bus. We went back to the roominghouse. Nobody said a word all the way there.

W hip the tail feathers off the Pueblo Chieftains? I hoped we could. But it wasn't one of those things that came with a guarantee, if you know what I mean. Up till year before last, Pueblo was in the Western League. That's Class A ball, the higher minors. But the league threw them out, and Denver, too, on account of most of the teams were farther east even though they called it the Western League, and taking the train out to Colorado cost too blasted much. That's the kind of thing the Big Bubble busting made leagues worry about.

Some of the guys who'd played for Pueblo in the Western League hooked on with other teams in the regular minors. Some of 'em like it there, though, and stuck around after the league pulled out. You can't blame 'em. It's pretty country. If you'd found a girl there, you could look for a job, too. And you could still play ball and put some extra cash money in your wallet.

So the Pueblo Chieftains were a hot team. They had some players who'd been maybe *that* far from the bigs once upon a time. They even had themselves a new ballpark. Runyon Field opened up not long before we got there. None of the players from the House of Daniel had ever seen it before.

"When we came through here last year, the Chieftains played at Merchants Field, where the Western League used to be," Eddie told me while we were going to the new place. "Oh, my, people were ticked off about getting dumped! It was even worse in Denver. The Denver folks tried to sue the league, but it got tossed out of court."

Runyon Field looked as though a team from the higher minors could play there. It held, I dunno, four or five thousand people. The grandstand ran a long way down the foul lines. Then bleachers took over. When Eddie got a look at them, he started to laugh. "What's so funny?" I asked—they didn't look like anything but bleachers to me.

"They took those out of Merchants Field and brought 'em over here," he said. "Waste not, want not."

"How do you know?"

"I remember that blue-green paint they've got on the benches. I thought it looked queer a year ago, and I still think it does."

"Oh," I said. *Waste not, want not* was about the size of it. If you were going to put bleachers in a new ballpark, why pay for new ones when you could move the old ones for a lot less? Of course, that was the same kind of thinking that made the Western League pull out of Colorado, but try telling the folks in Pueblo anything along those lines.

We got a run in the top of the first. Wes set the Chieftains down in order in the bottom of the frame. In the top of the second I came up with one out and Eddie on third. The Chieftains' pitcher threw me a changeup. I was out in front of it. I hit it hard, but way foul. It pinballed off one of the columns holding up the grandstand roof and smacked a fan in the back of the head. Poor guy never saw it coming. Just *wham!*, out of the blue.

"Way to go, Snake!" Harv yelled from the dugout. "You put a new crease in his fedora!"

I felt bad about it. I'd never done anything like that before. But after a minute or so the fellow waved to show he was all right. The crowd gave him a hand. He was tough. He stayed in the game—well, in the stands.

"Play ball!" the plate umpire said, and we got back to it.

The Chieftain threw me another offspeed pitch. I hit this one hard, too, but I waited on it and kept it fair. It dropped in front of the left fielder. Eddie could have walked home. The pitcher slammed his fist into his glove. He tried to fool me, doubling up on the slow stuff, but it didn't work.

Things kept going right for us and wrong for the Chieftains. They had a runner picked off second. They lined into a double play. They couldn't turn one when they needed it most. I don't think we exactly whipped the tail feathers off them, but we won it 6-3.

"Better. A *little* better," Harv said after the game. "But you've got to get better yet. Colorado Springs tomorrow. And we're still on our way to Denver."

He didn't say we'd go straight to Denver from Colorado Springs. I didn't know what he had planned. Probably we'd go some other places before we got there. It still wasn't tournament time. But we *were* on our way, even if it was a twisty way to be on.

Colorado Springs was another medium-sized town at the edge of the Rockies. The mountains marched across the western skyline as we rolled north up US 85. They were something to see, all right.

Colorado Springs was different from Pueblo and Denver—it hadn't had a real pro team for years and years. The old club was called the Millionaires. Anybody who's ever played minor-league ball will tell you what a silly nickname for a team *that* is.

But one of the guys who'd played for them stayed in Colorado Springs when the team folded. He ran a city league of semipro teams. A lot of people want to stay in the game somehow after they get too old to play. He'd found a way to do it.

We were going to play an all-star team from this league. We'd done that before. I figured we'd do it again after this, too. Towns didn't always think any one club of theirs was good enough to face us—and the other teams didn't always want one getting the glory if they won (and the big gate even if they didn't). So they'd split up the players and they'd share the money. It worked out.

Harv said, "All-star teams have better players on 'em, yeah. But they aren't teams the way we're a team. Their guys haven't played together for years. The shortstop doesn't know what the second baseman'll do on a grounder up the middle. If you push 'em, they'll make mistakes."

They did have a nice place to play the game. Spurgeon Field looked so new, they might've just taken it out of its box. If they wanted to get back into minor-league ball, they could do it as far as the park was concerned.

The Colorado Springs All Stars wore shirts and caps with stars on 'em. They really did. I don't know where they got 'em, but they had 'em. The old Millionaires player in charge of the city league managed them. He had an All Stars uniform, too, and a pretty good stretch of belly to pull it tight. He kept a big chaw in his mouth, and shifted it from one cheek to the other every so often.

All the people in the stands cheered when they took the field. Then . . . Well, by the time the game was over, they must've wished they'd picked a different batch of all-stars. They were pretty sorry. They threw to the wrong base not once but twice. Their first baseman dropped a perfect throw from short. Plop—it fell out of his mitt. He looked at the ball on the ground as if he couldn't believe his eyes. They had a runner get picked off first. One of their batters doubled but got thrown out trying to stretch it into a triple: this when he led off the inning. The play wasn't close, either.

We ended up winning 9-4. The game was easier than that. They hit a two-run homer with two out in the bottom of the ninth. It changed the final score, but both sides knew who'd played well and who hadn't.

Their manager came up to Harv after the game and said, "I didn't think I was sending out a high-school nine this afternoon."

Harv set a hand on his shoulder. "Happens to everybody once in a while," he said, and anyone who's played a little baseball knows about that. "Sometimes you're the windshield. Sometimes you're the bug."

"Splat!" the fat, old, ex-Colorado Springs Millionaire said. They both laughed. I'm sure it felt funnier to Harv, though. You lose a game like that, you want to go somewhere quiet and have a couple-three cold ones so you don't need to brood about it as much.

Afterwards, we celebrated at a spaghetti joint. Spaghetti and meat balls and that kind of stuff is cheap, but it fills you up. "I think we did play better today. I'm not what you'd call sure, though," Harv said. "When the other side turns in a game like that, you've got a tough time gauging how good you are."

Wes kinda coughed, but he didn't say anything. Harv had had kittens when we played two games like that. Of course, Harv was looking ahead to the tournament. We couldn't play like that in Denver, not if we wanted to go very far.

We got back on the bus. Harv drove us to the roominghouse where we were staying in Colorado Springs. The gal who ran it came out just about spitting rivets. "Mister Watrous," she snapped, "Mister Watrous, there's someone in the parlor who says he needs to see you."

"Well, all right. I'll see him. What's the matter?" Harv said. Pretty plainly, something was.

The woman made a horrible face. "I am not in the habit of letting persons of that sort enter my establishment. I don't know how he sweet-talked me into allowing it. Do your business with him and send him on his way, if you would be so kind."

"What's she going on about?" Eddie whispered. Eddie was a Northern fella through and through. He had no hint. I thought I did, but I could've been wrong, so I shrugged back at him. We all trooped in together. As soon as we got to the parlor, we'd know.

In there sat a colored fella. I nodded to myself; that was what I'd figured. He stood up when he saw us. He was tall—six-three, maybe six-four—and skinny. He wore a sharp suit. He might have been my age or he might have been twenty years older. You couldn't tell at first glance. He would've been handsome and to spare if he hadn't quit shaving a few days earlier.

He touched the brim of his Panama hat. He had long, thin fingers. *A pitcher's fingers*, I thought, not knowing yet how right I was. " "Which one of y'all is Mistuh Watrous?" he asked, his voice smooth as creamed coffee and full of the Deep South.

"That's me." Harv stuck out his hand. "And you would be—?" He sounded as though he knew, but he wanted to hear it with his own ears to make it official.

The colored fellow shook with him. His hand almost swallowed Harv's, which wasn't little itself. "I'm Carpetbag Booker," he said. "Mighty pleased to meet you, suh. I've come to pitch fo' your team through the tournament, like you asked me to."

Harv beamed just like Christmas. Everybody except Harv gaped at Carpetbag Booker. Fidgety Frank, Wes, Eddie, and I were maybe a little less amazed than the rest of the guys, but only a little. Yes, the four of us knew Harv had got a CC message connected to somebody from the Pittsburgh Crawdads, but we'd never dreamt he could've talked Carpetbag Booker into signing up with the House of Daniel, even for a little while.

Wes looked less happy about it than some of the others. He was our number two pitcher. Now he'd be number three, which meant he wouldn't pitch much. He played the outfield, too, but even so. . . . This bit a big chunk out of his pride.

But the first thing Harv had to do was get the lady who ran the roominghouse down off her high horse. The idea of a colored man staying in her place gave her conniptions. It did till Harv slipped her an extra ten clams, anyway. That and hearing how Carpetbag was a famous colored man sweetened her up. Mostly, though, it was the money.

Nobody asked me how I felt about things. I'd played against colored fellas a few times now. Play on the same team with one? He'd give us a way better chance to win the tournament. Any fool could see that. I'd been raised to think whites and coloreds playing together was wrong, though. No, it was worse than wrong—it was a sin.

Maybe it was . . . in Oklahoma. And in Texas. And in Alabama or Mississippi or wherever Carpetbag Booker came from. Not in New Mexico or Colorado. If these places could cope with it, maybe I could, too. Besides, Carpetbag had already put some extra money in the roominghouse lady's pocket. If we went deep into the tournament, he'd put more in mine.

And the way he acted, you didn't think of him so much as a colored fella. You thought of him as a ballplayer. He'd barnstormed with big-leaguers in the offseason. If they could play alongside him, I reckoned I could, too. Playing alongside him sure got them some extra cash.

So we all talked for a spell. Then he picked up the carpetbag he was nicknamed for and went to his room. He had one all to himself. The gal who ran the roominghouse insisted on it. Carpetbag, he didn't say boo. If he slept better than the rest of us on account of not having any roommates, he didn't say anything about that the next morning, either.

For that day's game, we went toward Denver by going away from it. Canon City is about forty miles southwest of Colorado Springs, most of it along a winding mountain road. They spell it the way they spell it, but they say it as though it were Canyon. It's at the start of the Grand Canyon of the Arkansas, which isn't in Arkansas and isn't as grand as the Grand Canyon of the Colorado, which isn't in Colorado. Names get confusing sometimes, don't they?

My guess is, Canon City used to have one of those Spanishy thing-umabobs over the first n so you could tell how you were supposed to say it. It doesn't any more, though, and it hasn't for a long time. They still say it as if it did. Spelling gets confusing sometimes, too.

The Grand Canyon of the Arkansas is a thousand feet of red granite carved by the river over Lord only knows how many years. A bunch of 'em—that's all I can tell you. The other thing you could see in Canon City was the Colorado State Pen. The walls there were all made out of gray stone, so I don't think they got carved out of the Grand Canyon.

Across from the prison was State Park. When we got there, trusties in striped jail suits were mowing the grass and trimming weeds and the like. In the middle of the park stood the field where we'd play.

Well, the ballpark stood and leaned and tilted. It was another old wooden place falling to pieces a bit at a time. For a little while, not long after I was born, Canon City had a team in the Rocky Mountain League. A very little while—it moved down to Raton partway through the season, and the league gave up the ghost before the season ended. So that's been a semipro park and a for-fun park ever since.

We were playing the Canon City Fylfots. That was the name of the pro team back when, and the semipro team hung on to it. You do see that here and there. And they had a hooked cross on each sleeve and FYLFOTS across the chest in black letters with red edging. They had got hold of the thing before that noisy fella on the far side of the ocean, and they were not about to let go of it for him or anybody else.

The stands were not great big. They were pretty full, though. The House of Daniel does pack 'em in. And everybody in them buzzed when Harv bawled out the last name in our lineup: "And pitching today for the House of Daniel, for the first time ever, is the one, the only, the great . . . Carpetbag Booker!"

Carpetbag tipped his cap to the crowd. They must have seen him there warming up, but not all of 'em would have known who he was. They'd heard of him—that was for sure. Most of 'em cheered. Some booed. A few yelled the kind of things colored fellas hear a lot.

Growing up where he grew up, Carpetbag must've heard 'em all a million times. If they bothered him—and how couldn't they?—he didn't show it. As far as anybody could tell by looking, they rolled off him like water off an oilcloth.

We staked him to a couple of runs in the top of the first. That's always good. He went out and put on a show. He kicked his leg way high in the air when he wound up, so the batter would see the sole of his shoe. He had a fastball that sank. He had a fastball that hopped. He had a changeup. He had a nickel curve. And he had the knack that good pitchers have, the knack for ruining a batter's timing. He had way more of that than anybody else I've ever seen.

When no one was on, he'd throw a hesitation pitch. Guys will do that now and then. But he was even better at it than Fidgety Frank. He could stop his motion at a different place each pitch, yet still throw hard and still throw strikes. You wouldn't believe it, but Carpetbag did it. He made it look easy, too.

It didn't seem fair. He was tougher than big-league hitters. The Canon City Fylfots couldn't touch him. Oh, it wasn't a perfect game or anything—they scratched out a few hits and even a run. That was something for the guy who did it to tell his grandchildren about when he had them. *I knocked in a run against Carpetbag Booker!*

But it wasn't any kind of contest. By then we'd got seven or eight, I forget which, and the poor Fylfots hadn't a prayer of catching up.

Carpetbag toyed with them. He started clowning. They still couldn't hit him.

The crowd ate it up. "Do the windmill!" some leather-lungs shouted from the seats. And Carpetbag would. He'd send his arm around three or four times before he turned the ball loose. And the hitter would swing and miss. Or else he'd stand there with his eyes wide and take it. The ump would call it a strike, because it was.

When the game was over, half the Fylfots crowded round to get his autograph. He signed and signed, a big old grin on his face. "Mistuh Harv, I had to get stretched out after the train ride west, but I reckon I'm ready," he said.

"I reckon you are," Harv said. "The teams in Denver, though, they'll be tougher than you had it here."

"Some of 'em will." Carpetbag knew how good he was. He didn't brag or boast nearly so much as he might have. He must've known that, if he'd been born white, he would've been even more famous than he was, to say nothing of a lot richer. Knowing that kind of thing would have soured a lot of men. It rolled off his back, the same way the nasty names did.

Nothing stuck to him. I guess that's what I'm trying to say. He was what he was, he knew what he was, and he was happy with what he was. You know what? You could do worse. Plenty of folks have, whatever their color.

When we went back to the boardinghouse in Canon City, the woman who ran it held a sealed CC envelope out to Harv and said, "This came while you were playing the game."

"Did it?" Harv answered with no expression in his voice. I mean, none. He looked a trifle worried while he opened the envelope. Carpetbag Booker seemed less cheerful than usual, too. What kind of finagling did he do to get out of his contract with the Crawdads and sign one with the House of Daniel? Had the Crawdads sicced lawyers on him to make him go back where they said he belonged?

"What's it about?" he asked Harv.

A big, slow smile spread over Harv's face once he read the message. "It's from the guy in Colorado Springs who runs their semipro league," he answered, nothing but relief in his voice. "Wants to know if we can play his All Stars again tomorrow. Says he promises a full house if Carpetbag pitches." He turned to the colored fella. "Don't want to wear you out ahead of the tournament."

"Reckon I can go a few, anyways," Carpetbag said. "Didn't have to work too hard today—no, suh. An' I done a lot o' ballplayin', Mistuh Harv. Soupbone ain't fallen off my shoulder yet."

"You know best," Harv said. "But sing out if you feel tired or sore, you hear? The tournament's more important than a warmup game."

"I will let you know," Harv said solemnly.

"Okey-doke." Harv turned back to the landlady. "Where's the CC office at here? I've got to answer this."

When we got back to Colorado Springs, we found a different roominghouse to lodge at. The old couple who ran this one didn't get shirty about having Carpetbag Booker staying at their place. He did wind up with a room of his own again, though. He seemed happier that way, and Harv wanted to keep him happy.

That old minor leaguer didn't miss a trick. He advertised the game in the town paper. Flyers all over said BALLGAME TODAY! COLORADO SPRINGS ALL STARS VS. HOUSE OF DANIEL AND CARPETBAG BOOKER! SPURGEON FIELD, 2:30 PM! In smaller letters underneath, it said *Admission only one dollar!*

Tickets two days earlier had been fifty cents, what the House of Daniel usually charged. If he could fill the ballpark at twice as much a head . . .

He could, and he did. People cheered when they saw Carpetbag getting loose. He tipped his cap to them, and they cheered louder. "I barnstormed through here—ain't been back for a few years, but I did," he said. Then he paused and thought about it and looked surprised and a little sheepish. "Reckon I barnstormed through just about everywhere. Everywhere they plays baseball, anyways."

The All Stars did better than they had the last time we faced 'em. You could see why the old ex-Millionaire thought they *were* all-stars. But they'd never faced Carpetbag Booker before. From center, I could see he wasn't throwing as hard as he had against the Fylfots the day before. But he didn't need to. When the All Stars weren't out in front on him, they swung late. He had 'em—what's the word?—mesmerized, that's it, like a bird in front of a snake.

Oh, not all of 'em, and not every pitch. One guy singled off him, then hit a two-run homer. Carpetbag tipped his cap to him, too, as the fellow rounded the bases. Baseball's a fair game. Even Carpetbag Booker made mistakes. If you could jump on one, more power to you.

Carpetbag might not have been so polite if we weren't still ahead, 5-2. After six innings, Harv batted for him and brought in Fidgety Frank to finish the game. Frank gave up a run, but we still beat the All Stars again.

Their manager took it like the pro he'd been. "Well, at least we looked like we belonged on the same field with you today," he told Harv.

"Your guys played a fine game." Harv was always willing to be generous, especially after we won.

Players from the All Stars did the same thing the Canon City Fylfots had. They crowded around Carpetbag to get him to sign things. Some people from the crowd came out on the ratty grass to get his autograph and shake his hand, too. They didn't care whether he was black or white or purple with orange stripes. With Carpetbag, what color he was hardly seemed to matter. What mattered was, he was a pitcher. And he was a showman.

Harv glanced over at him and smiled. Then he looked back to the All Stars' manager and smiled another kind of smile. "I really liked the way you plugged the game," he told him. "Admission *only* a dollar, you said, like they were getting a bargain instead of paying through the nose. Wish I would've thought of that, I do."

"Thanks. Much obliged. You're welcome to steal the stunt." The old minor leaguer shifted his cud of tobacco, spat a brown stream, and chuckled. "Like I could stop you from stealing it even if I wanted to."

"I may. I expect I will—long as Carpetbag sticks with us, anyhow," Harv said. "He's signed through the tournament. Afterwards . . . Afterwards'll just have to take care of itself."

"That's how you do it. Worry about one thing at a time." The ex-Millionaire looked toward the All Stars and Carpetbag Booker. "He's a piece of work, ain't he? I saw him up in Denver once. He was playing against a team of mostly big-leaguers, so he couldn't show off so much then. When he knows he's got the edge on you, like he did today—oh, my! He oughta be against the rules."

"I've gone against him a few times," Harv said. "Sure is more fun with him on my side."

"I bet it is!" the Colorado Springs manager said. "Play like you did today and you'll go a long way in the tournament."

"Here's hoping," Harv said. They shook hands. The All Stars' manager went to round up his team. Carpetbag had 'em just as much under his spell now as he had when he was pitching against them. He'd forgotten more baseball than almost anybody else ever learned.

After we showered and changed, we went back to the spaghetti joint where we'd had supper when we were in Colorado Springs two days earlier. The guinea who ran the place, he gave Carpetbag a funny look when he walked in with the rest of us. If he'd gone in there by his lonesome, I bet that guinea would've told him to get lost. But he must've seen we would've walked out with Carpetbag. He didn't feel like losing a whole team's worth of orders, so he kept his mouth shut. It's like that a lot, I reckon. One kind of people may not fancy another kind, but hardly anybody doesn't fancy money.

We filled ourselves up with noodles and meat balls and tomato sauce and flat cheese pies with sausage on 'em and what the guinea called vino. I don't drink a lot of wine—I like beer better. But it went with spaghetti and meat balls just fine.

While we ate, we hashed over the games we'd played and the games we'd be playing once we got to Denver. There'd be sixteen teams in all, and they'd draw who played who out of a hat once everybody got there. Win and you went on; lose and you were done. Win three in a row and you made the finals. That'd be a series, best two out of three. Win it and you were the champions. That's what we were aiming for.

I was sitting near the middle of the table, gabbing with Eddie and Azariah. Harv was at one end, Carpetbag at the other. Carpetbag had Fidgety Frank on his right, Wes on his left. He was going on about the Pittsburgh Crawdads and the Kansas City Regents, the two colored teams that were coming to Denver. He knew the Crawdads like his own team, of course, on account of they had been. But he knew plenty about the Regents, too. He'd played with them and against them, and he knew how to get them out. He knew how to get them out if you could pitch the way he did, anyhow.

Wes and Fidgety Frank told him about the Las Cruces Blue Sox, the only team we'd played lately that was gonna be there. He listened. He nodded. He asked a few questions. He listened some more. He asked more questions. He soaked up baseball the way a sponge soaks up water.

Wes sat beside me on the bus ride back to the new boarding house. He kept shaking his head as though somebody'd clouted him and he was trying to clear it. "The things that son of a gun knows!" he said, more to himself than to me. "Not just how to pitch to those colored teams, but how to pitch. I learned more at that restaurant than I did the past ten years."

"He looked like he knew what he was doing out there, all right," I offered.

Wes kinda glared at me. "You . . . outfielder," he said. "All you know about pitching is that you can't do it." *That you're too dumb to do it* was what it sounded as if he meant. "Pitching's about messing up a hitter's timing. Carpetbag, he's got more ways to do that than Jimmy's got little liver pills."

"Can he teach 'em to you, or can you work out some of your own when you know the kinds of things he does?" I asked.

"Maybe," he said. "Or maybe not. I'm a pretty fair pitcher, but that's all I am—a pretty fair pitcher. Take a pretty fair singer. Let Joel Alson give him lessons. He'll get better, yeah. But he ain't gonna turn into Joel Alson himself. I ain't gonna turn into Carpetbag Booker, neither, not even if they go and paint me black."

That made sense. If you could do it—and if you were white, so you got to do it—you did it and you made your living at it. If you were pretty fair, you played for a team like the House of Daniel. And if you were no darn good, you sat in the stands and second-guessed, the way most folks did.

Carpetbag plainly liked teaching. But Wes was right—all the teaching in the world only helped so much. You had to be able to *do* things, or the lessons were just talk. That gave me something to think on when we got back to the boarding house. It sure did, all right.

Next morning, we set out for Denver.

(XIII)

Denver was the biggest town I'd ever seen in person up till then. It had upwards of a quarter-million people, which put it ahead of Oklahoma City and Tulsa. You think stockyards, you think of Chicago or maybe Kansas City. Denver had 'em, too—big ones. Animals came in. Meat and hides and smells came out.

Till you've gone right by a stockyard, you don't think about the stinks. Those animals stay in the pens for at least a little while, and they do what animals do while they're there. They do what animals do in the stock cars that bring 'em there, too. Those have to get cleaned out before anybody can use 'em again.

Most of the cleaning crews were zombies. If you're already dead, how much do you care about shoveling manure all day? Not much. That was what the hiring bosses figured, anyway. They weren't as right as they thought they were. I was there to find out about that, and I wish I hadn't been.

But I won't get ahead of myself. When we drove past the stockyard, Carpetbag wrinkled up his nose and said, "Per-fume!" Something about the way he said it set us all laughing. He could take an ordinary word and put a little spin on it you'd never notice if you weren't listening. If you were, he'd have you holding your sides. He talked like a colored fella who'd grown up down where colored fellas couldn't get much school, but he was nobody's fool. Not even a little bit.

We didn't have a game that day. It was the first day we hadn't played since that big old rainstorm in Texas. That afternoon, we were supposed to go to the *Denver Post* offices for the draw and then to Merchants Park, where we'd play the games, for photos.

We pulled up in front of the boarding house where we'd be staying for the tournament. While we were getting off the bus, Carpetbag said, "Mistuh Harv, you don't mind, I'd like to go on up Larimer Street to the colored part o' town an' stay there. I gits everywhere I needs to be on time, I promise."

Harv frowned. "You got to understand, Carpetbag, we don't mind you stayin' with us. We truly don't."

"You can say that again," Fidgety Frank put in. "I ain't hardly started picking your brains yet."

"I hears you, an' I believes you, an' I thanks you," Carpetbag said. "But you gots to understand, friends. If I stays here, I'll be livin' in a boarding house. Well, I can do that. But if I goes an' stays amongst my own folks, I be livin' like a king."

We all looked at one another. Carpetbag Booker was such a great pitcher, even white people knew his name and some of his reputation. But I don't reckon we ever stopped to wonder just how famous he was with his own kind. As famous as the Bambino? Maybe. Or maybe a little more famous than that. He sure made it sound as if he was.

Harv coughed once or twice and peered down at his shoes. "You do whatever you think is best, Carpetbag," he said at last. "We've got to be at the *Post* at two o'clock. Then I'll drive us to the ballpark for photos."

"At the *Post* at two o'clock. I be there," Carpetbag said. Then he waved for a taxi. He was the kind of fella who always had one drive by when he needed it. Me, I would've waited a week before one came down that no-account street. Not Carpetbag Booker. He tossed in his luggage and rolled away.

"I hope he shows up," Wes muttered.

"I expect he will," Harv said. "He's here to do a job with us. Till he does it—till we do it—he doesn't get paid. I've never heard that he's got anything against money."

"Me, neither," Wes replied. "But hey, who does?"

Same way as Denver was a bigger city than I was used to, the *Post* was a bigger newspaper. It lived in a big, square building—a fancy one, I'd call it—with a big baseball diamond over the entranceway. You could follow a game from back East on one like that, with the plays coming in by Crystal message or then by radio. Or they could show what was going on in games from their own tournament.

Men in baseball uniforms filled the front hall. We were supposed

to wear them because we'd be taking the pictures at the ballpark afterwards. I saw Carpetbag as soon as I walked in. He'd beat us there.
He was joshing with the other colored players, especially the ones
whose shirts had *Crawdads* across the chest in script and who wore
caps with little red crawdad patches sewn on 'em.

One of the colored guys was short and stocky—built like a catcher,
in other words. After a second, I realized he only looked short 'cause
he stood next to the tall, tall Carpetbag. His shoulders were wide
enough for any two men, maybe two and a half. That had to be Job
Gregson.

The Kansas City Regents had crowns on their chests the way we
had lions. I'd seen the Las Cruces Blue Sox before. A couple of teams
were from Colorado. One had a brewery backing them; the guys on
the other worked for—or made like they worked for—a company that
made rubber half-soles.

If you put two half-soles in a zombie's head, would he turn back
into a human being? Yeah, my mind started wandering. Too many
strangers all at once.

There was a team from Wichita. There were the Rapid City Runners, from South Dakota. The Olympia Timbermen came out of Washington State. The Cheyenne Buffaloes were from Wyoming. The San
Diego Sailors had gold embroidery on the bills of their caps—scrambled
eggs, I heard one of 'em call it. Didn't look like scrambled eggs to me.

The Salt Lake City Industries wore a beehive patch on their sleeves.
I didn't know why then. The Reno Gamblers had a big ace of spades
there. I got that. There was a team from Phoenix, and one from Billings, Montana. They were Buffaloes, too, and kinda looked sidewise
at the Buffaloes from Cheyenne.

And there were the Waco Wildcats. What those Texans looked sidewise at were the Crawdads and the Regents. I knew what they'd be
feeling. I'd felt some of it myself. They were going to have to play
against colored teams? They must've known before they set out for
Denver. The rules and who all was coming weren't any secret. Only
now they were face-to-face with it, you might say.

A plump fellow in a suit and tie whacked a lectern with a pointer
to get us to pay attention. When we finally did, he said, "Hello, everybody. I'm Zeb Huckaby, sports editor of the *Post*. I want the manager

for each team to come forward, if you please. We've got sixteen teams. There will be eight games in the first round. You'll draw to see which game you play in and whether you're home or visiting."

Harv and the rest of the managers pushed up toward him. He had a big board behind him on an easel. Now he whacked the board with the pointer.

"Winner of game one will play the winner of game three. Winner of game two will play the winner of game four. Five will play seven, and six will play eight," he said. "Then the winner of one and three will play the winner of two and four. The winner of five and seven will play the winner of six and eight. And the winners of those games will play best of three for the championship."

His board had eight games on the bottom row, four on the next, two on the next, and then the last series. Lines made it look like a pyramid.

"If the managers will line up so you can choose your envelopes . . ." Zeb Huckaby said. They did. The envelopes were in a fish bowl. The managers came up one at a time.

The Crawdads' boss went first. He was a wiry little gray-mustached fella. He looked as though he'd been a shortstop till he got past forty and still knew how even if his body didn't let him. "Game six, visitin'," he said.

"Game six, visiting—the Pittsburgh Crawdads." Huckaby slid their name into the top slot for game six.

"Game one, visiting," the Las Cruces Blue Sox's manager said.

Harv went up two guys later. "Game one, home," he read. He and the fella who ran the Blue Sox nodded to each other. We'd get a rematch right away, and somebody would go home unhappy. I also figured out we wouldn't have to play the Crawdads till the finals, if we got that far.

But the Regents turned up in our half. And the Waco Wildcats' manager drew . . . "Game six, home." He looked ticked off for all kinds of reasons. He wasn't just playing a tough team to start with, he was playing a tough colored team. If he didn't like it . . . all he had to do was beat the Pittsburgh Crawdads.

When all the matchups for the first round were set, Zeb Huckaby said, "Thanks very much, everybody. Let's go out to the ballpark and take some pictures." So we did that.

Most of the other guys from the House of Daniel had seen Merchants Park before. It was my first look at the place. I'd have some patrolling to do, all right. It was 457 out to dead center. Somebody told me only three people had ever hit the ball over that fence. One was a Denver semipro. One was Job Gregson. And one was the Bambino. That Denver guy, whoever he was, traveled in some pretty fast company.

Left field was long, too. Right was kind of ordinary, which meant it'd play short in the thin air. The infield was all dirt—no grass on it anywhere. I hate skin infields. Most of the time, they were what you got when you had a lazy groundskeeper. But the Denver park had nice grass in the outfield. They just did it that way there.

A whole forest of pillars held up the grandstand roof. Outside, it had said HOME OF THE DENVER BEARS. They'd painted over that when the Western League threw 'em out, but not well enough to keep you from reading it.

Oh—and the park had lights. They were electrics, not salamanders. Still, I was glad I'd played at that park in Madrid, New Mexico. I had some idea what it'd be like. The odd-numbered games, like ours, would be in the afternoons. They'd play the evens at night. But if we won the first one, we might have to go under the lights for the next.

They took our pictures alphabetically by the town the team came out of. Billings, Cheyenne, and then . . . "The House of Daniel, from Cornucopia, Wisconsin," the photographer called. He grinned as we took our places. "Won't confuse you people with anybody else."

"That's on account of I'm so good-lookin'," Carpetbag Booker said. In a different tone of voice, it would've meant he had the biggest swelled head in the world. He *was* good-looking, but that isn't the kind of thing you want to boast about. But the way he said it, in among us long-haired, bearded white men, just set us giggling. The photographer, too.

When we could go, Harv said to him, "If you tell me where you're staying, I'll take you there on the bus."

"That's a kindly thing to say, but you don't got to trouble yourself none," Carpetbag answered. "If'n you don't mind, I'll jus' ride back to the boarding house with y'all. I tol' a friend o' mine to pick me up there when I reckoned all this foofaraw'd be over with."

"However you want," Harv said. "We're glad for your company."

Carpetbag pointed at me. "Even this Southern fella?"

He hadn't paid me a dime's worth of notice since he joined the House of Daniel, except when I caught a fly ball for him or threw a base hit back to the infield. How did he know where I came from? However he did it, he knew. Quick as I could, I said, "Even me. Maybe especially me. You're a whale of a ballplayer."

"I ain't no whale." His voice went high and shrill. He wanted it to carry. "Ol' Job on the Crawdads, now, he big enough to be one."

"Your granny, Carpetbag." Job Gregson slurred his words a little. It was early to start tying one on, but I recognized the signs from my pa. Job pointed at Carpetbag. His finger was bent—he had a catcher's beat-up hands. "Wait till we play each other. We see who goes jokin' after that."

"We sure do." Carpetbag didn't lack for nerve. He was a tall man, but there was more of Job Gregson all told than there was of him: I mean a lot more. Of all the fellas I wouldn't've cared to tangle with, Gregson stood high on the list.

It didn't come to that, though. They razzed each other some more, and then everything died down. Job Gregson wasn't the kind of drunk who had to show everyone within nine miles how right he was. Or maybe he just wasn't drunk enough to do that then.

Harv took us back to the boarding house. No more than a minute or two after we got there, a cherry-red Chevy, brand new, came round the corner. Driving it was about the cutest little high-yaller colored gal anybody ever saw. I got the feeling she might've been driving around the block for a little while by then.

Carpetbag tipped his Panama. "See y'all at the game tomorrow," he said, and hopped in the car. He sat real close to that gal. She was laughing as she whizzed away.

"Hope he ain't too worn out to pitch by tomorrow afternoon." Did Wes sound jealous? Oh, maybe a little.

Harv clicked his tongue between his teeth. "If that wore Carpetbag out too much to pitch, nobody would ever have heard of him," he said. Wes couldn't find any way to quarrel with that, so he didn't.

B y then, I wasn't used to getting into town the day before a game. Without a bus ride, without getting into a new room and running around and all, I hardly knew what to do with myself in the morning. Everything seemed to happen too slow. We lingered over breakfast instead of shoveling it into our faces quick as we could.

We got to Merchants Park with plenty of time to dress and loosen up. A taxi brought Carpetbag Booker a few minutes after the rest of us showed up. He looked happy and relaxed, but what did that prove? From what I could see, he always looked happy and relaxed. Whether he truly was or not, I can't tell you, but he always looked that way.

"They gettin' good money here," he said when he started to throw. "Dollar an' a quarter reserved seats, dollar general admission, sixty cents in the bleachers. An' this is a nice-sized ballyard. I bet you can pack upwards o' ten thousand in it."

Harv studied the sweep of the stands. "I'd say you're right," he answered. They might not have seen every ballpark in the country between them, but I bet they came close.

Some people were already wandering in an hour and a half before game time to watch the teams warm up. Carpetbag put on a show for them—and for the Las Cruces Blue Sox. He kicked his leg extra high. He hesitated here, there, anywhere. He threw over the top, sidearm, submarine, what have you. If he gave the Blue Sox a few things to think about, I don't expect he minded.

Their colored outfielder came over to me. He nodded toward Carpetbag. "You call him Tarbaby, too?" he asked.

"Nope." I shook my head. "He's on my side."

Willard tilted his head a trifle, eyeing me. Then he nodded. "Okey-doke. I'll take that. Between the white lines and outside 'em, they're not the same thing." He smacked me on the hip with his glove, easy-like, and trotted away.

Merchants Park wasn't sold out for the first game of the tourney, but they must've had 8,500, 9,000 people in the place. Harv and Carpetbag agreed on the crowd, and grinned at each other when they did.

Since we were the home team, we took the field first. That felt funny, too—I'd got used to being on the road. I played deep: it was a big outfield. If a dinker fell in front of me, well, fine. But Carpetbag didn't let it faze him. He got the Blue Sox out.

They sent a different pitcher against us, older and stockier than the fella they'd used in Las Cruces. He was careful and smart. He had good control, too, almost as good as Carpetbag's. I haven't said much about that, but it was a big part of what made Carpetbag what he was. He could put a ball where he wanted it like nobody's business.

We got a run. An inning later, the Blue Sox did. We got another one. One of their big left-handed hitters knocked one over the short right-field wall. Carpetbag kicked at the rubber. No, even he wasn't perfect. Close, but not quite.

So it was 2-2 in the bottom of the eighth. I worked a walk to lead it off. Carpetbag bunted me to second. Then Eddie hit a sharp grounder to the third baseman. Only it hit a pebble on that skin infield and kangarooed over his head. I scooted in with the go-ahead run and Eddie had himself a bad-hop double.

Carpetbag set down the Blue Sox one-two-three in the ninth. They were out. We moved to the next round. With a grassy infield, it might've gone the other way. We'll never know now, will we?

Afterwards, we cleaned up, changed into our street clothes, and went to a steakhouse around the corner for some grub. The waiter almost got snotty about serving Carpetbag, but he didn't have the nerve, any more than the dago in Colorado Springs did. Carpetbag, he took it all in stride.

Then we went back to the ballpark to watch the second game. Except for the one where Rabbit and Double-Double smashed together, I couldn't remember the last time I'd watched a game I wasn't playing in. But Harv wanted to scout the other teams. We weren't the only players doing it, either. We even paid a buck and two bits apiece for good seats.

This was the Regents and the Denver Half-Soles. The Denver semipros wore road grays, but the crowd cheered them like there was no tomorrow. Some of the stuff they yelled at the colored players was worse'n anything I'd heard before, and I'm from Oklahoma.

It didn't do them or the Half-Soles any good. The Regents chewed 'em up and swallowed 'em. The colored team pitched better, fielded better, and hit better. They ran 'em ragged on the bases. They stole third. They pulled off a double steal, second and home. The Half-Soles' catcher threw one into center trying to nab a runner. Their poor pitcher tried like anything to hold the Regents' runners close. For his trouble, he had not one but two balks called on him.

When it was all over, it was 11-4. Anyone who watched it knew the Half-Soles didn't belong on the field with Kansas City. But they were from Denver . . . and they were white.

Did *we* belong on the field with Kansas City? We could give them a better game than the Denver team did—I knew that. With Carpetbag pitching, we always had a chance. But I don't think I'd ever seen such a quick team before.

Over the next three days, we went to six more games, three in the morning and three at night. The Crawdads beat the Waco Wildcats even worse than the Regents roughed up the Half-Soles. They did it the same way, too: they ran 'em out of the ballpark. The final was 12-1, and it wasn't that close.

As things wound down there, I asked Carpetbag, "Do all the colored teams steal like that?"

"If you reckon you can get away with it, why not?" he said.

When the Texans saw they'd lose, they started throwing at the Crawdads. The Pittsburgh pitcher threw back. He hit one Wildcat in the ribs and one in the arm when the guy threw it up to protect his face. There were some hard slides, too. They didn't quite out-and-out brawl, maybe for fear they wouldn't get to come back next year if they did. Not a pretty game, though.

We had a night game against the San Diego Sailors. The day game that day was the Regents against the Cheyenne Buffaloes. We all went and watched it. We figured we needed as many looks at Kansas City as we could get.

Cheyenne started a little blond lefty who looked like nothing much till he took the hill. The first colored fella who reached against him got his lead . . . and the little southpaw picked him off. It wasn't even close. He had a demon of a move. Just to prove it, he picked off another guy the next inning. *That* slowed down the Regents' running game. But good, it did.

Those Buffaloes were a big step up from the Denver Half-Soles.

They weren't fast like Kansas City, but they had power and they didn't make mistakes. If you don't beat yourself, the other side has a harder time. Nothing fazed their pitcher, either. They knocked out the Regents, 5-2.

A lot of the Pittsburgh Crawdads sat right in back of the Kansas City dugout. They laughed and yelled and whooped and hollered and carried on to watch the other colored team in the tournament lose to a bunch of cowboys from Wyoming. They thought it was as funny as the Regents would have if Pittsburgh had gone out.

We had sandwiches after the day game. You don't want to fill up too much when you'll be playing soon. The Sailors, remember, were the team with the scrambled eggs on their caps. Those looked silly, but they could play some.

Carpetbag said, " 'Cept fo' when I come out here on the train, don't hardly remember the las' time I don't pitch fo' three days."

"Yeah, but did you get any rest?" Wes asked, deadpan.

Carpetbag sent him a sharp look, then broke up laughing. He knew we'd seen the girl with the red car. "Got me some," he said, and mimed going limp as a dishrag. He was good. If he hadn't been a pitcher, he could have gone on stage.

And he was good when he pitched. Yeah, the Sailors could play some, but they'd never come up against anybody like Carpetbag Booker before. There isn't anybody like Carpetbag Booker. He made one bad pitch that a guy hit in the gap for a run-scoring triple, but we were up 3-0 by then. We won, 4-1.

When we went back to the boarding house that night, a different pretty colored woman in a Buick drove off with Carpetbag. He grinned back at us before he slid in with her. "Ain't it nice to be in demand?" he said.

"He'll pitch day after tomorrow," Harv said, more to himself than to anyone else. "I hope he remembers."

Carpetbag did remember, of course. He knew what he had to do. He knew when he had to do it. And he did it. In between times, he enjoyed himself.

Our game against the Cheyenne Buffaloes was the afternoon semifinal. The night game matched the Crawdads and the Salt Lake City

Industries. We'd play the winner for the title—unless the Buffaloes beat us.

They threw that little blond lefty at us. They called him Whitey. People called Carpetbag Booker a whole bunch of things, but I would have bet nobody ever called him that.

We weren't gonna run much on Whitey. We'd seen what he could do. He picked Harv off first base anyway. Harv went back to the dugout covered in dirt and shaking his head. By the look on his face, he came mighty close to cussing then.

We kept getting guys on and then stranding them. Carpetbag wasn't as sharp as I'd seen him—or else the Buffaloes wouldn't swing at so many pitches that looked like strikes but weren't. They held a 1-0 lead through six.

I tried to bunt leading off the seventh, but it went foul. I did draw their third baseman in a couple of steps, though, and got one past him for a single. Whitey looked over at me. I took off on the first pitch. If he'd come to first, I was hung out to dry. But he went home. I ran. I slid. The tag got me up near the hip.

"Safe!" the base umpire yelled. Their shortstop didn't argue, so I guess I was.

Carpetbag sacrificed me to third. Eddie hit a fly ball, and I scored. We'd tied it, anyhow. In the eighth, Wes hit one down the left-field line that barely got over the wall. The Buffaloes made it hard, but Carpetbag hung on. We beat 'em 2-1.

"This looks way too much like work," Harv said, which was about the size of it.

After supper, we went back to see who'd face us in the finals. The team from Salt Lake put me in mind of the Buffaloes. They weren't glamorous. They just got the job done. Industries was a good name for them.

A team like that stood a chance against the Crawdads. The colored outfit had better players, but they were flightier. If they got down and got rattled, they might give the game away. But they didn't. They scored two in the first, two in the third, and another one in the fourth. After that, they played not to lose. They didn't do that, either. They breezed. The final was 6-2.

"See you day after tomorrow at eight o'clock for the first game of

the final series between the House of Daniel and the Pittsburgh Crawdads!" the announcer boomed through the PA system. "Get your
reserved seats early—we expect to sell out!"

Still in his catcher's gear, Job Gregson pointed at Carpetbag and
shouted, "Gonna take you over the fence!" He thumped his chest protector with a big, knobby-fingered fist.

"Good luck, fool," Carpetbag shouted back. "I'm here to tell you,
you gonna need it."

"We beat you so bad, we put you in the hospital," Gregson yelled.

"Talk is cheap," Carpetbag said.

His onetime catcher pointed at him again. "You oughta know."

If I ever saw Carpetbag Booker mad, it was then. Good thing he
didn't have a baseball handy, or Job Gregson would've been stretched
out in the dirt, a knot—or maybe a hollow—right between his eyes
to show where Carpetbag drilled him.

"That man don't respect me," Carpetbag muttered. "He be sorry
he don't respect me. I *make* him sorry he don't respect me."

"Save it for the game," Harv told him. "Don't use it all up here."

"I be fine, Mistuh Harv," Carpetbag answered. "You don't got to
worry 'bout nothin', on account of I be jus' fine."

Before the first game, Zeb Huckaby told both teams all three games
were sold out. "Better than eleven thousand tickets a game," the
sports editor said happily. "So speaking just for myself, I hope it goes
three. It will add to the pot, and we won't have to give back any
money."

The Crawdads' manager was called Quail Jennings. "All the same
to you, we'd rather end it quicker," he said, his voice as dry as the New
Mexico desert.

"Now that you mention it, so would we." Harv didn't have the
drawl, but that was the only difference in the way they sounded.

We won the coin toss. We'd be the road team in game one and at
home for two and three, if there was a game three. Carpetbag went
up against Lightning Washington. I'd seen him pitch. He threw hard,
all right. He could hit his spots, too. He set us down with no trouble
in the top of the first.

Carpetbag got through the first, too, but he walked two doing it.

He was missing the corners instead of kissing them. His control was off. In the dugout, he complained, "Umpire's pinchin' me, doggone it." But the ump wasn't, or it didn't look that way from center field. Carpetbag hadn't found his good stuff.

Other thing was, the Crawdads knew him. If it wasn't a strike, they laid off. He kept walking people. Then he *had* to come in. Job Gregson clouted one into the gap in left-center with two men on. I ran as hard as I could, but it shot by me and rolled all the way to that faraway wall. Job ran like the catcher he was, but he got a standup triple. A second later, the next guy singled him home and we were down three.

We ended up losing 5-1. It was about as dismal as it sounds. After our last out, the Crawdads shook hands with one another and patted one another on the back as they walked off the field. They figured they had the prize and the trophy and the glory. In their cleats, I would have, too.

"I'm sorry, Mistuh Harv," Carpetbag said softly. "I done let you down."

"There'll be another game tomorrow—and one more the day after that." Harv wasn't happy, but he hadn't given up. He went on, " 'And these three men, Shadrach, Meshach, and Abednego, fell down bound into the midst of the burning fiery furnace.' But after a bit, Nebuchadnezzar said, 'Lo, I see four men loose, walking in the midst of the fire, and they have no hurt, and the form of the fourth is like the Son of God.' If God's with us, we can't lose."

"You is a believin' man, Mistuh Harv." Respect filled Carpetbag's voice. "God weren't with me today—God and that umpire, neither."

"We'll get 'em tomorrow, then," Harv said.

But when tomorrow came, he put the ball in Fidgety Frank's hand. "I can go, suh," Carpetbag said.

"I know you can. If I need you, I'll bring you in," Harv answered, salving his pride. "Let's see what they do against somebody they haven't met so often, though."

Carpetbag nodded, but you could tell how much he wanted to be out there. "You the manager," he said. No, he didn't think Harv was doing the right thing.

Harv saw it, too. "Look, if this doesn't work out, you can say, 'I told you so, you stupid jerk.' I'll sit still for it. I'll have earned it."

"Well, that's fair," Carpetbag allowed. "We win today, you run me out there tomorrow?"

"You bet I will!"

"Let's win, then."

Something funny happened when we headed for the bus for the second game. A tall guy was walking down the street—almost dancing down the street—juggling three oranges and whistling. He was having himself a great time. If he wasn't a pro dancer, he should've been. He was good.

Just for the heck of it, I tossed him a baseball. He didn't miss a beat. It went right into the stream. Three or four steps later, it came back out—straight to me. We all clapped for him. He grinned and tipped his hat, also without dropping an orange, and kept on going.

"Maybe he'll bring us luck," Harv said.

I hoped he would. We needed it. And I hoped Fidgety Frank wouldn't be off because he hadn't pitched for so long. I really hoped he wouldn't worry that he—a semipro pitcher—was out there in place of somebody who'd be pulling down a fat salary in the big leagues if only he were pinker.

Fidgety Frank got through the first mostly with fastballs. The Crawdads started a left-hander who went by Two Lemons Ellis. When I asked Carpetbag how come, he started giggling and wouldn't tell me. Two Lemons threw slow, slower, and slowest. He couldn't blow it by you, but he could drive you nuts.

It was one of those games where you knew somebody would catch a break sooner or later, but you didn't know who. I stopped the Crawdads from getting theirs by running down a long drive in center with two out and two on. It would've gone out of some parks. In Denver, as long as I could get to it, it wasn't a tough catch.

"Yeah, Snake!" Fidgety Frank said when I came in.

Two innings later, we loaded the bases with two out. Harv hit one right up the middle: between Two Lemons's legs, past the Crawdads' diving shortstop, past their diving second baseman, and into center. A seeing-eye single, good for two runs. Wes singled in another one, and we had ourselves a lead. Out on the mound, Two Lemons cussed like a muleskinner.

All that rest must've helped Fidgety Frank, not hurt him. He threw a four-hit shutout, and we won by those three runs. Everything was on the line the next day.

Carpetbag was gracious. He mostly was. "Well, Mistuh Harv, you tol' me so," he said. Then he turned to Fidgety Frank. "You kin do that to my ol' team, why ain't you a fo'-true pro?"

"I like what I'm doing here." Fidgety Frank must've known he couldn't pitch like that all the time. But he'd done it once, when it counted most. If he was proud of himself, he'd earned the right.

Carpetbag nodded seriously. "That's impo'tant," he said. "Now I got to pitch me a better game yet. Can't let the Crawdads say some white boy showed me up."

"I'm no boy." Fidgety Frank had a few gray hairs in his whiskers. Carpetbag just grinned a sly grin. I still had no idea how old he was. I wondered if anyone but his mother did.

I had a thought before the last game. Remembering Amarillo, I asked Carpetbag, "Reckon the Crawdads have a conjure man helping 'em along?"

"They don't do that much," he said. "An' no conjure ain't never caught up with me yet. I ain't lookin' back to see if one's gainin', but I ain't hidin' under the bed, neither." I had to be satisfied with that. I guess I was.

The Crawdads ran Lightning Washington out there again. So it was a rematch of the first game. Only it wasn't. This time, Carpetbag Booker had his good stuff and Lightning didn't. We had a different plate umpire, too, and Carpetbag got the calls on the corners. Give him good stuff and that ump, and all we had to do was get some runs and try not to throw the game away.

We scored two in the third. One was mine. I'd bunted my way aboard—the Crawdads weren't the only ones who could use the speed game. Carpetbag got into hot water in the top of the fourth. One guy singled, and another walked. With two out, Job Gregson hit a screaming liner, but right at me. I didn't have to move more than a step and a half. You could hear the *thock!* when the ball smacked my glove all over Merchants Park.

That was the only hot water Carpetbag saw. He was as good as he'd promised he would be. We took this game 3-0, too, and he gave up that hit in the fourth and only one more. Eddie caught a popup for the last out, and we'd won ourselves the *Denver Post* Tournament.

The roar there was 11,000 people cheering their heads off. We all doffed our caps to them, and they cheered louder. I'd never played in front of such big crowds till Denver. Plenty of big-league games don't have nearly so many people in the stands. When you stop and think about it, that's pretty amazing.

Zeb Huckaby came out and made a speech about how wonderful the tournament was. Well, what would you expect him to say? Then he gave the Pittsburgh Crawdads the runner-up trophy and a check. The crowd applauded them no matter what color they were. That was good. They played some fine ball. They were better than we were, I guess, but they couldn't solve Carpetbag Booker when it mattered most.

Then it was our turn. We got photographed. We got a bigger trophy. I don't know how much the Crawdads made, but I expect we got a bigger check, too. It came to about $150 a man. Not a lot for so many games, but some glory came along with the money. Now if only you could buy stuff with glory.

Almost everybody stayed in the stands to give us one more hand. I felt eight feet tall and solid as Job Gregson. He did shake Carpetbag's hand after the game. That was good, too.

As the clapping died down, we heard a different kind of noise from the direction of the stockyards. It was coming our way, and getting louder. I didn't know what it was, but it sounded scary. And that's how we—and Denver—got caught up in the Great Zombie Riots of 1934.

(XIV)

There in Merchants Park, you understand, we had no idea it was the zombie riots yet. We just knew we were hearing a whole bunch of people who sounded scared and angry at the same time. Then, through the middle of all that, a bunch of sharp *pop*s came through loud and clear.

"Those are guns going off," I said to Eddie.

"You sure?" he asked.

"I'm positive," I answered. Once you know what gunfire sounds like, you won't mistake it for anything else. Not even fireworks come close.

"You're right," Carpetbag Booker said. I wasn't surprised he'd heard gunshots, too. "What's goin' on?"

"Nothing good—can't be," I said. Well, I was right. I didn't know how right I was, but I'd find out.

A cop with his cap all askew on his head ran into the ballpark and handed Zeb Huckaby a sheet of paper. Then he ran right back out. He pulled his pistol from his holster as he hustled away.

"May I have your attention, please? Ladies and gentlemen, may I have your attention, please?" Huckaby said into his microphone. "The police have asked me to request that you leave Merchants Park quickly and in an orderly way. Be careful when you get outside. They have warned me that there are, ah, disturbances out there."

Naturally, that set off more hubbub than it stopped. But it might've been all right if the lights hadn't picked that exact minute to go out. I don't just mean the lights in the ballpark. I mean the lights all over town. All at once, without the slightest warning, Denver went black as the inside of a crocodile. The screams we were hearing got louder and shriller. The gunfire didn't let up, even a little.

Some of the ushers, bless 'em, had wills-o'-the-wisp they used to guide people to their seats. In a night game, it got dark under the grandstand roof—the lights were for the field. But it didn't get so dark then as it had now. Those little flickering lights were godsends.

"Will an usher please come to the field to guide the players away?" the *Post*'s sports editor shouted. The microphone was dead, of course. But either an usher heard him anyway or the fella had the notion on his own. In that sudden midnight, even a will-o'-the-wisp seemed wonderful.

"Come on, you guys," the usher said. "This way—and hustle, if you want to get away with a whole skin."

"What's going on, anyway?" Half a dozen people must have asked him the same thing at the same time. I oughta know—I was one of 'em. We didn't all use the same words, but it was the same question no matter who asked it, or how.

As we went down into a dugout, he said, "Maybe you should grab bats. I don't know if it'll help, but it won't hurt. What I hear is, all the zombies in town, and especially the ones from the stockyards, they've gone squirrelly. Wild. Outta control. Whatever you wanna call it. They're killing anybody alive they can get their mitts on."

I happened to be right by the bat rack. I grabbed me a Louisville Slugger. You bet I did. It was heavier than the one I hit with—probably belonged to Harv or Wes. Even while I grabbed it, I wondered how much good it could do. Zombies are already dead. If you hit one with a baseball bat . . . Well, so what?

I grabbed it, anyhow. Like the usher said, it couldn't hurt. So did the other players, from the House of Daniel and from the Pittsburgh Crawdads. You felt better with something like that in your hand. It was made for hitting things. And it sounded as though *things* were running loose. No—running wild.

Somewhere not far enough away, a machine gun started banging away. I'd never heard one before, but I knew what it was. It couldn't very well've been anything else.

"Do Jesus!" one of the Crawdads said. "That ain't gonna settle no zombies. They's already too dead to care if they gits shot." It was the same thought I'd had when I was taking hold of the baseball bat. If machine guns wouldn't stop zombies . . . In that case, we were all in a lot of trouble.

They wouldn't. And we were.

The will-o'-the-wisp gave us just enough light to see by as the usher led us down the tunnel and through our dressing room. Somebody—I think it was Carpetbag Booker, but it could have been one of the other colored fellas—said, "How'd them zombies go wild like that? They ain't supposed to be able to do nothin' but what their massas tells 'em, and not all that much even then."

"What somebody told me was, vampires been whispering poison in their ears," the usher said. "They want to see that red flag flyin' here like it does in Russia."

It made some kind of sense, anyhow. Vampires weren't dead like zombies, or weren't as dead as zombies, but they weren't exactly alive, either. If anybody or anything could get through to a zombie, a vampire could, or might be able to. That was how it looked to me, anyway.

Most of the time, zombies didn't want anything. Not to want anything any more was the whole point to becoming a zombie in the first place. Vampires, though . . . Vampires wanted blood. Everybody knew that. And if they could somehow get zombies to spill blood in rivers, we might have a mess something like the kind of mess Denver had right now.

When we got out of the clubhouse and out of the ballpark, the noise was a lot louder, a lot scareder, and a lot scarier. And it wasn't pitch-dark out there now. Here and there in the distance, fires were burning—I mean burning out of control. It wasn't enough light to navigate by, but it was there, and it kept on getting brighter. I smelled smoke, too.

Our bus sat only a few steps from the door we'd come out of. Harv said, "You Crawdads, you can pile in there along with us. It'll be jammed, yeah, but you'll have some iron between you and whtever's going on out here."

"Thank you, suh. We is much obliged to you," Quail Jennings said. And both teams got on. We had three on a seat, not two. We had guys standing in the aisle. We didn't have any oil on us, the way sardines do in their tin. But we all made it aboard.

Harv started up the engine and turned on the headlamps. By then, my eyes had got used to the dark. The beams stabbed out like spears. The bus grunted and groaned more than usual because it was carrying so much extra weight, but it went when Harv put it in gear. Slow and careful, he pulled out onto Broadway.

He needed to be slow and careful, on account of people leaving Merchants Park were going across the big wide street as quick as they could. Other cars coming by almost knocked them over. Everybody in the cars was honking his horn as hard as he could.

Harv drove north past a big Montgomery Ward's store next to the ballpark. That was the direction of our boarding house, and of the flea-bag hotel in the colored part of town where the Crawdads were staying. We were trying to make headway against the tide, though. That was also the direction the riots were spreading from.

People came driving down Broadway like maniacs. They were coming south on both sides of the street. It made going north, well, interesting. Exciting, too. Harv learned on his horn. My thought was that, if folks coming the other way couldn't see our big old bus, they weren't likely to hear it, either. I just thought it, though. I didn't say anything. I might've been wrong. Even if I was right, honking wouldn't hurt anything.

People came running down Broadway, too, on the sidewalk and in the middle of the street. Some of them were bleeding. Some had their clothes torn off. We saw all this in bits and pieces, as they got in the way of somebody's headlamps or as they ran past some house or shop that was on fire.

"I hope the ballpark doesn't burn down," Eddie said. "It's all wood—the stands, the fences, everything."

He was jammed onto the seat behind the one where I was practically sitting on a Crawdad's lap—or maybe the colored guy was practically sitting on mine. "Thanks a lot," I told him. "Now I've got something else to worry about."

Up ahead of us, a fire engine raced around a corner. It had its headlights on and its red light going, and its siren wailed like a lost soul. The guy in the Model A trying to get away from the zombies broadsided it even so. He was going way too fast to stop. I don't think he even had a chance to hit the brakes.

It was an awful crash. Pieces of metal and glass flew off the Ford and the fire engine and smashed and cut people on the street. Another car ran over one of the Model A's wheels. It went out of control, bounced up onto the sidewalk, and slammed into a telephone pole. Three or four people flew out of the car. They lay there thrashing. They might even have been lucky, because the car started burning like nobody's business.

Some of the firemen got knocked off their engine, too, when the Model A hit it. Harv pulled the bus over to the curb and stopped. "Come on," he said. "We have to help those people. It's the only Christian thing to do."

Right then, I wouldn't have been too disappointed if he hadn't been such a good Christian. But when the bus's door wheezed open, I jumped out with everybody else. I wasn't brave enough to stay behind when other people didn't. The bat in my hand felt as though it would do as much good as a fly swatter against a boa constrictor.

We were trotting toward the wrecks—and trying not to get run over ourselves—when I saw my first for-sure rioting zombie. He—no, she—wore shapeless, colorless coveralls, the cheapest kind of stuff you could still call clothes. She wasn't moving slow and stupid, the way zombies are supposed to do. Oh, no. Oh, Lord, no! She sprang on one of the people thrown from that car that hit the pole and started tearing and biting at him. He'd been groaning. Now he shrieked.

"C'mon!" Harv yelled, and ran toward her, waving his baseball bat. "Like I said before, remember the fourth man in the fiery furnace."

He had faith. Me, all I had was not wanting to look yellow to the guys on my team and to the Crawdads. That was enough to make me follow him. Go ahead, call me a fool. I sure was calling myself one.

The zombie looked up from what she was doing. Her face was all bloody from the nose down, but I knew that wasn't her blood. I don't think zombies have any or use any or however you want to put it. The fire from the burning car blazed out of her eyes. I know people's eyes don't shine like that. She wasn't a person. She was a zombie.

She yowled. I'd never heard a zombie make a noise before. I hoped I never would again, but I wasn't so lucky as that. Then she charged us.

Harv swung on her first. If he'd hit a baseball with that swing, he would've bombed it out of the park. He rearranged her face pretty good and knocked her back on her heels. But that's all he did. How could he kill her? She was already dead. She didn't care if she got uglier than

she was before. She just cared about ripping him—ripping all of us—
to pieces.

We all waded in. Some of us got scratched and cut a bit, but she
couldn't bite the way she had before thanks to Harv's home-run swing.
We kept at it, swinging from the heels. A zombie with face and arms
and legs all broken up may still want to kill you, but it can't move
any more to do what it wants.

Then Carpetbag pulled a book of matches out of his hip pocket. The
zombie knew what they were. She yowled some more with that ruined
mouth. Carpetbag struck a match and touched it to her.

She burned. She burned like you wouldn't think flesh and bone
could burn, so we all had to hop back to keep from catching fire ourselves. I suppose zombies aren't exactly flesh and bone any more.
Whatever they are, they're fire's friends.

"Now we know how to kill 'em—well, to end 'em," I said.

Carpetbag Booker whistled between his teeth: a low, flat note. "My
mama learned me that zombies'd burn when I was jus' a chile," he
said, wonder in his voice. "I ain't thought about that for years an'
years, but I ain't never forgot it, neither."

"Good," Wes said. "Good if we can make 'em hold still to get lit
up, anyhow."

"We'll worry about that later," Harv broke in. "We got out to help
these folks, remember?"

Well, we did what we could. Harv and Wes knew as much about first
aid as any ballplayer is likely to. They were the ones who tended sprains
and sore arms and the like. They could bandage cuts and even splint
up a fireman's busted ankle and a woman's broken arm. They couldn't
do anything for the poor son of a gun who was gunning the Model A
when it rammed the fire engine. He'd gone straight through the windshield and busted his neck on the engine's red-painted iron side.

Some of the Crawdads gave them a hand. The rest of us stood guard
with our bats. If the zombies came at us one at a time, we could mob
them and end them before they hurt us bad. And we did end a couple
like that.

But then a whole wave of people—live people, human people—rolled
down on us. "Run for your lives, you dummies!" a man shouted as he
ran. "They're right behind us!"

And they were. I don't know how many zombies there were. Probably not so many as I imagined I was seeing then. The only thing I'm sure of is, there were too many of 'em for us to deal with 'em the way we had been. And if we couldn't deal with 'em like that, they were gonna deal with us instead.

"Harv!" Fidgety Frank called. "Harv, we've got to get out of here right this minute. If we don't, we're gonna end up zombie food."

"Can't leave these folks here, or else they will," Harv answered.

"Put 'em on the bus, then," Frank said. "We'll do it some kind of way. We—" He broke off then, because two more zombies were coming at us. Job Gregson broke the leg on one of them, so it could only crawl. Carpetbag lit it up. Half a dozen of us smashed the other one down before it could do us much harm. But more and more of the horrible things were running toward us.

Some kind of way is about how we did it. I'd thought we were crowded before, with Crawdads and us on the bus. It was way worse now. If any zombies had got on, we couldn't've fought 'em off, on account of we couldn't have raised our arms to swing a bat.

Harv made a U-turn on Broadway. He saw he couldn't keep going north. Whatever happened at our boarding house was gonna happen without us. Same with the Crawdads' hotel. We'd sort all that stuff out later, if we stayed alive long enough to do it.

We did make better headway going south. Now we were in the flow, not trying to buck it. Harv blared away with the horn, clearing people on foot out of the bus's path. Sometimes they'd move aside in a hurry. Sometimes they wouldn't, and he'd come about *that* close to running them down.

And then he let out a whoop. I was standing close enough to the front to let me sorta see out the windshield. Those two shapes ahead of us weren't people. They weren't live people, I mean. They were zombies, out to turn live people into dead ones.

"Prepare to ram!" Harv sang out. He might have been at the wheel of a battle cruiser, not a semipro ballclub's bus. I just had time to grab the seat next to me before he hit those zombies. They went flying. I don't suppose he killed them or ended them or whatever you want to call it. They didn't catch on fire or anything. But they got pretty well smashed up. No matter how much they might want to go on killing live people after that, they weren't going to be able to go anywhere to do it.

After a mile or so, he turned off of Broadway. I saw why a second later—there was a hospital down the side street he turned on to. Lanterns and flashlights and wills-o'-the-wisp lit it after a fashion. Outside the building stood cops and ordinary folks. Some had pistols, some carried rifles, and one guy cradled a Tommy gun. They wouldn't kill zombies the way they would with ordinary people. Break arms or legs and you'd do some good, though.

Out the window, Harv called to them: "We got hurt people we need to drop off!"

I wonder how close he came to getting shot. A long-haired, bearded fella in a baseball suit—Lord, he was still wearing his cap—driving a bus with some brand new dents in the front end? They might've figured him for a zombie . . . or they might have started banging away without any figuring at all. Easy to be jumpy right then, mighty easy.

But they held fire. A burly cop with a sergeant's stripes on his sleeve came up. He looked us over, a revolver in his hand. Then he said, "You guys were in the *Post* tournament. I seen you play once."

"That's right," Harv said. "Can you let us get to the entranceway to unload these poor folks?"

"Yeah, come ahead." The cop turned around and shouted to his friends. Then he told Harv, "Once you do, keep heading south. Put some distance between you and this—this craziness."

"I'll do it." Harv drove up to the hospital entrance. He took everything slow and easy, so he didn't look dangerous. With so many frightened men with guns around, that seemed like a real good idea.

A nurse and a couple of doctors in white coats came out to give us a hand with the firemen and the people from that car that hit the pole. One of the docs had a cigarette in the corner of his mouth. I'm not sure he remembered it was there; it was almost singeing his lips. His eyes looked a million miles away, as though he'd seen too many horrors all at once. Well, on that black night I guess he had.

"Operating by candlelight," he said to nobody in particular. He sounded as dazed as he looked. "The lights went out, and we fell back a hundred years. If we get a generator, or a wizard who can call light . . ."

I don't know if they ever did or not. We shifted around on the bus now that it wasn't quite so jam-packed. Harv pulled away from the hospital. We headed south, the way the cop told us to. Like everybody else, we were trying to get away.

We drove down US 85 to Castle Rock, thirty miles south of Denver. That took us most of the night. I have never seen a road so jammed as that one, not in all my born days. I guess we went faster than the zombies did, because none of them broke into the bus and tore us to pieces. But I don't know why they didn't. All of Denver was trying to get away down a highway that wasn't wide enough for half of it.

Folks used both sides of the road to go south. That helped some, but less than you'd think. For quite a while, till they blocked northbound traffic farther south still, people who didn't know about the zombie riots were still happily coming north, bound for Denver. They were happy till they ran into our southbound wave, anyhow.

Some of them ran into some of us for real. Harv drove past some nasty head-on smashups that blocked half the road and made traffic even worse than it was without 'em. If one of those wrecks had blocked the whole highway . . . Well, in that case you'd likely be looking at some other yarn right about now.

It was getting light, and we were just about to Castle Rock, when he pulled off the road and onto the shoulder. Off to the side was a field, or maybe you'd call it a weedy meadow. "I think we've come far enough," Harv said. "We can maybe grab a little shuteye here and try to decide what to do next. House of Daniel is supposed to play in Greeley today, and if I can work out how to get there from here—"

"And if the zombies aren't tearing Greeley to pieces," Wes broke in.

"Yeah, that, too," Harv agreed. "If we can get there, and if the town's still all in one piece, we'll have ourselves a game."

"We got train tickets from Denver back to Pittsburgh tomorrow mornin'," Quail Jennings said. "Don't look like we'll be able to use 'em. Have to talk to the railroad, see how much extra they gonna charge us to change things."

"They shouldn't charge you a dime," Harv said. "Not your fault you aren't there. Not your fault the trains outta Denver aren't on time, either."

"You right, suh," the Crawdads' manager answered. "You right, but they ain't gonna care. Any time they think they kin screw some extra money out of somebody, they gonna do it."

Anybody who's ever had to rearrange a train ticket knows about that. It's not about whether the railroad'll screw you. It's only about how hard. That kind of thing runs all through too many different kinds of business. Maybe it's not such a wonder the zombies rose up. Maybe it's a wonder the people didn't rise up with 'em.

Vampires suck the blood out of people in Russia, they say. Over here, the railroads and other outfits like 'em do the job instead. That could be why the vampires got the zombies boiling, if that's what they did. They were jealous. They wanted the chance for themselves.

I wasn't worrying about that when I got out of the bus. I was worrying about whether the zombies had gone crazy everywhere at once, not just in Denver. And I was worrying about my stuff, back at that boarding house we couldn't get to. But the devil with stuff. Long as I was alive and able to play ball, I'd bring in a little cash, and sooner or later I'd buy more stuff.

We had a few blankets and things in the bus. Some guys lay on those. Some just flopped in the weeds. And some stood guard over the rest, in case the zombies came that far after all.

I was one of the guard-standers. I felt tired, yeah, but way too keyed-up to sleep. As the sky got brighter, you could see the smoke coming up from the north. Some of that smoke might've been from my burning stuff, or from Merchants Park. I couldn't do anything about it any which way. In my baseball uniform, with my bat at the ready like a gun, I could imagine I was a soldier on sentry-go.

Or I could till some real soldiers in khaki and some cops in dark blue marched past us, heading north. Two or three of the soldiers had metal tanks on their backs and things like hoses in their hands instead of Springfields. "What are them contraptions?" asked a Crawdad who was standing watch with us.

I had a notion, but I wasn't sure enough to say. Wes was: "Those are flamethrowers. When I was a green kid, I was in on the very end of the War to End War. Believe me, if anything'll settle a zombie's hash for good, it's one of those babies."

My punchy thought was *No, it'll turn 'em into hash, and overdone hash at that.* I didn't come out with it. You get really tired, it's like getting drunk. All kinds of stupid stuff bubbles up inside your head. If you're even halfway smart, you leave it in there and don't show it off.

We did a couple of hours watching. Then Wes woke up some of the guys who were sleeping so we could get some rest. I didn't know if I'd get any rest when I stretched out on the ground, but next thing I knew my face was on top of a weed and somebody was waking me up. It was Azariah.

"We're gonna get rolling," he said. "Harv wants to go down to Castle Rock and then head east on this road that runs that way."

"Okey-doke." I yawned. My stomach growled. "Maybe we can find something to eat, too."

"Maybe so," Azariah said. "C'mon."

Traffic had thinned out some when the bus got back onto US 85 again. We made it into Castle Rock in about forty-five minutes. Castle Rock was a tiny town. All the folks coming down from Denver just swamped it. Not enough food, not enough places to stay, not enough anything.

The Pittsburgh Crawdads got off there, anyway. Quail Jennings gravely shook Harv's hand. "I don't thank you for beatin' us, but I thank you for your kindness afterwards," he said. "They got phones here, an' a train station, an' a CC office. We kin get back east from here. May take a while, but we kin."

"You sure?" Harv said.

"I am," Jennings answered. "Had plenty o' time to think it through. Take a while, cost some money, but we'll make it back where we belong." His players nodded.

"Good luck to you, then," Harv said, and they shook hands again.

Carpetbag Booker got off, too. "You only sign me through the tournament, Mistuh Harv," he said. "You know that."

"I do know that." Harv nodded. "But I was hoping you'd stick with us longer once you saw the kind of ball we played."

"It ain't the kind of ball, suh." Carpetbag sounded a little embarrassed, but he plowed on anyway: "Easier bein' with my own kind— easier on everybody. Don't git me wrong. You been fair with me. I ain't never gonna say nothin' else. Still an' all, though . . . I gonna head

East, too, only I don't aim to go's far's them Crawdads. Gonna pitch fo' the Kansas City Regents fo' a spell."

"Well, I wish you luck, too," Harv said. Since Carpetbag wasn't under contract, what could he do but make the best of it? "Maybe you'll play for us again, or maybe we'll take our licks against you on the road."

"Could be. You travel all the time, an' there ain't hardly no good colored team that don't," Carpetbag said. "I would be pleased to go with y'all for a while some other time, an' that's a fact. Good luck to you, too. We licked the Crawdads. We licked 'em right out o' their spikes." He said that loud, so his old Pittsburgh team could hear.

I wondered if they'd jump him when he hopped down from the bus, but they didn't. Away he went, head up, stride bouncing, never looking back. All by himself, he was bigger than any team he played for. Maybe he wouldn't be if they ever let whites and coloreds play against each other in the bigs, but maybe he still would, too. He was one of a kind, Carpetbag Booker. I'm gladder than I know how to tell you I got the chance to play with him, even if it was only for a few games. Yeah, I'm from Oklahoma. I'm still glad. You don't like it, lump it.

From Denver to Greeley, if you go from one to the other the straight way, is around sixty-five miles. From Castle Rock, if you don't pass through Denver to get there, you have to drive around the other three sides of a big rectangle: east, north, and then back west again. The long way around? You bet.

Harv didn't care. Most of the refugees from Denver kept going south, along the eastern edge of the Rockies. When we headed east instead, we could make halfway decent time. And we were getting farther from Denver with every mile we drove, just the same as they were.

Colorado is a funny state. The western part is mountains. The eastern chunk, though, it's all prairie. Once you get a little ways away from the Rockies, you could've figured you were back in Kansas. Wheatfields and cows, that's what it was. A little cool and a little dry to be Oklahoma, but it wasn't all that different from the part of the country I came from.

We got stopped by two roadblocks before we got to Limon. That was where we'd start the northbound leg of our rectangle. The first block was cops. They looked over the bus to make sure we weren't hauling any zombies or vampires. When they didn't find any, or any coffins, they waved us on.

Eddie tried a laugh, but it sounded shaky. "Remember that bull session in New Mexico?" he said to me. "Ain't gonna see vampire outfielders flying after fly balls in night games any time soon."

"Well, that's what they get for firing up the zombies," I answered. We didn't know for sure that was what had happened. But we'd heard it, and it seemed to make sense, so we believed it.

The second roadblock was about ten miles farther east than the first. It wasn't the police. It was farmers and herders. The roadblock was hay bales and a tractor. The men carried hunting rifles or shotguns. A couple of them just had pitchforks. What good a pitchfork would do against a zombie, I can't tell you. Maybe they made the fellas toting 'em feel better, anyway.

Those cops had been men doing a job. The farmers were scared out of their wits. They made us all pile out of the bus. Then they searched it like you wouldn't believe. If we'd given them the least bit of backtalk, they would've shot us. They might have been sorry about it afterwards, but that wouldn't have done us any good.

"Them things, they're out there, and they're comin' to get us!" one of them said. He wasn't wrong, exactly, but he wasn't exactly right, either. Didn't seem to me there were enough people out here to draw cither rampaging zombies or hungry, twisted bloodsuckers, but what did I know?

I'll tell you what I knew. I knew I had a beard and longish hair in country where the menfolk didn't wear 'em. That was plenty to keep me quiet. If a couple of them hadn't heard of the House of Daniel, maybe even been to a game or two, we might've had a tougher time than we did.

Wes bought gas in Limon before we turned north. "Been a lot of people comin' through here. I'm almost out of fuel," said the fellow who ran the station. "Heard me a pile of crazy stories. Any o' that stuff true, or do the city folks have the vapors again?"

"Some of it's true," Harv said as he paid him. "I'm glad you've still got the gasoline." Limon was lucky to have one gas station. If it had run dry, where would we have got more? I had no idea. By the way Harv sounded, neither did he.

North of Limon, we came to another roadblock. This was more farmers, not cops. They didn't seem sure whether to block cars going into Limon or the ones coming out. To them, Limon was a big city, almost like Denver. It was a place bad things could come from, even if they weren't too clear on what kind of bad things those were.

"Gotta keep the devils away!" a farmer said. "I put some silver shot in with my double-aught buck."

I'm sure silver shot won't do anything special to a zombie. I'm almost sure it won't do anything special to a vampire, either. But, while I'm plenty dumb for all ordinary use, I'm not dumb enough to argue with a spooked farmer not quite aiming a double-barreled shotgun at my belly button.

We eventually got past those guys, too, and rolled north till the little road we were on joined up with US 34 just east of a town called Brush. They had a sugar-beet processing plant there. Some of the people doing the hard, brainless work at the plant, work nobody would want to do under the hot sun, weren't people. They were zombies. Whatever had gone wrong in Denver hadn't here. Not yet, anyhow.

One more roadblock, this one outside of Greeley. Cops manned it. We didn't have any trouble getting by. The cops knew we were ball-players. Some of them had gone down to Denver for tournament games.

One guy even knew we were supposed to play the Greeley Grays. "Didn't expect you'd be coming from this direction, though," he said.

"Yeah, well, we kinda had to take the long way around," Harv answered.

"I guess you did!" the cop said. "I heard you whipped the coons in Denver before things there went up the spout. Give the greasers here a dose of the same medicine, all right?"

Like me and the guy with the silver shot, Harv didn't say anything. He didn't care much about who was colored and who was Mexican. He cared a lot less than I did; I know that. All he cared about was who could play baseball, and how well. I would've liked to see the cop's face if Harv told him the guy on the hill when we won the championship was Carpetbag Booker. But Harv could see keeping his mouth shut was the best scheme, so he did.

Me, I hadn't even known the Greeley Grays were a Mexican team. They turned out not to be all-Mexican—just mostly. We saw in Brush they grew lots of sugar beets in those parts, and they brought in Mexicans from southern Colorado and Texas and New Mexico to work the fields. From Old Mexico, too. The ones who hadn't known about baseball before picked it up in a hurry.

A game against a town team on a shabby field in the middle of a city park . . . Quite a comedown from facing the Pittsburgh Crawdads in front of a crowd that wouldn't have shamed two big-league clubs. Harv had to know he'd barely make expenses here at best. But he'd signed up to play, so we'd play.

They had a decent crowd for a semipro game, but that's all they had. The Grays played like a town team. That afternoon, playing like a town team was plenty to beat us. They did, easy. We played like a bunch of zombies, and I don't mean angry ones. We weren't dead, but we were dead tired. We were slow. We were stupid. We gave it our best shot, and our best shot wasn't good enough.

The crowd cheered in Spanish and English. "Next year, you guys go to the tournament!" somebody called to the Grays. I hoped there was a tournament in 1935. I hoped Merchants Park was still standing, not up in smoke. I hoped the same for the *Denver Post* building.

And I hoped Harv knew what he was doing and where he was going next. Wherever it was, I was going there, too.

(XV)

Harv talked things over with the Colorado Highway Patrol in Greeley after the game. They weren't letting any traffic go through Denver, not till they either ended all the zombies there or got 'em back under control somehow. "Well, on the map it looks like there's another way to get to Grand Junction," Harv said. "If we go through the Rocky Mountain National Park—"

"Maybe Milner Pass is open, but maybe it isn't," the Highway Patrolman broke in. "It's almost eleven thousand feet. You can get blizzards any time of year there. I don't recommend it. And that road isn't easy for cars. If you're gonna try and take your big, clumsy bus through there, you've got to be out of your mind."

"But what am I supposed to tell the folks in Grand Junction?" Harv asked. "We've got us a game tomorrow."

"Tell 'em it's an act of God. It damn well is," the Patrolman answered. "It is if you think God and zombies have anything to do with each other, I mean."

"God has to do with everything that is and everything that happens," Harv said seriously. "And if that pass is open, I'm gonna go through it. We're gonna go through it. The bus is gonna go through it. We have a game in Grand Junction tomorrow."

The Patrolman looked as though he thought Harv was nine different kinds of idiot. I'm sure he did. He sighed and said, "I've got a friend on duty in the park. Let me call him and see how things are there. If he says it's no go, I'll shoot the tires out of your bus before I let you drive west out of here." He sounded as stubborn as Harv. They don't make many like that.

"Come on, boys. Let's get ready to leave in the middle of the night," Harv said as soon as the Highway Patrolman stumped away. "He won't shoot out our tires if we ain't here so he can do it."

"Harv . . ." Fidgety Frank said.

"Let's wait and see what he says," Wes added. "If we get stuck way up high in the mountains, we'll miss more games than just one."

They'd both played a long time for the House of Daniel. They were the pitchers, too. Both those things meant Harv had to pay more attention to them than he would have if, say, I'd sung out. He looked disgusted, but he nodded. "All right," he said. "All right, doggone it." No, Harv didn't need to cuss to let you know how he was feeling.

After half an hour or so, the Colorado Highway Patrolman came back. "Vern says they got six inches of snow today, and it isn't letting up. You go that high, summer's nothing but a faraway rumor."

"Shucks!" Harv said. Big Stu could've sworn for twenty minutes without sounding half so mad. Then Harv went on, "Let me use that telephone of yours, will you, please? 'Act of God' is what it's gotta be. Have to see what other kind of games I can drum up."

We ended up playing the Greeley Grays twice more. Crowds weren't great, because nobody knew about the games till too late to make plans to come. We won one and lost one, so the Grays could say they beat us in a best-of-three series. The Pittsburgh Crawdads couldn't make that boast.

When we weren't playing ball, we read the papers from Greeley and Fort Collins and we listened to the radio. The reporters going into Denver, they were like war correspondents. One poor fella for United Press, he got torn apart and chewed up and killed. Zombies didn't have any quit in them.

The soldiers and police clearing them out opened up every vampire's coffin they could find, too. Maybe the vampires had something to do with the riots and maybe they didn't. Nobody seemed to care whether they did or not. If they got caught, they got a finishing dose of sunshine. After that, you didn't need to worry about them any more.

On the third day, we played in Fort Collins, in the park on the west side of town. The guys we played against were a scratch team. Some of 'em, I think, never made a dime playing ball before that afternoon. By the way they played, some of 'em would never make another dime that way. We trounced 'em.

After the game, we ate fast and made darn sure we were back at our lodging before sundown. That was the night of the full moon. I felt sorry for the cops and soldiers in Denver, taking on not just vampires and zombies but werewolves, too. That stupid farmer's shotgun shells with silver pellets would've come in handy then, I bet. We heard some howling, but nothing tried to get us.

I guess the cops made it through the night, too, because roads through Denver opened up again the next morning. Harv phoned Grand Junction and had us out of Fort Collins faster than you could spit. Can't say I was sorry. Fort Collins and Greeley weren't bad towns, but I'd seen as much of them as I ever wanted to.

By what the radio said, traffic through Denver was allowed. Going off the through routes wasn't. Some zombies were still loose, and some werewolves didn't turn back into people the second the moon went down. The folks giving the orders didn't want anyone sticking his foot in the lions' den.

"Daniel put his whole body in the lions' den, and they didn't harm him," Harv said after we got going. "We all have things we want back at that boarding house. Let's see if we can get 'em."

"You think God wants us to have our stuff back as much as He wanted Daniel not to get eaten, Harv?" Wes asked.

"I don't think He needs to watch over us as much as He watched over Daniel," Harv answered, not bothered a bit. "Just a little will take care of it."

"You hope," Wes said.

"That's right. I do. Shall I let you off?" Harv said. Wes shook his head, so Harv went on driving.

Denver looked like I don't know what. No, I do: Denver looked like a city that had just been through a zombie riot. Parts were burned. Parts were smashed. Parts were burned *and* smashed. There weren't many bodies on the streets. The soldiers and police—and the zombies— must have got rid of most of them. Here and there, red-brown stains and splashes on sidewalks and walls told their own story. The air stank from sour smoke and the smell of rotting meat.

What I thought was a zombie trotted down a street. Then I realized he was a man. He had a hard sausage almost the size of a bat in one hand and a whiskey bottle in the other. A zombie wouldn't have needed either one.

I did see one for-sure zombie down an alley we passed. I only got a glimpse, so I don't *know* what it was eating. That's bound to be just as well. Harv didn't spot it, or he would've put another dent in the bus's front end.

Our boarding house was still standing. We piled out of the bus, Louisville Sluggers (and one Adirondack) at the ready. Harv knocked on the front door. When nobody answered, he tried it. It wouldn't open. He used the key. That got us in. No horrible smells inside. Whoever'd been in there wasn't any more, alive or dead.

Nobody'd plundered our rooms, either. The people who'd stayed at the place ran away, and no one else broke in. Things were the way they had been before we went off to play the third game against the Craw-dads. We gathered up what was ours and got out of there in a hurry.

"See? All hunky-dory," Harv said when we got on the bus again. "Now to Merchants Park. We've got stuff in the clubhouse there, too, if no one's stolen it and if somebody will let us in to get it."

But Merchants Park had burned. It was sad to see, the grandstand all black and crumbled, the entrance fallen in on itself. That's what happens to wooden ballparks. It's a shame, but it does. Which is why, ever since the time I was born, they've built big-league parks from cement and steel. You can imagine one of those lasting fifty years, maybe even a hundred.

Not long after we got back on Broadway, we drove by another squad that included a couple of men with flamethrowers. Maybe the burn-ing in Denver wasn't over yet.

I wondered how many people still hunkered down in their houses and flats, eating whatever hadn't spoiled in their cupboards and keep-ing their doors locked and maybe barricaded, too. And I wondered how many zombies still prowled the streets, looking for anybody they could kill. They'd go after soldiers, even soldiers with flamethrowers. Why not? What was the worst thing a flamethrower could do to a zombie? End it. You ask me, the guy with the flamethrower would be doing it a favor.

Not that anybody asked me.

We had to clear another checkpoint coming out of Denver. That one actually made sense. Denver was the heart of the riot. Anything bad would spread out from there. And cops and soldiers ran it, so they weren't shoot-on-sight jumpy the way rubes with varmint guns would've been.

They searched the bus. They searched our stuff. No zombies, no vampires. Not even any werewolves. "Did you see any . . . things when you came through town?" asked a soldier with two stripes on his sleeve.

"No, Corporal," Harv answered. I had, but I kept quiet. The zombie likely wouldn't be where I saw it any more. And we weren't supposed to have been there ourselves. Chances were the searchers would find it anyhow. Zombies weren't long on brains—unless they ate some-one else's.

The ride we did take to Grand Junction was wild enough. US 24 went over and through the most amazing mountains I'd ever imagined, much less seen. We never did have snow on the highway, but there was snow on the Rockies not far above us. This in the summertime, too! In the winter, they must close long stretches of road for long stretches of time. If we'd tried to go the other way, the one Harv wanted, we might be trying yet.

We had to stop for a couple of roadblocks along the way: nervous mountain folks, not police. One fellow was as shaggy as anybody who played for the House of Daniel. He thought that was funny. Me, I would've laughed harder if he hadn't been holding a rifle.

We got there. We got there on time—just barely, but we did. Grand Junction brags that it's the biggest town in Colorado on that side of the Rockies. I guess maybe it is, but that's not saying one whole heck of a lot. Still and all, Lincoln Park wasn't a bad place to play a game. It was short down the left-field line, then stretched way out in left-center and center. Right wasn't one way or the other, which meant it would play short in the thin air.

It was a city field—there'd never been a pro team in town. But it did have dressing rooms. That was good, because we went straight there. We didn't stop at our rooms to change.

They had a microphone at the place. When we came out, the an-nouncer said, "Here they are, folks! The House of Daniel! *Denver Post* Tournament champs and survivors of the Great Zombie Riots! Show 'em how glad you are that they could come out to Grand Junction and give the Falcons a game!"

Lincoln Park couldn't have held even a quarter as many people as Merchants Park did—I mean, had. But they all stood up and cheered for us. I didn't know what to do. You don't have that happen when you're the road team, and the House of Daniel was almost always the road team.

The other guys didn't know how to take it, either. It caught 'em by surprise. Finally, Harv took off his cap and waved it. The Grand Junction folks clapped harder than ever, so we all did that. After a bit, they quieted down, and we went ahead and played the game.

Fidgety Frank was pitching for us. He drove the Grand Junction Falcons buggy. He might've been a southpaw Carpetbag Booker out there, the way he had them eating out of his hand. They were young guys, only a couple older than me, and they'd never seen anybody like Frank before. They kept swinging off his motion, so they were way out in front.

We fell behind, 1-0, in the third, but we didn't worry. Their pitcher had a fastball and a change and a wrinkle of a curve. He pitched into trouble and got out of it a couple of times. Then he walked two guys and aimed a fastball to steal a strike instead of cutting loose with it. Wes hit it like he knew it was coming. He split the gap between their center fielder and the fella in left. That was the big part of the ball-park. Both runners scored, and Wes had himself a triple. A minute later, Harv knocked one through their drawn-in infield and put us two runs up.

Fidgety Frank kept the Falcons off balance, and we figured out what their pitcher had. I doubled and scored a run myself. I always felt good when I helped out with the bat, because I didn't do it as often as I wanted to. I was fine in the outfield, but you've got to hit some. So I was extra happy every time I got good wood on the ball.

We ended up beating them 7-1. Sometimes, you win by a score like that and you think *I dunno. They'd be trouble if we played 'em again.* It felt as though we could take the Grand Junction Falcons any time we pleased. That may not have been so, but it felt that way.

We didn't let on. When we came in after we got the last out, we waved our caps to the crowd again. They gave us another nice hand. The Falcons wanted to take us out to supper. They wanted to hear about the tournament—and about the zombies.

"Go if you want to," Harv told us. "I got to find me a telephone and see what we can do about fixing our schedule. If those doggone zombies weren't already dead, I'd want to kill 'em for fouling us up like this."

So after we all showered and changed, the Falcons took us to what they said was the best place in Grand Junction. It was pretty good, all right. They served big slabs of dead cow cooked just the way you wanted it, with baked potatoes or mashed potatoes or French fries on the side. Hard to go wrong with a menu like that, especially when the beer was on tap.

Some of the Falcons had played against Carpetbag when he came through the town with one barnstorming team or another. "No wonder you guys beat the Crawdads if you had him on the hill," one of them said. "That guy's murder."

"Hey, Fidgety Frank won a game against them, too, remember." I'd drunk enough beer to get talkier than usual.

When my mug got empty again, the cute little blond gal taking care of us gave me back my dime. "He already paid me," she said, nodding Frank's way.

I couldn't buy my own beer the rest of the night, it turned out. So I started buying Fidgety Frank's instead, to even things out a bit. He hadn't wanted to remind the Falcons he'd had something to do with the House of Daniel's hoisting the trophy. I wouldn't have guessed he was so modest, but there you are.

But they were more interested in the riots than in the baseball. They knew about baseball. The whole zombie business, though, that rocked them. "I took a magic class at Mesa State here," one of them said. "The prof said zombies couldn't go off the rails like that."

" 'There are more things in heaven and earth, Horatio, than are dreamt of in your philosophy,' " Azariah said. Where Harv talked Book of Daniel talk, he came out with Shakespeare. I didn't know he had it in him, not till then. All on his own, he added, "More things than are in your prof's philosophy, too."

"I guess so," the Falcon said. "Maybe the vampires know things Professor Houlihan didn't."

"Wouldn't surprise me one bit." That was Wes. If anybody was always ready to believe people were dumber than they thought, he was your man.

What surprised me was how little *we* knew about what all had happened in Denver, happened to Denver. We'd lived through it. If we didn't know, who did? Who could? But all we knew was our own little bit, plus what we saw when we drove through there early that morning. And we were too busy trying to stay alive to take a lot of notes.

Makes you wonder how anybody ever finds out anything about what happened a long time ago, or even day before yesterday. How can you tell? Even if you're sure your memory's perfect, wouldn't somebody else call you a lying fool and be just as sure about something completely different? You'd have to put together dozens of people's stories, wouldn't you, to have any idea of what really went on? Even then, it wouldn't be a neat jigsaw puzzle. Some of the pieces wouldn't quite fit no matter how you pushed them around. Others would stick out over the edges.

What *is* history, then? Whatever enough people say history is, that's what. If they make you believe their story, then it's true for you.

Enough. Too much, I bet. The Falcons took us back to Lincoln Park. We'd said we'd meet up with Harv there. He was sitting in the bus waiting for us and smiling like Santa Claus. "Well, boys," he said, "I know where we're going."

"Where?" Fidgety Frank sounded worried. Harv looked too cheerful for his own good, and maybe for ours.

"Salt Lake City tomorrow," he answered. "Go to bed early tonight, everybody. We'll be up early tomorrow. We've got a long trip ahead of us."

We had to get through one more roadblock before we could head on toward Salt Lake City. This one was just on the Utah side of the border with Colorado. The cops in charge of it were just as jumpy as any of the farmers with shotguns a lot closer to Denver.

"We don't want any of them zombie things sneaking into our state out of Colorado," one of them said.

I wondered how many were already in Utah, working in mines and factories and other places where all you needed was stupid muscle.

Every one of them saved some boss the expense of paying a live man's wages. The accountants with the glasses and the green eyeshades had to love them.

They had to love them till the zombies rose up and started slaughtering people, anyhow. That would put some red ink in your books in a hurry.

We stopped in Price, Utah, about seventy-five miles this side of Salt Lake City, for gas and a stretch. Price was a coal town. Some of the dust there was black from the mines. Some was red from the desert we'd been driving through. Desert and mountains, mountains and desert—we didn't seem to do anything else. It was all pretty country, but too rugged for me to want to live there.

Now the Great Salt Lake and the salt flats around it, that was something to see. Harv was practically cackling when he drove past Lehi and Provo on the last lap toward Salt Lake City. "We are going to make money like bandits in these parts," he said. "Like bandits, I tell you!"

"You mean we carry guns instead of bats?" Wes always tried to let the air out of Harv's imagination.

"Shut your face." Harv wasn't gonna let anybody rain on his parade. "Do you know where the closest pro teams west of here are at? In the Coast League, that's where! In California—well, Oregon and Washington, too. From here to there, semipro's the best ball folks can watch. And who's the best semipro team around?"

"We are!" we all chorused. And we were, too. We'd proved it in Denver. Fewer people knew we'd won the *Post's* tournament than they should have. Other headlines came out of Denver instead. But that didn't make winning it any less real.

"Right!" Harv nodded, luckily without turning his head. "The Coast League was in Salt Lake for a while, but then they pulled back to the coast. Town didn't draw well enough to suit their Majesties."

Harv sounded snottier and less charitable than usual. I think he was jealous. The Pacific Coast League is Class AA ball, only one level shy of the bigs. And because they are way out there on the West Coast, they get to do as they please more than any other minor league. They think of themselves as just about a big league, and maybe they aren't so far wrong.

After that, Salt Lake City was in the Utah–Idaho League, in Class

C, for two or three years. But it went under, so no pro ball was left around there any more. They had what they called the Utah Industrial League. In fact, we were playing the Salt Lake City Industries, the local team that had gone to Denver.

Salt Lake City was bigger than I expected, bigger not just for number of folks but for size, too. The blocks were long and the streets were wide. It spread out; there weren't many tall buildings.

That meant you could see the State Capitol from a long way off. The Mormon Temple, too, with the gold angel on the spire. I didn't know much about the Mormons then. Come to that, I still don't. I wondered whether Harv was jealous in a different way, though. Utah made me think of what the House of Daniel might be like if it had a whole state to play with, not just part of a small town in Wisconsin.

From the little bits I did find out, a lot of what I think the Mormons believe seems pretty silly. But whatever they believe, they mostly turn out nice people. Which counts for more? You'll have to decide that for yourself.

Bonneville Park probably held about as many people as Merchants Park had. But when they built Merchants Park, they at least remembered they were high up and made you hit the ball a long way before it went over the wall. Salt Lake City's about a thousand feet lower than Denver, but Bonneville Park would've been a hitters' heaven at sea level . . . or below it.

Left was 308; right went 320. And out to dead center? Only 360. The fences were at least twenty feet high—I will say that. Advertising signs, some fresh but more old and faded and peeling, covered them.

Wes shook his head when he looked out there. He'd pitch today, and he was as thrilled as you'd think. "I always try to forget ballparks like this," he said. "Somehow, they keep coming back to haunt me."

"Their guy has to pitch here, too," I reminded him.

"If he's a Mormon, he can't even drink afterwards, the poor son of a bitch," Wes said. "What'll you do out there? I don't need a center fielder—I need another second baseman."

One thing I will say is, the fans enjoy an 11-9 game more than one that ends 1 0. They want to see the ball flying around and the runners scurrying every which way. A pitchers' duel may be more interesting to play in, but not for the folks who shove quarters at the ticket-sellers.

Oh—I did find out how come the Industries had bees on their sleeves. To the Mormons, the bee stands for industry. The Salt Lake City PCL team was called the Bees, as a matter of fact.

We got the same kind of introduction and the same kind of big hand at the start of the game as we had in Grand Junction. One of the Industries said to me, "We were lucky to get out when we did, but I wish we'd been playing against you in the finals."

"I know what you mean. You always want to do as well as you can," I answered. He nodded.

When the Industries ran out to take the field, the crowd cheered them even louder than it had for us. Well, they were the town team, so that was all right. Getting hands on the road felt funny anyhow.

And the game was . . . what I thought it would be as soon as I got a look at that silly center field. Ordinary fly balls zoomed over the fence. When they didn't go over it, they banged off it. Wes hadn't been kidding about wanting a second baseman in center. The Industries' shortstop ran out and got a ball that caromed back over the left fielder's head. He grabbed it so fast, Eddie had to jam on the brakes and scamper back to first. The short fences gave bases, but sometimes they took them away, too.

Never a dull moment out there, and that's an understatement. I could state some other things, but I won't. When the smoke cleared away and the dust finally settled, we ended up on top, 13-10. Not a tidy way to win a ballgame, but you take what you can get.

"Beat 'em by a field goal," I said to Eddie when we went in after the last out.

"I wouldn't have minded a football helmet today," he said. "All those balls coming and going . . . I thought I was in the middle of a shooting gallery." He ducked, as though another line drive whizzed past him.

"Scary out there," I agreed.

Some of the Industries came over and told us what a good game it was. Mormons are polite and friendly. They work hard at it. It gets annoying every once in a while, but only every once in a while.

I nodded to the guy who'd talked to me before we played. "This park must drive you nuts," I said.

"Only if you're a pitcher," he answered. "To me, it feels like the happy hunting ground."

"I guess it would." If I played all my home games in Bonneville Park, I'd start thinking I was a power hitter. That's the kind of place it was.

We had a hotel in Salt Lake City. One step up from a boarding house, though Harv said it didn't cost any more. On the way there, we passed two different soup-kitchen lines, one at some government kitchen and one at a Mormon church. They did try hard to fight the mess that had the whole country wrapped up in spider webs. But when there aren't enough jobs for the people who need 'em, what can you do? Keep folks from starving—that's about it.

The main way the hotel was different from a boarding house was, the rooms had a bathroom with a toilet and tub. We didn't need to go down to the end of the hall to clean up. I liked that. I wished we'd live it up more often. If it was the same price, why not? But most of the time it wasn't. And Harv was a great man for tossing nickels around like manhole covers.

That was a terrific way for a fella who ran a semipro team to be. The guys who played on the team? Maybe they didn't enjoy it quite so much.

After we went over and up to Salt Lake City, we went partway back down to Provo. It's about fifty miles south of the bigger city. Would've been better if we could've played there before we went up to Salt Lake, but it didn't work out like that. Harv was still untangling the knots the Great Zombie Riots tied in our travel plans.

Provo's the home of BYU, the Mormons' college. There's a big Y on a mountain east of town that the students whitewash every year. Nobody on the bus got real excited when Harv told us about it, though. I don't think any of us had taken college classes. Some of us went to high school, but I don't think many came away with a sheepskin.

There was more to Provo than the college. We played the Timps at Timpanogos Park. They belonged to the Utah Industrial League.

I expect the name of the ballpark gave them their own handle. It was a fine place to play in, especially for a town that never had a pro team. The stands held 2,500, maybe 3,000 people. The outfield was a lot bigger than the one at Bonneville Park. That would warm the cockles of Fidgety Frank's heart.

And Timpanogos Park—the ballyard—was set smack in the middle of Sowiette Park, with trees and grass and tennis courts and a swimming pool and I don't know what all. Nice place to go on a hot summer afternoon. You could sit in the shade of the trees and enjoy a picnic. Or you could come to Timpanogos Park, set down half a dollar, and bake your brains out in the bleachers. Plenty of people did. If it wasn't a sellout, it came close.

The Provo Timps were like the Industries—like most of the teams in the Utah Industrial League. Some of their players worked in town. Some were pros who hadn't wanted to move away when the Utah–Idaho League folded: found work they liked, had a wife or girl close by, or came from around there and didn't feel like pulling up stakes. They played for the Timps to keep their hand in and to help keep the wolf away from the door.

Their pitcher, a lefty, had gray streaks in his sandy hair. He wouldn't beat himself—we'd have to do it to him. The whole team was like that. They knew what they were doing. Maybe the Crawdads could have rattled them with speed, the way they rattled the Industries in Denver. We didn't have that kind of speed ourselves, though. We had to play our game and hope we came out on top.

I did notice that their pitcher fell off the mound toward the third-base line more than some. So when I led off the top of the third, I pushed a bunt to the first-base side. As soon as it got past the mound, I knew I had a hit. Their second baseman picked it up and hung on to it.

A single and a sacrifice fly brought me home. "Yeah, Snake!" Harv whacked me on the behind when I came back to the dugout. "That bunting drives 'em bonkers. They aren't looking for it, and you fatten up your batting average."

"It needs some fattening up." I was just about good enough to play for the House of Daniel. Harv hadn't gone beating the bushes to flush out another center fielder. But he hadn't moved me up from eighth in the order, either. I didn't scare anybody with a bat in my hands. I could hurt people: I was fast, I knew how to bunt, and I could hit *some*. Scare 'em? Nope. That was a different kettle of crabs.

Then the Timps got a couple of runs. We tied it up, and it stayed tied at two into the ninth. About as different a game from the one at Bonneville Park the day before as you could imagine.

We had a guy on third with one out—a double and a long fly to right to move him along a base—when I came up. The Timps brought all their infielders in tight. Their third baseman was practically in my lap. He'd already seen that I could drop one down, and he didn't want me squeezing in the lead run.

More than one way to skin a cat, though. First pitch, I shortened up as if I was gonna bunt, then let it go by for a ball. That pulled their third baseman and first baseman in another half a step. I shortened up again on the next pitch, but instead of bunting I chopped down on the ball, hard. The bouncer went over the third baseman's head and out into left. The run scored.

"Butcher boy!" Harv yelled from the dugout. "Didn't know you had that in your bag of tricks!" I grinned over at him.

"Smart poke," the Timps' first baseman said when I took my lead. A second later, he added, "Dammit."

Their pitcher was wearing down. Two more singles brought me home. Fidgety Frank went out for the bottom of the ninth with a two-run lead. When he could smell a win like that, nobody was tougher. He set the Timps down in order. We had ourselves another one.

The crowd applauded us as we came off the field. Yes, Mormons are polite people. The Timps' pitcher came over to me. He already had a towel soaked in water and ammonia around his neck to help him cool off. "You oughta be against the law," he said. "Wasn't for you, we woulda won."

"You play with nine," I said. "You need all of 'em." I guess I sounded modest. But I meant it. Baseball's a team game. If Frank hadn't pitched well, if we hadn't made the plays with the leather, if there hadn't been a man on third for me to bring in . . . If, if, if. We would've been a different team then, and it would've been a different ballgame.

"Well, I hope they're paying you what you're worth," he said.

"Hey, Harv!" I sang out. "This guy says you oughta give me a raise."

Harv looked over to make sure I wasn't talking about anybody from the House of Daniel. When he saw who was standing next to me, he said, "Sure—long as it comes out of his pocket."

"See ya," the Timps' pitcher said, and walked away quick. We all laughed.

I wasn't really grousing about what Harv gave me, and he knew it darn well. I had more cash in my grouch bag than I'd ever had in my life before. Part of that was because I was getting paid more regularly than I ever had. And part of it was because I didn't have much to spend my money on. I still steered clear of the card games. If you know you're a sucker, that's the best thing you can do.

So I'd shell out for suppers and breakfasts and snacks. Now and then, I'd buy a paper or a magazine to read on the bus and make time go by. But that was about it. I hadn't visited a sporting house even once, the way some of the guys did now and then. Like I've said, if I end up with a girl, I want it to be on account of she likes me. Plenty of men don't care, or there wouldn't be any sporting houses. Hey, when I get horny enough, I don't care so much, either.

Sometimes after a game, the team you played doesn't want anything to do with you and you don't want anything to do with them, either. Sometimes you go out to supper with them and hoist a few. We went out to supper with the Timps. They were nice folks. We ate at a place with pot roast, meatloaf, fried chicken, that kind of thing. I had the chicken. It was fine—I've eaten plenty worse.

We told more stories about the Great Zombie Riots. Or rather, we were starting to tell the same stories over and over. One of the Timps said, "We don't have many zombies in Utah. They aren't against the law, but only gentiles use 'em here. If we do it, we get disfellow-shipped."

That took some straightening out. When he said *gentiles*, he meant any people who weren't Mormons. Even the old Jew who ran the Enid pawnshop counted for a gentile in Provo. And being disfellowshipped was the last step before you got tossed out of their church.

"Do some folks care more about money than about church

rules?" Wes asked. I wondered the same thing, but he came out with the question.

The Timp didn't look happy. Neither did his teammates. "It happens," he said after a pause. "Not too often, but it does. We've got greedy people, too." They were human beings just like the rest of us. Not a great big surprise, I guess.

(XVI)

We went through Salt Lake City again, this time on the way north to Ogden. "Yes, I know it ain't the smooth way to do things," Harv said, sounding put-upon. "I had it set up so we'd play Provo–Salt Lake–Ogden till the zombie riots knocked things sideways. Then the Timps had a game set for a day when the Industries were free, so we'll put some more miles on the bus, that's all."

Ogden is bigger than Provo, smaller than Salt Lake City. It has long blocks and wide streets running north-south and east-west, same as they do. The mountains spring up off to the east; the Great Salt Lake is fifteen miles or so off to the west. That stretch between the mountains and the Great Salt Lake, that's where most of the people in Utah live. It's pretty enough and then some. Mountains make a horizon interesting, don't they? Back in Enid, you could see every which way as far as things ran. Not like that in Utah, I found out.

We were taking on the Ogden Gunners. They had been in the Utah–Idaho League with the Salt Lake City Bees. When the pro league hit a rock and sank, most of the team stuck together. They kept the name. I think the uniforms were new, though. Newer, I should say. They still had the old style: white caps with blue brims, crossed rifles over the heart, and an O in a diamond on the left sleeve.

Lorin Farr Park had a short right field with a high fence and was long in center and left. Wouldn't you know it?—the Gunners sported three or four big, tall, strong-looking guys who batted left. That right there warned they knew what they were doing. If the park you play in favors one side over the other, a smart team will find players who can take advantage of it.

They started a southpaw, too, to make it tough on our left-handed swingers. We had Wes going, so we had to hope he was on his game.

It wasn't the kind of game you'd use to teach somebody how to play baseball. They threw at us. Wes threw at them—he was never shy about that. Fidgety Frank took out their shortstop with a body block to break up a double play. They had to substitute for the guy; he got a wrenched knee. Then one of their runners spiked Eddie trying to steal second. Eddie got it bandaged and stayed in. Both sides said some things neither church would've been happy with. Nobody threw any punches and the benches didn't clear, but that was about all we missed.

The fans loved it. They always get excited about games like that. They called us worse names than we called each other, things that weren't in the Book of Daniel or the Book of Mormon.

They liked the game even better 'cause the Gunners won it 7-5. We had a guy called out at the plate when he looked safe easy. Harv didn't cuss the umpire, but he called him hard of seeing so many ways that the jerk threw him out of the game anyhow.

We didn't go out to supper with the Gunners. Harv stuck around just long enough to collect our share of the gate. Then we went back to our motor lodge. We cleaned up there and found somewhere to eat. If the Ogden team was out celebrating somewhere else, that was its business.

"He robbed us! In broad daylight, he robbed us!" Harv must've said it eight or ten times.

"What can you do?" Fidgety Frank said when he'd heard it often enough to get sick of it. "I mean, Harv, what can you do? You'd best believe we're lucky that kind of crap doesn't land on us even more than it does."

"Shucks, I know one thing I can do," Harv said. "I can make con-sarned sure that squinting baboon doesn't work our game the next time we swing through here. I can make sure his guide dog doesn't work it, either!"

Well, we all started giggling. Not laughing. When I say giggling, I mean giggling. And the sight of two big tables' worth of long-haired, bearded ballplayers giggling like three-year-olds set the waiters giggling, too. One of them laughed so hard, he dropped the apple pie that was supposed to be part of our dessert.

He wasn't happy about that. The price of it would come out of his pay, and you can bet a waiter at a diner in Ogden, Utah, wasn't going to drive home in a Duesenberg. But Harv slipped him a half-dollar to go with his regular tip when we were leaving. The world suited him better after that.

"It was our fault," Harv said as we walked back to our rooms. "We broke him up and made him drop that pie. Scales oughta balance."

"You're got a soft heart, Harv," Wes said. "You've got a soft head, too." He was still out of sorts because he'd lost the game.

"It could be," Harv said. "But I don't care. I'm gonna do what feels right by my lights. If anybody else doesn't like it, too bad. No skin off my snoot."

Wes thought that over. He decided he didn't feel like picking a fight with his manager. The House of Daniel would have had a problem without him. But he would have had a bigger problem without the team. He had sense enough to see it. Pitchers, they're mostly smarter than position players. Mostly.

Next morning, we went to Logan, northeast of Ogden. They played their games on the football field at the agricultural college, but they weren't a college team. They'd played in the Utah–Idaho League, but they went under a year before it did. They went on as a semipro outfit and kept the Collegian name—another verse of that same song.

When you put a baseball field in a space made for football, you're going to have one field that's too short and one that's too long. At the agricultural college, left was the short field—it was only 251 down the line. They had a tall chicken-wire screen that they mounted on two metal posts to take away some of the cheap homers, but it wouldn't take away all of them. Meanwhile, you needed to climb on a horse to go to the fence in right.

Before the game, the Collegians' manager walked over to Harv and said, "Hear you had a run-in with the Gunners yesterday."

"That's right." Steam didn't shoot out of Harv's ears, but I don't know why not. "And if you want to play the way they did, we'll have another one with you fellas today."

"No, no." Their manager shook his head. "Those guys, they think they gotta show you how big it is every time they put on spikes. You don't throw at us, we won't throw at you. If you do, we can take care of ourselves."

"We aren't headhunters. You know anything about us, you know that," Harv said. "Frank may push you back from the plate, but—"

"That's not the same thing. Sure. I know the difference," the Logan man said. "Fair enough. If it doesn't start, we'll both be happy. If it does, we'll go on from there."

"Yup." Harv held out his hand. The Collegians' manager shook with him. *An eye for an eye and a tooth for a tooth* isn't Book of Daniel talk, but it'd be baseball Holy Writ even if it weren't in the Good Book some other place. They both understood it. So did everybody else on both sides.

The crowd cheered when the Collegians took the field. The cheers sorta faded away instead of coming down on top of us. They sounded lonely and far off. Football fields are different, that's all.

So are games you play on football fields. Wes hit a screamer that would have been out of most parks. I mean to tell you, he almost broke that baseball. It hit near the top of the screen and bounced down into their left fielder's glove. The guy knew his business. He fired it into second. Wes took a big turn around first, but he had to scoot back in a hurry. What should have been a homer turned into a single.

The screen tooketh away, and the screen gaveth. Yeah, I know that's wrong, but it was right, too. In the top of the second, Eddie hit a high, lazy fly ball to left. The Collegians' outfielder drifted back till he'd pressed his behind against the chicken wire. Then all he could do was look up and watch the ball sail about two feet over the top of the screen and out.

Eddie laughed all the way around the bases—not at the Collegians' pitcher, but at the park. He hustled around the bases, too. He had about as much power as I did. He didn't hit many home runs, and he didn't know how to act them out. It's the big, strong guys who get to practice the slow trot.

Then the Collegians tied it. They had a man on third and one out when their hitter smashed one into the gap in right-center. "I got it!" I yelled. "I got it! I got it!" I didn't know if I had it or not, but I remembered what happened to Rabbit and Double-Double. I didn't want another smashup.

And darned if I didn't have it. It wasn't quite as good a catch as the one I made in Ponca City, 'cause I could use both hands. But I covered a lot of ground to get there. The runner on third waltzed home, but if I hadn't caught it they would have had another guy there—or he might have come all the way around.

Their batter stopped about ten feet past first and stared out at me with his hands on his hips. "Call the police!" he hollered. "I been robbed!" He kicked at the dirt and trotted back to the dugout.

Some people threw me silver when I came in after the inning ended. "Obliged, folks," I said as I picked it up. "Much obliged." Two bucks and a quarter, it came to. It wouldn't go to waste.

"Nice one, Snake," Fidgety Frank said. "You might've saved us a big inning there."

"You can go get 'em, all right," Harv added.

What I wanted was to swing the bat. If Eddie could hit one out here, I could, too. I could, only I didn't. Their pitcher worked me away, away, away. I tried to pull one, but all I could manage was a grounder to short.

Next time I batted, we were down 3-2. We had a man on first. The pitcher went away from me again. I took one off the plate for a ball and fouled one back. Then I thought, *Hey, he just won't come in to me. So okey-doke, why don't I go the other way myself?*

Sure enough, low and away one more time. I golfed it into right-center, and it rolled between the two outfielders. I've got pretty fair speed. I tripled standing up and drove in the guy ahead of me. Then I scored on a fly to center.

"Lookit the Snake!" Fidgety Frank said. "Does it with the glove, does it with the bat, too!"

"Bat me cleanup!" I told Harv.

"You want to clean up, Snake, go get yourself a broom," he said. He knew I was joking. Good thing he did, too. A team with me batting fourth wouldn't be one anybody wanted to watch.

We won the game. The final was 6-4. The Collegians' pitcher came up to me and said, "I served up what you wanted there, didn't I?" He sounded ticked off at himself. Pitchers always figure they can out-think hitters and set them up.

"I was waiting for it, yeah," I answered. If we'd been in a league together, I would've put on a stupid expression and said something like *Huh? I musta got lucky.* But I wouldn't see him again for another year, if I ever did. So the truth didn't cost me anything.

He shook his head. "If I'd come in, though . . . I hate that stupid screen." Any pitcher would've said the same thing.

I patted him on the shoulder. "Sometimes it works, sometimes it doesn't. What else can you say? It's the same for hitters as it is for pitchers."

"I know. Not like I haven't been through it before." He made a sour face. "I thought you'd try and pull it again. Pitch inside to a righty at this field and you better make out your will beforehand."

I looked out at the screen. Not so long ago, people started calling Weeghman Park in Chicago the Friendly Confines. I've never been to Chicago, but Weeghman can't be as friendly as that.

You go north. You go south. You go up some highway. You come back down the same highway. Maybe Harv was still straightening things out after the Great Zombie Riots. Maybe he just got wind of another team that wanted a game with us. I dunno. I was starting to think he made up our schedule as he went along.

All of which is by way of explaining how we went up US 91 from Ogden to Logan and then halfway back down US 91 from Logan to Brigham City. We laughed about it some, but not too much. All the guys except me were used to it, and I was sure getting used to it in a hurry.

I hardly cared which way we went. This part of the country was new to me, and you notice different things going down a road from the ones you see coming up it. I had more money coming in than going out, and that was new to me, too. I liked it. I had enough to eat. I was playing. I was doing enough to help the team. So why should I have cared where I did it?

There were peach orchards all around Brigham City. They can 'em there, and make jam out of 'em. Some of them make moonshine brandy from 'em, too, and don't think that won't put hair on your chest even if you're a girl. And the town team, the team we were taking on, was the Brigham City Peaches.

Of course Brigham City was another Mormon-founded town. I was getting to know the look of them. I was getting to like it, too: the wide streets, the sycamores shading them, the greenery everywhere, the mountains always thrusting up in the distance. Plenty of worse ways to live.

One other thing I noticed—the Mormon cities didn't have any shantytowns outside of them. Part of that has to be because Utah has hard winters. Well, fine, but so does Colorado, and Pueblo and Colorado Springs and Denver had their share of those huts and shacks on the edge of town. The Mormons worked hard to take care of their own. They weren't perfect about it, but who is?

The Brigham City ballyard was another one in the middle of a city park. There were trees that weren't sycamores all over the park, and bees buzzing around them. Eddie said they were locust trees. I thought locusts was another name for grasshoppers, but what do I know?

It was a neat, pretty little place. The Peaches had PEACHES on their shirtfronts in orange letters. Their caps showed a B and a C, with a peach patch sewn on between them. I thought it was a silly name for a team, but they did all right by it.

Their pitcher was a kid named Heber Orson Woodruff. They introduced him by all three names, and I've never forgotten a handle like that. I've never forgotten the game he threw at us, either.

We did get a hit. It was a clean one—Azariah doubled inside of third. Heber Orson Woodruff walked three or four guys, and the Peaches kicked one behind him. But he blew fastballs past us all game long, and I'd never seen anybody else who could do that. I didn't see anybody after him, either.

Wes pitched a pretty fair game. We lost 3-0 anyhow. When it was over, Harv shouted at the kid: "Sonny, why ain't you pitching in Detroit or New York City?"

"On account of I like it here, sir," Heber Orson Woodruff answered. I've already talked about how polite the Mormons were. The Peaches' pitcher, he had it worse than most.

"Long as you stay healthy, you're good enough to go to the pros," Harv said. "Maybe outside of Carpetbag Booker, you're the best pitcher we've seen in I don't know how long."

"I couldn't help my family with the orchard then, sir," Heber

Orson Woodruff said. "And a pro team probably wouldn't like it when I went on a mission for a couple of years."

Harv started to say something to the Peaches' manager. Then he closed his mouth again. He could see he wouldn't change anything. Afterwards, though, when we found somewhere to eat, he was still shaking his head. "I don't know whether to admire that kid or smack him in the teeth," he said. "He's got no idea how good he is, and he doesn't want to find out."

"He has a life he's happy with. He plays ball for fun," Eddie said. "What's so bad about that?"

"He doesn't care to use a gift the good Lord gave him," Harv said. "If that ain't sinful, it oughta be."

I bobbed my head up and down. If I'd had Heber Orson Woodruff's talent, I would've ridden it as hard and as far as I could. But I didn't. I'd never be anything but a semipro outfielder. Seeing that arm go to waste made me want to cry. Some of the other House of Daniel players nodded with me. This was as far as they'd go, too.

Eddie said, "You don't know, Harv. Maybe he makes an even better peach farmer than he does a pitcher."

"What if he does?" Wes said. "Nobody prints peach-farmer cards for little kids to collect."

"Nothing wrong with being a peach farmer," Eddie said. "I'm gonna have the peach cobbler for dessert."

"I didn't say there was anything wrong with it—and I'm gonna have peach pie myself," Wes answered. "But the reason they don't make peach-farmer cards is, plenty of people can do a good job growing peaches. An arm like that kid's got comes along once in a blue moon. He made us look like . . . like . . ." He stopped, because he couldn't think of anything strong enough.

Harv could: "He made us look like a bunch of doggone semipros. The Pittsburgh Crawdads couldn't do that, and most of their team would be in the bigs if they were white." He shook his head. "What can you do?"

You couldn't do anything. As far as I know, Heber Orson Woodruff's still raising peaches in Brigham City. I suppose he's done his missionary work by now. Maybe he's still pitching for the Peaches; maybe he hurt his shoulder or his elbow. I don't know. All I know is, I follow the box scores pretty close, and I never saw his name in the bigs. You ask me, it's a shame. Heber Orson Woodruff didn't ask me, and I guess he doesn't think so.

I wondered where in Utah we'd bounce next. Somewhere halfway down the state, was my guess. We didn't, though. We headed up into Idaho instead. It looked like Utah, only with more pine trees. We had a Fourth of July game at Overland Park against the Pocatello Bannocks.

What's a Bannock? I don't know. I did find out Pocatello was in Bannock County. Maybe they were an Indian tribe. The Bannocks were one more team that had been in the Utah–Idaho League when there was a Utah–Idaho League. Now they played in something called the Twilight League. They called it that even though Overland Park had no lights. Why did they? I don't know that, either.

It was . . . a ballpark. It was big enough to have a covered grandstand. We played in the late afternoon—there'd be fireworks after the game—but it was a demon of a hot day. You think of Idaho, you think of deep snow. It's not hot for a long stretch of the year, but when it is, it *is*. The outfield fence was made from vertical planks. They weren't nailed together clinker style; there were spaces between them. I saw some kids, and some grown-ups, peering through, watching the game for nothing. Knothole gang, only more so.

One of the marks of a good team is that, when you lose, you want to come back and win the next day even more than you would if you'd won. That seemed especially true against the Bannocks. Heber Orson Woodruff had made us look bad in our own eyes. We weren't used to getting toyed with like that. So we took it out on the poor Pocatello team, no matter that they hadn't had anything to do with it.

We got two in the first, three in the third, and three more in the fourth. After that, it was all over but the shouting. We did some shouting, too, 'cause we kept tacking on runs. By the time it was done, it was 13-4. Fidgety Frank didn't work too hard the last few innings. He lobbed it in there, figuring they'd mostly hit it where somebody could run it down. They mostly did, too. Sometimes they didn't, so they scored a few late runs.

After the game, the Bannocks looked glum. We hadn't tried to run up the score on them or make them look bad. It was just one of those days where this side trounces that. "I see how you fellas won the *Post* tournament," one of their players said to me.

I shrugged. I hadn't done that much. I had a single and a walk, and I'd played all right in center. I stole a base early on. I could have swiped more—their catcher couldn't throw you out if you broke your leg half-way to second. But if you steal with a big lead, you *are* trying to show up the other guys. That's how beanball wars and fights start.

That Bannock tried again: "Does anybody know for sure what set off the zombies in Denver? Don't want anything like that happening here. It'd be terrible."

"It was terrible in Denver, all right," I answered. "People are saying the vampires fired them up, but I don't know if that's true. The best way not to have more zombie riots'd be not to have any zombies, you ask me."

"Sounds good. Those things aren't natural," he said. It sounded good to me, too. That doesn't mean it's happened, of course. We've had more zombie riots since Denver, though I've never got caught in another one. And we still have zombies. They make even more money for people who already have a lot of it. Anything that does that is tough to get rid of.

We stuck around to watch the fireworks show once it got dark enough. Enid put on a better one, you ask me. Well, except for one thing. A bomb bursting in air hit a vampire flying by. He went down in flames, just like an aeroplane in the War to End War. That was part of the show nobody expected, but people cheered plenty.

They fed the ballplayers on both teams free hot dogs and French fries. Not a great supper, but it didn't cost anything and it went with the Fourth—made it feel kinda like a picnic.

Next morning, we headed up to Idaho Falls. Another day, another game. That was what we did. I was grooved like a phonograph record by then.

It was only about fifty miles from one town to the other, but we took a lot longer getting there than Harv planned on. A Cooperative Construction and Conservation Project labor gang was tearing up the highway. Don't get me wrong—that road would be smoother once the CCCP finished with it: wider, better paved, better graded. In the meantime, what we had was more of a roadblock than a road.

All of those men, anywhere from sixteen to fifty years old, most of them bare-chested in the bright sunshine, working away with shovels and picks and mattocks and sledgehammers . . . It was impressive to watch, at least till you remembered that all the men in that gang, and in I don't know how many others like it, were doing that work in exchange for a full belly and a place to flop because they couldn't find anything better on their own.

Back in Enid, I thought about joining the CCCP. I thought about it, but I didn't do it. That outfit is like the Army: when you're in, you're in. And you're in all the time. They wouldn't have given me time off to play for the Eagles. Some CCCP gangs had teams of their own, but the Eagles played better ball—and they paid a little something.

So instead of talking with my CCCP recruiter, I talked with Big Stu. Yeah, and look how that turned out.

The Idaho Falls Spuds—well, what were they gonna call themselves, the Pineapples?—had also played in the Utah–Idaho League. One more outfit that went semipro after it couldn't make a go of things in the regular minors.

Highland Park was a good enough place for a game. From what one of the Spuds said, folks in Idaho Falls had been playing there since they dug up a beet field somewhere around the turn of the century and turned it into a ball field. It was another one of those wooden ballparks, the kind that last till they have a fire—and then you find out if whoever's running the place has the cash to rebuild.

Good-sized park, too. It was 350 down each line and 408 to center. The fancy grandstand roof covered most of the stands. Only the folks in the box seats down close to the field got wet when it rained.

And it was on-and-off drizzling, maybe more than drizzling, when we started to play. A big-league club or one in the Coast League, say, might've called the game and scheduled a doubleheader the next day. But the House of Daniel wouldn't be in Idaho Falls the next day. We had a game somewhere else.

What the Spuds had were 3,500 people in the stands—that was Harv's guess. They weren't about to give all that nice money back, not unless Noah's Ark floated by looking for Mount Ararat to anchor on. The crowd was all for going ahead, too. Some of the people in the boxes moved back under the roof. Some opened umbrellas. They'd come prepared. And some just didn't care if they got wet.

It wouldn't be a neat, tidy game. When the ball was wet and the dirt was muddy and the grass was slick, funny things were bound to happen.

And they did.

Harv biffed one up the gap in right-center. On that wet grass, it squirted through to the wall like a watermelon seed you shoot between your thumb and first finger. Harv's not swift on his feet, but he would've had a triple even if the Spuds' center fielder didn't fall on his can chasing the ball.

Their pitcher stood on the rubber cussing his luck and scowling at Harv. He squeezed the wet ball getting ready to pitch—and it wiggled out of his hand and fell on the ground, plop. "Balk!" the umpire on the bases shouted, throwing up his hands. "That's a balk! Runner advances one base!"

Head down so the Spuds wouldn't see him snickering, Harv trotted home and stepped on the plate. The pitcher yelled at the umpire. So did the catcher. So did the Spuds' manager, who was also their first baseman. So did the crowd.

But the ump was like the folks with the umbrellas. He came prepared. He pulled a rule book out of his hip pocket, opened it, and gave a shout: "Rule thirty-one, section eleven, says it's a balk 'If a pitcher, in the act of delivering the ball to the batsman or in throwing to first base, drop the ball, either intentionally or accidentally.'"

They shut up. They couldn't very well say he didn't drop it. He did. Their manager did say, "That's a new one on me. I've never seen it before, and I've seen a little." His belly hung over his belt. A lot of the time, first base is an old guy's position.

"Doesn't happen often," the ump agreed, "but it's in the book." He got points in my book for knowing the rule. He got more for explaining it instead of getting up on his high horse when they hollered at him. And he got some for carrying the book so he could cite chapter and verse.

That game had bad hops. It had bad throws. It had passed balls.

One of the Spuds pulled a hamstring trying to score on a short fly ball. He went down in a heap halfway between third and the plate. He tried to crawl home, but Amos tagged him out. His buddies had to almost carry him back to the bench, poor guy. He got a hand, but he would rather have had the run. He wouldn't play again for a while, either.

We came out on top, 6-5. The only thing that proved was that we came out on top that afternoon. "Wonder how we'd match up in a real ballgame," their manager said when it was over.

"Oh, it was real," Harv answered. "Not to write home about, maybe, but real."

"Still a shame it was raining," the Spuds' manager said.

"Always a shame when it rains," Harv agreed. "But we got the game in, and we had a decent crowd." That made the Spuds' manager quit grousing. Money took some of the sting out of losing. Did Harv know that? He just might have.

I've talked before about how Harv had a good dose of mother hen in him. He got his chicks on the road way too early the next morning. We had a game in Twin Falls, and we had to go back down through Pocatello to get there.

"Lord only knows how long that CCCP work will hold us up today," he said when he fired up the bus's engine. "Lord only knows if they're messing with the road somewhere west of Pocatello, too."

"It may not matter. We may not be able to play, anyhow," Wes said. The bus's windshield wipers were already flicking back and forth.

"You bite your tongue, you hear me?" Harv was mad as could be. "We won't draw real good this afternoon—Twin Falls ain't the big city. If we have to play tomorrow morning instead, before we go on to Boise . . ." He shook his head and looked up at or past the ceiling of the bus. If God listened to him—and who didn't?—that kind of disaster wouldn't happen.

Turned out to be just as well we started early. We had to hold up while the CCCP dynamited a boulder that was in their way. We were so far off, all we saw was a big cloud of smoke and rocks flying out of it. We were so far off, in fact, that we saw it before we heard the boom. Then we had to wait some more while the men without shirts cleared away those smaller rocks. They didn't clear them all; we bounced over some.

They stared in through the bus windows when we finally went by. Most of 'em looked green-jealous. We weren't working as hard as they were—nowhere near. But we were doing better on account of it. You could see them thinking *If only I was able to hit a decent curve, or throw one.*

There *was* more CCCP work west of Pocatello. Harv didn't say a word, but his back might as well have had an electric sign on it flashing I TOLD YOU SO! on and off in big red letters. Wes didn't say anything, either, which was bound to be just as well.

It was still drizzling when we got to Twin Falls, but that was all it was doing, drizzling. We wouldn't have any worries about getting the game in. Or I thought we wouldn't, till I got a look at where the Twin Falls Cowboys played. It was in a park by a canal that brought wastewater down from a mine in the hills outside of town. I don't know what was in that wastewater, but I know it smelled like a conjure man's kettle over a fire when he didn't like you one bit. And I know grass wouldn't come up anywhere near it.

So their field didn't just have a skin infield. It had a skin outfield, too. Except the skin was all over mud. If I was gonna play on that, I wanted a spoon or something in my hip pocket to clean my spikes with. And I was gonna play, because the stands were full even if they didn't boast a roof.

Harv pulled a rabbit out of his hat. Instead of spoons, he handed us all those flat wooden things docs use to hold your tongue down. I didn't know he had them till he pulled them out of a duffel. I mean, I had no idea. Even Mother Nature needed to work hard to get one past Harv.

The Cowboys didn't have any of those wooden doodads. But they did carry spoons or butter knives or shoehorns or anything else that could get the dirt out of their cleats. They knew what kind of ballpark they had, and they knew what it was like on a wet day.

And Fidgety Frank was just flat. His hesitation moves didn't fool the Cowboys. Neither did his curveballs. When we got down 8-3 after five, Harv took him out and let Azariah finish the game. He threw knuckleballs, only some of 'em didn't knuckle. So he got knocked around pretty good. He had a big old grin out there on the hill, though. He was just mopping up, but he was having a good time. The Twin Falls fans were, too.

Not Fidgety Frank. When the rest of the House of Daniel came back to the dugout after Azariah got the Cowboys out at last, he sat there with his head down and said, "What do you think, boys? Shall I catch a train back to Cornucopia and go into the secondhand inner-tube business?"

"Nope," Harv said. "Remember, you got the Pittsburgh Crawdads out in Denver. They're a lot tougher'n these guys'll ever be. Anybody can have a bad day once in a while. Everybody does."

"Those Crawdads feel like a million years ago," Frank said. "And my arm oughta be in a museum, 'cause it feels a million years old."

"That's why Azariah's finishing up for you," Harv said. "You've put a stack of miles on it. Give it some rest, and you'll be better next time out. Besides, next time you'll pitch in a park where the grass grows."

"I hope so." Fidgety Frank made as if to hold his nose. "That dang canal stinks, too—unless I'm just smelling my dead arm."

"It's the canal," Wes said. "I don't care how dead your arm is—it wouldn't stink like that."

We made the third out, and Azariah went back to the mound and took some more punishment. Our bats woke up a little, but not enough to make a real game of it. It wound up 13-7. The Cowboys were happy. So were the Twin Falls fans. They'd knocked off the mighty House of Daniel! It was as close to winning the Series as a place like Twin Falls could come.

In spite of the rain, in spite of the roofless grandstand, we had a better than decent crowd. We made enough to get through to Boise, no worries. We all had a little more cash in our pockets and grouch bags. You don't get rich playing in places like Twin Falls. You show the flag. You try to win. If you don't, you fool around so the fans enjoy it. We managed that.

Then you clean up and you get out of town. We managed that, too. There'd be a story in the paper about how the Cowboys pounded the stuffing out of us, but who twenty miles away read the Twin Falls paper? As far as the world knew, we were still the champion semi-pros. Next time we won, we'd believe it again ourselves.

(XVII)

Boise was another one of those towns that had been in the Utah–Idaho League till there was no Utah–Idaho League to be in any more. That team was called the Senators—Boise, I found out, was the capital of Idaho. When I went through there, two or three semipro teams played one another and the teams farther east. We were scheduled against the Boise Broncos.

We played at a field in the Boise Municipal Park, not far from the statehouse. I don't think that's where the Senators used to perform. It wasn't half bad, though. If they ever got a minor-league team back, they could spruce up the place, maybe put in some lights for night ball and make the grandstand bigger, and it would do fine.

I liked their uniforms—they had brown bucking broncs on their chests and on their caps, too. When I got close to one of the players, I saw it said *Bronco Bootery* under the horse in small letters. After that, I knew who was putting the money into their team.

Their pitcher looked as though he'd taken the mound for the Senators, and for all the pro teams Boise'd had before them. If he wasn't forty, he was forty-five. As soon as you saw him, you knew he'd throw junk and have good control. Against a team full of eager, free-swinging kids, he'd keep 'em off balance.

But we'd seen guys like that before. We hit him harder than the Twin Falls Cowboys had hit Fidgety Frank and Azariah the day before. He lasted three innings before the Broncos' skipper decided he needed to try someone else. It was 9-2 by then, and the new pitcher didn't help.

Their glovework didn't help, either. I don't recall whether they made five or six errors that day. I'm sure it was one or the other. You haven't got a chance when you do something like that. Somebody in the stands who know who their sponsor was shouted, "No wonder you play for the bootery! You boot it often enough!"

This was in the bottom of the eighth, mind. The crowd had been sitting on its hands since the fifth or sixth. The score, if I remember straight, was 16-4. It was one of those awful days any team can have. We'd had one ourselves against Twin Falls. So everybody who hadn't gone home by then heard this yell. And of course everybody who heard it laughed. Getting laughed at by your own fans is the one thing I can think of that's worse than having them boo you.

They booed plenty when we got the last out an inning later. Don't get me wrong—that's no fun, either. These are people who live with you. Their kids go to school with yours. You gas up your Plymouth at the service station one of them runs. Your wife buys pickles and flour at the grocery where another one stands in back of the cash register.

You think you won't hear about the kind of game your team played? You think your wife won't? And your son? You're dreaming if you do. Junior will come home from first grade and ask you *Daddy, why are you a bum?* You sure you want to play this game again?

Their manager came over to Harv and shook his hand. You could see he was a gentleman, but you could also see he was a gentleman who'd got thrashed. "You didn't try to run it up, and I thank you for that," he said. Then his mouth twisted. "You didn't need to. We did it for you."

Harv set a hand on his shoulder. "Hey, it happens to everybody once in a while. It happened to us yesterday down the road from here."

"I saw that," the Broncos' manager said. "If you really want to know, I thought the paper had the score backwards."

"Nope," Harv said. "We got waxed. I wasn't jumping up and down about it, but what can you do? The Cowboys didn't try and rub it in, either. We just played a lousy game, that's all."

"They wouldn't rub it in against you. Oh, no. They'll wait till the next time we play 'em, then rub it in on us." The Broncos' skipper sounded like the managers from La Mesa and Las Cruces, down in New Mexico. But we'd beaten both of them, so neither could boast. Wasn't like that here.

"Hey, tell 'em you've got a ballpark where the grass'll grow. That'll shut 'em up," Harv said.

A blue jay landed on the dugout roof and pecked at the peanut shells to see if there were any peanuts in 'em. Only it wasn't a blue jay like the ones in Oklahoma. Oh, it was a jay, a lot of it was blue, and it had a crest. It skrawked like a jay, too. But it was bigger than a regular blue jay, and its head was black. Isn't that funny?

Now that I think back on it, the jays in New Mexico didn't have crests at all. I'd done so much traveling, even the birds were getting peculiar. If I'd paid more attention, I'm sure I would've noticed more things like that.

While I was watching the blue jay that wasn't quite a blue jay like I was used to, the Broncos' manager chuckled. From a guy whose team made all those errors and who lost by twelve runs, that was something. "There you go," he said. "But they like that horrible place, you know?"

"They've probably got other things wrong with 'em, too," Harv said. The Broncos' boss man laughed out loud. If you've got to get KO'd, there are worse ways to climb off the canvas.

We hopped out of the sack early the next morning. We had a game in Lewiston against the Indians that day. I had no idea where Lewiston was. But Harv did, so we got up with the sun. We ate breakfast at an all-night diner, and poured down the coffee as if Prohibition on it started two days later. Then we got into the bus. North up US 95 we went.

The mountains in Colorado are higher than the ones in Idaho. The ones in Idaho have sharper edges, though. I noticed that especially because we were leaving the valley of the Snake River, where we'd spent most of our time in Idaho. Not many sharp edges there. It's as though some enormous fire elemental way under the ground melted everything in the valley till it got soft enough to lose those edges.

Going up through the mountains to Lewiston, we got them back. Boy, did we ever! Sometimes US 95 was narrower than you wished it would be. You paid attention to that most of all when the drop was on your side. There were guardrails a lot of the time, but you didn't want to think about what would happen if the bus chose just the wrong minute to blow a tire or lose its brakes. Guardrails would never hold it, and some of those drops went a long way down.

Right outside of Lewiston was the Nez Perce reservation. That made me wonder if the Lewiston Indians really were Indians. Plenty of

Indians in Oklahoma, of course. Most lived farther east than Enid, but some of the guys on the Eagles had a little Cherokee blood. They were proud of it—it wasn't the tarbrush or anything.

We drove past some Nez Perce kids playing ball on a schoolyard. They looked like Indians, all right, but they didn't look much like Cherokees. Well, you wouldn't expect a squarehead to look like a dago, either.

Lewiston's a nice little town. Idaho is a lot like New Mexico that way—it hasn't got any big cities. We were back in the Snake River valley again, but now we'd got north of the melty part.

The gal who ran our roominghouse looked to be part Indian herself. Most, I'd say, but she wasn't a fullblood, on account of she had blue eyes. Well, back in Oklahoma I knew some blue-eyed people who called themselves Cherokees, too.

We could relax at the roominghouse for a while before we went to play. The Indians had scheduled a night game to draw better. Their home field was the normal school's ballpark, and it had lights.

"Even if they don't have their own ballyard, they're one of the top clubs around here, so be sharp out there," Harv warned us. "I hear they're going into the Idaho–Washington League next year, and that's a real good semipro circuit. Wait till we get to Spokane. Some of the teams there already belong to it, and they play exhibitions against us and against the Seattle Indians from the Coast League and against the Tokyo Titans. Sometimes they even win."

Wes knew that stuff, but he started laughing anyway. "Wait a second," he said. "The Lewiston Indians play the Seattle Indians?"

"I'm not sure about that, but the Spokane clubs do." Harv took longer to see the joke than he might have. "Oh," he said when he did. "Yeah. The Indians always win."

"But they always lose, too," Wes said.

I had my own *Wait a second*. "Tokyo's in Japan, right?" I said. "Across the ocean and everything?"

"That's right." Harv nodded.

"They play baseball there?" I was a kid from Oklahoma. I didn't know anything. Till I joined up with the House of Daniel, I'd hardly even known they played baseball in Mexico.

"Yup." He nodded. "Sometimes the Titans come to America in the wintertime when their regular season's over. They barnstorm like us when they do. We played 'em a couple of years ago, down in California. We beat 'em, but it might've gone either way. They could play some."

"Baseball. In Japan! How about that?" I couldn't have been much more surprised if he'd told me the House of Daniel played a team from Mars. Green men with four arms didn't seem much stranger to me than Japs. I knew Japs looked pretty much like Chinamen, but I wasn't sure I'd ever seen one.

Some of the Lewiston Indians *were* Indians, all right. No matter what they were, they looked sharp loosening up. Salamanders blazed on top of poles outside the fences. I don't think the light they gave was as even as what we got from the electrics in Denver, but we could play by it. Now I had a few night games under my belt. I didn't feel as funny about the idea as I had in Madrid, New Mexico.

What I really wanted was to see whether Fidgety Frank could bounce back from the pounding he took in Twin Falls. If he was just worn out there and had a bad game, that was one thing. If something in his flipper had gone sour, though, we had worries. Wes couldn't go every day. If we had to run Azariah or Eddie or somebody else who wasn't a proper pitcher out there in games we wanted to win . . . No, that wouldn't be so hot.

Some of the crowd were really Indians, too. Not everything they called to their team was in English, or in any language I'd ever heard before. I guess it was whatever the Nez Perces used amongst themselves. Frank got the Indians on the field out in the bottom of the first. One guy hit the ball hard, but it was right at me.

"How you doin'?" Harv asked from the dugout—in fact, it was just a bench inside a chain-link cage with no ceiling and a couple of openings in the sides.

"Not too bad," Fidgety Frank answered.

We got him a couple of runs in the second. I singled in one myself. It was only a bloop in back of their second baseman and in front of the right fielder, but it did the trick.

Frank made the most of the lead. He kicked his right leg high in the air and waggled his foot. He hesitated here, there, any old where, in his motion. He threw slow, slower, slowest—except once in a while he'd sneak in a fastball when they weren't looking for it. He was *pitching*, was what he was doing. It may have looked funny, or even ridiculous, but it got the job done.

Their cleanup hitter was the kind of guy who looked like he had muscles in his sweat. Fidgety Frank made him break not one but two bats, curving him inside and getting him to hit it off his fists. The guy's fourth time up, in the bottom of the eighth, he hit one over the fence, but by then we were up 6-0. So 6-1 was how it ended.

After the game, that cleanup hitter aimed a finger at Fidgety Frank as though he wished he had a pistol. "Hope I never see you again," he said.

Frank blew him a kiss. "Thank you kindly. I love you, too."

"You made me guess wrong all night long, except when it didn't matter any more," the guy said. He had blond hair and pink skin, but something in the angles of his cheekbones and his chin told you he wasn't all one thing or the other.

Harv put his arm around Fidgety Frank. "Name of the game," he said.

"Yeah, it is." The big man nodded. "I saw Carpetbag Booker put on a show like that in Spokane one time, but nobody else till now."

That made Fidgety Frank touch the bill of his cap. "Obliged, friend," he said. "Carpetbag's the best there is. I ain't, but I do try."

The salamanders dimmed just then, to save the Indians the cost of feeding 'em so much. All the faces, even the white men's, went dusky orange. Shadows seemed thick enough not to need people to cast 'em. It was getting chilly; the heat of the day didn't last once the sun went down. Wish I could say that about summertime in Oklahoma.

The Indians' manager came up beside their cleanup hitter. He looked more like a real Indian than the other fella did. "You learned us a lesson today," he told Fidgety Frank. He turned his head toward Harv. "Your whole team did. You play as tight a game as the Seattle Indians."

"I don't know if that's true, but thanks for saying so." Harv touched his cap, too. "And now we're gonna scurry. We're going into Spokane tomorrow, and we'll play in those parts for a bit."

"I may come up there myself and catch a game or two," the Indians' manager said. "Like to see you play, and like to keep an eye on the teams there, too. We'll be in the league with 'em next year. The more you know, the better you do."

"There you go," Harv said. My head bobbed up and down with his. If I were a slugger like the Indians' cleanup man, I wouldn't have needed to worry about things like bunting and hitting the cutoff man and playing in the right place for the guy who was up. But I did need to worry about those things, so I noticed when other people paid attention to them.

Another hundred miles on the bus. What was that? Not a long ride, not a short one, not when the bus belonged to the House of Daniel. The trip up US 195 was mighty pretty, though. Eastern Washington—they called it the Inland Empire—had some of the finest farming country I'd ever seen anywhere. The wheatfields were green, green, green, just starting to go golden. The country gently rolled. It wasn't flat like the prairie. Here and there, brown squares of fallow land gave the picture a touch of variety.

Everything was just so. That impressed me, too. But for a few patches of mustard with those little yellow flowers, I hardly saw any weeds. All the houses were neat and looked freshly spruced up. Same with the barns and other outbuildings. I don't recall spotting a barbed-wire fence with a missing strand, or even one that sagged very far.

Spokane was the city where people from that whole Inland Empire came to do business. It was bigger than Enid, smaller than Tulsa. Seattle's bigger, of course, but Seattle's on the other side of the mountains, on the other side of the state. Spokane was just as happy *not* thinking about Seattle, thankyouverymuch.

We got to unpack in our roominghouse. We were going to stay in town for a while. We had games against three of the teams from the Idaho–Washington League. We were going to take on the Silver Loaf Bakers on Monday, the Bohemian Brewers on Tuesday, and Inland Motor Freight on Wednesday. They banged heads with one another on the weekends, and with the out-of-town teams in their league. In between times, they stayed sharp and made money with exhibitions against smaller clubs or against barnstormers like us.

All the games were at Natatorium Park—Nat Park, they called it.

They used to have a swimming place there before they built the ball-park. That's what a natatorium is: a fancy name for a swimming hole. And if you think I knew that before I got to Spokane, kindly think again.

Nat Park was in a bigger park. Big pines grew all around it. It was another one of those all-wood ballparks that don't last, and it was fall-ing to pieces right before our eyes. They'd run it up before I was born. Now it was running down. The stands held four or five thou-sand, though—not comfortably, but they did—so Harv stayed happy.

Wes took one look at the sagging, shabby grandstand roof before we even went inside and said, "Let's hope we can get these games in before the termites finish eating the joint." That was about the size of it.

The playing field had its quirks, too. The infield was all dirt, like the one at Merchants Park in Denver. It was only about 250 down the right-field line, but a lot longer out to center and left. I figured I'd shift a little into left-center to cover as much ground as I could.

Watching the Bakers take their warmup cuts, I wasn't amazed to see that they had four or five lefty hitters who looked strong. They were another team that had looked for players who could use what their park gave them.

The crowd cheered them when they took the field. The stands weren't full, but I'm sure we drew better than three thousand. The House of Daniel came through there every year, near enough. The fans liked to watch their home-town heroes square off against the traveling team, and Harv liked the money he made.

By the time the game was over, as many folks were cheering us as the Bakers. We beat 'em 5-2. Wes could've taught a class on how to pitch, the way he handled them. He worked those big lefty bats away again and again, so they couldn't pull the ball down the short right-field line. When he came in, it was in off the plate to jam them. He treated the right-handed hitters just the other way. He wanted them to hit to left. That was the big part of the ballpark. And he made it work all game long.

We had a better house the next day against the Bohemian Brewers. Their manager was a tall, skinny guy they called Sad Slim Smith. He looked the part; if you asked his face, it would've told you he was watching his house burn down with his family inside.

We brought Fidgety Frank out there, and the Brewers threw another southpaw at us. In Nat Park, lefties made sense. They were better against power hitters who swung from the left side, and those were the guys who could do you in there.

I wanted to see whether Frank could give us another good outing after the start in Lewiston. I'm sure Harv wanted the same thing even more than I did. Come to that, I'm sure Frank did, too. We got a couple of runs. So did they, on a long home run. Fidgety Frank didn't put that pitch where he wanted to, but anybody'll make a mistake now and then. Even Carpetbag did. What mattered was how long you put between *now* and *then*.

I singled up the middle to lead off the fifth. Then I lit out for second. Back in the day, everybody ran all the time. It's more a power game now. The steal catches the other guys napping. And it did that time. The throw from behind the plate came in way late.

Fidgety Frank flared a Texas Leaguer over the shortstop's head. I saw right away it would drop, so I was running almost from the crack of the bat. I scored standing up. Then the top of our order chewed up the Brewers' lefty. We came out of the fifth with a 7-2 lead. And Frank held on to it. We won that one going away, 9-3.

The Brewers were good sports about it. In fact, they'd brought along a few cases of what they turned out at work. Most of us—not all, but most—were ready to help turn 'em into cases of empties. I don't think anybody except maybe Wes got smashed, but we got happy for sure.

"How come a city this big doesn't have a pro team?" I asked Sad Slim Smith.

"On account of the minors say Nat Park's too rundown to play in," he answered . . . sadly. "Our team in the Pacific Coast International League pegged out fourteen, fifteen years ago, and nobody's wanted us back since." He gulped from a bottle; I hadn't realized what a nerve I'd touched. "It's better for guys like us. We draw more than we would with a pro team in town. But still . . . If they built a ballpark that didn't look like a shantytown reject, we'd get a club in nothin' flat."

Inland Motor Freight the next day. They wore IMF in big red letters on their shirts, and on their caps, too. When they went through their paces before the game, they didn't look any better than the Bakers or the Brewers. But they hit Wes as though they knew Amos's signs before he set 'em down. Maybe they had somebody peeking through a gap in the fence with field glasses. Things like that do happen. Maybe they just got lucky. Or maybe Wes was still hurting from the beer he'd put down the night before. No, he hadn't been shy about it.

Whatever the reason, they beat us 7-4. Harv fussed and fumed and carried on. He sounded as ticked off as anybody could without cussing up a storm. "Consarn it, I wanted to get outta here with a sweep," he growled inside our tiny little mildewed dressing room. "We shoulda done it, too." He took a deep breath. "Wes . . ."

"Yeah, Harv?" Wes sounded quieter than usual. He knew what was coming.

And it came. "Don't get plowed before you're gonna pitch, all right? Anybody could see you were still feeling it out there."

"Sorry, Harv." Wes looked like a schoolboy getting it from the principal. Well, as much like that as a long-haired, bearded guy with his shirt off and his hairy chest sticking out can look. Your schoolboy probably won't stink of sweat and liniment, either.

"Fudge!" Harv said. I'd never heard that one from him before. It sounded fierce.

"Oh, take it easy, Harv. So they got a win. We still took two outta three," Fidgety Frank said. He could afford to talk—he'd won his game in Spokane. He went on, "They'll want us back next year, and they'll all have something to shoot for."

"Something to shoot at, you mean. Us. Fudge!" Harv wasn't buying it, not even for a minute.

I enjoyed staying in Spokane. First time since the Great Zombie Riots wound down that we'd stayed anywhere longer than a day. First time since then that we'd just taken the bus to get to the ballpark. I liked relaxing that tiny bit. I could do the kind of traveling the House of Daniel had to do, but it wore on me. Some people liked it. Wes did, I think, and I'm sure about Harv. It drove others crazy. If they ever got on the bus, they didn't stay. I was kind of in between.

We rolled out of Spokane heading west on US 10. More of that fine, fine wheat country, with apple and pear orchards mixed in. After about sixty miles, at a little town called Wilbur, the highway swung from west to southwest. We went northwest instead, up a smaller road.

Our next game was at a place called Mason City—almost as often as not, they called it Electric City. The Mason City Beavers were another semipro team that played its regular games in the Idaho–Washington League.

Mason City was a company town, like Madrid, New Mexico. Only they weren't miners there. They were working on the Coulee Dam across the Columbia. When they got done, if they ever did, they said it'd be the biggest man-made thing in the whole world. When they said Coulee, I thought they meant Coolie. So I was surprised at first when I didn't see any Chinamen in Mason City.

But I knew—I mean, I knew for sure—how come they called their team the Beavers. After all, what else do beavers do but . . . ?

You could tell Mason City was a company town just by looking at it. All the houses were built to the same pattern. They were all painted white. They didn't seem like bad houses—don't get me wrong. But you had to do things the company way. Back when they made flivvers, you could get one painted whatever color you wanted, as long as you wanted black. It was like that.

After a while, Ford had to paint cars other colors or go under. Too many other people made cars, too. If you worked for a company that made dams, you had less choice.

When I first saw Mason City, I thought it was too small to let us get much of a crowd. But the place was baseball-crazy. They loved their Beavers. And Coulee City was only a mile away. That was the town where the engineers and the wizards working on the dam lived. They were talking about getting up their own team, but they hadn't done it yet. In the meantime, they pulled for the Beavers.

Mason City Ballpark was as neat and orderly as the rest of the town. It was made from concrete and steel, not wood. They were putting so much concrete and steel into the dam, I bet they didn't even notice a ballpark's worth. It was 335 down each line, 380 to left-center and right-center, and 405 in straightaway center. Like I said, neat and orderly. If it was less interesting than a lot of playing fields I've seen, the company likely didn't care.

The Beavers' pitcher fit the park to a T. He was a fastball, curveball, changeup guy who couldn't blow it past you but hit his spots. We nicked him for a run in the first, one in the third, one more in the fourth.

Meanwhile, Fidgety Frank mowed 'em down. With the herky-jerky windup and the leg kick and the waggle, he seemed as though he belonged in a tumbledown wreck of a place like Nat Park. But the Beavers couldn't solve him. They were out in front on his changeups, late when he came in with the heat.

Their crowd got quiet. Little by little, they saw how well we played even if we looked funny. The only thing wrong with the stands was, they didn't hold enough people. Official capacity was 1,500. They sold standing room for us, but we could've drawn more than we did if the park would've held 'em.

They batted for their pitcher in the bottom of the seventh. I don't know whether the guy they brought in had a tired arm or was just no good, but we hit him hard. It had been 3-1. It ended up 8-2.

They were good losers. We and the Beavers all ate supper at the company cafeteria, and the company sprang for our food. I had a pork chop with stewed apples on top, mashed potatoes, and peach pie. It was better than what the coal-mining outfit dished out down in Madrid.

They lodged us overnight, too. Harv was happy about that. It partway made up for the smaller crowd. The rooms were . . . rooms. They were newer and cleaner than a lot of the places we stayed at, but I've lain down on plenty of mattresses that made my back happier.

They fed us breakfast, too. That was nice of them. A plump fellow in an expensive suit said, "You fellas may look . . . different, but you sure can show people how to play the game." He meant *may look weird*, of course, but he did manage not to come out with it.

"Thank you, friend," Harv answered. We got on the bus and headed west down to Wilbur, then west on US 10 for Wenatchee. The mountains climbed up the horizon as we went toward them. They'd grown tall by the time we got to town.

Apple orchards all over the place there. The Wenatchee Chiefs played for an apple-packing outfit, matter of fact. Their crates had a solemn chief with a feather headdress and buckskin shirt on the ends. They were all over town, used for everything from apples to auto parts to secondhand books. The team played in Recreation Park. It was at the south end of town, and held about 3,500.

That was the good news. The bad news was, it was 320 down the lines but only 350 to center. The unpainted wood fence was low, too. "Oh, my aching back!" Wes said. "What did I do to deserve this?"

"Daniel said, 'My God hath sent His angel, and hath shut the lions' mouths, that they have not hurt me: forasmuch as before Him innocency was found in me,'" Harv quoted. How much innocency an angel would've found in Wes, I can't tell you. But I don't know that about the Chiefs' pitcher, either.

It was the kind of game you'd expect in such a silly little ballpark. We wound up taking it, 9-7. I threw a guy out at the plate from the warning track in left-center. I'd be prouder of the throw if it were longer, but it sure went straight.

And we headed straight out of town the next morning, early, bound for Bellingham.

US 10 went through the Wenatchee National Forest. More pines and firs and spruces than I'd ever imagined, let alone seen. I saw dryads flitting through the forest, too, looking for saplings to live in. There's an awful lot of logging in Washington state outside the places where it's against the law. Tree spirits without trees are as sad and desperate as people without jobs or houses. I don't know what to do about that, or how much trouble it may brew down the road.

We went over Stevens Pass and down the other side. It's only 4,000 feet, though—not half so high as the ones in Colorado. Where US 10 runs into US 99 outside of Seattle, we took the 99 north to Bellingham. And along the way I saw the ocean for the very first time. It was gray. It looked cold. But I saw it. In Oklahoma, I never reckoned I would.

Bellingham is a lumber town. I wouldn't care to think about how many dryads that spent a few hundred years in a fir are trying to make homes in shrubs and rose bushes these days. The world's hard on everybody—not just on people.

In Bellingham, I didn't just see the ocean. I smelled it. Now that I've had that thrill, I almost wish I didn't. It wasn't what you'd call real clean.

I liked the Bellingham Chinooks' uniforms. They had a salmon—a chinook is a kind of salmon, I found out—jumping over a baseball bat. They were different. Battersby Park, where they played, that was different, too. Never seen anything like it before or since.

The stands were fine. It held about three thousand, so it was a tad smaller than the ballpark in Wenatchee. But whoever laid out the field must've had his head on a slant. It was 290 down the left-field line, 350 to center . . . and 435 to right. It was shaped like a first baseman's mitt, in other words.

Harv took one look and said, "Snake, today you're a right fielder."

"Makes sense to me," I said. "Enough ground out there—you bet."

Fidgety Frank scratched his head, staring out at the funny field. "You know how I pitched in that Spokane park?" he said. "Well, today I gotta turn that upside down and inside out." I saw what he meant. He'd want the Chinooks' left-handed hitters to pull to the long field. Righties, though, he'd work away so they'd hit to the opposite field.

You can always make your plans beforehand. Whether you can do what you want is another story a lot of the time. So is whether following your plan will wind up working out the way you hope.

Clouds blew off the Pacific. It was cool and damp. We'd left the dry, warm weather on the other side of the mountains. People came to the game anyhow. Most of them wore checked wool shirts, red or green or blue, and dungarees. For once, I didn't sweat like a pig in my wool flannels.

When the home team took the field, one of those loudmouthed fans you run into sometimes bellowed out, "C'mon, Chinooks!" from behind their dugout. My head swung in that direction. He shouted again. He was a sandy-haired guy in his forties, dressed like a lumberjack. I didn't know what that proved, though, since so many others there wore the same kind of clothes.

He whooped and hollered when they got us out in the first without giving up a run. In between the hollers, he drank beer. That was like putting gasoline in the engine. It kept him running.

Their third hitter clouted one out to right. But he didn't hit it over that far-off fence, so I ran it down. The big-mouthed fan booed me. I felt like tipping my cap to him, but I didn't.

When I came up to lead off the third, I bunted. I hadn't tried that in a while. If you do it all the time, word will get ahead of you. They'll play close and make it hard. I caught the Chinooks by surprise, though. Their third baseman didn't bother throwing. He just picked up the ball. That loudmouth called me about half the names in the book.

He called me the other half when I scored after Azariah pulled one over the short left-field fence. It had a stretch of chain-link above the planking, but it still wasn't high enough to stop cheap homers.

"Boy, that guy sounds like he knows you," Harv said when old Leather Lungs wouldn't shut up no matter what.

"And loves you," Wes added. I laughed—more than he must've figured the joke deserved. But it tickled my funny bone.

The Chinooks got a run back in the fifth. The loudmouth did everything but hang on a big bass drum. They might've plated more, only I ran down a long line drive. The guy in the stand hadn't used up all his bad names. He found some new ones, just for me.

He found some more when I walked, swiped a bag, and scored in the seventh. We got a couple of more then, and another two in the eighth. A Chinook hit one over the center-field fence in the bottom of the eighth. The way it would have in Wenatchee, that sounds more impressive than it was. The fan with the big trap kept right on rooting.

It didn't help. They tried a ninth-inning rally, but that fell short. We came out on top, 6-4. I ran in from right as fast as I could. I didn't think the loudmouth would move real quick himself, not after all that beer, but you never could tell.

Everybody was staring at me as I hustled over by the third-base dugout. Wes and Eddie and Harv must have figured I wanted to punch out that guy. Not exactly. "Don't go!" I yelled at him. "You hear me, Pa? Don't you go!"

(XVIII)

He'd started up the steps, half a dozen rows toward the way out. Now he stopped and turned and looked me over. I wasn't sure he'd recognize me. He'd never seen me with whiskers before (he had some of his own, too, but just the I-didn't-shave-the-past-couple-of-days kind). And he'd been drinking all through the game, at least—I didn't know how long a running start he'd had before it.

"Jack?" he said while people heading to the exit tramped past him. "Is that you, boy?"

"It's me, all right." Hearing my own name felt funny. The House of Daniel guys, they called me Snake most of the time, and I was getting used to it. Hearing Pa's voice again, that felt stranger yet. It had all through the game. I'd known it right away, even if I hadn't heard it for years. It's not the kind of thing you're ever likely to forget.

He started coming down the stairs, toward me. "What the devil you doing here, Jack?"

"I could ask you the same thing," I said. "I thought you were in California."

"I was for a while, over near Eureka," he answered. I didn't know then where Eureka was; I've found out since. Pa went on, "Went up into Oregon, and then up here. Don't quite know how I got to be a lumberjack, but I did. It ain't a bad way to make some money, and there's lots of chances for jobs."

"If you say so." I wondered how they liked him crocked in the woods. Because he *would* drink. I knew that. He'd been drinking at least since Ma died. Maybe before then, too—I can't remember so far back. I asked him, "Have the day off today?"

He nodded. "Uh-huh—the whole weekend." I'd forgotten it was Saturday. When you were on the road, each day blurred into the next. He went on, "Wanted t'come out an' see the Chinooks play the House of Daniel. Never reckoned I'd be watching my own kid." He eyed me. "You look peculiar with a beard."

"It's part of the uniform, like," I answered. And it was, just as much as our spikes or the roaring lions on our shirts. We were the baseball team with the beards. The beards and the hair were what people knew us by.

From behind me, Eddie said, "This guy here is really your dad, Snake—uh, Jack?"

"That's right." I looked around. Half the team had gathered there. Having somebody they played ball with run into his old man out of the blue wasn't something that happened every day, or even every week. "This is my pa, Clayton Spivey. Pa, these're Eddie Lelivelt and Wes Petersen and Frank Carlisle and Amos Funkenstein."

"How about that?" Pa said. "How'd you get to play on a hot team like this, anyways? I didn't reckon you were that good."

"Thanks a bunch," I told him. He'd sure poured down enough so he didn't care what came out of his mouth. Trouble was, that didn't mean he had it wrong. I still wasn't sure I was good enough to stick with the House of Daniel.

Harv came over, too, so I introduced him and my pa. Harv said, "After we clean up, we're gonna have some supper. If you want to come along, Mr. Spivey, we'd be glad to have you."

I kinda wondered about that; Pa wasn't the sort who grew on you when you knew him longer. Before I could say anything, though, or even figure out what I should say, my father answered, "I dunno . . ." I understood what that little whine meant. I'd heard him sound that way when folks in Enid were dunning him. It meant he was busted, flat, broke, skint.

"I'll spring, Pa," I said.

Well, that put his nose out of joint. I might have known it would. "So you're a rich man now with your baseball, huh?" he said.

I laughed. I couldn't help it. And all the House of Daniel guys standing in back of me, they laughed, too. How could you do anything else? Nobody gets rich playing semipro ball. Nobody. Dang few—I mean *dang* few—make any kind of living at it. I knew how lucky I was to manage that much.

The laughs only made him huffier. I might have known they would.

"I don't aim to be any kind of bother," he said. Even drunk, he was proud, in his way. Maybe I get it from him. I don't know. How can you know something like that?

"Okey-doke," I said. "Tell you what, Pa. I saw some kind of joint over on Girard Street, maybe a block from here. Let's you and me go there by our lonesome. I can walk back to the boarding house after we eat. I know where it's at." Talking with him, more Oklahoma came out than it did with the team.

He finally decided that was all right. I cleaned up under Battersby Park and got back into my street clothes. Eddie took charge of my baseball stuff. That was nice of him. "Go on," he told me. "How often do you get the chance to spend some time with your father?"

"It's been a while, sure enough," I said. "Now I have to work out whether I want to."

Pa waited out front, near the ticket booths. He'd got hold of another bottle of beer from somewhere. He killed it when I came up to him, and tossed the dead soldier in a trash can. "Well, boy, let's get going," he said.

He ordered stuffed cabbage at that place I'd seen. I had liver and onions. He ordered a beer, too. So did I. The food came quick enough. It was . . . food. Not terrible, not worth remembering. He shoveled it in. He didn't talk.

After a bit, I did: "How come, Pa?"

"How come what?"

"How come what?" That made me mad. "How come you went and disappeared? That's how come what!"

He took a pull at his Olympia. " 'Cause I couldn't stand that stinking shack or that stinking town one more minute, that's how come. Plain enough for you, sonny boy? You didn't need me no more. You were old enough to get by on your own. You must've been, hey? You went and did it."

I bit down hard on that one. Except 'cause he took all the money in the place, I hadn't been any too sorry he was gone. Still . . . "You could've let me know where you went. Sent a CC message or had somebody write a card for you. Something."

"Like you cared," he said. I bit down hard on that, too. What was he, back in Enid? A no-account town drunk. I knew it. So did he.

One more time, though—still . . . "You're my flesh and blood. You're about what there is of it. And are you so much better off out here?"

That made him laugh. It was a nasty laugh, not one I cared to listen to. "Oh, you bet I am!" he said. "There, I'd been worthless Clay Spivey since I was twelve years old. Everybody had me tagged. Here, half the loggers are on the run from crap like that. And you've got your high and mighty nose in the air on account of I drink some? Oh, yes, you do—I can see it. But next to a lot of the fellas I crew with, I'm temperance. And you can take that to church, 'cause it's the Gospel truth!"

He meant it. He was too sore not to mean it. "Lord help 'em, in that case," I said.

"Lord helps him who helps himself." He waved to the fella in the greasy apron behind the counter for another bottle of beer.

I'd wondered if he would want to know about what had gone on in Enid since he pulled up stakes. He didn't care. As far as he was concerned, he'd made a clean break. As far as he was concerned, he'd made a clean break with me, too. It was odd that we'd run across each other, and kind of funny, but that was all it was to him.

Was it that way to me? The longer we sat across from each other, the more I saw it would have to be. "Well, I'm glad I got you here for a supper, anyways," I told him: a last try.

"Yeah, you got me, and a hell of a git you got," he said. It wasn't the kind of father-son reunion they put in stories and films. I wanted it to be. Some of me did, anyhow. But it just wasn't.

"Here." I put money on the table for both of us. "I better get back to that boarding house. We'll be heading . . . wherever we're heading pretty early tomorrow mornin'."

"Thanks," Pa said. "I'll do the buying next time we meet up."

"Sure." I pushed back my chair and stood up. I held out my hand. Pa shook it. I turned around and went on out. I haven't seen him since.

I had a ways to walk before I got to the boarding house. Bellingham's not the big city, but it's no tiny little town, either. It's the biggest place north of Seattle and the towns around there.

Because it was so far north, summer sundown came late. Sunlight still slanted across the sky while I mooched along. I wouldn't have to worry about vampires jumping out at me, not unless I was walking the wrong way and had to waste a lot of time backtracking. And I wasn't. That was good, because I had plenty of other things on my mind. One of those critters could've sunk his teeth into my neck before I even noticed he was around.

There were a lot of things I'd wanted to tell Pa: things I'd done, things I'd seen, things I'd thought, things I'd felt. But to tell him things like that, I needed him to be the kind of man who cared about them. I needed him to be the kind of man who didn't walk out the door without telling me he was leaving.

He wasn't that kind of man. He never had been. He never would be. He didn't give a damn. He never was gonna give a damn. And I couldn't do one thing about it.

To be fair, he didn't look for me to give a damn about him, either. I wanted to, but how could I when he pushed me away as hard as he could without using his arms? There was nothing between us. There never had been, not since I was tiny. There wouldn't be. It wasn't over. How can something be over when it doesn't start?

Shadows kept getting longer, but the sun's gotta be up to cast shadows. I almost would've welcomed a vampire, if I saw it before it got me. It would've given me something to fight, and I was looking for something to fight just then.

Maybe, instead of buying Pa supper, I should've punched him in the nose. That might've got through to him. Nothing I said to him while we were eating did—I'll tell you that. What can you do? Sometimes things don't work out the way you imagine they might. Then you're stuck with it. There I was, walking through Bellingham, stuck with it.

The rest of the guys were already back at the place when I finally got there. Some of them had already gone to bed. Some were sitting around in the parlor, looking at papers or magazines or playing hearts.

Wes looked up from his cards. "How'd it go, Snake?"

I'd known he would ask, or somebody would. I kind of spread my hands. "It didn't." I stopped for a second, trying to find a way to put it. "The bridge is out."

"There's no there there," Wes said. "Somebody said that about

somewhere or other. It stuck in my head. I'm not sure what it's supposed to mean, but it sounds like it oughta mean something."

"It does, doesn't it?" I thought about it. Then I nodded. "It's pretty
close. There's no connection between me and him, for sure."

"That's too bad. That's a crying shame, as a matter of fact," Wes
said. "Long as you've got a father, you ought to have one who's worth
the paper he's printed on."

"It's no big surprise," I said. "I wish he was different, but he ain't.
He'll do whatever he pleases, and he won't think about me or anybody else before he does."

"Almost better to have no father at all than to have one like
that," Wes said.

I won't try and tell you the same thought hadn't crossed my mind,
because it had. It's a miserable thing to think, a miserable thing to
say, about the fella who's half the reason you're in the world at all.
But what can you do? Things happen the way they happen, not the
way the folks they happen to wish they would. Everybody would be a
lot happier if that worked the other way round.

All I could do there in the parlor was shrug. "I wish things were
different," I said. "I won't try and tell you anything else. But at least
now I've got some answers instead of questions. They may not be the
answers I want, but I've got 'em. Did Harv tell you guys where we're
going next?"

"Down to Tacoma," Wes answered. "We might not go there if
Seattle was in town, but they're on the road. Me, I think Tacoma'd be
worth stopping at even if the Indians were at home. It's Seattle's kid
brother, and it doesn't like the big city up the road even a little bit."

I could laugh when I wasn't thinking about Pa. "Where have we
seen that before?" I said.

"Only everywhere," Wes answered, and that was about the size of it.

Tacoma's pretty near the size of Spokane. Wes put it just right:
that's the right size to remind it it's not nearly as big or as important as Seattle right next door. Tacoma is a port, a lumber town, a
fishing town, a railroad town, and a town that works metal. One
great big smelter has a tall, tall stack that spits out a smoke trail you
can see for miles.

Trouble is—at least if you're Tacoma—that Seattle does all the same things, and more besides. Other trouble is, when the Big Bubble popped, it put the screws to the port and to the logging business. Swarms of people went on the dole. Others turned parks into gardens. They had teams of beggars who shared what they got. They did whatever they could, in other words, same as everywhere else.

If you're gonna be broke, you could pick plenty of worse places to do it than Tacoma. It's not too hot; it's not too cold. It's as green as any place could want to be. You've got the bay on one side and the mountains on the other. Mount Rainier is as big and beautiful a mountain as anybody would ever care to see. When you could see it through the haze, I mean. Even when it's not raining around there, the air's damp. No wonder it's all so green.

Tacoma was Seattle's kid brother when it came to baseball, too. Seattle had the Coast League Indians. The PCL is Class AA, like I said before. Out on the West Coast, the PCL might as well be the bigs. The closest big-league teams are in St. Louis, more than half the country away. Only one team in the whole PCL has any kind of arrangement with the bigs. The rest go their own way, as much as they can.

Tacoma . . . isn't like that. The Tacoma Tigers were in the Western International League once upon a time. That was just B ball, a long way down from AA. And the team and the league hit a mine and sank halfway through the season a dozen years earlier.

So semipro teams had played in Athletic Park ever since. Tacoma was like Spokane—it was big enough for a local league. The first team we played down there was an outfit called McNulty Transfer.

They had a script *McNulty* across their chests in red, and a red McN on white caps with blue visors. One guy looked scary taking batting practice. He wasn't especially big, but he hit the ball hard. It jumped off his bat with the kind of *crack!* you don't hear very often. He'd been around; you could see it in his face. He looked head and shoulders more dangerous than anybody else on the team.

"Who is that fella?" I asked a fan sitting in back of our dugout.

"The one who's up there? That's Vic. I forget his last name—something Eye-talian," the fan answered. "He played a couple years for the Indians. He wasn't a regular or nothin', but he did. Then he messed up his knee, and they didn't want him back after that. He's falling to pieces, just like the stands here."

Sure as the demon, Athletic Park had seen better years. Nobody'd bothered painting advertisements or slapping posters on the outfield fences for a long time. Nobody'd bothered painting them at all, to tell you the truth. The planks were faded and warped. You got the feeling you might be able to charge right through them.

I also got the feeling I might have to try it. Down the left-field line it was 312, and 324 to right: a trifle short. But center was more than a trifle short—it was only 374 out there. That isn't far enough, not if you're a center fielder and especially not if you're a pitcher.

And the grandstand roof was even older and more decrepit than the fences. Moss grew on the shadowed parts. I hoped the logs in the columns holding it up hadn't started rotting. All in all, that roof looked more as though they meant it to keep off the rain than the sun.

They had a decent crowd under it, though, and out in the bleachers in the watery sunshine. The McNulty Transfer team trotted out. They had Vic playing first, a sure sign of somebody who could hit but couldn't run any more. Their pitcher was a freckly, redheaded southpaw.

"Boy, he's got the map of Ireland on his mug," Wes said as the guy warmed up.

Harv hit a pretty good drive off him, but the ball didn't carry for beans. Their center fielder had to go back to the track to haul it in. He didn't have any trouble, though. We weren't playing somewhere with thin, dry air any more.

They scored a run off Wes in the first. We came back with three in the third and one more in the fourth. That redhead was wild as a bobcat. He kept walking guys, and we kept making him sorry.

They got one back in the bottom of the sixth. Vic came up with two on and two out. Wes didn't put a curve where he wanted it, and Vic hit a long, high one to center. I had time to get back to that fence, and then up against it. It must've been about eight feet high. I jumped and got my glove above the top of it. The ball hit and stuck. A split second later, I had my meat hand on it, too.

Vic had already gone into his home-run trot. The ump on the bases didn't know I had it, either, not till I threw it back in. That's when he brought up his right fist.

Vic stopped dead, about fifteen feet past first base. Nothing makes an outfielder happier than seeing how disgusted a batter can get. "Oh, for Christ's sake!" Vic hollered. But when I came by him, he swatted me on the butt and said, "Hell of a catch, ya bastard."

"Thanks." I went on into our dugout.

When I got there, Wes squealed, "Oh, Snake! My hero!" like a girl in a dumb movie. He made as if to kiss me like one of those girls, too.

I pushed him away. "If I'd known you were gonna do that, I woulda let him have his homer," I said. We both laughed. Laughing's easy when three runs for the other side don't go up on the board.

We ended up winning the game 6-3. McNulty Transfer got their last run when Vic hit another curve way over the fence in left-center. "Bring that one back, you something-or-other!" he shouted at me as he rounded second. I would've needed a long-handled net, or maybe wings, to do it.

"Well, Snake, you do keep finding ways to earn your keep," Harv said when he paid me.

"Good," I answered. I was extra happy about the catch because I didn't get any hits. I was glad for anything I could do to show him I belonged on the House of Daniel. If I'd had to, I would have run through that fence, or more likely mashed my nose trying.

We stayed in Tacoma two more days. We beat Superior Dairy— trounced 'em, in fact. And then, just to remind us not to get cocky, the team from Kimball Gun Store beat us. Harv hated that. Harv hated to lose any old time, of course. But he hated losing to a team he didn't think was good enough even more.

"They aren't fit to carry our jocks!" he shouted after the game. "Heavens to Betsy, they aren't fit to carry guts to a bear! We've got no business losing to a club like that! We've—" He broke off and glared at us in a different way. "What's so funny, you goose twits?"

That only set us off some more. The guys who didn't start giggling about *Heavens to Betsy* did over *aren't fit to carry guts to a bear*. Sometimes you truly do need to cuss to get across what you're driving at. This seemed like one of those times. He sounded mad, yeah, but he sounded silly, too, and you can't sound silly when you're trying to scorch the paint off somebody. *Goose twits* made things worse, not better.

"Harv, honest to God we know they ain't supposed to beat us," Fidgety Frank said. "Things just didn't go right, that's all."

"I hope to kiss a catfish, they didn't!" Harv yelled. By then, everybody who wasn't already laughing his head off was stuffing a towel in his mouth so he wouldn't. Harv threw his hands in the air. "All right, you pack of mangy clowns—I give up. But you better look like you don't have your heads in your backsides when we go to Yakima tomorrow."

I'd guessed we would go to Olympia and play the Timbermen, the Washington team that went to Denver. Olympia's just the other side of Tacoma, after all. But it turned out the Timbermen were on the road themselves, so we headed for Yakima instead.

Yakima was southeast of Tacoma. They grow fruit around there—apples more than anything else—and hops and wheat. Toward the end of summer, it's like cotton-picking time in Georgia or somewhere like that. The town fills up with farm workers—there are more of them than the folks who live in the valley year-round. The House of Daniel got there before the big inflood started. Even so, there were guys in straw hats and denim shirts and dungarees wandering in and out of the movie houses and saloons, and gals wearing overalls and bandannas looking for packing-plant work moseying down the street peering into shop windows.

At the motor lodge where we stayed, the geezer who ran it said, "I wouldn't have room for you in another six weeks. Everything goes crazy at harvest time. The lodges all fill up. We got shacks, we got tent villages, we got people in bedrolls sleeping out in the open. When they do sleep, I mean. Whole place works its head off."

"Work is a Christian virtue," Harv said.

"Don't reckon slaving is, and what we got then ain't far from it," the old man answered. Harv didn't have a good comeback for that one.

We took on the Yakima Indians at Athletic Field. Not Athletic Park—that was back in Tacoma. Athletic Field. The pro Yakima Indians had played there till they folded about the same time as the pro

Tacoma Tigers. One more semipro team carrying a dead pro team's name. One more ballpark falling to pieces a bit at a time on account of the semipros didn't have the money to keep it up—and on account of wooden ballparks just do start falling to pieces even if you are able to take care of 'em.

Athletic Park had been on the small side. Athletic Field was big: 345 to left, 420 to center, and 353 to right. The fences were high, too. I couldn't hope to stick my glove over the top and swipe a home run. That kind of park meant lots of doubles and triples—plenty of room for the ball to rattle around and to bounce off the fences and away from the outfielders.

Fidgety Frank looked out to the far-off right-field fence and said, "Glad I'm on the hill today. Wes can go chase my mistake, and I don't got to run after his." For some reason or other, Wes didn't jump up and down and dance about that.

By the way the Indians loosened up, they seemed better than any of the teams we'd played in Tacoma. They had a kid shortstop who vacuumed up anything anywhere close to him. But I figured it would come down to pitching in the end. Most of the time, it does.

Most of the time, but not always. A fellow was dancing in the stands. He was red-brown, with black, black hair under his wide-brimmed Stetson. He wore a collarless work shirt and blue jeans and boots like everybody else's, but not everybody wore a coyote's tail sticking out from between the shirt and the dungarees. It wasn't just an ornament, either, or it didn't seem to be. It had as much wiggly life as if it were really attached to him.

No one in the stands got in his way as he capered up and down the aisles. The more he danced, the more he sang—the words weren't English, or anything like English—the better their guy pitched and the more funny hops the ball took.

I wasn't the only one who'd noticed. "What's going on with that fella?" Eddie said to Harv after we went down a run on a ball he should have fielded with his eyes closed.

"Well, I don't know for sure, but it kinda looks like a Yakima Indian giving the Yakima Indians a helping hand, don't it?" Harv said.

"Do something about it," Fidgety Frank growled. "If they beat us, he won't get the credit—I'll get the blame."

"I'll do what I can," Harv answered, "but it's his home park more ways than one."

I needed a second to see what he meant. How long had the Yakima Indians lived right around there? How in tune were they with every little Power that had lived there just as long? Those were more questions where the exact answer didn't matter much. *A long, long time* seemed close enough. So did *mighty in tune*.

But there are little Powers, and then there are big Powers. The little Powers draw their strength from where they're at. The big Powers have strength enough to use it wherever they go. That's what makes them big Powers. And there isn't any Power much bigger than the one they talk about in the Good Book.

Harv looked toward the Yakima with the coyote tail, and he said, " 'How I am come to make thee understand what shall befall thy people in the latter days: for yet the vision *is* for *many* days.' "

He didn't talk loud. The Yakima couldn't have heard him, not with ordinary ears. But he all of a sudden stopped dancing. His tail twitched up, the way a dog's or a coyote's will when it takes a new scent.

" 'And a mighty king shall stand up, that shall rule with great dominion, and do according to his will. And when he shall stand up, his kingdom shall be broken, and shall be divided toward the four winds of heaven; and not to his posterity, nor according to his dominion which he ruled,' " Harv went on. " 'And when he had spoken such words unto me, I set my face toward the ground, and I became dumb.' "

The Yakima with the coyote tail didn't set his face toward the ground. He didn't become dumb, either. He let out a startled yip, the way a dog will if it's running and it slams into your foot when you've got it up to take a step. And his tail went down, down, down like an unhappy dog's. He took off as though he had ants in his britches.

"That Book of Daniel, that's strong stuff." By the way Fidgety Frank said it, he might have been talking about 120-proof rotgut. His voice had the same mix of admiration, respect, and fear.

"You bet it is. Nothin' stronger," Harv answered. Believing it was was what brought you into the churchy part of the House of Daniel and kept you there. By the way Harv handled conjure men, the Book of Daniel had something going for it, all right. He nodded to himself and added, "Let's go play ball."

So we did. Maybe 'cause we were ticked off, maybe just 'cause we were the better ballclub, we won the game 7-5. We should've won by more than that, but the quick kid they had at short made a couple of plays that might've been magic all on their own. I didn't know if he could make it as a pro—one game isn't usually enough to judge how somebody swings the bat. But he could field with anybody. I knew that.

After it was over, Harv told the Indians' manager, "Shame your dancing buddy had to cut out early."

"Mrm." The noise the guy made and the face he pulled might've come when he bit down on something he didn't fancy. He could have been a quarter Indian himself. Or maybe not—you never know for sure. After a few seconds, he decided he needed to say something more: "I didn't put Ralph up to trying his Spilyay routine. He did it on his own hook."

"Trying his what?" Harv asked.

"His Spilyay routine," the Indians' manager repeated. "Means 'coyote' in Yakima. The coyote's always full of tricks and practical jokes, like."

"How about that?" Harv said. I kind of pricked up my ears when I heard it, because some of the Indians back in Oklahoma believed the same thing about the coyote and used him to help make their magic. Anybody who's ever had anything to do with coyotes would believe it.

After the Indians' manager lit a cigarette, he went on, "So I'm sorry about that, but it wasn't my fault. Anyway, looked like you took care of it pretty good."

"Yeah. We did." Harv nodded. "But we shouldn't've had to. Baseball oughta be about what happens in between the white lines, not outside 'em."

"I think you're right. Ralph, though, he's a home-town fan like you wouldn't believe," the Indians' manager said.

"Uh-*huh*." By the way Harv said it, he didn't believe the other fella but didn't need to bother proving he was a liar. He nodded back toward the ticket counters. "Well, let's go split the take. And no—what did you call 'em?—no tricks and practical jokes, all right?"

"Sure," the Indians' manager said quickly. He'd want the House of Daniel back in Yakima the next year so he'd have another big gate to split. And . . . "Even if I aimed to cheat you, put us in a room together and I bet I'd come out without my skivvies."

"The dickens you would!" Harv said. "I don't care what kind of drawers you wear—I don't want 'em."

While they dealt with that, the rest of the House of Daniel cleaned up and got into our regular clothes. "You know," Fidgety Frank said, "sometimes I wonder what would happen if Harv used his Book of Daniel stuff on some team first instead of waiting till they tried to lay spells on us."

"He'd never do that!" Azariah sounded shocked. "It would be sinful. And you heard him—he wants it to be about the game between the lines."

"Yeah, I heard him." Frank sighed. "And I know he wouldn't pull it out first. He wouldn't be Harv if he did. But that doesn't stop me from wondering, or even from wishing. Things sure would be easier if he did."

"For a little while, maybe," Azariah said primly. "Then pretty soon there'd be three or four conjure men and wizards and I don't know what all pulling and tugging every which way at all the ballgames. You wouldn't be able to tell where the baseball started and the magic stopped."

"Who says you can now?" Fidgety Frank answered. "Shove enough money into the pot—big-league money, I mean—and anything can happen. And it's liable to. Don't you know people who swear up and down the Bambino couldn't have hit as many homers as he did without some fancy magic giving him a hand?"

"Just 'cause they swear it doesn't make it so," Azariah said. "I've heard all the big-league parks have wards against that kind of thing, wards set by the best wizards they can hire."

"I've heard the same thing. So what?" Fidgety Frank said. Azariah blinked at him. He said it again: "So what? Whatever one wizard builds up, some other wizard'll find a way to poke a hole in it. Gamblers and fixers can hire strong sorcery, too. You were still a kid when the Black Stockings mess came along, weren't you?"

"I know about it," Azariah said. "Everybody does."

"Well, all right, then," Frank said. "I don't care how good the wards are. People will always find some way to cheat."

"They shouldn't. The game ought to be out on the field, not with some guy dancing in the stands or going to an office and working a spell on a player," Azariah said.

"Yeah. It oughta be. But tell me this—if you found a conjure man who could work a magic that made you good enough to play in the big leagues, would you let him do it?" Fidgety Frank asked.

"He'd have to be quite a conjure man. I know what kind of ball-player I am," Azariah said.

"We all know what kind of ballplayers we are on this team," Frank said harshly. "But you didn't answer my question. Let's do it a different way. How about if you already played infield for the Seattle Indians?"

"If I played for Seattle, I might not care whether I went to the bigs or not," Azariah said.

"You're being a pain in the neck." Fidgety Frank didn't exactly say *neck*, but that's close enough. "If you were almost good enough to play in the bigs without the magic, wouldn't you get it so you could and then worry later about whether it was right or wrong?"

"I . . . hope not," Azariah answered after what looked like a real pause to think.

"Could be you wouldn't. You're too clean for your own good. I'll tell you, though—plenty of people would. If I was almost good enough myself, I might. But I ain't, so I don't have to fret about it," Frank said.

Was I too clean for my own good? Big Stu would've thought so. But if I was all that clean, how come I ended up doing things for him to begin with?

(XIX)

After a while, the towns started running together. If you ask me whether something happened in a game in Richland or Pasco or Kennewick or Walla Walla, I can't tell you for sure. We lost one of those games, or it might've been two.

One thing I can tell you is, the fellow who managed the Walla Walla Bears was named Cliff Ditto. He really really was was. I think that was a game we lost. The ballpark there was at a college, and they used it for baseball and football. It made a better baseball field than the other one like it that we played at. The stands in Walla Walla were farther from where they put the football gridiron, and that gave them more room in the outfield.

From Walla Walla, we could've gone back to Lewiston, Idaho, as easy as not. Instead, Harv took us on the Columbia River ferry, down to Pendleton, Oregon. We beat the Pendleton Buckaroos at another one of those wooden ballparks where it was even money whether a fire or the termites would finish the place for good. Pendleton cared more about its big rodeo than it did about baseball.

After we beat 'em, we ate supper at a place that served venison steaks. That was something out of the ordinary, anyhow. Most of the time, I'd sooner chow down on cow. I'm glad I tried the other that once, though. Gives me something to talk about I wouldn't've had without it.

At the restaurant, Eddie said, "Looks like we'll do pretty much the same thing we did last year."

"What's that?" I asked. The other guys on the team knew what they'd done then, but I didn't.

"Work our way down through the smaller towns in Oregon and California till the Coast League season ends, then play against barnstorming teams in the bigger places—San Francisco, Los Angeles, San Diego," he answered. "You can play the year around down there. It rains some in the wintertime, but it never snows. Things stay green all the time—it doesn't freeze."

"That'd be something to see," I said, thinking about how the trees around Enid lost their leaves in the fall and how the grass and bushes went yellow.

"It is," Eddie agreed. He came from a lot farther north than Oklahoma. Snow in Enid was a once-in-a-while nuisance. Snow in a place like Cornucopia, Wisconsin? Even I didn't want to think about that.

"Who all plays on the barnstorming teams?" I asked.

"Everybody you can think of. Lots of guys from the Coast League, natch. A bunch of them live down there fulltime. Some big-leaguers come out to make extra money and just to stay sharp. Sometimes Negro League teams go out there the way we do, too."

"Carpetbag was talking about how they stayed on the road all the time," I said.

"That's right. He was." Eddie nodded. "And some colored guys from teams that don't go barnstorming come out on their own and join up with mostly white outfits." He poked me in the ribs. "They do, even if you don't like it."

"Oh, give it a rest, why don't you?" I poked him back. He wiggled—he was more ticklish than I was. I went on, "Folks don't mix that way where I come from. But I played against colored guys, and you'd have to be nuts not to want Carpetbag Booker on your team."

"Can't tell you you're wrong about that." Eddie nodded again. "Carpetbag's different, though. When he's with you, you're playing with Carpetbag Booker. You're not playing with some ordinary colored guy."

"He's not ordinary—that's for sure," I said. "Funny you should put it that way, too, 'cause I had almost the same thought when he was pitching for us."

"I wish he would have stuck around after the tournament," Eddie said. "With him throwing, we'd really be ready to take on some of the hot barnstorming teams we'll run into." He shrugged a sad shrug. "Now he's mowing people down for the Regents instead."

"Uh-huh. That was interesting, wasn't it? What color Carpetbag was didn't matter so much to us. But what color we were mattered to him. He was happier with his own folks."

"I don't think we bothered him so much: the team, I mean. I sure hope we didn't," Eddie said. "When he was with us, though, he had to put up with all kinds of garbage he didn't need to worry about in his own part of town. The landlords who didn't want to let him stay in their places, the waiters who didn't want him eating in their restaurants—"

"The crowds calling him names, too," I put in. I won't tell you I never called a colored man a name. I could. You wouldn't know I was lying. But I would know. When you listen to other people do it, though, you start hearing how ugly it sounds.

"Yeah, that's one more thing he doesn't have to hear when he plays for a colored team in front of a colored crowd," Eddie said. "They won't razz him for being colored. They'll just razz him for playing on the road team."

"That's bad enough," I said. The House of Daniel heard that kind of thing all the time. We'd heard some in Pendleton that afternoon. What the people in Enid yelled at the Ponca City Greasemen, and what the Ponca City fans called the Eagles, that was worse. But none of it came close to the things a white crowd shouted at colored ballplayers.

The *Tarbaby* I'd hung on Willard, it was nothing much, not as those things went. Still, I wondered how come he hadn't hauled off and decked me. Only reason I can think of is, he knew how much hot water he would've landed in if he had.

It hardly seemed cause enough to hold back.

O ur next stop was The Dalles, on the Columbia. Of course, we'd crossed the river to get down to Pendleton, but I don't think I said anything much about it before. That is one *serious* stream, with a lot of water in it. I suppose the Mississippi's bigger, but I bet the Columbia runs faster.

We played an all-star team in The Dalles on a high-school field with some extra portable bleachers set alongside the ones that were usually there. The all-stars didn't all have one uniform, the way a lot of those teams do. They wore the home whites for their own clubs. Guys played for teams from a salmon-packing plant, an outfit that brined cherries, a butcher shop, a railroad, and I don't know what all else. It was quite a sight.

Put them all together . . . and they weren't very good. We were up something like 13-2 after six, so Harv took Fidgety Frank out and let Azariah finish the game with his knuckleball. He gave up three or four runs, but we had the game in hand anyway. He might have given up more, only Eddie pulled the hidden-ball trick on a runner at second base. He made as if to throw it, the way he would with nothing when he did the phantom infield during warmups. That was what he threw this time, too—nothing. Azariah pretended to catch it on the mound. The runner took his lead . . . and Eddie tagged him.

Oh, that guy was mad! And he was embarrassed, too. He couldn't seem to decide whether to murder Eddie or just sink down into the ground and disappear. The way he walked back to the dugout—slow, slow, slow, his chin on his chest—he might have been going to meet a firing squad. By how the manager tore into him, he might really have been going to meet one next.

"That wasn't very nice," I told Eddie after the last out.

"Yeah." His eyes twinkled. There was just a little bit of devil in Eddie. Not much. Most of the time, his sober side ran things. But that devil bubbled out once in a while. I could see it right then. He went on, "Figured I'd give it a try. If he didn't fall for it, fine. But Azariah played it up neat as you please, so he got suckered."

"I guess he did!" I said. "Maybe you should try it more often, you know? These guys aren't looking for it. Who would? We had this one in the bag, but you might be able to steal an out that matters."

"Huh!" His eyes twinkled some more. "You've got some of that old original sin left inside you, don't you, Snake?"

"Funny," I said, "but I was just thinking the same thing about you."

The Dalles was about as close to Portland as Harv wanted to play. He didn't plan to go into Portland, any more than he'd gone into Seattle. The PCL teams in those towns ruled the roost. There were plenty of semipro teams in both places, but they were more semi than pro. In a smaller town, one where there's no team in the regular minors, the semipros can be cocks o' the walk. But the Indians and the Beavers had Seattle and Portland sewed up. They got all the newspaper ink. Their games were on the radio.

And they played better ball than we did. Oh, we were good enough to stand a chance against them. But if we played a season in the PCL, we'd finish a lot closer to the bottom than to the top. You've got to keep your limits in mind.

So we played in Salem after The Dalles. And we played in Corvallis, and we played in Eugene. We got a day off in Eugene, too, because it poured rain. Just as well, too—the night between those days had a full moon. You want to stay inside with things locked up tight when werewolves prowl.

Harv fidgeted like a cat with fleas even so. He was the one who had to fix up our schedule, and the one who had to shell out for our lodging with no money coming in that day. I have to say, though, the rest of us weren't too sorry. Rain was about the only thing that kept us from going out on the field every doggone day. Wes put it best: "Weather's been too damn good lately. We've been working our fannies off."

"You've still got a good bit left of yours," Harv said. No, he didn't need to swear to needle.

Wes looked wounded to the core. He looked so very wounded, he probably practiced in front of a mirror somewhere. "I've got big bones," he said, as dignified as an English butler only without the silly accent.

We went over to Springfield the next day to play the Booth-Kelly Axemen. They were—surprise!—a sawmill team. Their uniforms had a red diamond with a white BK in it on the left breast. Some people from Eugene were in the crowd. The two towns are only a few miles apart. You could tell the fans from Eugene—they booed the Axemen and cheered for us.

If I remember straight, we won that one. I know I remember the muddy field. It wasn't like playing in the mud in Texas. This stuff was chilly. So was the weather. People from Oregon told me it could get hot there. I don't think anybody told the sun, though.

We took US 99 down to Medford. The highway crosses one branch of the Umpqua River or another three or four times. We liked the name. Every time we went over the river, we'd all start going "Ump-qua! Ump-qua! Ump-qua!" like a bunch of bullfrogs. You spend that much time riding in a bus, you find ways to make your own fun. You'd better.

Medford's town team was called the Nuggets. They played at a fairgrounds ballpark with an auto-racing track around it. Harv kinda clucked when he took a gander at the stands. "I thought this place was bigger," he said sadly. "I bet it don't even hold two thousand."

It was packed, though. In a town like that, a long way off from any-where big, the House of Daniel was something to come out and see. So we put on a special show for 'em. We did a fancy phantom infield. We even ran a phantom outfield, going back under flies that weren't there and firing 'em to the bases, where the guys pretended to catch 'em and slapped tags on imaginary baserunners.

The game turned out to be tough. The two things I recollect about their pitcher were his jughandle ears and his fastball. He smoked it in there, and he didn't have bad control. Amos caught one square and hit it out, but most of the time we flailed away.

We were hanging on to a 2-1 lead in the bottom of the ninth when a Nugget doubled with one out. I got the ball back in to Eddie. He car-ried it over to Frank, then walked back to second base. Frank strad-dled the rubber and peered in at Amos for the sign. He shook his head.

If you stand on the rubber without the ball, it's a balk. You can straddle it all you please, though. The Nugget led off second. Fidgety Frank ignored him and kept shaking Amos off. Eddie strolled over to the runner and slapped him on the can with his glove.

Then he showed the base umpire the glove had the ball in it. "You're out!" the ump shouted, and held his fist in the air with his thumb sticking up.

"I'm what?" the Nugget yelled, even louder. Eddie showed him the ball, too. The Nugget didn't walk off the field as though he'd just watched zombies eat his ma. He hollered something that dented four or five commandments all at once, and he tried to knock Eddie's block off.

Everybody on both sides ran out to second base. Most of it was push-ing and shoving and wrestling, nothing more. At the bottom of the pile, Wes ground that hotheaded Nugget's face in the dirt, accidentally on purpose. After a while, we untangled. The ump threw the hothead out of the game, and we got on with things. Fidgety Frank made their next hitter bounce back to him. That was the ballgame.

Eddie had a bruise on his cheek. That haymaker got at least part-way home. He was grinning all the same. He slapped me on the back almost as hard as the Nugget had swung on him. "Try it when it counts, you told me, Snake," he said. "They won't be looking for it, you said. Boy, did you hit that one on the button!"

"Hey, I'm glad it worked," I said. "Two outs with nobody on is a lot better'n one out and a man on second."

"You betcha!" He pounded me on the back again.

The Nuggets' manager wasn't so happy. "Of all the chickenshit things to do—" he growled at Harv.

"I can't help it if your guy went to sleep out there," Harv said sweetly.

"But the hidden-ball trick? C'mon! Nobody uses the hidden-ball trick! Is it any wonder that Olaf got sore at your second baseman?"

"He made the bonehead play. Eddie didn't. And when things started up again, your old Olaf looked worse'n Eddie. We don't want to play rough, but we'll finish anything you start," Harv said. Baseball's Golden Rule is *Do unto others as they do unto you.* Somewhere or other, *as you would have them do unto you* got changed a bit.

"Aw, manure!" the Medford manager said. Something like that, anyhow. Harv smiled back at him. You win the game, you can afford to smile. You win the game because you worked the hidden-ball trick, you can *really* afford to smile.

We drove east to Klamath Falls through the forested mountains. They've done a lot of logging in Oregon, but they've still got a demon of a lot of trees left. The ones covering those mountainsides were firs and spruces and pines and hemlocks and oaks and others I couldn't name. The shrubs underneath the trees were wild lilac and manzanita and something that grew lots of little red berries.

There wasn't much traffic. Deer kept bounding across the road. Once Harv screeched the brakes so hard, he spilled half of us out of our seats. If he hadn't, we could've brought some more venison into Klamath Falls tied to our fender. Deer are stupid. They don't look both ways, or even one way, before they jump out. They just do it, and sometimes they pay the price.

I saw a black bear in a roadside clearing, making a pig of itself on a carcass. Maybe it had killed that deer a little while before, or maybe it was filling up on carrion. Bears are fussier than buzzards, but not always a lot fussier.

And I saw . . . Well, I saw two or three of 'em before I decided my imagination wasn't playing tricks on me. Even after I decided it wasn't,

I had no idea what in blazes to call 'em. So I asked: "What's eight or nine feet tall, all covered over in shaggy brown hair, and walks on its hind legs?"

"That would be Harv's uncle," Wes answered. "Didn't you hear? He's playing left for us when we get to Klamath Falls."

"Looked more like your grandpa to me," Harv said, and turned some of the laughs back on Wes.

Laughs were fine, but I still wanted to know. "C'mon, you guys," I said. "What's the right name for those—things? Whatsits?"

"You said your grandpa was called Elmer, didn't you, Wes?" Harv said. Once those two started going at each other, they didn't want to stop.

Eddie actually answered my question: "Around here, they call 'em bigfoots, or sometimes bigfeet or bigfeets. The Indian name for 'em— or *an* Indian name for 'em, anyhow—is sasquatch."

"Are they people or animals or devils?" I asked.

"Somewhere in there," Wes said, which didn't help at all. He went on, "Probably closest to people. But what are people except animals with some devil in 'em?"

Harv breathed out, hard. "You need to read the Good Book more, Wes."

" 'What is man, that thou art mindful of him?' " Wes quoted, to show Harv that he did—and to annoy him. Then he said, "That always seemed like a real good question to me." It must have seemed like a good question to Harv, too, because he didn't try to answer it.

Klamath Falls sits by the southern tip of Upper Klamath Lake (Lower Klamath Lake is on the far side of the California line). Swarms of white pelicans floated in the lake and flew above it—when they did, they seemed nearly as big as a small aeroplane. They raised their chicks there. As soon as I saw 'em, I understood why the team we'd be playing was the Klamath Falls Pelicans.

Out in back of the motor lodge where we were staying, a bigfoot or sasquatch or whatever you wanted to call it was chopping a big oak log into firewood. The axe it swung could've cut off an elephant's head. No, not *it*. In spite of the long hair all over, that bigfoot was definitely *he*. His feet weren't the only big thing about him.

He stopped and stared at us when we got out of the bus. "Boy," he said in a high, thin, piping voice that didn't go with his bulk, "you guys are almost as furry as I am! How'd that happen?"

"We're the House of Daniel." Harv sounded calmer than I could have. "How'd it happen that you're here in town and not up in the mountains somewhere?"

"I love waffles," the bigfoot said. "Pancakes, too, but waffles even more. You have no idea what a nuisance it is to make waffles in the woods. And whipped cream! Whipped cream is *impossible*! So I work in Klamath Falls and I get waffles at the diner."

"You don't, uh, play baseball, do you?" Harv asked. Yeah, the sasquatch had a big strike zone. But if he ever got good wood on one, no ballpark would hold it. Lordy! No county would.

"Not me. I'm kinda slow," he answered. "But Klamath Falls has a basketball team that hasn't lost for years." He mimed dropping the ball in the basket. With hands that size, he could treat a basketball the way Carpetbag treated a baseball.

After we put on our uniforms and headed over to the ballpark, we saw a few more bigfoots going on about their business in Klamath Falls. I don't know whether they loved waffles, too, or if they had different reasons for coming to town. But they made themselves at home, and the ordinary people there took 'em in stride.

Pelicans Field was wooden, but pretty new and well kept up. It held maybe 2,500. The team played in a semipro league with the Medford Nuggets and other outfits from towns in southern Oregon and the northern chunk of California. A game with us was an extra payday for them, and a bigger one than they got most of the time.

While we were coming in from our warmups and they were going out, one of them said to me, "Hear you had some fun in Medford yesterday."

"Fun?" I gave him a crooked grin. "Yeah, you could call it that."

"What touched it off?" he asked.

"We pulled the hidden-ball trick in the bottom of the ninth, and the fella who got caught didn't much like it."

His mouth fell open. "I bet he didn't! I've never seen anybody try that, let alone work it."

I wondered if I should've kept quiet. Now we wouldn't be able to spring it here. But if he knew there'd been a dustup in Medford, somebody on the Pelicans probably already knew why. That was how it looked to me, anyway. And with a little luck, we wouldn't need it.

As the park filled up, I noticed it had a few extra-big boxes by the dugouts. The seats in 'em were extra big, too. And sure enough, three sasquatches sat down behind the Pelicans' dugout. Klamath Falls worked to help 'em fit in if they wanted to. Plenty of worse ways to go about things. In a bit, one of them went up to the concession stand and came back with three of the biggest mugs of beer you ever saw. I wouldn't have wanted to mess with a drunk bigfoot, but they didn't get drunk. They behaved better than most ordinary people. You could hear 'em, though. They all had those squeaky voices.

The Pelicans beat us, 4-3. They got a well-pitched game, and they made some good plays when their guy got in trouble. Wes pitched fine for us, too. It was one of those games where somebody had to lose, and that afternoon it was us. Not even Harv could get too upset about it. We didn't do anything wrong. We just didn't win.

When we went to a diner for supper, I almost ordered some gooey waffles. But I didn't. I had fried fish and French fries instead. I was cleaning my plate when Eddie said, "I wonder if the bigfoots who live in town have to pay taxes like everybody else."

"If they do, it's the best reason I can think of for moving back to the woods." Wes didn't like taxes. He liked the people who collected them even less.

"But then what would they do for waffles?" Fidgety Frank asked.

"And beer," I said. "Don't forget beer."

"I never forget beer," Frank said seriously. "They sure could put it down, couldn't they?"

"They've got bigger boilers to fill up," Wes said. "They didn't get out of line or anything."

"Good thing they didn't," I said. "I wouldn't want to try and make anything that size shut up, not unless I had some bigfoot cops with me. Even then, I'd like it more if they got out in front."

"Me, too," Eddie said. He was about as big as I was: not very, in other words. Most of the other guys on the team were taller or wider than the two of us, or taller and wider. Of course, put anybody from the House of Daniel alongside a sasquatch and he'd look nine years old, tops.

"We want to get an early start tomorrow," Harv said. "Next game is down in Redding, against the Tigers, and it's a longish way. California, here we come, with our spikes and chewing gum!" Have I said before that Harv couldn't carry a tune if he had a pail to put it in? In case I haven't, he couldn't. That didn't stop him from trying, however much the rest of us wished it would have.

California! For a long time, I'd thought my pa settled there after he got out of Enid. I might think so to this day if he hadn't gone to that game up in Bellingham—about as far from California as you can get and still stay on the West Coast.

Maybe Mich Carstairs still was somewhere in the Golden State. I hoped she was, for her sake. She'd got out of Ponca City, anyhow, even faster than I had. For all I could prove, she'd headed for New Hampshire. But I liked thinking she might be in the same state I was in. I liked thinking we might bump together some way, too. I didn't figure the odds were good, but I didn't do a lot of calculating about odds. Did she ever go see a ballgame? I had no idea, which didn't keep me from thinking about it.

Crossing from Oregon into California wasn't anything special. It wasn't like taking the ferry across the Columbia to get from Washington into Oregon. It was more like going from Colorado into Utah. The only difference between the start of the one state and the end of the other was the line on the map. If I hadn't seen the sign next to US 97, I never would've known where that was.

Even after we crossed the border, we had more than 120 miles to go before we got to Redding. California's a big state. All the states out West are big, but California's big even compared to the rest of them. After Texas, it's the biggest in the forty-eight. And it's about as tall as Texas. It's just skinnier.

Weed was the town where US 97 ran into US 99. Dunno how come they called it that—it was a harmless enough little place. We went on down US 99. Off to the east and south, Mount Shasta got bigger and bigger. It's not as tall as Mount Rainier, up by Seattle and Tacoma. But you can see it better because the air is dry, not hazy and misty and foggy.

Redding sat at the upper end of the Sacramento Valley, with

mountains to the east and west. It wasn't much bigger than Weed, but they knew about the Tigers all the way up in Oregon. Tigers Park had gone up ten or twelve years earlier. The team or whoever backed them had money. Everything was clean and freshly painted. The plumbing worked. The showers had hot water. A team from the regular minors would've been happy to play there.

The Tigers handled themselves like a team from the regular minors. They wore pinstriped uniforms with a tiger's head on the left breast. I'd wondered if that would ever happen. Now here it was. Their tigers against our lions. The two biggest cats facing off.

It was a hot day—up in the nineties, maybe over a hundred. The heat felt more like New Mexico than Texas or Oklahoma, though. The air stayed dry, so your flannels didn't stick to you and get all soaked with sweat. That made the weather easier to take. Not easy, but easier.

At least half the Tigers could've played pro ball, or had a few years earlier. They weren't a young, quick team. They knew what they were doing, though, and they hadn't got too creaky to do it. Their second baseman had one of the sweetest pivots I'd ever seen. The crowd cheered 'em on. The park wasn't great big—like the one in Klamath Falls, it held 2,500 or so (no bigfoots, or none I saw). Against us, they filled it up. It was another one of those ballyards with spaces between the planks on the outfield fence. Kids—grown-ups, too—peeked through them.

Fidgety Frank kept the Tigers guessing. They threw a lefty at us, too, only one who didn't fidget so much. Their guy tried to fool us with his pitches, not with his motion.

That works the first time through the lineup, especially if you've never seen a pitcher before. The fellow on the mound has to be better to make it go the second time around, and the third pass is harder yet. Besides, he's starting to tire out himself by then.

So they went up on us, 2-0, after four. But we tied it in the fifth and got a run in the sixth. Then *they* tied it. Yeah, they could play. We got four in the eight, though, to grab some breathing room. I knocked in two of those myself with a single to left. They plated one in the eighth and one in the ninth, but we won it, 7-5.

They were good sports. They all shook hands with us. They didn't like losing any more than anybody else would have, but they didn't waste time moaning about it. "You got us," their manager said. "We like to take on the best teams that'll play us. We sent letters to the Seals and the Oaks in the Bay Area, and to the Sacramento Senators, but we couldn't get a game with any of 'em."

"We've had the same trouble with Coast League teams," Harv said. "Seems to me like they think they're supposed to beat us. So if they do, it's nothing special. But if we beat them, they look like chumps. The only thing that might bring 'em is if you can promise a big house. They like money as much as anybody else."

He didn't tell the Tigers' manager to go on the road against the PCL clubs. That was a bad bet. Fans in Frisco and Oakland and Sacramento are spoiled. They wouldn't want to watch their darlings take on a no-account team from a whistle-stop town. The people in charge of the big-city teams knew what was what. If they didn't care to play against the House of Daniel, they weren't likely to take a chance on the Redding Tigers.

"Where do you guys go next?" the Tigers' manager asked.

"Red Bluff," Harv answered.

By the face the guy from Redding made, I guessed that was the next town down the road. They must have loved each other like Pampa and Borger in Texas. As soon as the fella opened his mouth, I knew what he'd say. And he did: "You beat those damn Stags, you hear?"

"We'll give it our best shot," Harv said. "We always do."

Red Bluff. Chico. Yuba City. I don't know how many other Sacramento Valley towns we played in. Lots of them. We kept working our way south. Redding was hot. Red Bluff was hotter. Chico was hotter yet. If you felt like baking yourself, central California was the place to do it.

We stayed away from the coast. It was kind of a shame. On that side of the mountains, the weather wasn't much different from what they got in Seattle. It was cool and damp and foggy. On the side of the mountains where we were at, the weather wasn't much different from what they got in hell.

And we kept working our way down into it, too. Stockton. Modesto. Those were towns that had had pro teams years earlier but lost them again: towns like a lot of the ones in Texas and Utah and Idaho. Even now, when one of the semipro clubs in those places found somebody good, the Coast League teams would hear about it quick. The semi-pros made money selling contracts to the PCL teams. The big leagues had chains of farm teams in the regular minors. The Coast League used some of those semipro teams in the medium-sized towns in California the same way.

The baseball there was tough even before the barnstorming teams got going. We lost more often than Harv liked. The trouble was simple: they had lots of good players. If a guy lost a step or two and couldn't stick with the Seals or the Beavers or the Hollywood Stars, he wouldn't drop down to a lower minor league. There were no lower minor leagues on the West Coast then.

No—he'd get on some hot semipro outfit and make it hotter, the way that Vic guy had with McNulty Transfer in Tacoma. He might not be a topflight pro any more, but that didn't mean he couldn't play. I was glad to be a center fielder. You really needed to cover ground out there. Some old pro who'd got slow couldn't steal my job. A good thing, too, 'cause plenty of those fellas hit harder than I did.

Oakland, now, did its spring training in Fresno. And the semipro team we played there, which was probably the best one in town, was called the Fresno Acorns. The Oaks played them every spring, getting ready for the Coast League season. And the Oaks' young players, the ones who weren't ready for the PCL, played for the Acorns and learned whatever they needed to know.

One thing I don't reckon they ever did learn was how to stay cool in Fresno. I don't believe there is any way to do it. Fresno isn't just hotter than Texas. Fresno's much hotter than Texas. If that doesn't scare you, you must never have been to Texas. Or to Fresno.

Fresno is also the raisin capital of the world. You put grapes out under that sun and they shrivel to raisins in nothing flat. If you put me out under that sun with no clothes on, I'd shrivel to a raisin in nothing flat, too.

You'd think—you'd hope—a team in a place like that would play in a ballpark with lights and schedule as many night games as it could. You'd be disappointed. I sure was. We beat the Acorns 4-3. It was an-other one of those games where at the end you aren't sure of anything except that you won. You don't go away thinking *We were better than the team we beat*. I'd got used to that feeling playing for the House of Daniel. The longer we played in California, the more air leaked out of it.

One of the things you'll see in Fresno is wreaths of garlic bulbs around doors and windows. A lot of the people there are Armenians. The men are hairy and dark and they've got big hooked noses, so they look like Jews. But they aren't. Armenians are like Greeks—they use garlic to keep vampires away. You smell it all over the place.

They cook with it, too. They put it in lamb and in chicken and in salads—in everything but ice cream and soda pop. They put tarragon in soda pop instead. After a while, garlic grows on you. I don't know but what I'd sooner flavor lamb with it than with mint jelly.

Visalia is another one of those towns where they play good ball. Porterville is, too. We won a game in Visalia and lost one in Porterville—or it might've been the other way around. Neither one of those ballparks had lights, either, and oh, they were hot. We kept pouring down water and gulping salt pills.

From Porterville, we went down to Bakersfield. That's an oil town, the last town of any size before you go over the high pass there and come down the other side into Los Angeles. I hadn't done that yet. I wouldn't have believed it if I hadn't seen it with my own eyes.

Game first, though. We were playing against the Coca-Colas—the company had a big bottling operation in town. The ballpark was horrible. I don't know who laid it out, but the sun shone straight into the batters' eyes. It was another one that ran only 354 to center, too. It was so short there, *I* hit a home run, and I don't hit many.

We beat the Coca-Colas something like 11-2. I had spare ribs for supper (dunno why they call 'em that—I bet the pig they come from doesn't think they are). Then, instead of letting us overnight in Bakersfield, Harv put us on the road after dark and started for Los Angeles. He wouldn't say why. He just did it. We grumbled all the way. We wanted to *sleep*, dammit!

(XX)

We rode and we rode, still grumbling. Then after a while, when we were on one of the last downhills before the city, Harv pointed out the windshield and said, "Take a gander at that, boys."

All those lights spread out for miles and miles, every color you could imagine, some steady, some blinking . . . Los Angeles has way more than a million people, and it's almost the size of a small state. The city lights looked like stars, but there were more of them and they were brighter and closer together than the ones up in the sky.

It was just about worth seeing by night. In the daytime, the magic would go out of it. We'd see buildings, not lights. We didn't let on we were impressed, though. Oh, no. We went right on complaining. If ballplayers aren't playing, they're grousing about something.

Then we got in amongst the buildings. They looked like buildings with lights on them, all right, except for the ones that looked like buildings without lights on them. They were lower than you'd expect for such a big city. When I said so, Wes told me it was against the law for any building except the city hall to go up more than twelve stories.

"How come?" I asked him.

"They've got quarrelsome earth elementals, that's why," he said. "They had a big old earthquake last year, and they expect more. None of the elementals will admit the quakes are their fault—they all say they're the other guys' fault. So nobody human here wants a big old skyscraper to fall over in the next one and kill a bunch of people."

"Ah," I said. "Thanks. That makes sense."

"I know." Wes sounded even gloomier than usual. "But they do it anyway."

I take back what I said a minute ago. Not all the Los Angeles buildings looked like buildings. We went past a hat store that looked like a fedora and a fried-chicken place that looked like a drumstick and a place that sold boats that looked like a cabin cruiser and a doughnut house with a giant doughnut on top of it. I don't even want to guess what the building that looked like the Sphinx sold. Mummies? Pyramids? Cripes, maybe it was another fried-chicken place.

So we got into Los Angeles, and we drove and we drove, and we didn't drive out of it again. Sometimes it was more built up, sometimes less. There were small farms and orange orchards among the houses and shops, but not too many.

We didn't go past the city hall. I think I got a glimpse of it, way off to the east of the street we were driving on. If I did, it was miles away. We just kept chugging along.

After a while, Harv said, "This isn't Los Angeles any more. We're in the suburbs now, heading down to Long Beach."

"What's Long Beach?" I asked. "Is that where Los Angeles goes for a swim?"

"It's a city all by itself—an oil town and a port. It's got something like 150,000 people in it," Harv said. "And you know what? Hardly anybody who doesn't live in this part of California even knows it's a town."

"I sure didn't," I said.

Wes chipped in again: "Other thing you need to know, Snake, is that you can't just charge into the Pacific and go for a swim. Well, you can, but I promise you won't do it more than once."

"Why? They have sharks that eat you or something?"

"No, or no worse'n anywhere else. But the water's *cold*. All up and down the West Coast, you'll freeze your pecker off except for maybe two weeks a year. Maybe."

"Plenty warm on land," I said.

"Oh, yeah." Wes nodded. "The ocean, though, the ocean feels like there oughta be polar bears coming out of it."

The cabins at the motor lodge where we stayed looked like cabins—I mean log cabins where you might meet up with Honest Abe or somebody wearing fringed moccasins and a coonskin cap. They weren't. The logs that made the outside walls were painted stucco, and the bark shakes on the roof were just as fake. Inside, the cabin had smooth plaster walls and electric lights and running water and anything else they would have had in Spokane or Amarillo . . . or Chicago, come to that.

"Pretty crazy," I said.

"It is, yeah," Eddie said. I reminded myself this wasn't the first time he'd seen Los Angeles in all its glorious weirdness. I was the new fish. I wasn't used to such things. He flopped on the bed. Around a yawn, he went on, "Mattress feels good. And we won't have to get up early to go somewhere else. We're already here."

"Uh-huh." I yawned, too. I was ready for a good night's sleep.

Being ready for one didn't mean I got one. Some time in the middle of the night, a vampire tapped on the window. I was mad when I woke up. You'd think a place like a motor lodge would be properly warded, especially after the Great Zombie Riots. You'd think so, but no such luck.

"Go tell it to get lost, Snake," Eddie said. I'd done it before, so he knew I wouldn't just let the thing in. And I was still the new guy on the team. Annoying crap like that landed on me.

"Let me in!" the vampire said when I went to the window. Moonlight glowed in its eyes. They're supposed to be able to mesmerize you, but not that night. I was ticked off, not mesmerized.

"Get lost," I said. The cross under my shirt gleamed. You could see that, but you couldn't make out what it was. The vampire didn't have to flee.

And it didn't. "Let me in!" it said again. "Let me liberate you from bourgeois respectability. Keep your own company! Keep your own hours! Meet the people you want to meet, not the ones your boring business makes you deal with. Meet them, and set them free, too!"

I laughed. I couldn't help it. Bourgeois respectability! Boring business! That vampire hadn't tried biting any semipro ballplayers before, had it? It had no idea how fouled up it was. "Get lost, I said," I told it, and started to reach under my shirt to bring out the cross and make it go.

Quickly, it said, "Wait!" I didn't mean to hesitate, but I must've, because it went on, "With your looks, I can get you going in Hollywood if you let me make you a blood brother. Honest, I can! I've got connections up there—so help me, I do."

Honest? That was funnier yet, coming from a vampire. It was trying anything to sink its fangs into my throat, same as a guy will try
anything to lay his girl. Of course, there are so many bloodsuckers in
Hollywood, what the thing said had maybe a quarter of a chance of
being true. If only I'd wanted to break into films, that might've made
a difference. But I didn't, so it didn't.

I pulled out the cross. It shone like a flashbulb, hot and blue-white.
The vampire's scowl of pain showed off its long, pointed teeth. "Go
away!" I said one more time. "You can't come in here." The flash faded.
When I looked out the window again, the vampire was gone.

"Was it talking about the movie business?" Eddie asked. "Did
I really hear that?"

"You sure did," I said.

He whistled. "That's a line you'd only get here. Is the thing gone
now?"

I checked one more time to make certain. No glow from the cross.
No vampire outside the window. "It's gone, all right."

"Okey-doke. C'mon back to bed, then," Eddie said. And I did.

There's a part of Long Beach they call Semaphore Hill, because a
signal tower stood at the top before Consolidated Crystal and the
telephone put those out of business. These days, it's all over oil wells
and derricks.

Shell Field sat at the bottom of Semaphore Hill. We were taking on
the Shell Oilers there. It was as nice a ballpark as most small-town
minor-league fields. Wooden roofed-over grandstand. Bleachers.
Roofed-over dugouts, too, so you didn't bake your brains under the hot
sun. Wooden fences.

One of the Oilers told me the Bambino and Larrupin' Lou barnstormed through there. Carpetbag Booker, too, though not on the
same tour. Where *hadn't* he been? Along with guys who worked on
the wells and derricks, the Oilers had fellas who'd played in the bigs
or the Coast League. They were at least as good as most small-town
minor-league teams.

Their pitcher wasn't old enough to have bounced down. By the bite
on his curve, he was on the way up. If he stayed sound—you talk about
pitchers the way you talk about racehorses, because both kinds of

critter are always breaking down—he wouldn't have SHELL OIL on his chest and the Shell shell on his sleeve much longer. He'd play for the Hilltoppers or the New York Titans or the Bengals or Buccaneers.

Fidgety Frank gave it everything he had. By his wiggles and thrashes out on the mound, he was coming down with St. Vitus' Dance or Saturday Night Fever, one. He would have confused a lot of semipro hitters if he couldn't have got them out any other way. The Shell Oilers, though, they'd been around the block a good many times. They'd seen guys like Frank before. They waited for the ball, and then they clouted it.

After a while, I started wishing for a bicycle out there in center. I kept dashing into the gaps, now to my right, now to my left, and trying to hit the cutoff man with my throws. Sometimes, for a change, I'd run straight back when an Oiler smashed one over my head.

They thumped us to beat the band. And they had a band, down by their dugout: trumpets and clarinets, a banjo, a fiddle, and a drum kit. The guys in it wore white musicians' uniforms with the Shell shell on their jackets. Like the guy in New Mexico who sang, they were semipros, too.

It got bad enough so Azariah came in to finish it off and make it worse. The final, unless I misremember, was 12-5. You couldn't have proved by the way we played that those Oilers were too washed up for the Coast League or even the bigs.

"Well, that was horrible," Harv said as we got into our street clothes. One thing about Harv: he didn't waste time beating around the bush. He went on, "The worst part is, we got to come back here tomorrow. We play Chancelor Canfield/Midway Oil tomorrow. We better not look like a bunch of jerks in that game, too—that's all I got to tell you. If the folks around here decide we're lousy, they won't want to book matches with us. And that'll skinny up our wallets pretty blasted quick."

If Harv wanted me to be worried when we went back to Shell Field the next day, he knew how to get what he wanted. The guys from the other oil company might lick us the way the Shell Oilers had. If they did, we really would look like a team that made its name beating up on nobodies. We knew better, but the Los Angeles people and the barnstorming teams wouldn't.

Most of the time, Fidgety Frank was a better pitcher than Wes, too. Nobody said anything like that, but I couldn't have been the only one thinking it. Well, all we could do was play the game and see how it came out.

The guys on the Chancelor Canfield/Midway Oil team had a big C over their hearts, so I'll just call 'em Chancelors from now on. They looked sharp getting loose. Their pitcher made the catcher's mitt pop when he fired 'em in.

Then he made Azariah's ribs pop. He drilled him with the second pitch of the game. Azariah went down in a heap. He got up and walked to first real slow. Amos hit a chopper to short. Azariah broke up the double play and spiked their second baseman doing it.

"Hoo boy! Gonna be a warm afternoon." Harv wasn't talking about the weather.

Wes took the mound. His first fastball lowbridged the Chancelors' leadoff man. His second pitch caught the guy square on the kneecap. They had to run for him. Wes picked the runner off. Yeah, a warm afternoon, all right.

We were up 1–0 in the sixth when the real fun started. One of their big galoots threw a body block into Eddie at second base. That wouldn't have done the trick by itself, but the Chancelor kinda kicked at him while he was on the ground. Eddie bounced up and swung—not smart, maybe, but brave.

Lots of fights start around second because there are so many chances to do that kind of thing. Everybody on both teams swarmed into this one. I wanted to take a shot at their pitcher, and I guess they were gunning for Wes. But Wes could take care of himself. He coldcocked a Chancelor with a right to the jaw. The guy went down and stayed down. After that, they decided maybe they weren't gunning so much for Wes after all.

"Break it up! Knock it off!" the umps yelled. When we felt like it, we did.

They threw Eddie out of the game, and the guy who knocked him halfway to shortstop. Wes stayed in—don't ask me how or why. Maybe they didn't see him flatten that Chancelor. The fella did wake up and get back in the game, but he spat out a tooth, too. He'd be paying his dentist for some bridgework.

The crowd loved it. They cheered us as much as the Chancelors. Those guys were just using Shell Field. It belonged to the Oilers.

I was first guy to the plate in our half of the seventh. Their pitcher threw behind my head. You only do that when you're really out to hurt somebody. I froze. I was lucky. If I'd ducked, I would've gone straight back into the baseball.

I looked out at him. If he wanted to play like that . . . I dropped a bunt down the first-base line. He ran over to field it, and I gave him a better shot than their guy did with Eddie. I stepped on his foot, too. That was just by accident. Of course.

He got up and charged me, and the benches cleared again. When the dust settled this time, I got run and so did their pitcher. We hit their reliever hard, and ended up winning 9-1.

"Hey, Harv, I think people here will notice us now," Wes said after the game.

"Could be." Harv was grinning wide as a bullfrog. He turned my way. "Snake, I didn't know you had that in you."

I shrugged. "He was trying to put me in the hospital. Hit me in the ribs or on the elbow? Okey-doke. You can get away with that. Throw behind my head? You got to pay the price."

"Amen!" Wes said, as if he was shouting out for a preacher in a colored church. I didn't look for us to have any more games like that one around Los Angeles. Word would spread fast. This year's House of Daniel didn't turn the other cheek. It hit back, hard.

Those two games were the only ones we played at Shell Field. That was bound to be just as well. We went north and west for one against the Torrance Columbias. Their guys worked at the Columbia steel mill there. Some of 'em didn't work real hard. They were another semipro team where half the players had been pros not long before.

We beat 'em anyway. Fidgety Frank pitched great. You never can tell, that's all. Maybe he hadn't had his good stuff the last time out. Maybe it was just horses for courses, and the Oilers thought he made a tasty snack while the Columbias couldn't figure him out for beans. The harder you try to understand why baseball works the way it does, the loopier it'll drive you.

Oh. It was about as polite a game as any you'll see. No brushbacks.

No rough slides around second base. After it was over, their manager said to Harv, "The Chancelors always try and push teams around. A little bird told me you pushed back. Good for you."

"I'd sooner play baseball than basebrawl any day," Harv answered. "But some people, if you let 'em have an inch, they'll grab for a mile. Not against the House of Daniel, though."

"Fine by me," the Columbias' boss man said. "I wish we didn't come out on the short end today, but we played the best we could. Anybody can see the stories are true, and your guy on the hill's been keeping company with Carpetbag Booker."

"I heard that!" Fidgety Frank said. "Thanks!" The stories the Columbia was talking about had to come from Denver. Nice to know some news about the *Post* tournament leaked out along with all the stuff from the Great Zombie Riots.

We went north again the next day. Not far, just up to a little town called Gardena. Some of it was suburbs—houses of clapboard or stucco, a lot of them with roofs of the half-round red tiles they call Spanish. Some was truck farms and chicken ranches. Japs had a lot of the farms; most of the guys who raised chickens were Mexicans.

They had themselves a fine ballpark there. Todd Field sat at the corner of two streets named Redondo and Vermont Beach. Vermont doesn't have any beaches that I know of. Didn't stop whoever gave the streets their handles. It was only 303 to the right-field line, but they had a thirty-foot screen to cut the homers down to size. Left was 340, and it went out to 417 in center. Wood pillars held up the tin grandstand roof. Every so often, a foul pop would clank back onto it.

That place couldn't have worked out better. Our motor lodge was right across the street from Todd Field. On one of the other corners of that intersection was a feed store. Most big-city suburbs, you wouldn't expect to see something like that. But what with the little farms and the chicken ranches, J. N. Hill's made a go of it.

Seeing the feed store put me in mind of Charlie Carstairs back in Enid. He ran the same kind of business. I hoped Big Stu never did manage to get his pound of flesh out of Charlie. I hoped his goons never caught up with Mich Carstairs, too. His other goons, I should say. Big Stu's goon was what I started out as, after all.

Our first game at Todd Field was against the Strawberry Park Pickers.

Strawberry Park was the section of Gardena where they raised, well, strawberries. The Pickers were a Jap team. They all spoke English, and most of 'em were born over here, but they still looked like Japs. If the House of Daniel had squared off against the Tokyo Titans—Japs from Japan—then Japs from Gardena wouldn't faze Harv. They didn't bother me, either. Going up against colored guys had felt a lot more peculiar.

More of the crowd was white folks than Japs, but not a whole bunch more. The Japs all yelled for the Pickers, in English and in Japanese. The whites seemed split. Some rooted for the Pickers 'cause they were the town team. The rest cheered for us because we looked like them.

The Pickers weren't as good as the oil-company clubs or the Columbias. It wasn't because they were Japs. It was because they *were* a town team. They were guys who liked to play and got together. None of them had ever pitched at the Cricket Grounds or caught in Weeghman Park.

We beat 'em 6-2. They seemed happy they'd had a game against us, and happier that we hadn't clobbered them. They had fun. So did I—I picked up a single and a triple and grabbed everything they hit my way.

Just down Redondo from the ballyard was the Tijuana Inn. Wherever you've got Mexicans, you'll have Mexican food. It wasn't quite the same as what they dished out in New Mexico, but it tasted good and it doesn't cost much. Can't knock that for a combo.

We were gonna play at Todd Field again the next day, against the Redondo Beach Sand Dabs. Since all we had to do to get to the ballpark was cross the street, we had the morning to ourselves. The Tijuana Inn wasn't open for breakfast. A diner a few doors down was, so I had ham and eggs there with Eddie (well, he had bacon and eggs, if you're feeling exact). Then he went back to the motor lodge.

I started to do the same thing, but I stopped before I got there. "Go ahead," I told him. "I'm gonna look in the feed store." They sold pets, too—I noticed that painted on their side window.

Eddie gave me a sly smile. "Feeling homesick?"

"Something like that," I said. I'd missed Enid and Oklahoma now and then. I'd sure never missed my old shack. I don't reckon a mouse or a cockroach could've missed that miserable place.

"Have fun," he said, and kept walking. He didn't care about cows or chickens, at least before they got cooked. He didn't have a dog or a cat or a goldfish. J. N. Hill's wasn't his kind of place.

I also had no pets. You can't, not on the road. I'd done some hired-man work on farms outside of Enid, but I was never a farmer. So what drew me into Hill's? I had to be thinking about Charlie Carstairs and his business again.

A bell over the door rang when I walked in. It smelled like . . . a shop that dealt in animals and their food. The green notes of alfalfa, whatever goes into chicken feed, cat box, bird cage—all that kind of stuff. And there were spades and rakes and hatchets on the walls. Half a dozen dowsing rods pointed at a glass of water on a counter. I smiled to myself. No, I wouldn't have been surprised to see Charlie Carstairs talking with a farmer in overalls, explaining which rod would suit him best and why.

A couple of farmers in overalls were in J. N. Hill's. One of them was smoking a cigarette. They were talking to each other . . . in Japanese. I guess it was Japanese, anyway. They looked just like the Pickers we'd played the afternoon before. But they could've been speaking Yakima and I wouldn't have known the difference.

One of them looked my way and said something that had *House of Daniel* in the middle of it. Maybe he'd been in the stands at Todd Field yesterday. Anyone who wears a beard that isn't white is liable to get asked if he belongs to the House of Daniel, of course. If you don't think of cough drops when you think of beards, you'll think of the traveling baseball team.

I looked at the burlap sacks of feed piled almost man-high. No, I didn't get homesick much, but that whole place stabbed at me. Not much around Los Angeles is like things in Enid, but that store could've belonged to Charlie Carstairs as easy as not. It caught me by surprise, so I felt the stab worse.

Going over to the pets didn't make things any easier. Canaries and parrots, those didn't do anything for me. Neither did the little green turtles swimming in a galvanized washtub. But puppies and kittens are like babies. They can't help being cute.

I bent down and stuck my finger out at a red tabby kitten. Then I jerked it back in a hurry—the kitty took a swipe at it with a paw full of little needles. I'm sure it didn't mean to hurt me, which didn't mean I wouldn't've got hurt. Some ways, cats are more like people than you'd think.

"Would you like to hold him?" a girl asked. She smiled at the kitten and at me. She was tall and slim, with wavy hair a little darker than honey blond. Her crisp white blouse had J. N. HILL'S embroidered over her heart, the way a ballplayer might wear his team's emblem there on his shirt. She filled the blouse better than any ballplayer would have, though.

I straightened up in a hurry—so fast that I had to work my arms to keep from falling down again. I'd been thinking about Charlie Carstairs and his place back in Enid. If I hadn't been thinking about it and him, I wouldn't have gone into J. N. Hill's to begin with.

But thinking about Charlie wasn't enough for . . . this. I'm about as sorcerous as your average two-by-four, but . . . this had me wondering if maybe I wasn't a wizard after all.

"Are you all right?" she asked. Some of what was going through my head must've shown on my face. She sounded honest to Pete worried about me. Well, I was probably either white as gypsum sand or else green like a lime.

I tried to talk, but all I managed the first time was a cough. I tried again, and this time I was able to come out with it: "You're Mich Carstairs." I've seen guys who just got beaned steadier on their pins than I was then.

An up-and-down frown line came and went between her eyebrows. "That's right. I am. But I don't reckon I know you."

She'd seen me once, for a couple of minutes, months earlier. I hadn't had a beard then. Now . . . Now I hadn't shaved since a few days after that. No wonder she didn't recognize me.

"I'm Jack Spivey," I said. I almost said *Snake Spivey*, which wouldn't have helped. But, naturally, she didn't recognize my name, either. So I went on, "I'm the fella in Ponca City who told you to come to California. I'm mighty glad you did, too."

Her eyes went wide. They were even greener than I remembered. "You *are* that fellow," she said, more to herself than to me. "Nobody else would know about it." She took a different kind of look at me. "But what are you doing with that hair and those silly whiskers?"

The Jap farmers might know why I looked the way I did. Mich hadn't the faintest idea. "I play ball for the House of Daniel," I explained. "That's why I'm in Los Angeles myself—the team'll be around for a while."

"How crazy!" she said. "I knew there was a game across the street yesterday, but I never imagined anybody I'd, uh, met was in it."

"What are you doing here?" I asked. "I mean, here at J. N. Hill's, not here in Los Angeles. I know about that."

"You know some of it," Mich said. "After you went away, I found a telephone booth and telephoned Charlie. He said getting away might be a good notion—he was having trouble with that fat thug in Enid, so staying in Ponca City wasn't safe for me." That fat thug! Nobody in Enid would've dared call Big Stu any such thing. Plenty of folks might've thought it, but they didn't say it. Well, we were a long way from Enid now.

"But . . ." I looked back at the dogs and cats. That marmalade kitten seemed ready for another crack at my finger. "You still haven't said why you're *here*."

"I needed a job when I got out to Los Angeles," she said. "I saw this place, and I came in looking for one. They asked me if I'd worked in a feed store before. I told 'em I'd spent years helping my brother in Enid. They sent him a CC message and found out I wasn't making it up. I think that startled Mr. Hill enough to get him to hire me."

Now I wished I'd spent more time, or any time, in Charlie Carstairs's store. I would've met Mich sooner. Of course, she would've met me as the town drunk's kid. That would've put two strikes against me in a hurry. Oh, wouldn't it just!

"You like it in Los Angeles?" I asked her.

She shrugged. "I'm still getting used to it. It's not like Oklahoma, is it? Los Angeles isn't like anything else that I know of. So many people here, but it doesn't seem like a big city. Big pieces of it hardly seem like a city at all."

"This Gardena place doesn't, or not very much," I said. "I was down in Long Beach for a couple of days. That had more of a city feel to it."

"If you say so. I haven't been there yet." Mich studied me. "Can I ask you something now?"

"Sure. Go ahead."

"When you knocked on my door in Ponca City and told me to get out of town, did Big Stu send you there to do something else?"

"I don't want to have to lie to you, Miss Carstairs," I said after I thought for a few seconds. "So if it's all the same to you, I'm gonna pretend I didn't hear a word you said."

She clicked her tongue between her teeth. Then she asked, "Why didn't you do whatever he wanted you to do?"

So much for me not hearing a word she said. But that one I could answer: "Because he thought you were Charlie's brother, not his sister, that's why. I couldn't do anything like that to a lady."

"Oh." She looked down at her shoes. Then she managed sort of a smile. "I didn't know Big Stu hired gentlemen."

"Heh," I said—sort of a chuckle, to match her smile. "Till you opened the door, neither did I. And neither did Big Stu. You'd better believe that."

Mich said "Oh" one more time. She seemed to think of something else. "Did you, uh, get into trouble with him because you didn't do whatever that was?"

"Nothing I couldn't handle," I answered, which was close enough to true. His strongarm boys hadn't broken my ribs, and they hadn't punted my balls, either. Not from lack of effort, but they hadn't.

"Mich!" a man called from the front of the store. "We need you at the other register!"

"Coming, Mr. Hill!" She hurried away. Her skirt swirled around her legs. She had nice ones. I hadn't noticed that in Ponca City, which only goes to show how shook up I was when she opened that door and turned out not to be Charlie Carstairs's kid brother.

She took care of whoever was buying something up there. Me, I let the little orange kitty try to murder my finger some more. If she wanted to come back and talk a while longer, she could do that. If she didn't . . . then she didn't, that was all. I couldn't blame her. The only way we knew each other was that I hadn't slugged her with brass knucks or blackjacked her. It wasn't exactly what the women's magazines called a formal introduction.

She did come back. Something warm happened inside my chest when she did. It told me she didn't think of me as one of Big Stu's slimy guys who wasn't quite slimy enough for that particular job. You don't want a pretty girl thinking about you that way, even when she isn't your pretty girl.

"I guess I'm glad you made me pull up stakes and come out here," she said. "I do think there are more chances in Los Angeles than in Oklahoma."

"You've been here longer than I have, but I wouldn't try to tell you you're wrong," I said. The kitten meowed at me—I wasn't paying attention to him. I stuck my finger down there again. He almost got me that time.

"Careful!" Mich said.

If I was careful, would I have gone gallivanting all over everywhere with the House of Daniel? Oh, who knows? All my other choices looked worse. I said, "The team will be in Southern California through most of the winter, looks like. Lots of teams and players come here then, 'cause the weather stays nice. If I'm, um, close to Gardena, could I maybe take you to dinner and a movie?" If I was careful, would my mouth have gone gallivanting all over everywhere?

Well, what was the worst thing she could do? She could tell me to get lost and walk away. If she did, I'd go back to the motor lodge and not talk about how I struck out when I wasn't even up.

But she said, "Wait a second." She came back with a pen and a sheet torn from a scratch pad that had J. N. Hill's name and address and telephone number printed at the top. She wrote another address under it. "This is where I'm renting a room," she said. "You can write me there. They don't have a telephone, but you can call me here during the day if you want."

"Thanks! I'll do that, promise." I folded the sheet and stuck it in an inside pocket. "Thanks very much, uh, Mich." I think that was the first time I ever used her name.

"Jack, I ought to be thanking you." She used mine, too.

I shook my head, because I knew what she meant. "Not for that," I said quickly. "Only a skunk woulda gone through with that."

"Big Stu could have found one," she answered. She didn't say *He thought he had found one*. We both knew that. One of the reasons she'd left Ponca City in such a tearing hurry was that, even though Big Stu was wrong the first time he thought he'd found one, he would've made sure he was right the next time.

"This isn't how I ever figured I'd meet somebody," I said.

"Well, neither did I," she said. "We'll see what happens, that's all. We'll see if anything happens."

"Sure." I nodded. You never can tell how you'll get along with some-body before you try and do it. Sometimes you can't tell how you'll get along with somebody even after you've been doing it for a while. If it were simple, everybody'd get along with everybody else, right? You know as well as I do how that works out. So it ain't simple, and a lot of the time I think that's the only thing anybody knows about the whole business.

Mr. Hill called Mich up to the front again. I figured it was time for me to get out of there before she wound up in trouble for wasting time with a customer. Except I wasn't even a customer, because I didn't buy anything.

I felt as though I didn't need a carpet to float back to the motor lodge eight or ten feet above the street. Good thing I didn't try it, though, or a car would've taught me different in a hurry.

A bunch of the guys were gathered together when I came back. After a little bit, I noticed that one of the long-haired, bearded men wasn't anybody I knew. About the same time, they noticed I was there.

"Hey, Snake," Harv said. "Got somebody here you need to meet." He nodded to the stranger. "This is Rabbit O'Leary. Rabbit, this here's Snake Spivey."

(XXI)

We shook hands. "Good to see you back," I said, for all the world as if I didn't feel a goose walking on my grave. "How you doing?"

"I still get headaches," he answered with a shrug. "I don't remember running into Double-Double. From what the docs say, I probably never will. I woke up a little when they were carrying me off—"

"I saw you wave," I said. "I was there."

"Yeah, that's what the guys were telling me. I passed out again pretty soon, though. Next time I came to was quite a while later, in the Ponca City hospital."

"How's Double-Double coming along?" I asked.

"He still needs one crutch or a cane to get around," Rabbit said. "Maybe he'll heal up all the way and maybe he won't. He'll be able to walk—the doctors are sure of that. They still don't know if he'll be able to run fast again."

"You guys smashed into each other like two trains on the same track," I said. "It was horrible."

Harv set a hand on my shoulder. "Snake, you and me need to talk."

"Okey-doke," I said. The goose's footfalls felt heavier. If he was gonna cut me loose, this was how he'd go about it. But you don't let on you care about anything like that, the same way you don't show a pitcher he's hurt you even if he just bounced a fastball off your elbow.

He took me aside a few steps. The rest of the guys drew back to give us room. Some of them would have had managers tell them things like that. The ones who hadn't, would. Baseball isn't forever. It's only as long as you're good enough. The old PCL guys on the semipro teams could testify to that.

Harv said, "Snake, for now I'm gonna leave you in center and put Rabbit in right. That'll let Frank and Wes concentrate on their pitching and not have to play the outfield part-time. In a while, though,

I may move Rabbit back to center and shift you over to right—see if we're better that way. Suit you?"

I gaped at him. I'd been so sure the news was gonna be bad, I could hardly make sense of it when I found out it wasn't. Even though Rabbit was back, Harv didn't want to throw me on the street. No matter that he was a guy, and a shaggy guy at that—I almost kissed him.

You don't let on when you're happy, either. *Wouldn't say shit if he had a mouthful.* I took a deep breath. "However you want to do it, Harv, it's fine by me," I answered.

"I was sure you'd say that, Snake, but I didn't want to catch you unawares or anything," Harv said. Harv was a good manager all kinds of ways.

"Thanks," I told him. "Thanks a lot." That was twice in just a few minutes that I'd said it and really meant it. I patted my jacket, right above where I'd stashed Mich Carstairs's address.

"Sure," he said. Maybe he didn't know how relieved I was. He went on, "Now—are we gonna knock the scales off those Sand Dabs this afternoon?"

"Uh-huh." To tell you the truth, I'd almost forgotten about the game.

"Oh. One other thing," Harv said. "I'm gonna give number fourteen back to Rabbit, if you don't mind. Got any other number you want?"

"Whatever you have that'll fit me," I said. I didn't care at all. As long as the shirt had a lion embroidered on the front, the number on the back didn't matter for beans. Some guys got fussy about that kind of thing. I didn't.

So I wore 23 on my back against the Redondo Beach Sand Dabs. The shirt was on the baggy side, but that didn't matter, either. It was a House of Daniel shirt. *That* mattered.

The Sand Dabs looked and talked as though they were mostly fishermen. They were tan, with sun-bleached hair, and they swore even worse than pro ballplayers. They were bigger guys than the Pickers, but I'd bet on the Pickers every time. Those Japs had forgotten more about defense and teamwork than the Sand Dabs ever learned.

We had another good crowd, a full house or close to it. It was a different crowd from the day before, though. There were some Orientals in the seats, but a lot fewer than had come out for their own kind. Whites made up for it, whether from Gardena or that Redondo Beach place I couldn't say. Nothing wrong with any of that. I did think it was interesting, though.

I had my head in the stands more than I usually do. I hoped I'd spot Mich coming out to watch me play. Nope. Maybe she couldn't get the afternoon off. Maybe she didn't care about baseball. Or maybe she didn't care that much about me but was just being polite at J. N. Hill's.

I can't tell you how good having a real outfielder in right felt. Fidgety Frank and Wes could throw, of course, and a right fielder needs to be able to do that. But they were both slow out there, and Frank didn't hit much. Rabbit made the team better with the glove. His first time up, he ripped a double into the right-field corner. He didn't have much rust to knock off.

We beat the Sand Dabs 11-3, I think it was. Their manager shook his head when he came up to Harv. "They said you were good," he said as they shook hands. "They knew what they were talking about, I guess. You could've made it look even worse than it does."

"Can't tell much from any one game." Harv stayed polite. They hadn't done anything to tick him off.

"Nice of you to say so," the Sand Dabs' boss said. He had sun-furrows on his forehead and cheeks. His eyebrows were paler than his leathery skin. "No matter what you say, though, we were welter-weights up against a top big man."

I'm sure Harv answered him, but I have no idea what he said. I did spot Mich then, still in the white blouse that said J. N. HILL'S. She was heading for the way out, but looking back at the field. I waved to her. She waved, too, but she kept going.

"Got a girl here, do you?" Rabbit said.

"I'd met her before, back in Oklahoma. We happened to bump into each other again this morning." That was all true, even if it left out most of what livened up the story. I could say more later if I felt like it, but I didn't have to.

"Lucky you. She's pretty." He couldn't have got more than a glimpse of her. Well, so what? Ballplayers notice good-looking women. Good-looking women notice ballplayers, too, but not so often. Still and all, we do all right for ourselves.

There are so many places to play ball in Southern California, I started losing track of them. We went up the coast to Santa Barbara and Ventura and Oxnard. We played in Pasadena, which was about as snooty as a town could get when it hadn't been there all that long. We went inland to San Bernardino and Riverside. I don't think they were as hot as Fresno, but they came close.

We went one county south to towns like Santa Ana and Fullerton and Anaheim. On the way there and back, I saw more orange and lemon trees than I ever had before. They call it Orange County, and it's got a little city named Orange in it, too.

And we went farther south, all the way to San Diego by the Mexican border. San Diego was a good-sized town: bigger than Spokane or Tacoma, for instance. But it didn't have a pro team then. Semipros and barnstormers played at Navy Field—San Diego's a big Navy town— or at Balboa Stadium in Balboa Park.

We took on a team of San Diego all-stars at Balboa Stadium. It was right next to their zoo. That was top-drawer: the snake house even had a baby dragon in it. He was something to see, all right. They made sure you stayed back far enough so he couldn't singe you when he spat fire. He wasn't much bigger than my arm. I don't know what they'll do when he grows up. His range will get longer. They can take their time figuring it out, though. The sign by the enclosure said dragons live hundreds of years.

That all-star team had its own baby dragon. The guy playing right for them was so young, it was ridiculous. Sixteen, tops—I'd be amazed if a razor ever touched those cheeks. He was skinny as a splinter. You could drop him down a soda straw and he'd never touch the sides.

"Hey, kid!" Wes called, watching him shag flies. "Does your mommy know you're here?"

He said something about Wes's mother that would've made one of those Navy men in San Diego turn puce. "Punk's not real smart, is he?" Rabbit said. "Five gets you ten Wes plunks him his first time up."

"I won't touch that," I said. I knew Wes, too.

The kid was hitting third for the All Stars. That should've told us something right there. He batted left. He came up with one out and a man on first base in the bottom of the first. Sure as the demon, Wes's first fastball spun his cap. He got up, dusted himself off, and climbed in again. "Is that all ya got, you old fart?" he yelled.

The next one would've played xylophone music on his ribs, but he twisted out of its way, too. Dunno how—Wes meant for it to get him. He sent some more compliments out to the mound.

Wes threw him a nasty curve on the inside corner. *Crack!* As soon as the kid swung the bat, he didn't look sixteen any more. He uncoiled faster than one of the snakes in the zoo. The line drive split the gap between Rabbit and me. By the time we ran it down, the kid loped into third. He was laughing his behind off.

He singled his next time up. Time after that, Wes *did* hit him. He went down to first cussing a blue streak. When he came up again, there were All Stars on first and second, so Wes had to pitch to him. The kid worked the count to two balls and a strike. Then he hit another one. I went back a few steps, but it was over my head and over the fence. Wes threw his glove ten feet in the air.

The kid came up one more time, in the bottom of the eighth. Wes gave him nothing good, and he tossed away his bat and took his walk. Thanks mostly to him, the All Stars beat us, 5-3. A kid, yeah. A splinter, yeah, but a splendid one.

He turned pro before his eighteenth birthday. By then, San Diego'd joined the PCL. A season and a half for the Friars, and the Boston Golden Cods bought his contract. They shipped him to Minneapolis. He tore up the American Association for the Mooses, too. Now he's smacking line drives all over the Fens. The way he swings the bat, he may keep doing it for the next twenty years.

You know what, though? From everything I hear, he's still a first-class son of a bitch. Not that his billfold cares.

Back then, what Wes said was, "That guy'll go far—if somebody doesn't kill him first." That was about the size of it. No one has yet, and the kid's still going.

But we kept coming back to Los Angeles. The Seraphs won the PCL pennant that year by thirty-five and a half games. I know the Coast League plays a long season. That's still preposterous. They split the season, winner of the first half playing against the winner of the second for the league title. Since the Seraphs walked away with both halves, they had a best-of-seven series against the top players from the rest of the league. They took that in six.

After the playoffs finished, the barnstorming teams from back East and up the coast started coming to town. We played a few games in Weeghman Park ourselves then. No, we didn't go back to Chicago. Los Angeles has a Weeghman Park, too. The Seraphs are a farm team for the Square Bears (sometimes people call 'em the Cubes for short), which is how that happened.

Weeghman Park—Los Angeles's, I mean—though, now *that's* a ballyard! They say it's the best minor-league park in the country. For once, I think they're right. It holds twenty thousand, and it's double-decked.

It did have its quirks. It went 340 down the left-field line, 339 down the line in right, and 412 to center. That sounds like a fair-sized field, doesn't it? Well, it was only 345 to right-center and left-center. They put bleachers back of the right-field fence, which cut the place down there. The fence in left ran along the street. So what would've been ordinary fly balls in most places went out of that one.

Still, if you spent most of your time going from a beat-up wooden park with benches that put slivers in your butt to a high-school field fenced off with chain-link, the way the House of Daniel did, that two-decked grandstand with the tall white clock tower sticking up behind it was something to see.

"Guys in the bigs can't have it *much* better'n this," Eddie said. I figured he was right. The clubhouses had lockers in 'em, not just nails, and they had room to turn around. If you'd seen some of the places that called themselves clubhouses that I had, you'd know how great that seemed.

And I'll tell you what else seemed great. The House of Daniel couldn't play at Weeghman every day. Too many other hot teams were in town. A lot of the time, we'd stay at that motor lodge by Todd Field in Gardena. When we did play at the fancy park, we'd ride the trolley up. Transfer to the S line, and it dropped you right by that clock tower (which was also a memorial to the men who died in the War to End War).

When we didn't play at Weeghman Park, we'd have a game in Gardena or Torrance or at Shell Field or Recreation Park in Long Beach or up in Pasadena or wherever Harv could promote one. And because we stayed right there so much of the time, I had a fine chance to spark Mich Carstairs.

Back in Enid, Mich wouldn't have looked at me twice. Hey, let's not kid ourselves. Back in Enid, she wouldn't have looked at me once. Her brother ran one of the biggest businesses in town, a business that kept going strong even after the Big Bubble popped. Me? I was a drunkard's boy, the kind of guy no respectable girl wanted anything to do with.

But you know what? Everything's different in California. Pa was wrong about an awful lot of things, starting with the bottle, but he got that one right. Go out to California and it's like starting over. Everybody comes to the plate with no out, no balls, no strikes. What you were, who your people were, back wherever you came from, that doesn't matter. Almost everybody in California comes from somewhere else, and most folks go out there to get away from whatever was wrong with where they came from.

So it wasn't the drunk's son and the businessman's kid sister. It was a guy who played ball for a pretty fair traveling team and a gal from his home town who'd found work at the feed store across the street from the ballpark. If we messed it up, it wouldn't be because of who our kin were. It would be because we didn't get along, just the two of us.

Only we did get along. First time we went out, we had a Saturday-morning picnic at Meade Park, up the street from the motor lodge. Had to be a morning picnic, 'cause I was playing that afternoon. A loaf of bread, cold cuts, soda—she could've drunk beer, but I didn't want to before a game.

We ate. We talked—more about California and where we wanted to go than about Enid and where we'd been. We found out we laughed at some of the same silly things. I held her hand a little. Nothing fancy, but we enjoyed it.

We went dancing. I'll never put Fred out of business, but I don't glump around out there like a zombie, either. Mich seemed happy I made the effort. Seeing her happy made me happy. So did any excuse to get her in my arms.

Gardena had a movie house on Renshaw Boulevard. You could go there on a bus from the corner with the motor lodge and the ballpark and the feed store. That was good, since Mich didn't have a car and I didn't have anything I couldn't carry with me. She was saving money to buy a secondhand machine. Los Angeles is so spread out, a car really helps you get around.

We would sit in the parlor at the house where she rented her room. The lady whose house it was would sit across from us. She didn't like my beard one bit, not even after I explained how I needed to wear it to fit in on my team. I never found out what Mich's room looked like. That gal would've thrown me out, and Mich, too, if she'd caught me in there. That was another reason to wish one of us had a car. You can find all kinds of quiet, private places if you do.

Just after the turn of the new year, Carpetbag Booker came through Los Angeles with a barnstorming team split about fifty-fifty between colored guys and whites. Los Angeles was tougher on colored folks than a lot of places I'd seen on my travels. It surprised me some, but that's how it worked.

The night before Carpetbag's team played us, the House of Daniel took him out to dinner. We'd found what we thought was a pretty good rib joint. Carpetbag didn't seem so impressed. His standards might've been higher than ours.

He didn't fuss about it, understand. He was always polite. And he ate his fill—it wasn't that bad a place, just maybe not quite so good as we thought. Afterwards, he waggled a finger at us. "Y'all can butter me up all you pleases, but I'm still gonna whup you tomorrow afternoon. That there's my job."

"Wouldn't think of buttering you up," Harv said. Carpetbag laughed—he knew better. Harv went on, "And it's our job to try and beat you, too."

"Sure enough. You kin try," Carpetbag agreed. "But I'm gonna whup you anyways."

And he did. We had a good crowd at Weeghman Park—seven or eight thousand. The payday made losing hurt less, but it still did. The other guys had faced him before. It was my first try. Oh, he was nasty! I figured I'd drop down a bunt, but he remembered I did that, doggone him. He threw me nothing but rising fastballs my first at-bat. When

I squared, I popped one up. From then on, I took my regular hacks. That didn't help, either. Well, misery loves company, and I had plenty.

In games like those, where nobody was the proper home team, winners got sixty percent of the gate, losers forty percent—that was after the Seraphs took a cut for letting us use their ballpark. "Sorry I cost you money, Mistuh Harv," Carpetbag said, "but I ain't real sorry, 'cause I made it myself."

"If you stick around here, maybe we'll get some revenge," Harv told him.

"We is in Bakersfield tomorrow, Sacramento the day after, an' Oakland the day after that," Carpetbag answered. "I'm a travelin' man, Mistuh Harv. Don't stick around nowhere fo' long."

Not many could say they traveled more than Harv. Carpetbag Booker was one of them, though. Back when I first met Eddie, he called himself a baseball bum. Next to Carpetbag, though, he was only a beginner.

Somewhere around that time, I realized I was serious about Mich. I can tell you just what made me see it. I started reading the want ads in the papers, looking for work in that part of town. Nothing paid as much as I was making for the House of Daniel. But before too long the team would travel on. If I had to choose between going with them and sticking around with Mich . . . If I was reading those want ads, that pretty much answered that question.

If we wound up together, she'd be bringing in some money from J. N. Hill's, too. And I figured I could catch on with one semipro team or another around there. That would add some. Not a lot: we'd play once or twice a week, not every day. And a town team wouldn't draw the kind of crowds the House of Daniel did. Still—some.

I had some other things to worry about, too. I knew what topped the list. Because I was serious about Mich, that didn't have to mean she was serious about me. If she wasn't, then sticking around in Los Angeles and finding myself an ordinary job weren't things I wanted to do any more. I'd go out on the road again with the House of Daniel, and I'd stick with them as long as Harv wanted me around. If anybody asked me, I'd say the same thing Eddie had. I'd tell him I was a baseball bum.

So I needed to see where I stood. Before I asked, I paid a call on a jeweler I'd found on Gardena Avenue. It wasn't a great big diamond. To tell you the truth, it was a little tiny diamond, on account of that was what I could afford. It did have a nice sparkle to it, though. Or I thought so. I hoped Mich would, too.

We went to the Tijuana Inn for supper. It was close to J. N. Hill's and to the motor lodge. They could do regular steaks, even if they spiced 'em Mexican style. We had a table in the back, where it was quiet. Well, it was pretty quiet all over. The waiters were always glad to see us. They liked regulars. They would've liked it better if they'd had more of 'em.

After we ate, I took the little velvet box out of my pocket and set it on the table. Mich stared at it and stared at me. She knew what it was likely to be. "Go ahead," I said, my heart pounding about a thousand a minute. "Open it."

She did. Then she stared some more. "Oh, Jack," she whispered. "It's gorgeous."

"You're gorgeous, honey," I said. "Try it on." I'd just been guessing about the size of her finger, but the jeweler promised he'd fix it for free if she couldn't wear it.

Either I was a good guesser or I got lucky. It slid onto her ring finger and didn't fall off again. She moved her hand this way and that so the stone caught the light from different angles. "It *is* gorgeous," she said.

I thought her eyes shone more than the diamond did. My heart kept thudding away, though, 'cause I still hadn't found out what I needed to know. I took a deep breath to steady myself, the way I would have stepping up to the plate with the game on the line in the late innings.

"Do you want to marry me, then?" There. I'd said it. Scarier than that fastball behind my bean? Now that you mention it, hell yes. All that fastball could've done was knock me sideways. It wouldn't have left me eating crow, the way she would if she said no.

But she nodded. "Sure," she said, which wasn't yes but was close enough. Then she came around the table, plopped herself down on my lap, and kissed me. I hadn't expected that, not even slightly, which isn't the same as saying I didn't like it.

The other folks in the restaurant shouted congratulations. All the waiters clapped their hands. The headwaiter went to the bar and brought us two rum-and-Cokes that could have brought a zombie to life and then put him back to sleep.

"On the house," he said gravely.

"Thank you!" Mich and I both said.

Those were mighty fine drinks. Oh, yes. When we left, I walked as though it was blowing a gale out there, even though it wasn't. Mich could've been steadier, too. But all I had to do was make it to the motor lodge up the street. Her bus stop was right at the corner there. The bus would drop her off less than a block from the place where she rented her room.

I stood with her at the stop till the bus pulled up. Nobody else was waiting there, so we found something to do with the time. We might've found something more if the bus had run late. But it came right when it was supposed to. Stupid thing.

"Love you," I said when she got on.

"Love you, too." She put a dime in the fare box. The door closed behind her. The bus growled away.

I navigated back to the motor lodge. The fella who ran it nodded to me and said, "How's your gal, Snake?" By then, we'd been staying there so much that he knew as much about what was going on with the team as any of us did.

"Couldn't be better," I answered. Was I wearing a silly grin? I couldn't see it for myself, but I know darn well I was.

Next morning after breakfast, before we got on the bus to go down to Recreation Park, I told Harv, "Need to talk with you for a few minutes."

He nodded. "About your girl, is it?" No, it's not like I surprised him.

"Uh-huh." I nodded. "I asked her last night, and she said yes. So—"

"So you'll be getting off the bus," he finished for me. He laughed at the look on my face. "What? You think you're the first one who played with us for a while and then decided he wanted to do something else instead?"

"I guess not." I hadn't thought about it at all.

Plainly, Harv had. "How long do you aim to stick around?" he asked.

"I was hoping till you guys head out of this part of the country,"

I said. "That'll give you time to look for a new center fielder—or a new right fielder if you put Rabbit back in center."

"I'm kinda thinking a right fielder, but I'll take what I can get," Harv said. With right fielders, he could go after more hitting in exchange for a little less glovework. He'd lived with the way I hit because I could run and throw and catch, but he'd never been thrilled about it.

"I know you know, but I want to say it anyway—I'm not leaving 'cause I'm sore at anybody or 'cause I think anybody did me wrong. Just the opposite. You guys saved my life." Ballplayers leaving the team might've told that to Harv before. I bet none of 'em meant it as literally as I did, though.

"I do know, yeah, but I'm glad to hear it. Well, you helped us out of a jam, too. You can go get 'em with anybody. And you found ways to chip in with the bat, probably more than I expected. You've got your head in the game all the time, and that's good. If you want to, you might make a pretty decent manager one of these days."

"Don't know that I'd want to," I said. "I've seen what a pain in the neck keeping track of a herd of ballplayers can be."

"You think it looks bad from the outside, just wait till you try it for real," Harv said with one of his crooked grins. He eyed me. "You *will* come down to Recreation Park this afternoon?"

"Oh, yeah!" I said.

We played another oil-company team. This one was from Onion Oil, or something like that. We'd bumped into them before. They had some old pros out there, the same way the Oilers and the Chancelors did. (We hadn't played the Chancelors since that one game at Shell Field. They didn't want anything more to do with us. If you want to think it worked both ways, I won't try to tell you you're wrong.)

The city of Long Beach ran Recreation Park. Some of the money from tickets and concessions went to it. It used that money to help people in town who were down on their luck. Nobody grumbled about it, not on our side and not on the Onion Oil team, either. It made our cut a little smaller, but we could put up with that. Plenty of folks needed money worse'n we did.

We beat the Onions. It was 5-3, 5-4, something like that. I'd like to say I hit three homers 'cause I was so happy Mich told me yes. I'd like to, but I didn't. I walked once. I bunted a couple of runners along, and one of them wound up scoring. I made two decent catches in center, and one throw that persuaded a runner of theirs not to try to come in on a fly ball. It was an all-right game, not a great one. You take what you can get.

And when we got back to the motor lodge in Gardena after supper, the man who ran it handed me an envelope. "You've got mail," he said.

"Oh, yeah?"

I wondered if Mich had sent me something. She'd know the motor lodge's address. But it wasn't her handwriting—and it wasn't addressed to the lodge. It was to me, all right, but in care of the House of Daniel baseball team, Los Angeles. The post office came through on that one in a big way.

Then I saw it was from Rod Graver, back in Enid. He'd done enough things for Big Stu to know I was with the House of Daniel. And he was enough of a ballplayer to know that the House of Daniel wintered in Southern California.

I opened the envelope. Inside was a folded note. *Jack—Hope this will interest you—Rod* was all it said. With the folded sheet was a little story clipped from the *Enid Morning News*.

Restaurant Owner Found Dead, the headline read. The story went on, *Stuart Kesselring, who owned the popular diner on Independence, was found deceased in a back room of that establishment yesterday afternoon. Police say the cause of death was three bullets to the back of the head. They are treating the case as a suicide.*

Kesselring? I don't think I ever knew his family name. He was always just Big Stu to me, and to everybody else. I read the last sentence about five times. Either it meant they were crazy or it meant somebody with all kinds of clout didn't want any questions asked. I couldn't be sure, not from halfway across the country, but I knew which way I'd bet.

"You all right, Snake? Is it bad news?" Eddie asked.

"Nooo," I said slowly. And it wasn't, even if it made me feel funny. I went on, "Just a line from somebody in my home town who figured out how to get hold of me. News from back there startled me a bit."

He knew I wasn't telling everything there was to tell. Eddie was no dope. But he was a gent. He didn't push me about it. Neither did anyone else.

M ich heard about Big Stu from me, and then not long afterwards from her brother. She wasn't sorry to find out she didn't have to worry about him any more. Well, neither was I. I did kinda wonder, though. Did Charlie Carstairs have enough clout to arrange something like what happened to him? I never said anything about that to her. If she wondered, too, she never said anything to me, either—or, as far as I know, to Charlie. That was bound to be just as well.

As things worked out, I quit playing for the House of Daniel about ten days before the bus headed off to Arizona or Nevada or wherever it was going next. By then, Harv had found a guy he could put in the outfield without wanting to slit his wrists, so he didn't grouse. I left early because J. N. Hill, who owned the feed and pet store, knew a fella who had a building-supply business and was looking for a man with a strong back to give him a hand.

I went down to talk to the fella. His place was on Redondo, a couple of miles south of Todd Park. It was at the edge of a slough. Big white egrets and even bigger herons stood in the muddy water amongst the reeds, waiting for a fish to swim by.

Ken Howard—that was the fella's name—took one look at me and said, "You'll lose the whiskers, right?"

"Huh?" I rubbed my chin. I was so used to them, half the time I forgot I had 'em. "Oh, sure. Whatever you want. I grew 'em for the baseball team."

"That's fine. But you'll be working for me from now on." He was a great big, burly man, but he looked sharp, too. "Here. I'll take you around, show you what you'll be doing."

Most of it was getting bricks and sacks of cement and lumber and the like into a truck, driving 'em where they needed to go, and taking 'em out again. I'd have a forklift to help at his end, but only a wheelbarrow at the other. It was a lot harder than playing center for the House of Daniel. It paid worse, too. But I'd be in town with Mich, and I'd have Saturdays and Sundays off, or time and a half if I had to go in on Saturday.

I took the job. If that wasn't love, I don't know what would be.

First thing I bought was a pair of sturdy leather gloves. Ken Howard didn't bother with 'em. He had calluses so thick, he could stub out a cigarette in the palm of his hand and not hurt himself a bit. I needed a good feel, though, if I was gonna keep playing ball.

I rented a room, too, a bigger one than Mich's. After we got married a couple of months later, she moved in with me. When we weren't too tired on account of we were both working our tails off, we were very happy together. We were still happy even when we were too tired to do anything about it, only in a different way.

And I got back to playing ball again. A company not far from where I roomed turned out what they called drizzle boots. Yeah, they were just what you'd think: rubber overshoes to keep your feet dry when it rained. They sold 'em all over the country, not just in Los Angeles, or they wouldn't have stayed in business long.

They had a team, called, naturally, the Gardena Galoshes. When I wanted to join, they asked me where I'd played before. I told 'em about the Enid Eagles, and I could see that didn't mean much one way or the other. Then I said, "And the House of Daniel." As soon as they decided they believed me, they wanted me, all right.

They weren't *much* of a team. Even next to the Eagles, they seemed pretty sorry. I hit second for them. With just a tad more power, I could've hit third . . . and I've already told you, any team where I hit third wouldn't be much. But you know what? I didn't care. Just getting out there was fun, and we picked up a few extra bucks.

And pretty soon, I was driving a forklift at the drizzle-boots factory, and doing the other odds jobs around there that needed doing. They paid me better than Ken Howard did. The work wasn't as wearing, either. I'm not knocking Ken. He gave me a job when I needed one bad, and he didn't have me do anything he wasn't doing himself. But he was six inches taller than I was, and outweighed me by seventy-five pounds. It came easier to him.

We needed the money that came with the new job. Pretty soon, Mich found herself in a family way. That kept her from working for a good while, and we started renting a house instead of a room. I would've liked to buy, not rent, but you do what you can, not what you'd like to.

If Sarah Jane Spivey wasn't the cutest baby ever born, I have no idea who could've been. Maybe her ma. But having a baby complicates your life all kinds of ways. Some you can see ahead of time. Some are surprises. You worry about the future even if you'd never thought past day after tomorrow, for instance. You get more frazzled than you ever had before, too. So does your wife.

We're still going. Dunno how Mich does it. Me, I try to take it the same way I took playing for the House of Daniel. You can have yourself a good game, or you can have a lousy one. Either way, though, you can't let it get to you too much. Because you always have to remember: there's another game tomorrow, and one more the day after that. So you go on. And we're going on. Another baby due in a few months. Maybe this one'll be a boy.

Author's Note

The House of Daniel never would have happened if Peter Beagle and I hadn't talked baseball through dinner at a Korean barbecue place in Los Angeles. Peter is the same kind of obsessive fan I am. His memory goes back even further than mine does, and we both know a lot about things neither one of us can remember. The conversation got me thinking, and this book sprang from those thoughts. Peter isn't to blame for any infelicities and mistakes here. They're all mine.

Obviously, *The House of Daniel* isn't set in our world. We have no zombies, vampires, werewolves, elementals, and the like. The guy juggling oranges in Denver springs from my wife's evil imagination, not mine. And nothing I say about the fictional House of Daniel and its beliefs should be taken as reflecting on the real House of David and its . . . although the real House of David did sponsor a real semipro team of long-haired, bearded baseball players.

By the same token, my fictional 1934 *Denver Post* Tournament is not set up the same way as the real 1934 *Denver Post* Tournament. Not all my participants are the same or modeled after the same real teams. The House of David did win the real tournament, with Satchel Paige and Grover Cleveland Alexander on their pitching staff. They did beat the Negro League Kansas City Monarchs for the title. So far as I know, there were no zombie riots in the real Denver.

Up into the early 1950s, semipro baseball was a huge part of the sport. It never quite disappeared altogether, but television killed its importance in the larger scheme of things. Most towns of any size at all in the 1930s would have a semipro team; most medium-sized cities would have semipro leagues. They were talent sources and sometimes farm teams for the minors and the majors. A lot of minor leagues were fly-by-night operations, and the Depression hit them hard, as it hit the whole country hard. Where what they called organized baseball failed, less organized and less expensive clubs carried on.

Most of this is forgotten now. Hardly anyone who played then or who watched those games is left alive. Statistics and records were kept erratically or not kept at all. Even when they were kept, many of them are lost now or buried in microfilm of small-town papers. Some do still survive, though. I've mined what I could for team names and park names and dimensions. Baseball is the game for historians. If you dig, you can often find things. And I'll say what shouldn't need saying: for anyone writing about the United States in the second quarter of the twentieth century, WPA Guides are absolutely indispensable.

But *The House of Daniel* is fiction. I am allowed to make things up, and I have. Do your own digging before you trust anything I say in here about some vanished team or ballpark. I will tell you straight off the bat that Todd Field in Gardena is entirely fictitious, and I've scrambled the streets and how they run. That's the town I grew up in, and I take a native's privilege in goofing with it. I sure wish that ballpark had been there, though!

Two names in *The House of Daniel* are real, because I couldn't make up any so perfect. Sad Slim Smith really did manage the Bohemian Brewers in Spokane in the mid-1930s. And Cliff Ditto did manage in Walla Walla . . . but in the 1970s. I hope his shade won't mind my moving him in time.